# The Moores, the Merriers

Holly Bebernitz

*For Vic*
*Holly Bebernitz*
*Proverbs 3.27*

Quinn Rose PRESS

*The Moores, the Merriers* is a work of fiction. Names, characters, businesses, places, events, locales, and incidents are either the products of the author's imagination or used in a fictitious manner. Any resemblance to actual persons, living or dead, or actual events is purely coincidental.

Copyright © 2019
Holly Bebernitz
All rights reserved.

Published in the United States by QuinnRose Press

ISBN: 978-0-9891721-3-4

Cover design: Michael Regina

Printed in the United States of America

www.hollybebernitz.com

## Acknowledgments

**Kathy Combass and Rachel Hozey:** my critique group, who supplied encouragement and helpful suggestions.

**Anna Harmon:** for providing information about the legal matters which affect the characters.

**Michael Regina:** cover artist.

**Wanda Violet:** for taking me on several tours of Madison, including the Oak Ridge Cemetery, and Cherry Hill and for answering all questions about the geography and history of those towns.

**Aaron & Haley, Aidan & Allison; Paul & Heidi, Ryland & Ella; Ethan & Lindsay & Audrey:** in all ways, in all times, my joy.

**Faithful readers:** who keep me encouraged and motivated enough to continue writing this series.

For more on men and women who rode the rails during the Depression era and Franklin Roosevelt's Federal Emergency Relief Administration, which purchased the property to establish Cherry Lake, see:

Michael Uys. *Riding the Rails. American Experience.* Boston, Massachusetts: WGBH Boston Video, 2003.

"Cherry Lake." Florida Memory Blog. Florida Memory. State Library and Archives of Florida.
http://www.floridamemory.com/blog/2015/07/21/cherry-lake/

# Also by the Author

*Trevorode the Defender*

*Road to Briarwood*

*Tea at Kimball Pines*

*Tales of the Peregrine Inn: Olivia's Escape*

Dedicated to Rachael Stringer, former student, fellow teacher, steadfast friend, without whose advice and expertise in proofreading and formatting, none of these books would have been possible.

# Chapter 1

# The End
**Jacksonville, Florida**
**September 1979**

By five minutes past noon, I knew something was wrong.

My neighbor Franny Moore had not arrived for our Labor Day cookout, and she was *never* late. Grabbing her house key from the pegboard in my kitchen, I called to my family as I opened the front door.

"I'm gonna check on Franny. Be right back."

My daughter Anne yelled from the dining room. "Make sure she brings the *pie*."

"Ha-ha," I said. Franny detested sugar and never brought anything but fruit to a dinner.

I stepped outside, wilting in the Indian summer heat, and started down the sidewalk.

Two doors down Ruby Simms, neighborhood matriarch, was watering her zinnias. "Hey, Babs. Got both kids for the cookout today? Or did Anne have to work?"

"She has the day off," I said. "Tom's manning the grill. Seen Franny today?"

"Early this morning when she came out for her paper. Haven't seen her since, but you know how she is about staying out of the sun. That *delicate* skin of hers."

We laughed. While the rest of us grubbed in our flower beds and pulled weeds, Franny would watch from her front porch, offering advice, as she wagged an Oriental fan back and forth.

## The Moores, the Merriers

The Southern belle of Lomax Street. Mid-60's. Every silver hair always in place, sprayed stiff. Perfect nails, French-manicured. Pink blush on high cheekbones.

"Can't blame her," I said. "We're eating *inside*."

I crossed the street. When I reached Franny's front walk, I called her name as usual. A widow for many years, she lived alone, was skittish, and asked that we "let her know" when we were on the sidewalk. I called again.

"Franny. Lunch is ready."

Strange. I still remember stooping down to pull up a dandelion growing through a crack in the sidewalk. I had it in my hand, roots dangling, as I unlocked her door and stepped in. Dirt showered on the braided throw rug. I winced.

Could I slip into the kitchen, toss the weed in the trash, snag a paper towel, and stroll back to wipe up the mess before Franny noticed? I hid the yellow blossom behind my back and started across the living room.

"Franny? Got your cantaloupe cut up? Franny?"

Through the kitchen door, I saw her, slumped on the table, left hand hanging limply by her side. I dropped the dandelion on the Persian rug as I ran forward. Lifting her head, I eased her off the chair and onto the floor.

She whispered, "Barbara."

Proper—to the end. She had never used my nickname, even when I was a child.

I snatched a dishtowel, hanging on the oven door handle, and tucked it beneath her head. "I have to get help, Franny. I'll be right back."

Racing out to the front porch, I yelled the news to Ruby. She dropped the garden hose. Her straw hat flew off as she ran into her house.

Hurrying back to Franny, I knelt beside her. "Don't worry. Someone will be here in a few minutes. We'll get you to the hospital. You'll be all right."

"No. No time. Promise…"

"Shh. Don't talk. Just rest."

"No." She gripped my hand. "Promise…you'll find my girls. Take care of my house till they come home. Find…" She gasped. "Find Justine. And Ivy Leigh. Tell them I'm—"

And she was gone.

That night, too upset to sleep, I stared at the ceiling fan and went over the instructions Franny had outlined years before. I could still picture her, sitting primly on her brocade sofa, the list clutched in her delicate, liver-spotted hand.

## Chapter 1 ~ The End

"First, take my obituary to the *Florida Times-Union*"—she held it up for me to see—"invite these women to my funeral"—a list of guests for a private graveside service in Madison—"contact Sanford Felsch to conduct the service"—her former pastor, now living in Pinetta—"and I want *you* to read the eulogy"—the last sheet in the stack of paper. "Everything's here. I've already been to the funeral home to make all the arrangements. Bury me in the pink dress, the one I wore to Cab's funeral."

"Are you sure you want *me* to do this?" I had asked. "One of your daughters should—"

Tight-lipped, brow drawn, she shook her head. "You've been more of a daughter to me than either of them. They don't know anything about my business affairs, and they've *never* loved this house…or appreciated my things…like you do."

No argument there. If I had not watched the Moores move in when I was seven, I would have been convinced Ivy Leigh and I had been switched at birth with her across the street, living the life that should have been mine.

Though I felt awkward taking charge of Franny's arrangements—much less being executor of her will—I would carry out her wishes to the letter. An elementary school secretary for more than 20 years, I thrived on "To Do" lists.

But "find her girls?" Justine had not been home in 10 years. Ivy Leigh—I couldn't remember. Of all Franny could have requested with her dying breath, it had to be that?

Three days later, Ruby and I in my car, followed by Linda Faye, Linda Jo, Jean, and Viola, from the "over-60" ladies' Sunday school class at our church, headed toward Madison to bury Franny in the Oak Ridge cemetery. We journeyed through the Osceola National Forest, over the Suwannee River, and then exited off I-10 West and drove into Madison. Entering the cemetery, we located the blue funeral home canopy and reluctantly climbed out of our air-conditioned cars. Then we lined up on the front row of chairs and waited for Rev. Sanford Felsch to arrive for the service.

Viola Banks, Franny's Sunday school teacher, leaned in and whispered in my ear. "Who in their right mind plans a graveside service in *September* in *Florida*? Everyone knows it's still hot in September. This isn't Vermont. And *out* of town? What in the world?"

"She couldn't possibly know she'd die in September," I said.

"And who leaves behind a guest list for a funeral?" she asked, tossing one end of her lime green scarf over her shoulder…onto mine. "I had a time explaining to the rest of the class—"

"Franny was a very private person," I said, brushing away her scarf. "You know that."

Viola wiped sweat from her forehead and flicked it off her fingers. "She *should've* been buried with her *husband*. Not over a *hundred* miles away. It's not right. What God hath joined together, let no man put asunder."

"I don't think that applies once both parties are dead."

Ruby shushed us and nodded at the pastor, approaching from his car. We bowed our heads out of respect, but did not weep. Not one of us said so, but we were relieved Franny was at rest. She had been unhappy for so long.

And never stopped reminding us.

Bible open to Psalm 23, the pastor read of green pastures and still waters while we swatted mosquitoes. Ruby sang two verses of "In the Garden," instead of three. Then the portly Rev. Felsch removed his blue suit coat, draped it over the empty chair next to Linda Faye, and loosened his tie.

"I hope you'll excuse me, ladies, but it's wa—ay too hot for a coat. Franny would object, but she's not here now, is she?" He chortled. "And, bless her heart, she won't mind as she peers over the ramparts of glory. Amen?" He scraped a wrinkled handkerchief across the back of his neck and announced, "Mrs. Barbara Allgrove, Franny's neighbor, will deliver the eulogy."

Leaving my seat, I stood next to him behind the casket and began to read the speech Franny had composed. "Francesca Elizabeth Hibbs Moore was born in Columbia, South Carolina, on August 23, 19—"

Barking interrupted me. Viola, terrified of dogs, half stood, ready to run. I scanned the cemetery. Half a dozen graves away stood a tall, rail-thin man in faded jeans, dingy white shirt, and black bowtie, ball cap held over his heart, Doberman—unleashed—at his side.

"You might want to hurry up," the pastor said from the corner of his mouth. "I was afraid he'd show up. I was hoping I wouldn't have to deal with him."

"The dog?" I asked, confused.

"Not the dog. He's the least of our problems."

Clutching my speech, I peeked at the Doberman. Sleek. Well-fed. This dog did not live on the street. So, why did his owner look like *he* did? I raced

## Chapter 1 ~ The End

through Franny's high school graduation, debutante ball, and onto her wedding.

"Francesca married Jon-Cabot Moore on July 22, 19—"

More barking shattered the hot, stifling air. I froze. Viola zeroed in on my panicked expression and turned to look behind her. The mammoth dog, ears up, legs flailing, was loping toward us like a stampeding buffalo.

Ruby gripped Viola's arm. "Keep still. Bad idea to run."

I was bending my knees to duck behind the casket—not hard, since at 5'2", I did well to see over the colossal spray of pink roses—when the stranger's voice thundered.

"Here. Caesar." He reached into his pocket, pulled out a tattered toy, and waved it high overhead, its loose, fuzzy legs flapping. "I've got your baby." Caesar skidded, whirled around, and charged after the "baby" his owner catapulted in the opposite direction.

The stranger caught my eye and held out his hand, palm up, as if to say, 'Go on.'

At that point, cutting the speech short and asking the pastor to close in prayer seemed like a good option, but I knew I'd never be able to live with myself. Reading these words was my last chance to honor Franny, the woman I had admired my whole life.

"Babs. *Babs*." Ruby jarred me from my thoughts. "Keep going."

Straightening up, I gazed at the page, impossibly out of focus, and tried to remember where I had left off. With a quick check on Caesar, lying down and gnawing his toy at a safe distance, I plowed ahead.

"Francesca's family settled in Cherry Lake in 1935, later moving to Madison. The family relocated to Jacksonville in 1941—"

"It was '40," Viola said, adjusting her rhinestone-studded glasses on her perspiring nose.

"No, it was '41," I said. "I remember, because—"

When I looked up at Viola, I noticed our visitor had slipped in closer.

"It doesn't *matter*," Ruby said. "They moved in. Go on."

"—to care for Jon-Cabot's aunt, Mumsie Murphy, stricken—"

"Stricken," Viola mumbled. "Only Franny would say 'stricken.'"

With each interruption, the man edged in, closing the distance between us. I glanced at Rev. Felsch. Feet planted like a gunslinger at high noon, he was staring down our unwelcome guest. His meaning was clear: *Don't take another step or else.*

"—with rheumatic fever. After Mumsie's death, the family inherited the home, which Francesca transformed into a haven of—"

"*Haven*," Viola said, snickering.

The Lindas shifted in their chairs. Jean cleared her throat.

"—of culture and...*haute cuisine*," I said, flinching. Even Ruby rolled her eyes.

By now the man was at the corner of the canopy, close enough I could tell he had gone to the trouble of making himself presentable. His craggy face was dappled with tiny specks of dried blood, the work of a dull razor. His sandy brown hair, streaked with gray, had been smoothed with a wet hand, his jeans and shirt creased with a hot iron.

This was no curious bystander. He had come to pay his respects. But why?

The ladies, annoyed by the heat, the bugs...and Viola...dabbed damp Kleenex on their faces and flapped their funeral programs to stir up a breeze.

Two paragraphs to go. "A member of the Jacksonville Historical Society, Garden Club, and Woman's Club, Francesca was known for her civic pride."

I peeked at the man again. His hazel eyes—familiar, somehow—were locked on mine. Head tilted, he tapped his finger on the back of the nearest chair. I nodded once. He winked, slipped in, and sat down. Sanford Felsch snorted.

"Franny brought up two girls—"

"And where are they *now*?" Viola asked, too loudly.

Ruby's patience was gone. "This is *not* the time to bring that up. We've *all* made mistakes with our kids."

"Hmm," Viola said, in a huff. She crossed her arms and inched away from Ruby toward Jean, jostling her into Linda Jo.

"Franny brought up two girls. Ivy Leigh and Justine,"—the stranger lifted his head—"born the same year. So near the same size, people often asked if they were twins." He leaned forward, elbows on his knees, cap dangling from his fingers. "Ivy Leigh married a veteran; Justine, a businessman. Grandchildren...followed."

The words, choked out, were accurate...but so far from the whole story I felt like I was lying. Even worse, every straight-faced, strait-laced lady knew the truth, and Franny's role in what happened. Mercifully, Viola was still pouting and did not comment.

No shipwrecked sailor, sighting an approaching sail, could have been happier than I was to see the last sentence come into view.

## Chapter 1 ~ The End

"Francesca hopes you will honor her memory by keeping our neighborhoods beautiful, and Jacksonville, the premier city of the South."

Finished, I surveyed my audience: Linda Faye, Linda Jo, Jean, Viola, and Ruby, red-faced, sweating, and all mad as wet hens; and behind them, unobserved, the other mourner, elbows still propped on his knees, head down, twisting the faded cap in his hands.

"That will conclude the service," the pastor said. "Join me in a word of prayer."

The ladies stood and bowed their heads, while I kept watch.

"Heavenly Father…" Rev. Felsch began.

The stranger steadied himself on the chair next to him and stood. He swiped the back of his hand across one cheek and then the other. He was weeping.

Prayer concluded, Rev. Felsch tucked his Bible under his beefy arm and approached the mourners. The stranger stepped back and whistled to his dog. My heart ached. I could not let him leave without a kind word. Who, but me, would say one?

Before I could think twice, I scooted around the coffin and stepped into the blinding sun. Shading my face with the eulogy, I hurried after him. Only then did I notice he was limping.

"Sir. Sir," I called.

He stopped. The dog and I converged on him at the same time; the three of us forming a tenuous circle among the tombstones.

"Yes?" the man said.

"I…I…wanted to thank you for coming."

He wrenched the toy from Caesar's mouth and returned it to his pocket. "Nice speech."

"Franny wrote it. I just read what was there."

"Sounds like her. Planning everything out. Nothing left to chance." He smiled. A sweet, sad smile. "Did she leave you a 'To Do' list?"

"Sounds like you knew her well," I said, laughing.

His mood changed. "Tell me. Was she…still beautiful?"

"Oh, yes. Timeless." Caesar nuzzled my hand. I patted him absent-mindedly. "We've been neighbors since I was a little girl. I still live in the same house I grew—"

His eyes brightened. "Then you knew Justine."

"Yes. And Ivy Leigh. But how do you know them?"

"I'm…Hank Merrier," he said, as if the name were as familiar to me as my own.

"Who?"

His shoulders drooped. "Sorry. The way you looked at me, I thought you knew who I was. That Franny had told you…and that's why you let me stay for the service."

"No, Franny never mentioned you. I didn't want you standing out in the sun."

"Babs," Ruby called.

I looked back. She was hurrying in my direction, Felsch following.

Hank took in the scene. "I gotta go. I shouldn't have come, but I thought there'd be more of a crowd and I could blend in. In the back."

"Babs," Ruby called again. "Come on. Let's get some lunch and cool off."

She was trying to sound casual, but her voice was tense—not like her.

"Go on home, Hank," Rev. Felsch yelled. "Show's over."

*Show's over?* I thought. *Who says that after a funeral?*

Hank edged backwards. "Thank you…for your kindness. I won't forget it."

"Hank," Felsch yelled. "That's enough. She needs to get on the road."

*That's enough? I wasn't a child who needed to be told when to leave. Much less by him.*

Hot, tired, and annoyed, I reached out to Hank. "If you want to say goodbye to Franny, I'll walk over there with you. Felsch doesn't bother me."

Hank put his hand, rough as sandpaper, in mine. "Don't worry about me. I'll come back this evening after everyone's gone." He put on his cap. "Franny's home now. I can see her every day, if I want. Well, goodbye. Come on, Caesar." He called out. "See you later, *Reverend*."

Ruby called again. "Babs. Come on. Let's go."

Watching Hank go, I fanned myself with the eulogy to chase away the simmering heat *and* cool my simmering temper. Franny had prepared me for what might go wrong on the day of her funeral. *Viola will be in a snit over not running things,* she warned. *But I don't want a church service or a big to-do afterwards—no green bean casserole or macaroni and cheese. You and Ruby go to Smith's Drug Store. Order the chicken salad.* All this was part of the plan. Along with the white coffin and pink roses. But Franny never mentioned Hank Merrier or advised that Sanford Felsch was insufferable. What did he have against Hank?

Ruby laid her hand on my shoulder. "Are you all right?"

## Chapter 1 ~ The End

I whirled around to lecture Sanford Felsch on compassion, but he was already headed back toward his car. "Of course, I'm all right. Why wouldn't I be all right?"

She shrugged. "When the pastor saw you with that man, he said we had to come get you. That there was 'no telling' what he'd do."

"That's ridiculous. He's just a friend of Franny's who wanted to come to the service. Honestly. Some pastor he is. Refusing to let a poor, old man—"

Ruby grabbed my arm. "That was no poor old man. That was Franny's first husband."

# Chapter 2

## Nancy Crisp's Sister
**Madison, Florida**
**September 1979**

"Hank couldn't be Franny's first husband," I said, whining like a second grader. "She would've told me if she'd been married before. We told each other *everything*."

"Apparently not," Ruby said, half-smirking. "I always knew there was *something* about Franny…something that didn't quite add up. Now I know what it was."

"You don't know any such thing. Who *told* you Hank and Franny were married?"

"That preacher."

"He just waltzed up to you and said, 'Oh, by the way, see the homeless guy? He was Franny's first husband.'"

If I'd used that tone when I was a kid, Ruby would've warned me not to be sassy.

"You've been out in the sun too long," she said, tugging on my elbow. "I'll tell you all about it when we get in the car, where we can cool off. I'm *dying* in this heat."

Ruby in the lead, we wove our way among the graves. Ancient stones, cracked, leaning, names eroded. Pristine markers, resolute, glaring in the mid-day sun. Our path bordered by faded silk flowers, years old; small American flags on veterans' plots; brown flowers, brittle leaves, drooping, dangling from standing wreaths, evidence of recent funerals.

And over us all—the dead and living—a cloudless blue sky.

"Where'd everybody go?" I asked. "I thought we were all going to have lunch."

"Don't know where the preacher went—"

"Some preacher," I said. "Wouldn't invite poor Hank to come in out of—"

Ruby spoke over me, "—but the girls left for Gainesville. Art gallery at the university."

"Art gallery? Viola wouldn't know fine art if it fell off the wall onto her head."

Ruby glanced over her shoulder. "Who put a burr under your saddle?"

I rubbed my forehead to ease the dull ache between my eyes. "I'm just *so* disappointed. I had everything worked out. I even practiced saying Franny's name like she told me to and—"

Ruby whirled around, her normally placid face contorted with anger. "*Disappointed*? Because some random man interrupted your little speech? Have you forgotten what happened at *Jack's* funeral?"

My mouth fell open. I had known Ruby since I was a child, and she had never once raised her voice at me. "I'm sorry…I should've thought…"

But she didn't hear me. She wasn't even *with me* any longer. She was back in Jacksonville, a year ago, on the front row of our church, her husband's coffin an arm's length away, flanked by mountains of sweet-smelling flowers.

"That thunderstorm during the service?" Ruby said. "The lights went out, and it was so dark we could hardly find the door? Took us *forever* to get to the cemetery because the streets were flooded. We all got soaked on our way to the grave, and I got sick the next day."

She stopped, wrung out, exhausted, like a Florida thunderstorm that billowed, blustered, and blew itself out, leaving wilted plants and fallen limbs in its wake.

I tried to slip my arm around her, but she put her hand up and kept going. I followed, regretting how thoughtless I'd been, hoping Ruby would still be willing to buy into the plans I'd made for the rest of the day.

As we neared Franny's grave, I spotted a faded red Volkswagen Beetle idling behind my car. When the driver caught sight of us, she pulled away, but not before I caught a glimpse of her—petite with short, graying hair, wire-rimmed glasses.

"I suppose you want to say goodbye one more time," Ruby said.

## Chapter 2 ~ Nancy Crisp's Sister

Nodding, I pulled a single rose from the spray. "Bye, Franny. Francesca...Elizabeth...Hibbs...Moore." I turned to Ruby. "There was never a 'Merrier' in there. Franny wouldn't have kept a secret like that. All these years?"

Ruby shrugged. "We all keep secrets. Could we go? I've had enough."

"There's one more thing," I said, ducking my head. "I promised Franny...after her funeral...we'd have lunch at Smith's Drug Store. She said—"

Ruby shook her head. "Oh, Babs. When will you *ever* let yourself out of prison?"

"What?"

"Franny's *gone*. You don't have to be her little shadow anymore. Hanging onto every word she says. Not making a move unless you get her approval first."

"What's that supposed to mean?" I asked.

"She wasn't the sum of all wisdom. She was fragile as a hothouse flower with *half* the good sense your own mother had."

My stomach flipped over; I broke out in a cold sweat. "How *long* have you felt like this?"

Ruby heaved a long sigh. "It doesn't matter. I'm sorry. I never should've said that."

I hesitated, snagged like a sweater on a rusty metal chair. Nicked. Unravelling. But I wasn't ready to give up yet.

"Maybe you'd feel better if you ate something," I said, "and I did promise Franny we'd eat chicken salad after her funeral."

"All right," Ruby said, glancing at the coffin. "It's a long way home, and I *am* hungry."

We reached an unstated truce and rode toward the center of town, neither of us speaking. I drove slowly, gazing from side to side, noting street names, trying to identify landmarks Franny had told me about. The courthouse. The park. The old Episcopal church. The Wardlaw-Smith house, once a Confederate hospital during the Civil War. Franny had relived her Madison memories so often, I had no trouble recognizing the places she had described. Why had she never brought me here? A "secret past" would make perfect sense, but I did not want to admit the possibility.

"Are you sure you're going the right way?" Ruby asked. "You've made a lot of turns."

"I was just looking around. It's a beautiful place, isn't it? You gotta love a small town."

"Yes. Beautiful. But maybe you could come back *by yourself*...to pay homage."

Ruby's words were biting enough, but her tone was withering. Franny had warned me *Viola* would be "out of sorts," take it personally she hadn't been left in charge of the funeral arrangements. But Ruby? Furious? This was one wrinkle too many.

We pulled into a space on SW Range Avenue and entered Smith's Drug Store. Heeding the sign, "Please Wait to Be Seated," we remained on display as a dozen pairs of inquiring eyes turned in our direction. A bald man, hunched over a salad bowl, fork poised in mid-air, mumbled to his wife, who swiveled around to get a peek at us. A busty woman in a pink t-shirt, two sizes too small, stared so hard, she missed the baby's mouth she was wiping and swiped the napkin over his forehead instead.

"I feel like we're intruding," I whispered to Ruby.

"Like you said, 'You gotta love a small town.' They know who doesn't belong."

A prissy young woman, wearing a black bib apron monogrammed *Lottie*, greeted us. "Two?" She grabbed menus and napkin-wrapped silverware from the counter by the door and led us to a table in the center of the room. "Your server will be right with you."

Relieved the day was half over, I sipped my water and tried to calm down. Ruby studied the menu; I studied her. She was always predictable (till today, anyway). Reveling in simple joys. Cooking. Gardening. Sewing. Permed salt-and-pepper hair. Wardrobe, decades old, consisting of tasteful, standard outfits for every occasion. Navy blue Christmas sweater, embroidered with holly and poinsettias, red trim at the cuffs. Pink chiffon dress for Easter, spring weddings, and baby showers. Today she was wearing her funeral dress, black polyester, tiny white polka dots, white collar, matching belt, and her mother's hand-painted brooch pinned to her left shoulder.

Ruby had always been a steadying influence, my barometer for good behavior and social protocol. Always there. No-nonsense. Plain vanilla. Sturdy. 'Miss Ruby,' I called her, taking forever to switch to just plain 'Ruby,' even years after I was grown. Franny, on the other hand, was exceptional, poised at the top of the social ladder with the rest of us several rungs below. She never bought clothes from the bargain rack or clipped coupons. Her home had been my refuge, a gentle world full of beautiful things, a short walk across the street from the second-hand world I lived in.

Our server, Mandy, a petite brunette with a button nose and big brown eyes, filled our water glasses and described the specials.

"Does Miss Louise still make chicken salad?" I asked.

"Oh, yes, ma'am. Every day. But how did you know? You're not from around here."

"No," I said. "We're in town for a funeral. An old friend. She told—"

Mandy's eyes grew wide. "Not…Franny. *Her* funeral?"

"Yes," Ruby said. "Do you have any—?"

"Oh, wow," Mandy said. "Franny's friends." She nodded slowly. "So, *she* told you about Miss Louise. That makes sense."

"Yes," I said, handing over the menu. "We'll both have the—"

Ruby cleared her throat. "I'd like a few minutes, please."

Wincing, I smiled sheepishly at Mandy, who tucked her ticket book in her apron pocket and retreated. She made a beeline for Lottie and whispered in her ear. Lottie peered at us.

Hoping to breach the chasm between Ruby and me, I drew in a quick breath, about to say, 'Lunch is on me,' when a man's voice from the table behind me caught my attention.

"Heard Franny Moore was buried today."

"Yeah. I saw the obituary in the paper," said the other, fork clinking against his plate. "Buried *here*. Don't that beat all?"

I glanced at Ruby to see if she had picked up on Franny's name, but she was still hidden behind her menu. Desperate for more, I dropped my napkin on the floor to have an excuse to scoot back my chair and hear better. I bent over, snagged the napkin, and pretended to be occupied with my shoe, while the men kept talking.

"Think Hank showed up at the funeral?" He snickered.

I flicked away an imaginary speck of dust from my shoe and sat up, still sideways, leaning into the conversation as I feigned interest in a faded seascape on the wall.

"Don't know. He mighta slipped in. What with his trailer bein' only a stone's throw away from the cemetery. Pass the ketchup."

The other man lowered his voice. "I *heard* he moved his trailer there to be closer to Clarissa. Think that's true?"

*The Moores, the Merriers*

"Don't know. My missus told me Hank puts roses on Clarissa's grave twice a year. But I don't believe it." He slurped his coffee. "He couldn't afford *roses*. He's dirt poor. I told her that."

"Dirt poor. I don't think so. I heard he got money from the family business after his father died."

"He blew through that in no time after the accident. No matter how much money you've got, it ain't gonna last long if you never add to it. Know what I'm sayin'?"

"It's a shame. All that talent. Gone to waste and all because of—"

"You ladies ready to order?" Our perky server had returned. Too soon.

Still facing the wall, I pointed at Ruby with my thumb—"Go ahead"—and draped my arm over the back of my chair, straining to hear the rest of the story.

"—whatever happened to Cab and the girls—"

"I'll have soup and salad," Ruby said. "Do you have—?"

"—younger girl went *way* off the deep end. That's what I—"

"Thousand Island," Mandy said, scribbling. "Ma'am? You ready to order?"

"—cryin' shame…two families torn up—"

"Ma'am?"

"Umm," I spluttered. "Chicken salad."

"Sandwich or bed of lettuce?" Mandy offered.

"—mama still talks about it once in a while. Biggest scandal to—"

"Babs," Ruby said. "Lettuce or bread?"

"—and in only a few weeks' time, it was all—"

"*Babs.*"

Dazed, I gaped at Mandy. "I'm sorry…what?"

She repeated the question. I chose lettuce. Then she stepped toward the men and offered dessert, ending their conversation. Stymied, I turned back to our table and squeezed lemon into my ice water. Stirring. Thinking. Stirring. *Clarissa? Who's Clarissa? Scandal?*

"I'm glad you insisted on lunch," Ruby said. "It's good to sit down and relax."

Olive branch. I accepted. "And we won't have to clean up, like we usually do after a funeral," almost adding—*Franny was right. It's nice to skip the covered dishes*—but stopped myself in time. From now on, I'd have to keep Franny references to a minimum.

## Chapter 2 ~ Nancy Crisp's Sister

Ruby unwrapped her silverware and spread her napkin on her lap. "Babs, I'm sorry…about what I said." She sighed. "I thought I could handle another trip to a cemetery. I know it's been a year, but it's still too soon after Jack…I loved Franny, too, you know."

Reaching across the table, I laid my hand on hers. "It's been a hard day for—"

Over Ruby's shoulder, I spotted the woman I had seen driving the old Volkswagen. Alone at a table by the kitchen. Our eyes met; she looked away. Had she followed us here?

"What's wrong now?" Ruby asked. "What are you looking at?"

I leaned closer. "Did you notice that other car in the cemetery? When we were leaving?"

"You mean the preacher's?"

"No. After Hank left and you and I walked back to the grave. There was a red VW bug parked behind mine. The woman who was driving it is over there. She's staring at us."

Mandy returned with our orders. Ruby bowed her head to say grace. Propping my elbow on the table, I covered my eyes and peeked through my fingers at the woman in the corner.

"Heavenly Father," Ruby said, "thank you for the food. Please keep us safe as we drive home and help us get *back to normal tomorrow…*" Like other Baptist women, she often used "leading in prayer" as a covert means of lecturing.

While I watched, the woman carefully folded her napkin, stood, and walked toward us. I ducked my head and clamped my eyes shut, hoping to appear pious.

"Amen."

We opened our eyes. The woman was standing next to us. Solemn-faced, slim hands clasping a tattered leather purse, looking for all the world like the deprived matron of a Charles Dickens orphanage, except for her eyes. Kind. And brimmed with tears.

"Excuse me," she said, in a wispy voice. She propped her purse on the table, unzipped it, and pulled out an envelope. Head ducked, she looked at me over her glasses. "Justine, now that this is all over, Ivy Leigh should have this. When you see her, could you—?"

If only I'd kept my mouth shut and let her talk, I would've saved myself so much trouble, but, no, in typical Babs fashion, I just had to interrupt and correct her.

"I'm not Justine," I blurted out. "I'm Babs." I pointed. "This is Ruby."

"Oh." Her shoulders slumped. "When I...saw you at the cemetery... Your auburn hair. Like Justine's. You're the right age. Naturally, I thought Justine would show up for—"

"Would you like to sit down?" Ruby asked her. "You look worn out."

Ruby never minced words. Even with strangers.

Pulling out a chair, the lady sat down, envelope resting on her purse in her lap.

"You knew Franny?" I asked.

"A long time ago. I'm Nancy Crisp...used to be 'Murphy.' Clarissa...was my sister," she said in that same "once-you-know-you'll-understand" tone Hank had used in the cemetery.

There was the name again. *Clarissa.*

We waited for Nancy to collect herself. I signaled Mandy, who trotted over.

"Hello, Miss Nancy," Mandy said, laying a familiar hand on Nancy's shoulder. "You know these ladies?"

"We just met," I said. "Would you bring her lunch to our table?"

"Of course." Mandy winked. "You three must have a *lot* to catch up on."

Nancy remained silent, crushed under the weight of her errand. Whatever it was.

Ruby stabbed a bite of romaine "Who's Clarissa?"

Eyes wide, Nancy gaped at Ruby, then at me, then back at Ruby. "You...don't know?"

"No," I said.

Pushing back from the table, Nancy tucked the envelope into her purse. "This was a mistake. I shouldn't have bothered you."

Without thinking, I grabbed her arm and squeezed. "Please don't go. I was hoping to meet some of Franny's friends today. You're the first—"

A scream rose above the clatter and chatter. "Help him. Help him." Three tables away, a pale-haired woman leaped up, toppling her chair. She darted to the man on the other side of her table. Hands to his throat, panic in his eyes, he was gasping for breath. She pounded on his back.

Everyone stared, suspended. Everyone except Ruby. She took one look, marched over, and rapped on the woman's shoulder.

"Help me get him up," she said, cool as a cucumber. The lady obeyed. Ruby stepped behind the choking man, wrapped her arms around his rib cage, placed a fist firmly above his stomach, grabbed her fist with her other hand, and squeezed. Again. Again. Till a chunk of meat catapulted from his mouth. He sank into his chair. The lady wept.

Diners erupted into applause. I left the table and took Ruby by the shoulders.

"That was amazing," I said. "Where'd you learn to do that?"

"Jack and I took a CPR class, in case one of us ever needed it. Heimlich maneuver was part of the training. Never dreamed I'd use it on a stranger."

"You see," I said, "we were *supposed* to eat here today. Now we know why. You saved that man's life."

When we got back to our table, my heart fell straight into my sensible taupe patent leather pumps. Nancy Crisp had slipped away during the confusion. I was heartsick but said nothing. This was Ruby's moment. I wasn't about to spoil it.

Ruby sank down and pressed her napkin to her forehead.

"Are you okay?" I asked.

"Too much adrenalin," she said, her voice muffled by the napkin draping her face. "My heart's pounding right out of my chest."

I slid her water glass toward her. "Take a drink, and we'll go home."

"Give me a minute. I couldn't walk to the door. I'm shaking."

Mandy scurried over with two pieces of three-layered chocolate cake. "Lunch is on us today, ladies. And complimentary dessert."

Onlookers, still gazing at Ruby, nodded approval.

I was relieved to have an excuse to stay. Maybe Nancy had only gone to the bathroom and would come back. If we waited…

"We'll take it to-go," Ruby said, still hiding her face.

"I'll box it up," Mandy chirped, and swished away.

Eyeing Ruby, I nibbled at lunch and watched the ladies' bathroom door, which did not open. Nancy was gone. Another bungled opportunity to unravel the mystery of Franny. First, Hank. The strangers' conversation. Sanford Felsch. Mandy. Lottie. They all knew *something*.

Franny was a legend in this town. But why? She hadn't lived here in years.

"Excuse me, ladies." A rumpled man in a striped shirt, tie loosened, stood by us, a stubby pencil poised over a pocket-sized spiral notebook. "I'm with the *Madison News*. Could I get your names, so I can report this story?"

Ruby lowered the napkin. "Why?"

He smiled broadly. "It's not every day one of Madison's most prominent citizens gets snatched from the jaws of death. Where you ladies from?"

"Jacksonville," I said.

My mind was whirring. When I came back to Madison...and I *would*...I could refer to this incident to identify myself. I'd be a celebrity—not a stranger. People would be eager to talk. Help me find Nancy. Maybe even Hank.

Ruby stood. "I'm sorry." Her voice wavered. "I can't do this. Barbara can tell you what you need to know." She held out her hand. "Give me the keys. I'll start the car. Cool it off."

I fumbled for my keys in my purse and looked up at Ruby's blotched face, tears pooling in her red-rimmed eyes.

"Want me to come with you?" I asked, hoping she'd say no.

She shook her head as she left. "I need a minute..."

I should have asked the reporter to wait while I went with Ruby to the car. But I didn't. I watched her go and asked the reporter to sit down. Then I told him the story, our names, and longtime connection to Franny.

Right eyebrow raised, he scribbled furiously. "This is your first time in Madison?"

"Uh-huh. And if you're wondering why Franny never brought me here, I—"

"Hmm. Worked out well for the Donaldsons, didn't it?"

"Who?"

He stuck his stubby pencil behind his ear. "Donaldson. The man your friend saved."

"Oh. Yes. I said that to Ruby. That we were 'supposed to eat here' today."

"Well, thank you, ma'am. I need to get back to the office."

"Could you send me a copy of the article?"

"Sure. What's your address?"

He thanked me and left. I picked up the cake and started to the door. Lottie was waiting.

"Have a safe trip home," she said. "Come back when you can. Do a little shopping."

"Oh, I'm coming back," I said. "I love this town. I only wish I'd come sooner."

Cake boxes in hand, I strolled to the car. The engine was idling. I spotted something on the windshield—an envelope wedged under the wiper. It must be from Nancy. Hurrying, I stepped off the curb and opened the rear door. Ruby was sobbing—bent over double, elbows propped on her knees. I

## Chapter 2 ~ Nancy Crisp's Sister

deposited the cake on the rear floorboard, closed the door, and took the envelope from under the wiper. I slid under the steering wheel and left the envelope unopened on my lap. Now was *not* the time to look inside. I laid my hand on Ruby's shoulder.

"I'm so sorry, Ruby," I said. "I should've thought..."

She sat up and faced me. "Why couldn't I save *Jack*? I took that class, so I could help him if he ever needed it...but *he* died...and I ended up saving some man I don't even *know*."

"Jack died in his sleep. You couldn't have saved him. It wasn't your fault."

"It *was* my fault. If we'd been in the same bed, I would've known...but I made him sleep in the other room...because he snored like a freight train."

"Oh, Ruby," I said, patting her shoulder, "lots of people your age sleep in separate beds. That's no crime."

"Well, if I had it to do over again...I'd stay awake all night if it meant having Jack for one more day."

I opened the glove box, pulled out a handful of napkins saved from fast food stops, and pressed them into her hands.

"Close your eyes and rest," I said, reversing the car. "I'll have you home in no time."

She leaned back her head. "There was an envelope on the windshield. Did you see it?"

"I got it."

"Was it from Nancy?"

"I think so."

"What was it?"

"It can wait," I said, thinking anything but that.

I drove out of Madison, south on FL-53 toward I-10. It was a lovely drive on a two-lane county road, through fields, farms, bordered with wildflowers, shaded by massive trees. Air conditioner blowing cold, radio off, Ruby resting, I tried to piece everything together.

Hank—Franny's first husband? He was glad she was "home," so he could "visit her." Would he put flowers on her grave like he did for Clarissa? Or was that even true? Why had he asked about Justine, but not Ivy Leigh?

What had Nancy said? *Now that everything's over, Ivy Leigh should have this.*

Once we were up on I-10, cruising on a nice straight stretch, and Ruby's regular breathing had convinced me she was asleep, I propped the envelope

21

on the steering wheel, opened it, and pulled out a black-and-white photo. It was the image of a couple, in their 20s, arms around each other, gazing into each other's eyes. The man was holding a curly-haired toddler, her chubby arm around his neck. Glancing up and down at the road, I flipped the picture over. On the back—lower right-hand corner—were three names and a date.

*Cab, Clarissa, & Ivy Leigh Moore. 1935.*

Stunned, I read the names again.

Clarissa. With Franny's husband and Franny's daughter. It made no sense.

From somewhere, miles away, I heard Ruby's voice. "…hate to sound like a kid, but I need to go to the bathroom. Can we stop?"

I slid the photo under my seat. "Sure. There's a rest stop right up here."

"Do you have a mirror?" she asked, rifling through her purse. "I thought I'd try to fix my face a little."

"Use the one on the visor. But I don't think we'll see anyone we know."

She flipped down the visor and straightened her hair. "I'm doing it for my sake. I'm a mess. So," she said, eyes fixed on her image, "was the note from Nancy?"

"What note?"

"The one you just stuck under your seat."

"It's not a note," I said, pulling onto the exit ramp. "Just an old picture of Cab. I guess Nancy thought the girls should have it. Little does she know they never come home anymore."

The moment I parked, Ruby swung her door open. "Would you lock the car? I'm going to leave my purse here. I've read about people snatching purses from under stall doors."

"Good idea. I'll lock both our purses in the trunk."

Perfect solution. Put photo in purse. Lock purse in trunk. Once Ruby was back in the car, I'd peel out of this parking lot and get back on the interstate. If she asked about the photo, well, I couldn't get to it, could I?

Enough of my sacred cows had died today. I was not about to watch Ruby feel smug over the story she'd figure out as quickly as I had. Scattered facts were one thing. Offhand comments, rumors, another. They might be exaggerations. Misunderstandings.

But there could be only one reason for the look on Cab's face, preserved in that golden black-and-white moment. He was deeply in love with Clarissa. In all the years I'd known him, I'd *never* seen him look at Franny that way.

*Two families torn up.* That's what the men at the next table had said.

## Chapter 2 ~ Nancy Crisp's Sister

Still brooding, I retrieved the photo, gathered up our purses, got out of the car, and opened the trunk. If only I had not paused, hiding behind the raised trunk lid, to linger over the photo one more time, Ruby, returning for her wallet ("There's a Coke machine. Want one?"), would not have slipped up on me, grabbed my hand, pulled the picture closer, adjusted her bifocals ("Let me see that"), and gasped ("Oh, my word. That's not Franny"). She would not have been startled when I jerked my hand away, shoved her purse at her, and slammed the trunk.

Not a word passed between us all the way to Jacksonville. When I pulled into her driveway, I tried the apology I had been practicing in my head.

"Ruby, I—"

But she cut me off. "Thank you for the ride."

As polite and disinterested as if she were thanking a stranger.

# Chapter 3

## Houseguests
### Jacksonville, Florida
### September 1979

Dressed in blue gingham pajamas, I drove Nancy Crisp's red Volkswagen Beetle through the streets of Madison. Next to me, Franny, wearing the pink dress she had been buried in, held a curly-haired child in her lap. The cemetery appeared on our right.

*Stop here, Barbara,* Franny said. *Thank you for the ride.*

*Here?* I asked. *I can't leave you here. By yourself?*

She handed over the little girl and opened the door. *It's all right. Hank's waiting.*

Jerking awake, I threw back the sheet and sat bolt upright. My back was drenched with sweat, head pounding. The digital clock glowed 5:20. I turned on the lamp and took the black-and-white photo from my nightstand. Relieved I had only been dreaming.

"That's what I get for keeping this by my bed," I said, opening the nightstand drawer. I flipped the photo face down, slid it to the back of the drawer, and shut it. But not before my eye fell on the caption again.

*Cab, Clarissa, & Ivy Leigh Moore. 1935.*

Squeezing my eyes closed, I gripped the edge of the bed. "All this time...*Why* didn't Franny tell me?"

I changed from my damp pajamas into my housecoat and headed downstairs. Still repeating, *It was a dream.* But the house felt strange, empty, even though I flipped on every light switch I passed by. I wished the sun would come up.

When I walked outside to pick up my paper, I saw Ruby's kitchen light was on. I knew perfectly well she was at her table, drinking coffee, reading her Bible. It would be a simple matter to walk over, tap on the door…and say…

*Sorry about yesterday.*

But I wasn't up to it. Ruby *probably* wasn't either. We both needed some time. Leaving my apology unsaid, I retreated to my kitchen for breakfast.

While coffee perked, I poured a bowl of raisin bran, which I ate every morning, seated in the same *chair* every morning, at the same *time* every morning. My way of chasing away the noisy ghosts of my chaotic, disordered childhood.

Just because I still lived in the home I'd grown up in didn't mean I had to run the house like my mother had. Even now, I could picture her at the kitchen sink. Wispy dyed-black hair, threadbare housedress, sun-flowered apron, pudgy feet in furry slippers, swaying to some Irving Berlin tune she was crooning, while my little sister Janie tugged on the apron hem. Janie. I should call her, tell her Franny died. I used to take her with me to visit Ivy Leigh. I'd knock on the door, squeeze Janie's hand, and remind her not to say the house smelled funny.

*Moth balls*, I had explained. *Some people have nice clothes they try to take care of.*

But Janie had not been impressed. She had never loved the Moore house like I did.

Sometimes I thought the *Moores* didn't love their house as much as I did.

Their house was everything ours was not—quiet, orderly, pristine. Ours was loud, messy, chaotic. Franny was tall and graceful; our mother, Gladdie, short and disheveled. Franny had only two daughters, each with her own room. Our mother had five children and supplemented our father's janitor pay by "managing" the *River's Edge Inn*, her fanciful name for the rundown boarding house we lived in. Rooms labeled "spare" could be rented, so our three brothers were crammed into one room, and Janie, as a colicky baby, moved into my room when I was 14, the year I began planning a getaway.

At 18, I came close. Enrolled in Jones College, I was learning shorthand so I could get a job. I was going to marry J. Michael Ford, an artist with a "studio" on Riverside Avenue. We would move to Atlanta where he had a commission restoring mosaics in a Greek Orthodox church. That's what he *said.*

## Chapter 3 ~ Houseguests

But it didn't work out that way. Embarrassed, I came home, never to leave again. I married my high school sweetheart, Harry, who forgave me for throwing him over for "that artist." Our children, Anne and Tom, were born within three years.

My father got sick. We moved in to help my mother. Harry lost his job. My father died. My mother begged us to stay. Harry thought it was the "only sensible thing to do—huge house, no mortgage, a godsend."

The End.

Stuck, I worked tirelessly to impose my style on this house. But all these years later, the slightest sensation, like the sickly-sweet scent of my mother's gardenia bushes (Anne loves), can yank me up and plop me down in a memory, so thick—

The phone rang. I glanced at the clock over the back door. 6:10. Anne? Calling from the hospital? Or to let me know she was home? What shift was she working, anyway? I could never keep track.

"Hello?"

"Babs?"

Viola. *Was there no escape from this woman?*

"Something wrong?" I asked. "It's so early."

"Oh, I knew you were up. I know you can't *wait* to get into Franny's house today"—she giggled—"and I wanted to remind you about our yard sale a week from Saturday."

"Yard sale?"

"I'm sure Franny told you. To raise money for our class trip. We're going to Boone this year. So, as you're going through Franny's…"

Viola was the pushiest woman I had ever known, but I still couldn't believe she had the nerve to ask me to set aside…

"…castoffs to sell. Franny and I talked about it the week before she died. She said she had several things she would donate. She was going to give me a list…but, of course, she—"

"*I can't do that,*" I said. "Sell what belonged to Franny?"

Even over the phone I could hear her little huff of disapproval. "She *told* me you would be in charge of her estate."

"I *am*."

"She *also* told me she needed to get rid of some things…that Justine and Ivy Leigh had never appreciated her taste and wouldn't have the *slightest* idea what to do with her Lenox figurines when—"

"Well, I know what to do with them."

I had already pictured the Nativity scene I had coveted since I was 10 on *my* piano this Christmas. Mary. Joseph. Jesus. Shepherds. Boy with dog. Wise men. Angel. Palm trees. Donkey. Sheep. Two camels. Ox. The stable Cab had built.

Deadly silence. Slight sniff and then…'tsk.' The phone fairly froze in my hand.

"Will you be at Franny's all day?" Viola asked, high-handed.

"Yes," I said, unbowed.

"Then I'll be over—after lunch?—to see how many tables we can setup in the yard."

"What?"

"For the sale. Franny said she'd host this year. We thought if we had it on a Saturday, we could put up signs on Riverside and get a lot of the foot traffic from Memorial Park."

"You honestly think people are going to walk *two* blocks from the river in the heat just to buy a bunch of our old junk?"

"*Junk*? Linda Faye crocheted three Florida Gator afghans, and Linda Jo is donating 12 jars of her chow-chow. You can hardly call that—"

"Listen, Viola, could we talk about this later? It was a long day yesterday, and I have an appointment with Franny's lawyer at 11:00. It's not like your yard sale is tomorrow."

Another weighty pause. "You know, Barbara, Franny wasn't your mother. In fact, we've always thought if you'd tried to be more like your *own* mother, you'd have been more content."

Since, at that point, the room turned white and my pulse was pounding, I can't remember what I said. Something about, 'If I'd been like *my* mother, *my* daughter would be here cleaning up after me, instead of at the hospital assisting with *cardiac surgery*.'

"Your mother," Viola said, "was a good woman who took care of your grandmother and anyone else who needed it. She never understood why you refused to—"

"I have to go. I'm meeting Tom for breakfast."

This was a lie and we both knew it, but it got me off the hook. For the time being.

Before noon, everyone in the "Over-60's" class would know Viola had put me in my place. Gossip would be disguised as "a prayer request Babs will change her mind about the yard sale and not ruin our trip to Boone."

## Chapter 3 ~ Houseguests

My mood was as soggy as the raisin bran I scraped into the trash. Heading to the stairs, I paused to gaze at the place where the "check-in desk" had once stood. My mother and children loved that old counter my father had built from discount lumber, so I let the eyesore stay long after our "inn" became just a house. Two weeks after my mother died, I had it torn out and carpeted the scuffed wood floor. Now, in that very spot, was an antique marble-topped table between two French walnut armless chairs, four botanical prints on the wall.

But in the early morning light, Viola's words throbbing in my ears, *your mother was a good woman...* I could almost see my mother poring over the tattered green guest ledger, hear her calling, *Barbara June, come figure up Mr. Benson's bill.*

That was the problem with cemeteries and vacant rooms and voices from the past. Prod one memory, and they all wake up, start shoving each other, like my three brothers, legs and arms slung every which way in the same double bed.

Climbing the stairs, I stopped at their room on my way to take a shower. This was the same room where my own son used to live. Tom's trophies were still on the bookshelves, his high school and college diplomas on the wall. He was an accountant now, married, and the father of two-year-old triplet sons, Max, Charlie, and Ben. They were the reason I retired—to help their overwhelmed parents through the infant stage.

I stepped to Anne's room, where Janie and I had slept under a faded orange chenille bedspread from the thrift store. Anne's bed still had a pale pink comforter, ruffled shams, and quilted throw pillows. In place of my old desk, ink-stained and water-ringed years before I sat there practicing my Gregg shorthand, was a white French provincial desk. My mother had grumbled when I sent the old desk back to where it came from.

*I don't know why you're giving away perfectly good furniture,* she said.

Mother could squeeze a nickel till it screamed. That's why nothing in our house was ever new. But Franny...spared no expense making her home beautiful. Brocade sofa. Tasseled pillows. Pewter candlesticks. Tiffany lamps. Fresh flowers in ginger jars. Gilt-framed paintings.

I showered and returned to my bedroom—once my parents' room and later where I slept with Harry until he died in his sleep at 40. I had tried fresh paint and a new bedspread to make the room "mine," but it still felt empty.

Crossing to the window, I stared at Franny's house—dark and still. Her voice came back to me from a long-ago April morning when we were spring cleaning her kitchen. She stopped, brushed her hair from her face, and leaned on her mop.

*Who am I doing this for?* she asked. *My girls are gone. I have no one to take care of my home after I'm gone...like you're doing for your mother's house. What will happen to my house when I'm gone?*

I promised I would take as much care of her house as I did my own. Shortly after that, she told me she had made me executor of her will. I said I was willing but didn't entirely understand what my responsibilities would be.

"After I'm gone," she said, "go to Charles Hart. I've left everything you'll need with him."

The morning sun cast a gentle pink glow over the street. The day grew brighter. I gazed at Franny's house—the paired porch columns, Palladian window in the dormer, bay windows with decorative lattice, front porch running the length of the house.

Who might buy the house? I could not watch a stranger move in, paint it some other color, remodel. Would I as executor have a say-so in the asking price? Maybe I could price the house high enough to discourage unacceptable buyers. Or maybe...the thought stirred...I could price it low, sell my house, and buy Franny's. My heart raced as I considered it. I was financially stable with Harry's social security, life insurance, my retirement. No one was dependent on me. I didn't know what my house was worth, but way more now than when my parents had bought it.

Tom could advise me. He was a financial genius. Would I use my furniture or Franny's? Had Franny left me her furniture? An itemized list with my name on it? Left with Charles Hart like Franny said? *Everything you'll need is with him.* That must include the deed to the house. Had she left the *house* to me? I was getting ahead of myself. Turning from the window, I went back to the bathroom to dry my hair. I snapped on the dryer, and my mind snapped back to the possibilities. Move into Franny's house? Did I dare dream *that*?

How would I tell Anne? She would be heartbroken. She loved this house.

Anne. My beautiful, capable daughter, who had succeeded at everything she had ever tried except motherhood. After three miscarriages, she and her husband were pursuing adoption. Since I was going to the lawyer anyway, I was going to talk to him about that, too.

The doorbell? I turned off the dryer, waited. Nothing. Squinted at the clock by the sink. 6:45. Nobody would come over at this hour. Except maybe

## Chapter 3 ~ Houseguests

Ruby. Then a knock. Another. Louder. I tied the sash on my housecoat and started downstairs.

Through the oval window in the door I spotted a shabby woman on my porch. Facing the street, she swayed side to side on swollen feet, her puffy ankles spilling over the edges of worn out black orthopedic shoes. A pink polka dot bookbag, soiled, ripped at one corner, was slung over her shoulder.

Not the first time a homeless person had knocked. Our neighborhood was within walking distance of downtown and the bus station. My corner house easy to get to. This happened often enough, I kept $4 worth of quarters on a table in the foyer.

Leaving the safety chain hooked, I opened the door. She turned around. *Wreck* was the first word that came to mind. She was my age, maybe older. Heavyset. Wearing baggy tan polyester pants and a yellow t-shirt adorned with teddy bears and hearts. Face etched with wrinkles from too much sun, too much smoking, or both. Dingy, gray/blonde hair, shoulder-length, parted down the middle and held back by enormous jaw clips, one red, one green. In her arms was a sleeping baby, its nose, lips, and chin, chapped and red. Laboring to breathe. Three? Four months old?

"There's a rescue mission downtown," I said. "Wait here. I can give you bus fare—"

"Thank God," she said, voice trembling. "You're still here." She nodded in the direction of Franny's house. "I went home, but Mother won't answer the door. I need help with Topeka."

This made no sense. "I can't pay your way to Kansas. I meant I can give you bus fare to the *mission* downtown. Sit on the porch swing. I'll bring you a glass of—"

She laughed. "You haven't lost your sense of humor, Babs. *Kansas*...I don't want to go to Kansas." She turned the baby to face me. "I meant Topeka, my granddaughter. Topeka Hope."

I did not know what to address first. The fact she knew my name...and my nickname on top of that...or that some innocent child had actually been named 'Topeka.'

"Do I know you?" I asked.

"Of course you know me. We grew up together, silly. I know you were better friends with Ivy Leigh, but for pity's sake. Don't you recognize me? Open the door."

What was she up to? I shook my head. "Listen, ma'am, I'm sorry. I have an appointment this morning, and I really don't have time for this. Let me get you some money—"

She planted her feet. "Babs, stop foolin' around. I was on a bus all night. I can't get in Mother's house. Topeka's burning up with fever. I have to get her to the doctor. *Today.*"

"I'm sorry," I said. "I'm trying to tell you where to go for—"

She raised her voice. "All right. How's this? We moved in across the street when I was seven. I had a crush on your brother Archie. My dad gave you your nickname 'Babs.' You broke your arm when you were twelve. Fell off this porch into that bush right there."

My mouth dropped open. Knees buckling, I leaned against the door. "Justine?"

"Yes. Could I *please* come in till Mother wakes up? You don't know what I've been through." She broke down, her stooped shoulders heaving with sobs. Topeka coughed and cried.

Removing the safety chain, I opened the door and stood aside. The odor of "several days without a bath" wafted in. I could not bring myself to hug her. "I'm sorry. Come in."

"Could I lay the baby down? I'm so tired of carrying her."

"Of course." I took a quilt from the linen closet and arranged it on the sofa. Justine dropped the pink bag on the floor and laid Topeka on the quilt. We propped throw pillows around her. She whimpered in her sleep.

Justine shuffled to the kitchen. I followed, trying to convince myself this dejected creature was the same prissy girl in the portrait over Franny's fireplace. Plaid satin skirt. White ruffled blouse. Red hair bow. I had looked at her image for years.

"Coffee?" I asked.

"Yes." She sank down at the table and pulled out the chair next to her. Lifting her feet onto the chair, she leaned back. "Do you have any eggs?"

"Yes. How many would you like?"

"Three. Scrambled. I haven't had anything but raisins since lunch yesterday."

I was grateful for a reason to keep busy so I could turn away from Justine and collect my thoughts. "So," I said, opening the refrigerator, "it's been a long time." I broke the eggs into a bowl and whisked them furiously. "Hasn't Jacksonville changed since you left? Where are you living? A long way away? I mean—" I glanced over my shoulder. Head drooped, arms

## Chapter 3 ~ Houseguests

folded over her ample stomach, Justine had dozed off. I finished making breakfast, poured a glass of milk, and nudged her knee when I set the plate in front of her.

She sucked in a lungful of air and leaned forward, propping her elbows on the table. "Sorry." She held her fork like a shovel and hunched over her plate. "Got any ketchup?"

My mind hurtled forward, like an old jalopy dodging potholes on a dark road in a hailstorm. What to say first? *What happened to you? Where have you been? Your mother's dead? Where's J. Michael Ford?*

"So…" I said, leaning against the sink, "how—"

"Don't look at me like that, Babs," Justine said, a stray bit of egg on her upper lip. "I don't always look like this, but I had to leave in a hurry. And it's a long way from Buckhannon."

"Where?"

"West Virginia." She slurped her coffee. "That hits the spot. Could I have a couple of pieces of toast? Does your mom still make watermelon rind preserves?"

"No," I said. "She died several years ago."

Justine heaved a sigh. "Oh. Sorry to hear that. I always loved Miss Gladdie. She was so…comfortable." She laid down her fork. "So…where's Harry?"

"He's not here. He died of a heart attack."

Another heartfelt sigh. "You're just full of bad news, aren't you? Woke up dead?"

"What?"

"Did Harry die in his sleep? My third husband did that. Woke up dead." She swiped her napkin across her face, shifting the egg from one corner of her mouth to the other. "Never saw it coming. He was years younger than me. Seven. No. Wait. Eight."

"Third husband?" I sank onto a chair. "What happened to J. Michael?"

Justine drained her coffee cup and slid it toward me. "Who?"

"J. Michael Ford," I said. "The artist you ran away with."

"Oh. Jimbo." She shoveled the last of the eggs into her mouth and talked around them. "His name wasn't 'J. Michael.' He made that up." She chuckled. "He left me in Moultrie after six weeks. Pregnant with my first."

"Moultrie? I thought he had a job in—"

We heard Topeka coughing. Justine planted her hands on the table and pushed up. Wincing, she rubbed the back of her thigh. "Sciatica. You think

Mother will be awake soon? I've got to get the baby to the doctor. I think it might be croup." She sniffed under her arm. "Maybe I should take a shower first. I have enough formula for a couple more bottles. If you would feed Topeka, I could clean up and—"

I took her hand. "Come in the living room and sit where it's comfortable. I'll fix the bottle. We need to talk."

She walked with me. "Okay. But *no* third degree. I'm way too tired. And Mother will grill me. That's for sure." She backed up to my sofa and plunked down, jostling the baby. Then she picked up Topeka and settled her on her shoulder, patting and cooing. "There, there, Toppy-girl. We're home now. It's all better. No bus ride today."

I carted the soiled pink bag, smelling of grease and cigarette smoke, to the kitchen counter. The bottle was in a side pocket. I ran soapy water in the sink to soak off the dried milk from the last feeding and nearly gagged as I searched the bag for the formula. Underneath an XXL green and yellow Hawaiian shirt was a copy of the *National Enquirer,* an apple core wrapped in a brown paper towel, an empty raisin box, a honey bun wrapper, a plastic sandwich bag containing more than a dozen prescription capsules and tablets, two disposable diapers, and a baby's sleeper, crusted with spit-up and a brown stain down one leg.

Pushing the debris aside, I prepared the bottle and rejoined my visitors. I settled in a chair across from them and watched Topeka guzzle, pausing to catch her breath. Her nose was so stuffy, her chest heaving. My heart ached for her.

Justine looked up. "How do you think Mother will feel about being a great grandmother? Does she still hate to admit her age?"

I shrugged. "Is this your first grandchild?"

"Good grief, no. My 11th. And there's a 12th on the way. Even dozen."

"*Eleven?*"

"All my kids married young, and all the girls are Fertile Myrtles. I think I'll hold off on telling Mother that bit of news till later. The number, I mean." Her voice broke. "Fact is I'm scared to death to face her. But Topeka shouldn't have to suffer for the mistakes I've made." Brushing away tears, she lifted her eyes. "Do you think Mother will help her?"

"Listen…Justine. There's no easy way to say this. Your mother…died. We had her funeral yesterday."

Justine threw back her head and wailed. "Oh no. I'm too late. What am I going to do?"

## Chapter 3 ~ Houseguests

Skirting the coffee table, I eased down next to Justine. "Here. Let me take the baby."

I took Topeka in my arms, startled at how hot she was. "She's burning up, Justine. We have to get her fever down."

But Justine did not hear. Bent double, elbows propped on her knees, she was sobbing. "All those days on the bus…I thought if I could only get home, Mother would help us. But she's gone…Daddy's dead, too. I'm an orphan."

There was no time to console Justine.

Laying Topeka on the floor, I knelt and removed her sleeper and soggy diaper. Terrible rash. "Poor baby," I whispered. We headed to the kitchen. I ran tepid water into the sink and lowered her in, cradling her head in the crook of my arm. I scooped up cool water and gently poured it over her. She sighed, caught her breath, whimpered. "There you go," I said. "We'll get you in a clean diaper, and you can lie on Aunt Babsy's bed while your Granny gets ready. Then we'll get you some medicine, and you'll be all better. You'll see."

All this I said by instinct, until I realized—dumbfounded—I was hearing my mother's voice, soothing *her* child, and later, *my* child—same method, same sink, same tone.

I called to Justine to bring a towel from the bathroom. No answer. Topeka shivered. Called again. Silence. *Maybe she cried herself out and dozed off,* I thought. I yanked a dishtowel hanging on the oven door and wrapped up Topeka the best I could. Then I grabbed the diaper I had taken from the pink bag and started back to the living room. I lifted Topeka to my shoulder, pressing my cheek against her forehead to check her fever. "She's cooled down. I'm going to lay her on—"

The front door was open.

Justine was gone.

Hurrying onto the porch, I surveyed the street. Maybe she was taking a walk to clear her head. Maybe she was at Franny's—in a futile attempt to feel near her mother. No sign of her. Something warm and wet soaked my housecoat.

"Well…that was a rookie mistake," I said. "Let's get a diaper on you, little rascal."

Back inside, I closed the door and noticed the quarters from the candy dish were gone. *Maybe she was out of cigarettes,* I thought, *and walked to the 7-11.* That made sense. I put a diaper on Topeka, laid her on my bed, got dressed, and waited.

And waited. But an hour went by, and Justine did not return.

So, I did what I always did in a crisis. I called Ruby.

"Hello," she said.

Squeezing my eyes shut, I said sheepishly, "Ruby?"

Pause. "Oh. Hello, Barbara."

*Barbara.* The last time she had called me 'Barbara' was when I was in 5th grade and chucked a softball through her bathroom window…by accident.

There was nothing to do but charge forward. "I was going to write you a note to say how sorry I am about yesterday, but there's no time now. Justine is back, and—"

"Justine? When?"

"This morning. She's got a sick baby with her. Her granddaughter. We were going to take her to the doctor, but…" I spilled out the story, ending with… "I can't wait any longer for her to come back. But will a doctor treat Topeka without permission from a relative. Do you know?"

"Topeka?" Ruby asked. "That's the baby's name?"

"Yes. Topeka Hope. Ironic…under the circumstances."

"Oh, dear. Can you imagine what Franny would've said?"

"Well, I can tell you this. If she could see Justine, she'd flip over in her grave several times. I didn't even recognize her."

Ruby sighed. "Are you ready to walk out the door right now?"

"Yes. I've been ready."

"I'll be right there. We'll take the baby to Dr. Bailey."

Dr. Eben Bailey lived a few blocks over on Goodwin Street and had an office on Park.

"It's too early for him to be in his office," I said.

"We're going to his house," Ruby said flatly.

"His *house*? Don't you remember when I took Anne over there when she got that cut over her eye? He told me, 'This is my home. Not my office.' And packed me off to the ER."

"He's mellowed since then. Besides, after Jack died, Eben told me if I ever needed anything to let him know. Well, I *need* something. You still have one of the car seats you used for the boys? We'll need it."

My apology, never uttered, had been accepted.

A car seat was in the garage. I had kept it for when Anne had a baby.

Ruby (as usual) was right. Dr. Bailey did not turn us away. The good news was Topeka did not need a prescription. The illness was viral. Dr. Bailey told me to 'keep doing what I was doing.' Tylenol for the fever. Keep her

## Chapter 3 ~ Houseguests

hydrated. Keep her cool. Let her rest. He pressed me for details about Justine (who had been his patient as a child) and added sternly, "When she comes back, tell her if she's going to be responsible for this child, she has to have proof of guardianship. I won't see her again without it. Do you understand?"

"Yes, sir," I said. "Thank you."

Ruby took us home. She stayed with Topeka while I went shopping. Diapers, formula, bottles, pacifiers. Baby wash, Desitin, Vicks VapoRub, Children's Tylenol. Onesies, t-shirts, socks. A little blue whale rattle. Tiny stuffed terrycloth bear. Just enough to get by for now.

When I returned, I found Ruby and Topeka on the sofa. Ruby was dabbing the baby's forehead with a damp washcloth and singing, "Jesus Loves Me."

"Can you stay long enough for me to put all this away?" I asked. "Then I need to call the lawyer and cancel my appointment."

"Of course," Ruby said, still soothing the baby. "I'll go home and look through the yard sale stuff. I think there are some sleepers that will fit her. I'll bring lunch later."

Sick and half asleep, Topeka had won Ruby's heart.

"Thank you." My voice caught in my throat. "Ruby, I'm sorry—"

She held up her hand. "Go on now. Get those bottles washed. She's hungry."

Depositing the bags on the kitchen table, I removed the formula and bottles. I mixed the formula, delivered a clean bottle to Ruby, and went back to the kitchen. Lining up my supplies on the counter, I glanced at the junk I had taken from Justine's bag. I threw away the apple core, raisin box, pastry wrapper, *and* sleeper. The shirt smelled so bad I tossed it out the back door. When I lifted the *National Enquirer,* a long envelope fell out. Addressed simply to *Mother,* the envelope was printed with a return address, *Legal Aid of West Virginia, Inc.*

"No time for protocol," I said, and opened it without a second thought. Franny certainly couldn't read it. Unfolding the documents inside, I found a note attached and read it.

I should have sat down first.

Papers in hand, I returned to the living room and sat across from Ruby. The bottle, half full, was on the coffee table. Topeka was on Ruby's shoulder.

"If you want to finish burping her," Ruby said, "I'll go home and start"—she looked up—"what's wrong?"

I displayed the envelope. "I found this in the diaper bag."

Ruby squinted at the inscription. "Mother? What is that?"

"Justine never intended to stay."

"What do you mean?"

"Listen," I said, and read the note.

*Mother: Sorry to leave without saying goodbye. But if you and I couldn't live together when I was a kid, we can't do it now. I hope you can find it in your heart to help Topeka. She deserves more than I can give. Her mother doesn't want her. Her new boyfriend hates kids. So, I went to Legal Aid and got custody. Everything you'll need is here, including her birth certificate. If you can't keep Topeka, turn her over to social services. Maybe a nice family will adopt her. Justine.*

I folded the letter and put it back in the envelope. "Apparently, she was going to do the same thing to Franny she did to me. Bring Topeka into the house and the minute Franny's back was turned, take off."

Tears in her eyes, Ruby held Topeka closer. "How could a grandmother do that?"

"If you'd seen her, you'd understand. Justine was a mess. Probably spent her last dime getting here. She took the quarters out of my candy dish before she left."

"Poor girl."

I didn't know if Ruby meant Justine, Topeka, or me.

# Chapter 4

# Broken China
**Jacksonville, Florida**
**September 1979**

"Should we call the police?" I asked Ruby.

"What for?"

"To report an abandoned child."

Ruby laid Topeka next to her. "She's not abandoned. She has us. Justine may be back."

"She *stole* my money and *sneaked* off when my back was turned."

Ruby rolled her eyes. "I'd hardly call a handful of quarters a heist. She's in shock. She didn't know her mother was dead. Once she has a chance to think, she'll come home."

Snatching up the papers, I waved them like a wild woman. "Looks to me like she *already* had a chance to think. She knew perfectly well what she was doing."

Ruby laid her hand on Topeka's chest. "Lower your voice. You'll wake up the baby. Get ready and go to the lawyer."

"Go to the lawyer? I can't go now. I'm a foster mother."

Ruby stood, pulled the coffee table next to the sofa, and arranged throw pillows around the baby. "Don't exaggerate. You're not a foster mother. You're babysitting for a friend. Go to the lawyer. At the very least, he can tell you what to do about Topeka...if worse comes to worst."

"How did this happen?"

Ruby walked to the door. "You were home, and Franny wasn't."

"You *really* think Justine will come back?"

Ruby shrugged. "No idea. I'm going home to find some clothes for the baby. Then I'll come back and stay with her while you're gone."

I went upstairs to the bathroom, wet my hair again, and snapped on the hair dryer for the second time that day. The dryer whirred; my mind whirred. *Ivy Leigh should have this.* That's what Nancy Crisp had said. I snapped off the dryer and went to my room to get the photo. Then I propped it up next to the faucet and studied it while I did my hair. Cab held Ivy Leigh (about 2, I guessed) in his left arm; Clarissa was drawn in close with his right, her hand on his chest. The photographer caught them mid-laugh.

I had known Cab Moore for years, but I had never seen this kind of joy on his face. He had always been cordial, pleasant. But in quiet moments an abiding sadness shadowed him—an attitude I did not recognize as "melancholy" till after I realized J. Michael Ford was a con man, and I crept back home brokenhearted. *Look,* I thought, *how close they're standing.* Another memory flickered—Ivy Leigh remarking, *I love how your mom hugs your dad when he comes home. My mother never does that.* It was true. Cab usually kept a respectable distance from Franny.

When I finished my hair, I dabbed makeup on my face, lamenting my puffy bloodshot eyes. *You knew Justine,* Hank had said. Why mention her, but not Ivy Leigh? He left flowers on Clarissa's grave, but was glad Franny was "home." *Two families torn up. Scandal.* I brushed blush on my cheeks and reached for the eyebrow pencil. Leaning close to the mirror, I outlined one eyebrow, then the other. "Cab, Clarissa, and Ivy Leigh Moore," I whispered. "So…were Hank and Franny Justine's parents?" If that were true, how had Cab and Franny ended up together with both girls?

Having made myself presentable, I returned to my room. I was taking my blue dress off the hanger when I heard the rumble of an engine, squeal of brakes. Garbage day. I rushed downstairs and outside, wheeled my trash can to the curb, and sprinted across the street to put out Franny's trash. As I rolled her garbage can to the street, my toe caught on the crack in her driveway. Down I went. The lid popped off. Plastic bags spilled out. The burly garbage man, placing an empty can at the curb, saw me fall and ambled over.

"You okay, ma'am?"

I lumbered up, knee scraped and bloody, housecoat gaping open, revealing my slip. He politely ducked his head and reached down for the bags which had tumbled out. Grabbing two bags in one hand, the man wheeled the can to the truck. I tied my sash and eased my foot into the slipper which

## Chapter 4 ~ Broken China

had flown off. Sweat dripping down my face, bottom lip quivering, I waited while my rescuer finished his work. He brought the empty can back to me, reached down for the lid, and snapped it back on.

He smiled. "Here you go, ma'am."

It was the nicest thing that had happened to me in two days. "Thank you," I said, voice shaking. What could I say to such chivalry? "Stay hydrated."

He hopped onto the back of the truck with the agility of a knight mounting a noble steed. "Yes, ma'am." And waved the driver forward.

Grasping the black handle, I limped back up the driveway. I left the can next to the house and glanced at Cab's workshop in the backyard. I walked over and peered through the smudged window. Cab was always working on a project, squirreled away in this little wooden building—even in summer, a rusty box fan stirring the hot, sawdusty air, or on a frosty January day with a space heater at his feet. For love of his hobby, I had always thought, he preferred long hours in *here* to the comforts of the house. Or was there another reason?

Right knee throbbing, I started home. Blood trickled down my leg. I lifted the hem of my housecoat, so it wouldn't get stained, and crossed the street. Ruby, baby clothes draped over her arm, marched toward my house.

"What in the world happened to you?" she asked, nodding at my knee.

"Forgot it was garbage day. Tripped over that crack in Franny's driveway."

"You have Band-aids? I can go back home and get some."

We walked up the porch steps. "I have three grandsons. I'm never out of Band-aids."

While Ruby sorted baby clothes on my coffee table, I went upstairs to doctor my knee and touch up the makeup I had sweated off. Then I slipped on my dress and came downstairs.

Ruby pointed to three piles of clothes. "T-shirts. Sleepers. A couple of dresses. I'll wash them while you're gone." She glanced at Topeka. "When was her last dose of Tylenol?"

"An hour ago."

Grabbing my car keys, I limped to my car. I backed out and looked in the rearview mirror at Franny's house. Would I bring home the deed today? Could I move in by Thanksgiving? Would my children—grandsons in matching sweaters—come through that door to eat turkey in Franny's dining room? Then reality hit me like a clap of thunder. What was I thinking? If anyone was going to have Thanksgiving in that house, it was *Justine. She was home.* Executor or not, I had no right to make a claim on the house when the *heir* was present.

Car A/C on high, I drove over the Fuller Warren bridge to Charles Hart's law firm on Atlantic Blvd. and was ushered into his office. Dressed in a gray suit, sandy hair slicked into place, Mr. Hart motioned me to a leather chair facing his desk.

"Was Franny's funeral conducted according to her standards?" he asked, straightening a stack of documents on his desk blotter.

"Not exactly," I said, lifting my shoulders. "Too hot. Too many mosquitos. When Franny planned a graveside funeral, she never stopped to think what time of year she'd die."

"Hmm." He closed his eyes and tugged on his right earlobe. "We have a lot to go over."

*More than you know,* I thought, picturing Topeka on my sofa, but only said, "I'll save my questions till you're finished."

Pursing his lips, he glanced out the window at the massive magnolia tree on the side of the building. He seemed to be debating with himself about where to begin.

"Mrs. Moore," he said, "was a very private person."

"Yes," I agreed.

"But Mr. Moore's death a few years ago made it necessary for her to be more candid with me. I assume you're aware she had hoped to re-unite with her daughters before her death?"

"Yes," I repeated.

*Should I tell him Justine was somewhere in town this very moment?*

"Franny made you executor of her will because she was confident if either of her daughters re-appeared, you would give them whatever assistance you could."

"Of course. I grew up with them. We were all best friends."

*In fact, Justine's granddaughter is at my house. I took her to the doctor this morning.*

"Disposition of this estate"—he leaned forward and opened the folder—"is not going to be straightforward. There are issues to be resolved, and Franny stipulated they could be revealed only upon her death."

Out of nowhere the niggling sense of resentment I had been nursing flickered and flamed to life. Tired of feeling like the stupid kid in the room, I took the upper hand.

## Chapter 4 ~ *Broken China*

"You mean that Franny had been married before?" I asked.

His eyes widened. "You knew?"

I crossed my arms. "Hank Merrier showed up at the funeral."

Charles sank back into his chair. "And he told you who he was?"

"No. The pastor told Ruby who he was, and she told me."

"Ruby?"

"My neighbor. And," I said, feeling smug, "we met Nancy Crisp at lunch. Is that name familiar to you?"

"This meeting is going to be more streamlined than I thought," he said.

"There's more," I said officiously. "*Justine* came to my house this morning."

If a freak wind had toppled the magnolia tree onto the roof, Charles couldn't have been more surprised. Sitting bolt upright, he scooted to the edge of his chair and propped his arms on his desk. His glasses slipped down his nose.

"*What?*"

For some reason I myself did not understand, I relished the power I was wielding. "Justine's been married multiple times," I said, "and has a *passel* of grandchildren."

Charles rubbed his chin. "Where is she now?"

"I don't know. She took off while I was in the kitchen with the baby."

"Baby?"

"Her youngest granddaughter. Topeka."

"Topeka?" His upper lip curled slightly.

I related the story of Justine's arrival. Charles tried to keep a judicial bearing, but his fiddling with papers and drumming his fingers on his desk gave him away. He was rattled.

"If Justine doesn't come back," I concluded, "I need to know what to do about the baby. If she does come back, she may very well want to move all 11 grandkids into Franny's house. Will that take care of the disposition of—?"

Charles interrupted. "Justine has no right to the house."

"She's Franny's daughter," I said, failing to consider I was lecturing a jurist on the fine points of property inheritance. "She has as much right as—"

He rested his hand on the folder. "Franny made Justine the beneficiary of her life insurance policy, but the house belongs to Ivy Leigh." He swiveled his chair to face the credenza behind him. "Would you like some water?" he asked, pouring from a clear glass pitcher.

## The Moores, the Merriers

"No. What I'd like is the *truth*." I almost added: 'the whole truth and nothing but the truth,' but thought that was going a bit too far.

He set the glass on his desk. Opening the top drawer, he took out a King Edward cigar box and passed it across the desk. A mauve envelope addressed to "Mrs. Barbara Allgrove" was secured to the box with an aging rubber band.

"Franny gave this to me after Cab's death," he said, "and told me to turn this over to you after she died. She said she didn't want to leave without someone knowing who she really was."

The box smelled faintly of cedar and moth balls; the mauve envelope, newer, was scented lavender. My mother had kept 'important papers' in cigar boxes, but I had never pictured Franny doing something so mundane. She had three velvet-lined pewter jewelry boxes.

I removed the rubber band and slipped it onto my wrist. Then I tucked the envelope into my purse and lifted the lid of the box.

On top of pieces of paper and fragments of dried flowers was a photo of Justine's high school graduation. I recognized the photo. Franny had asked me to take it with her camera. At the time I thought nothing of the way the Moore family had dutifully "lined up," but now…knowing what I did…the image sent a shiver up my spine. On the left were Cab and Ivy Leigh, holding hands, smiling at each other. On the right, Justine and Franny had their arms around each other, the corner of Justine's mortarboard brushing the top of Franny's perfectly coiffed hair.

Between the pairs—father and daughter, mother and daughter—was a gap—subconscious or intentional? I peered closer at Ivy Leigh…Clarissa's likeness still fresh in my mind. There was no denying Ivy Leigh was an almost exact copy of her mother.

"It's true," I whispered.

"What's true?"

I turned the photo around. "Franny wasn't Ivy Leigh's mother. Clarissa was."

Charles nodded.

"And Cab was not Justine's father."

"No."

I returned the photo to the box and closed the lid. "The Moore girls were stepsisters. And 'the scandal' everyone in Madison is *still* talking about…Hank and Clarissa ran away together."

"Yes." His nonchalance was exasperating.

"Then, later Clarissa died."

## Chapter 4 ~ Broken China

"Correct."

"How?" I demanded.

"Car wreck. Six weeks after she and Hank left. She was killed instantly. Hank was badly injured. In the hospital for months."

"That's why he has a limp," I said.

"He almost died."

"So, Hank buried Clarissa, and sometime after that, Franny divorced Hank and married Cab." I sneered. "A case of 'if you can't be with the one you love, love the one you're with'?"

"After Hank and Clarissa left, Cab and Franny came to depend on each other. Cab had to work, so Franny would babysit Ivy Leigh, which gave her some means of financial support. The girls loved each other like sisters, so it only made sense for Cab and Franny—"

"To get married and pool their resources," I said. "Sensible. Not romantic, but sensible."

"Remember…it was the Depression. Being 'sensible,' as you put it, meant the difference between eating and having a roof over your head and doing without. Especially for the children."

"That still doesn't explain why Franny's house belongs to Ivy Leigh. Surely she'd want her *own* daughter to have a share—"

"How old were you when the Moores moved onto your street?"

"Seven."

"Do you remember *why* they moved into that house?"

"To help Mrs. Murphy. Cab was her favorite nephew. She was recovering from rheumatic fever and asked Cab and Franny to move to Jacksonville to take care of her."

Charles shook his head. "Mrs. Murphy wasn't Cab's aunt. She was his mother-in-law. Or used to be."

My pulse pounded. "Mrs. Murphy was Clarissa's *mother*?"

Charles steepled his fingertips. "Yes."

Propping my elbow on the armrest, I covered my eyes with my hand. "What a mess. *As the World Turns* going on across the street, and I never knew." I looked up. "Did *anyone* know?"

"Not that I'm aware of."

I leveled my gaze at Charles. "So, the house belongs to Ivy Leigh…because Mrs. Murphy was her *grandmother*?"

He nodded. "Mrs. Murphy was devastated by the scandal...and Clarissa's death, of course. Having Ivy Leigh with her gave her comfort and kept her family legacy intact."

"Did Franny *know* the house would be left to Ivy Leigh?"

"Yes."

"That's a low blow," I said. "Especially when Franny was good enough to become Ivy Leigh's mother."

"It was a perfect contract. Everyone got what they wanted. Franny could start a new life. Mrs. Murphy had a caregiver and a relationship with Clarissa's daughter. All parties satisfied."

"What about Cab? How did he feel?"

"I can only surmise. But...no rent? No mortgage? The women in his life all happy with their living arrangements? The girls provided for? It would work for me."

"Worked for my dad, too. We moved in with my grandmother when I was a baby. I still live there." Suddenly exhausted, I reached for my purse and took out my car keys. Then, hitching the purse straps over my arm, I grasped the cigar box, stood up, and marched across the room. "Could we finish this another day? I need time—"

Charles followed me to the door and opened it. "Of course. I know it's a lot to take in."

One foot in the hall, I whirled around and nearly collided with Charles. "Wait a minute. What about Nancy Crisp? Clarissa's sister. Did her mother leave anything to her?"

"Nancy got the family farm. That's a whole other story. I can give you the details."

I held up my hand. "Never mind. That's enough for one day. Thank you."

Half-sick, I maneuvered through the lobby and out the door. The moment I ventured into the steamy mid-day heat, my sunglasses fogged. I shoved them to the top of my head, slammed the cigar box onto the roof of my car, and fumbled to unlock the door. When I jerked the door open, the box slid down the windshield and crashed onto the hot pavement. The lid popped open. Contents cascaded out, scattering. Rolling my eyes at the rubber band still adorning my wrist, I retrieved the box and bent down to gather the pieces and put them back in.

Dimly...I heard Franny's voice.

*Careful.*

## Chapter 4 ~ *Broken China*

All at once I was back on Lomax Street—a teenage girl in a starched white eyelet-ruffled apron tied tight around my waist. I was helping Franny arrange her fine bone china on the long dining room table draped with a royal blue cloth.

Justine's high school graduation dinner.

A dessert plate sat too near the edge. When I leaned in to pick up a stray piece of greenery which had fallen from the centerpiece, I bumped the table leg. The plate careened to the polished hardwood floor and broke into four pieces.

I knelt to gather up the fragments. "I'm sorry, Miss Franny. I didn't mean to—"

"Careful," Franny said, standing in front of me.

I was touched—soothed by her soft voice. She hadn't lectured me about being clumsy. She was worried I would cut my hand on the sharp edge. But I couldn't have been more wrong.

"Give those to me," she said, hand outstretched, fingers wiggling. "I'll glue them."

I placed the pieces in her delicate hands. "Shouldn't we throw them away? Even if you glue them back together, the cracks will show."

Studying the pieces, she began to fit them together, a jagged edge pricking her finger. A drop of blood seeped up.

"Part of a set," she said. "There's no way to replace it. I'll glue this and set it at my place. I'll know the cracks are there. And *you* will. But no one else will. It'll be our little secret."

# Chapter 5

# Stormy Weather
### Jacksonville, Florida
### September 1979

A black Cadillac pulled into the parking lot. Still bent down, I glanced back, but kept to the business at hand, wiping sweat from my face as I scrambled after a stray bit of pink paper.

"Our little secret," I grumbled. "For cryin' out loud, Franny, how many did you *have*?"

The door of the Cadillac opened, closed. Footsteps.

A man's voice. "Looks like you could use some help." He reached under my car and picked up a photo lying face down next to the rear tire. "Here's one you missed."

Back still turned, I picked up the pink envelope flap with a scribbled telephone number. "Thank you," I said, shaking the box to shuffle the items into place so the lid would close. "I should've left the *stupid* rubber band on the box till I got home, but…" I looked up. My jaw dropped. I was staring into the smiling face of Mayor Jake Godbold. "Mr. Mayor. I'm sorry. I should've recognized your voice. I…I…voted for you."

Chuckling, he held out the photo. "My grandma left a box like that with her lawyer. Only it was a shoe box. I bet there's a good recipe for cornbread in there."

I slipped the rubber band back around the box. "I don't think so. Franny had her cornbread recipe memorized. And it was a secret." *Like everything else*, I thought.

"That wouldn't be Franny Moore, would it? I saw her obituary in the paper."

"Yes. She was my neighbor."

"Lovely woman," he said. "She and Cab were great friends to me and my wife. We loved their girls. Such a nice family."

"I don't remember seeing you at their house. I mean…I knew she was a big fan of yours. But I didn't know you were friends."

"They always came to *our* house." He paused. "Not to speak ill of the dead…but my wife never much cared for going over to Franny's. She was so…particular…if you know what I mean." He winked and extended his hand. "Well, have a nice day, Mrs.—?"

"Allgrove. Barbara. Nice to meet you, Mayor. And congratulations on the election."

He lifted his hand to wave goodbye as he walked toward the office. I slid behind my steering wheel and placed the cigar box on the passenger seat.

*Franny knew Jake Godbold. She was full of surprises.*

Back over the river I went—no better off than when I had left home. Turning onto Park Street, I thought of finding a shady spot where I could pull over to the curb and read the letter in the mauve envelope. But I had a baby to get home to. How had that happened? And why had Franny left me in the dark all these years? Even if she could not face telling her daughters who their parents were, she could have told *me*.

"After all," I mumbled, "I'm the executor. More like ex-eh-KEW-tor. I'm the one who's got to find everyone and kill their misconceptions about who they are."

I pictured myself facing Ivy Leigh…once I found her.

"Your mother died on Labor Day," I rehearsed, warming to my cynical tone. "Only she wasn't your mother. Clarissa Moore was your mother. Can we find her? Sorry, she's dead, too. Killed in a car wreck after she ran off with Justine's father, Hank. You thought Justine was your sister? No. Not even by half. She's your stepsister. She's got eleven grandchildren. Left the youngest one with me. I don't suppose you'd like *to adopt her, would you*?"

When I turned onto Lomax, I saw two cars parked in front of my house. I grabbed my purse and the cigar box and limped—my banged-up knee growing stiffer by the moment—up my porch steps and into the house.

Linda Jo, plump, pink-cheeked, pleasant, was sitting in my living room with Topeka cradled in her arms. "Hello, Babs," she said. "Ruby called and said you needed help."

"What's going on?" I asked, hearing racket upstairs and bustling in the kitchen.

## Chapter 5 ~ Stormy Weather

"Ruby and Jean made lunch. Richard brought in the crib from your garage. Ruby told him where it was. He's putting it together in Anne's room. Viola couldn't make it. She said she'd come by later."

Ruby, wiping her hands on a dishtowel, appeared in the doorway to the kitchen. "You're back. Everything go okay with the lawyer?"

"No. Everything did not 'go okay' with the lawyer. Richard's putting up the crib?"

"You can't very well sit and hold the baby all the time."

"I won't argue with that," I said, "but you didn't need to go to all this trouble." I lowered the cigar box to my side in a futile attempt to 'hide' it.

Ruby noticed but did not comment. "You weren't planning on taking care of a baby…and a sick one on top of that. Come eat lunch and don't argue."

"Be right there," I said, starting toward the stairs. "Let me get out of this dress. So *hot*."

Entering my bedroom, I set my purse on the dresser and then slid the box under my bed with as much stealth as if I had been hiding state secrets from the KGB. I changed clothes and went downstairs.

Lunch—egg salad sandwiches, watermelon, and iced tea as only Ruby could make it—soothed my nerves. The ladies let me eat without quizzing me. Ruby gave the kitchen counter a final swipe with a dishcloth and took the bottle of aspirin from the cabinet. She opened the bottle, shook out a tablet, and laid it by my glass.

"Take this," she said. "Once we put the baby to bed, you need to take a nap." I swallowed the aspirin. "You and Topeka can come to my house for supper at 5:00."

Tears seeped into my eyes. "I don't know what I'd do without you, Ruby."

She laid her soft hand on my shoulder. "We're all going to help till Justine comes back."

Richard, Linda Faye's husband, peeked in from the living room. "Crib's all set up. Wife put the baby down. We're gonna take off. Call if you need anything else."

Jean followed them out. Ruby told me where she had stored the baby supplies and with yet one more reminder for me to "take a nap," went home.

As I was leaving the kitchen, the phone rang. "Hello."

"Hi, Mom."

My daughter Anne. I was glad to hear her voice. "Hey. How are you?"

"Good. I was up all night, but I've been asleep since I got home so I feel better. Have you had lunch yet?"

"Just finished."

"Oh, okay. Well, want to get together for supper? Scott's working late."

"Ruby already invited us over," I said.

"Us?"

"Me and...Topeka."

There was no easy way to bring up the subject, so I simply blurted out the name.

"Who?"

I related the events of the morning, leaving out my trip to the lawyer and my increasing disillusionment with Franny.

Anne's sternness startled me. "You can't keep that baby. You have no legal right."

"I know that. I'm babysitting till Justine comes back."

She scoffed. "Babysitting...Justine could be halfway to who-knows-where by now."

"No, I don't know, and I'd appreciate it if you didn't use that tone with me."

Anne ignored me. "You *have* to report this to social services. I know what I'm talking about. I'm a medical professional."

"*I know that,*" I said, in no mood for her petulance, "but I'm not going to jump the gun. What would Justine say if she walked through the door in an hour and Topeka wasn't here...that I'd turned her over to the authorities like she was some kind of stray dog?"

Anne's voice rose again. "How *long* has Justine been gone?"

"I don't know. Since before the garbage man came. I don't remember the *exact* time."

"Mom...*think* about what you're doing. This has 'disaster' written all over it. What if that baby gets sick?"

"Her *name* is *Topeka,* and she's already sick. We took her to Dr. Bailey right after—"

"You took her to a *doctor* without parental consent?"

This condescending lecture from my own child got on my last nerve.

"Listen," I said in my most withering motherly tone, "I've had a purely awful day. I fell and nearly broke my knee." The moment called for exaggeration. "I have a terrible headache, and I'm not going to discuss this with you any further. Call back when you've calmed down."

## Chapter 5 ~ Stormy Weather

"All right," Anne said, meaning, *Have it your way.* "Bye." Click.

Exasperated, I slammed down the receiver, nearly dislodging the harvest gold phone from the wall. I stomped to the sink and gazed out the window at my car.

"If I wanted to," I said, "I could get behind the wheel, take I-10 West, and drive till I got to Houston…or Albuquerque…somewhere. No one could stop me."

But Topeka was upstairs, and…I reminded myself…none of this mess was her fault.

On the way to take the nap Ruby had ordered, I stopped to check on the baby. She was still congested but resting comfortably. I felt her forehead. Cooler. She was on the mend.

"At least I've done *something* right today," I whispered.

Stepping into my room, I took the mauve envelope from my purse and padded toward my bed. I fluffed the pillows and plopped down, heaving a deep sigh. Maybe…maybe…I could have a few uninterrupted minutes to myself before another crisis erupted.

I opened the envelope. Bits of lavender showered onto my bedspread as I unfolded Franny's note—tantalizingly brief.

> *Dear Barbara, I could not leave this life without someone knowing the truth. That Cab and I were married before and cruelly abandoned by our spouses, Clarissa and Hank, who broke their marriage vows and our hearts. Though I meant to, I never found the courage to tell the girls who their other parents were. Please don't judge me too harshly. Know that I've paid dearly for the choice I made—lived in constant fear they would find out. By now you'll know I died a coward leaving the secret with you alone. Do with it as you think best.*

Putting the letter aside, I lay back and closed my eyes. Only a week ago my biggest worries had been refilling the propane tank for the barbecue grill and chasing after a mole cricket on my driveway. Now, I was saddled with a sordid past that wasn't even mine. My perfectly ordered little life was in tatters. How was I supposed to find Ivy Leigh? I was no private eye, and I couldn't hire one. And what if Justine didn't come back? Anne was right. I'd have to report Topeka, and the poor baby would be shuffled off to someone else.

The house quiet and cool, I gradually relaxed, letting my mind wander— half-dreaming, half-imagining—as the ceiling fan whirred. I pictured Hank, left hand on the steering wheel, right arm around Clarissa, as they sped away from Madison on Highway 90. Snuggled close to him, her dark hair glistened on his strong shoulder under the brilliance of a full moon. In the distance a train whistle broke the stillness of the night. Farther, farther away the train sped, the whistle growing fainter as distance increased. And into the darkness on the two-lane highway, Hank and Clarissa rode, rode…leaving behind….

A little girl crying…a young woman's voice cooing, *Don't cry. Don't cry.*

My eyes popped open. Topeka was awake. I sat up and swung my feet onto the floor.

"Don't cry. It's okay." A sweet voice I knew well.

I scampered down the hall and found my Anne sitting on her old bed with Topeka's little head pressed against her shoulder. Anne was rocking back and forth, back and forth, her face and the baby's both wet with tears. There was no need to ask what was wrong. I knew. Anne had been longing for a child of her own for years. Sitting there on her pink bedspread with a baby in her arms, she was my little girl again, loving her dolly, her heart broken over some childhood disappointment, feeling helpless. Without looking up, she spoke softly.

"Sorry I was such a brat"—she wiped away tears—"on the phone. But it made me furious some family would simply throw a baby away when I want one so much."

Grabbing a handful of Kleenex from the pink flowered box on the nightstand, I sat next to her.

"I understand," I said.

She shifted Topeka to me and took the Kleenex. "You can't possibly understand. You got married and bang…spit out two babies within three years. Do you have diapers? She's wet."

*Spit out? There's more to it than that,* I thought, but decided not to argue.

"Downstairs in the kitchen. I bought supplies this morning. I'm glad you're here, so you can look her over. See how she is."

Anne stepped to the crib and rested her hands on the railing. "Don't you think it's a little premature to put up the crib?"

"It wasn't my idea," I said, patting Topeka's back. "Ruby said I can't sit around and hold a baby all the time."

Anne smiled. "Miss Ruby's always right." She started toward the door. "Come on. I still haven't had lunch. Do you have anything to eat?"

## Chapter 5 ~ Stormy Weather

"Oh, yes. Ruby called the ladies and said I needed help. They brought enough food for ten people."

We went downstairs. While I fixed a bottle, Anne changed Topeka's diaper and then took her usual place at the kitchen table.

"Now," Anne said, easing the bottle into Topeka's mouth, "start from the beginning."

As I busied myself with egg salad and watermelon, I told the story, peeking over my shoulder at Anne with Topeka in her arms.

Even on ordinary occasions like this—lunch in the kitchen—Anne had a professional bearing. Tall, willowy-figured, dark brown hair, high cheek bones, porcelain complexion, deep brown eyes, she could have been a model (everyone said). But even as a little girl, she wanted to be a nurse so she could "help people," which she had done her whole life. Whether she brought in a baby bird fallen from a nest, a stray cat she begged to keep, or a playmate with a scrape on her elbow, Anne had always been on the lookout for the wounded and forlorn.

She was my own daughter. I knew all her idiosyncrasies and flaws. But I admired her more than any woman I knew.

"And that's it," I said, setting a sandwich in front of her. "Till Justine comes back."

"Have you thought about what you'll do if she *doesn't* come back?" Anne asked.

I took Topeka and sat across from Anne. "I was hoping *you'd* tell *me*."

She picked up her sandwich. "It'd be complicated. But you're right. If Justine went to all the trouble she did, she wouldn't walk off and leave her granddaughter."

After lunch Anne brought in her medical bag from the car. I laid Topeka on the sofa and watched as Anne examined her. When she finished, she draped her stethoscope around her neck.

"Except for the congestion, she's in great shape," Anne said. "Justine has done a good job with her." She caressed Topeka's face. "Wonder how long she's had her."

"Didn't stay around long enough to tell me the whole story." I nodded at the manila envelope on the coffee table. "She left all those documents."

Anne sorted through the papers. "Everything is here. Even the shot records. All up to date." She returned the stack to the envelope. "Have you told Tom yet?"

"No. I try not to call him when he's at work."

"Well, you'd better call him tonight. You don't want him showing up here with no warning. You know how he overreacts."

"Unlike you?" I asked, grinning.

She rolled her eyes. "Yeah, unlike me." She stood. "I think I'll go home and make a few phone calls. It won't hurt to be prepared…in case Justine stays gone any amount of time."

"You sure you're okay?"

"I will be. I just need a little time alone." She leaned down to hug me. "Don't worry about me. You've got plenty to do to take care of this baby."

After Anne left, I took Topeka upstairs and laid her in the crib. "Lucky for you," I said, opening the closet door, "I haven't given up on more grandchildren. I still have everything."

I moved aside Tom's guitar case and pulled out the wind-up swing I had stored for the next baby—Anne's, I had hoped. I carted the swing downstairs to the living room, went back for Topeka, carted her downstairs, and slipped her into the swing. She jumped when I cranked it, but soon settled in, delighted at the gentle swaying. The look of contentment on her face brought back soothing memories of heady, bewildering days, when I had put one grandson after another in this swing. Topeka brought her hands to her mouth, nuzzled, and finally found her thumb.

"Be right back," I said, and went upstairs to get the cigar box from under my bed. Then holding the box like a sacred offering, I descended the stairs, set it ceremoniously on the coffee table, and settled on the sofa. "Well…" I said to Topeka, "shall we open—?"

At that moment the sky went dark. Lightning tore across the sky. A clap of thunder rattled the house. We both jumped. Topeka, wide-eyed, did not cry, only went back to her thumb with more vigor. She was less startled than I was.

In September, afternoon thunderstorms were predictable, especially if the weather had been extremely hot all day. Any self-respecting Floridian could "feel it in the air." Still…thunderclouds blotting out the sun, rain blowing sideways…the second I lifted the lid?

I reached out and jiggled Topeka's foot. "I think your great granny is trying to tell us something." She smiled back. My heart melted.

Scooting to the edge of the sofa, I leaned over the open box and took out a scrap of paper written in pencil so faint I could barely read it. "Cranberry Orange Cake. Don't remember eating this. Wonder why she saved the recipe?"

## Chapter 5 ~ *Stormy Weather*

On I went, examining each memento, mystified why Franny had placed value on such random items: phone numbers, unidentified; photo of a Model T, the driver wearing a Panama hat tilted jauntily; a soldier in a WWI uniform, barracks behind him. But halfway down the pile, I struck gold. Franny's wedding announcement—*Mr. & Mrs. Eldert Hibbs request the honor of your presence at the marriage of their daughter Francesca Elizabeth to Mr. Henry Fitzsimmons Merrier IV*; play program—*Abie's Irish Rose*, Hank and Clarissa listed as "Abie" and "Rosemary," a souvenir postcard, dated 193_ (postmark blurred), from Sweetwater, Texas.

By then the clouds were so black, the rain so heavy, it was too dark to read. I edged toward the end table and turned on the lamp. The card addressed to "Francesca Merrier" was printed in a small, firm hand.

> *Dear Franny, By the time you read this, I will be almost home. I've been a fool. I hope you can forgive me. For Justine's sake...please try. Love, Hank*

The narrative I had stitched together was wrong. The collision—killing Clarissa, crippling Hank—had not happened during the escape, but on the *return*. They had repented. At least Hank had. Flipping the card, I stared at the photo of the Nolan County Courthouse. How did Franny react when she read this? Plan to welcome Hank home? Urge Cab to do the same with Clarissa? Had she stood on her porch—her little girl straddling her hip—clutching this card, whispering, 'Daddy will be home soon'? Had she called to Ivy Leigh, and said, 'Your Mama's on her way back'?

Only to have her hopes destroyed by news of the accident. Had she thought of rushing to Hank's bedside? Have second thoughts about marrying Cab? Why did she stay with him? For his sake, because Clarissa was dead and Ivy Leigh needed a mother? I gazed at Topeka, lulled to sleep by the rain—safe from the storm. She was the next chapter in this sad story—*another* castoff child. Was this a Merrier family trait? Did someone in every generation walk away from the children who needed them? Leaving them behind for someone else to love and care for?

Propping my elbows on my knees, I gazed at Topeka. Her head drooped to one side, wet thumb, half-in-half-out, stuck in the corner of her mouth. She had settled in so easily. Was she that accustomed to adapting to a strange place?

"Well, I promise you one thing," I whispered. "As long as you're in my house, nothing's going to happen—"

A sudden gust of wind roared past. Rain pelted the house. I hurried to the door to stare out the oval window. Ruby's wooden garden bench was upside down in my front yard. My birdfeeder, suspended from a wrought iron pole, danced in the wind like Dorothy's house in a Kansas tornado. Empty garbage cans and lids tumbled down the street, littered with branches and leaves. The hanging baskets on my porch pirouetted from their hooks like clumsy ballerinas, a profusion of pink and purple impatiens showering down. I opened the door and stepped out to peek at Franny's house.

There it stood—resolute, unscathed. The lawn was saturated, puddles forming, but everything was still in pristine order. The tidy boxwood shrubs stood at attention on either side of the front steps. Franny had no outdoor furniture—"might mildew," she reasoned—to overturn. Not a leaf or twig cluttered the ground. Franny had ordered the beautiful live oak in front of her house cut down while I was still a child. When the house had belonged to Mrs. Murphy, my brothers and I played tag around that tree, hid there, rested in its shade. I still grieved over its loss.

Once, when Ivy Leigh and I were doing geometry homework at the kitchen table, I was foolish enough to ask Franny why she "got rid of the tree." Ivy Leigh kicked my shin and shook her head, but the question was already out.

Stationed at the sink, drying a clear glass with a white towel, Franny did not answer at first. Not unusual—she was often detached, musing. It appeared I had dodged a bullet, till she stiffened, the space between her shoulders narrowing.

"Have you been through a storm, Barbara?" she asked, as if I were on a witness stand.

"Yes, ma'am. This is Florida."

Back still turned, she set down the glass and placed her hands flat on the counter. "What happens?"

Her tone was blistering. I cut my eyes over at Ivy Leigh to guide me through the minefield I had ventured into, but she pretended to be busy bisecting a right angle.

"Depends on how bad it is," I said. "The street floods. Or—"

Franny took another glass from the drainer. "Have you seen a tree *fall* on a house?"

"No, ma'am."

"I have. It came right through the roof and into our attic." She turned to face me, twisting the dishtowel inside the glass with such force I thought it

## Chapter 5 ~ Stormy Weather

might shatter in her hands. "Crushing the cedar chest where Mama's wedding gown was stored. Ruined. She had saved it for me…for years…" She said all this, voice quivering with fury, as if accusing me of the deed. Then she fell silent, hands still. "It was a sign…and I ignored it."

I gulped. "I never thought about it…like that…I guess…"

Franny placed the glass on the counter, folded the towel in precise thirds, and draped it over the oven door handle. "Every day of your life you have to prepare for any eventuality. Think ahead to what *might* happen and don't be caught off guard." Eyes straight ahead, she walked past us to the living room. "That's why I had the tree cut down. It *might* have fallen."

When Franny was safely out of range, Ivy Leigh leaned in to whisper. "I tried to warn you. Don't *ever* mention Grandma's wedding dress. Mother never got over it."

"It's not my fault," I said. "I thought we were talking about a *tree*."

"You'll learn. The simplest thing can end up back at that wedding. I don't know what happened, but it must've been bad, whatever it was."

"She can't still be upset about *that*. After all these years? It's just silly."

Ivy Leigh shrugged. "All I know is there was no big church wedding. They got married in somebody's living room. I've never figured out why. Mother's family was so stuffy and formal."

"Whose house was it?"

"No idea. There's only one picture of the wedding. She had on a straight skirt with a jacket over a white blouse. Dad wasn't in a tux, like you'd think. Just an ordinary suit with a striped tie. He won't talk about it either. I've asked."

"Weird. I guess wearing that wedding gown was her dream. If she couldn't have that—"

Ivy Leigh closed her book. "Thing is…I've seen a picture of her in a wedding gown. Bouquet, veil. The whole thing. Standing under an arch all decorated with flowers. Candles lit. Looks like a wedding to me. I've never been able to figure it out."

"Maybe she posed for the picture before the dress got destroyed. You know, official bridal portrait. For the newspaper, maybe?"

The wind gusted, blowing rain in my face, stirring me from my reverie. I was opening the door to retreat inside when I spotted a Volkswagen Beetle putt-putting down our street, spraying water in its wake, leaving ripples in the puddles.

A VW Bug. Red. Faded. It couldn't be…the same one from the cemetery?

Nancy Crisp?

I ducked inside, leaving the door ajar, so I could peek out. Sure enough, the car pulled into Franny's driveway. The door opened. An enormous black umbrella popped up. Nancy Crisp emerged. As she hurried toward the porch, another burst of air blew her umbrella sideways. She held on the best she could, her thin arms straight out, straining, but the umbrella was ripped from her hands. It somersaulted into the neighbor's yard. Without thinking, I dashed out, limped off my porch, and, for the second time that day, hurried across the street.

Nancy chased the umbrella; I chased her.

She—tall, angular, elbows and knees flailing. Me—short, squatty, still hobbling from my morning fall. Wet hair plastered to our faces, feet sloshing through soggy grass. Feminine facsimiles of Laurel and Hardy.

Finally, the umbrella lodged against a sundial. Nancy grabbed it and whirled around, not knowing I was behind her. The metal tip of the umbrella whacked me in the left temple and scraped all the way down my cheek to my chin.

Howling, I clamped my hand over my face and bent over double.

"I'm sorry," Nancy said, stepping closer to hold the umbrella over me. A useless gesture too late to do any good. "I didn't see you. Let me help you up." She gripped my elbow with her slender fingers and tugged. Thrown off balance, I plopped down in the sodden grass and, for the first time since Franny died, laughed out loud. Nancy mistook my hilarity for weeping. "You're hurt. I'll get help." Off she ran toward the house next door.

I rolled onto my hands and knees and yelled. "Nancy. Come back. I'm all right."

By the time she returned, I had managed to lumber up. Again, she held the umbrella over my head. Did she not notice we both looked like drowned rats?

"I'm so sorry," she wailed. "Your poor face. It looks *awful*. Your eye is bleeding."

"I'm fine. What are you doing here? Franny's dead. There's no one home." This was no time for subtlety. I put my arm through hers—unsure which of us was supporting the other—and we started back to Franny's house.

## Chapter 5 ~ *Stormy Weather*

"I don't know why I came," Nancy said, "It's not like me to do something so impulsive. But I couldn't stop thinking about Ivy Leigh. When I didn't see her at the cemetery, I thought maybe she left before I got there. I hoped…she might be here. I couldn't miss my one chance to see her again. She's all I have left of my sister."

We reached the little red car. The door stood open. The inside was drenched.

"Ivy Leigh hasn't been home in nearly 30 years," I said, closing the car door. "I'm sorry." Nancy's head drooped. "Come to my house. We'll get dried off."

"I didn't bring a change of clothes. I was going to start home before dark."

"It's already dark," I said, guiding her across the street. "This storm isn't going to blow over any time soon. Stay with me tonight. You can drive home tomorrow."

"I wouldn't want to impose. I only met you yesterday."

We stepped onto my porch. I closed the umbrella and leaned it against the wall. "You're not imposing. In fact, you're doing me a favor."

"How's that?"

"You're saving me the trouble of driving back to Madison to find *you*."

# Chapter 6

# Dinner with Nancy
### Jacksonville, Florida
### September 1979

The minute I closed the door, the phone rang.

"Be right back," I said to Nancy and rushed to the kitchen to answer it.

"Do my eyes deceive me," Ruby asked, "or was that Nancy Crisp running down our street?"

"It was," I said, tearing off a paper towel to dab blood from the corner of my eye.

She whispered as if Nancy could hear. "What's *she* doing here?"

"Looking for Ivy Leigh," I whispered back.

Ruby sighed. "Poor thing. She had no idea. I was just thinking that baby doesn't need to be out in this weather, so when this lets up a little, I'll run the soup over to you."

"Great. I talked Nancy into spending the night. I thought I'd have to go back to Madison to find *her*, and she showed up on my own doorstep. I think it's a sign."

"A sign of what?" Ruby asked. She never let me dream for long.

"I don't know, but it's the first good thing that's happened since Franny died."

When I came back to the living room, I found Nancy cooing over Topeka. "Cute baby. Your grandchild?"

"No. Justine's."

She whirled around. "Justine is...*here? Now?*"

"Yes. No. I mean she *was* here...this morning. But she left."

"Where did she go?" Nancy demanded, hands outspread.

"I don't know." I told her the story, concluding with, "Ruby's sure she'll come back."

"You're not?" she asked, sinking onto my sofa.

My jaw dropped. Sorry as I was for Nancy, I was not about to stand by and let her rain-soaked dress leave a watermark on my taupe Ethan Allen cushions. I didn't care how skinny she was. A stain was a stain.

I managed an even tone. "No idea. But…we should change out of these wet clothes, don't you think?"

Taking the hint, she hopped up. "I'm so sorry." She examined the place she had vacated, brushing at moisture with her fingertips. "I can't change clothes. I didn't bring any. This whole trip was a mistake. I don't know *why* I came." She started toward the door.

"Wait," I said, motioning her to stop. "I have clothes that'll fit you. My daughter jogs in our neighborhood. She leaves workout clothes here."

Reluctantly, Nancy followed me upstairs to Anne's room and watched as I rifled through the bottom dresser drawer. I offered black nylon shorts and a hot pink Minnie Mouse t-shirt.

She held up her hand. "Oh, *no*. I never wear shorts. Not with my bird legs."

"How 'bout stretch pants?"

Frowning, Nancy brought her hand to her chin. "All right. But in those tight pants and that pink shirt, I'm going to look like a flamingo."

"Nobody here but us and the baby," I said. "I'll get you a towel. You can change in the bathroom. Then bring your wet clothes down, and I'll put them in the dryer."

While Nancy changed, I returned to the living room and inspected the sofa. No stain. Thank goodness for Scotchgard. The contents of Franny's cigar box were still scattered on the coffee table. Put them away? Or invite Nancy to examine them and ask her to explain? Might be too much at this point. I gathered up the pile, arranged the items in the box, and, slipping into the kitchen, slid the box behind my mother's Betty Crocker cookbook on top of the refrigerator. Nancy brought her wet clothes downstairs. I put them in the dryer, and we settled on the sofa with iced tea.

She folded her paper napkin in half and wrapped it around her glass. "This is a lovely house. How long have you been here?"

"All my life. Moved out for a while when I got married. But moved back. Stayed."

## Chapter 6 ~ *Dinner with Nancy*

"Same with me and my house," she said, smiling. "Don't you wonder how people just pack up and leave their past behind?" She set her glass on the coffee table. "I couldn't do it. I don't know how my mother did. Do you remember her? Bess Murphy?"

"Bess? No one called her that. We called her 'Mumsie.' I didn't know her all that well. She was nice but kept to herself."

"Mama hated leaving Madison. It was because of Clarissa. She was so embarrassed about her running off with Hank."

"It wasn't her fault. Clarissa was a grown woman."

"You know how people are…always want to speculate about 'what went wrong.' Assign blame. Everyone said it was because Mama handled Clarissa like a china doll."

"She didn't treat you the same way?"

She laughed bitterly. "No. I was the dutiful elder sister. Responsible for everyone else."

"I know what you mean. I'm a firstborn daughter."

"Mama never said so, but I often thought she would've been happier if I'd been killed in that car wreck instead of Clarissa."

Safely on the subject, I ventured further. "So, tell me. How—?"

The phone rang. Ruby. Again.

"It's only sprinkling now," she said. "I think I'll make a dash for it. Open the door."

When I said Ruby was on her way, Nancy hopped up. "That's the lady who was with you yesterday, isn't it? I'll get the umbrella and walk with her. Which way will she come?"

I pointed her in the right direction. Nancy darted out, popped her umbrella open, and met Ruby on the sidewalk. I held the door for them.

Ruby ferried in the stainless-steel pot. "What in the wide world happened to your face?"

"I did that," Nancy said.

"I'm not even going to ask," Ruby said and made her way to the kitchen.

We moved Topeka's swing into the kitchen and sat down to turkey vegetable soup. Perfect on a rainy afternoon. Blowing on a spoonful of soup, I glanced around the table. Until yesterday I had not known Hank Merrier and Clarissa Moore had ever been on the planet, but here I was having supper with Hank's great-granddaughter and Clarissa's sister.

*You couldn't make up a story like this*, I thought. *No one would believe it.*

Tired and hungry, we ate without speaking for a few moments until Nancy broke the silence. "I wanted to tell you, Ruby, how much I admired you for helping Mr. Donaldson."

"Who?" she asked.

"Donaldson," Nancy said. "The man at Smith's Drug Store…the one who was choking. You were so cool and level-headed. I'm useless in a crisis."

Ruby ducked her head. "Just instinct. I hopped up before I knew what I was doing."

"Well…" Nancy said, reaching for the saltines. "It was amazing."

"How is he, by the way?" Ruby asked. "Do you know?"

"He's fine. I heard from Mrs.—"

The front door opened. "Mom?" My son Tom. "Mom." Louder.

"In here," I called, flinching.

He started lecturing as he stormed across the living room. "Anne called. Said some woman left a baby with you." Arriving at the kitchen, he skidded to a halt. "What's up with your face?" When he saw I had company, he lowered his voice. "Oh. Hello, ladies."

He had come straight from work. Still in business attire—creased khaki pants, crisp long-sleeved blue shirt, Ralph Lauren tie—he was the quintessential upwardly mobile young professional. Like his sister, Tom was tall, dark-haired, and brown-eyed. Unlike her, he was impetuous and plain-spoken. Anne was right. I should have called him at the office, but it was too late for that now. I could tell from his harried look he had come to warn me about my reckless behavior.

Since his father died, Tom had held the opinion he was "responsible" for me—a point of view I found both endearing and irksome.

Ruby spoke up. "Hello, Tom. How are those boys of yours?"

"Fine," he said, cutting his eyes at Topeka. "Mother"—he was struggling to be civil and polite in front of my guests—"Anne said you're…babysitting?"

"For a while," I chirped. "You haven't met Nancy. She's…" *How could I sum her in a few words?* "…you remember me talking about Mrs. Murphy?"

Tom rubbed his forehead. "No…"

"Sure, you do. She lived across the street. She was the lady who owned the house before Franny moved in. You remember."

"That was a long time ago," he said, closing his eyes. "How could I possibly—?"

"Anyway, Nancy is Mrs. Murphy's daughter. We met at Franny's funeral." Hinting, I nodded slightly in her direction.

## Chapter 6 ~ Dinner with Nancy

He got my meaning and approached, extending his hand. "Tom Allgrove." Then he pointed his thumb at Topeka. "And who's *this*?"

"You remember me talking about my friend Justine?" I asked, an octave higher.

"No…" he said, pursing his lips.

Nancy leaned over and whispered to Ruby, who held up two fingers in reply.

*Nancy asked how many children I have,* I thought.

"Yes, you do," I said to Tom. "Justine was Franny's younger daughter. We were friends when we were little. Me and her and Ivy Leigh…"

"I can't remember the names of every little old lady in the neighborhood," he said. "There were too many."

"He has a point," Ruby said, grinning.

"Justine wasn't a little old lady," I said. "I told you we were friends when we were *kids*."

He scratched his left eyebrow. "I didn't come *all* the way over here *after* work to stroll down Memory Lane, Mom. I just want to know who this kid belongs to and why she's *here*."

If we had been alone, I would've warned him not to talk to me like an employee. But I did not want to cause a scene in front of Nancy. As it happened, there was no need to worry along those lines. She wasn't even listening. Turned sideways in her chair, bony elbows propped on bony knees, she was speaking to Ruby in a hushed confidential tone. I was dying to get in on their conversation, especially when Nancy said, "—my mother's fault our family didn't stay together. When Clarissa was gone, Mama left me without looking back."

From somewhere miles away, I dimly heard Tom's voice. "Mom. *Mom.*"

"What?" I asked.

"Who does this child belong to?" he demanded.

"I told you. Justine."

"—my mother was the same way," Ruby said. "That's why I never played favorites with my four girls."

"So…this Justine woman is the mother?" Tom asked.

"No. Grandmother," I said. "She's been gone a long time. Showed up this morning, looking for Franny…"

"She didn't know her own mother was *dead*?" Tom asked.

I frowned. "You don't have to put it like that."

67

"—have to find Ivy Leigh," Nancy said. "She's the closest thing I have to a daughter. I just hope there's some clue in—"

"—Bobby's working now, but I'll call him tonight—" Tom said.

"—talk to Viola while you're here," Ruby said. "She knew your mother best, but not even she knew Franny had been married before. None of us did."

I clenched my teeth. What was Ruby thinking? I was not about to invite *Viola* over here.

"Mom," Tom said. "*Mom.*"

"*What?*" I asked, so loud that both Nancy and Ruby looked up. Topeka, startled, began to cry. I stopped the swing and took her out, holding her close.

"I *said* Bobby's working now, but I'll call him tonight and tell you what he says."

I carried Topeka around the table and stood next to Nancy. "Would you like to hold your niece? Uh…great-niece, I guess?" Not really the case, but it didn't matter.

Nancy sat back in her chair. "I'm a little rusty at holding babies."

"Like riding a bicycle," I said, setting Topeka on her lap. "You never forget. Would you like to feed her?"

Nancy slipped her arms around the baby and kissed the top of her head. I took that as a yes and went to the dish drainer for a clean bottle. Tom followed, still talking.

"What time are you going to bed?" he asked.

I measured water into a bottle and added formula. "Same time. Why?"

"I told you. I'm going to call Bobby at home tonight and find out what you should do."

"*Who's Bobby?*" I screwed on the cap and shook the bottle to mix the formula.

"You remember," Tom said. "He used to come over all the time. We graduated together. He's a sergeant with the Jacksonville Sheriff's Office now. He'll know what to do."

"About what?" I asked.

"An abandoned child," Tom said, voice rising.

"Topeka has not been *abandoned*," I said. "How many times do I have to—?"

"Topeka?" Tom asked. "Is that her name? What in the blazes kind of name is that?"

I brushed past him and handed the bottle to Nancy.

## Chapter 6 ~ Dinner with Nancy

"Lots of babies are named after towns," I said. "It's trendy. Savannah. Charlotte. Madison. Dakota."

"That's a state," he said, smirking.

"Sierra," I said, pleased I had struck a nerve.

"That's a mountain range."

"There's a Sierra City in California," Ruby said, eyes twinkling.

She knew Tom as well as I did. He hated not being taken seriously.

"I had a cousin named Augusta," Nancy said, eyes fixed on Topeka.

"Cheyenne," I added.

Tom, not at all amused, gave up. "I'll call tomorrow. Good night, ladies."

"Didn't you forget something?" I asked, holding out my arms.

He came back, hugged me tight, and kissed my cheek. "Bye, Mom. I love you. I'm just trying to look out for you, but you sure make it hard."

"I know. But I've got everything under control."

Which was not even *close* to the truth.

Left alone, Nancy, Ruby, and I shifted into the rhythm women waltz to when cleaning up after a meal, sharing tasks without being assigned. Nancy tended the baby. I ferried dishes from the table. Ruby set the soup pot on the stove. When I refilled Nancy's tea glass, she set down Topeka's bottle long enough to hand me her bowl. Ruby turned on hot water, squeezed dish soap into the sink, lowered glasses and silverware into mounding suds. Engaged in these time-honored rituals, the three of us shifted imperceptibly from "hardly knowing each other" to being friends on common ground.

Rain pattered. Nancy hummed. Ruby scrubbed. I swept. Two old friends, a stranger, a baby, enfolded by Franny's past. Only 24 hours after we buried her in Madison, her long-kept secret had hounded and overtaken us, collided with the present, drawn us together.

"I envy you, Barbara," Nancy said. "This lovely house." She nodded at Ruby. "Good neighbors. Your children close by. Your mother must have been so proud of you."

I stopped mid-sweep. "I…guess she was. Trust me. This house looks *nothing* like it did when she—"

Catching my eye, Ruby cleared her throat. This was not the time to deliver my favorite lecture on how I had transformed my mother's "rundown boarding house" into a model of "Southern Living" and impeccable taste.

Nancy gazed around the room. "Even if you change a house, you can't get rid of the memories. Do you mind being alone, Barbara? Must be hard after living here with a big family and lots of company all the time."

*The Moores, the Merriers*

"I'm hardly ever alone," I said, propping the broom in the corner. "My grandsons come over at least once a week. And everyone on the block keeps an eye on each other."

"We wander in and out of each other's houses all the time," Ruby said, sitting across from Nancy. "Sometimes we don't even knock."

The doorbell. Not a polite pressing of the button, followed by a respectful pause, but insistent jabbing, like someone hammering a bent nail. On the fourth ring, the knocking started, the door swung open, our visitor bellowing as she entered.

"BAR-brah. Bar-BRAH."

Viola.

Before I could intercept her, she appeared in the kitchen door, a blue-corn-flowered Corning Ware dish sealed with Saran Wrap in her manicured hands. Ambrosia. That concoction of canned fruit, marshmallows, coconut, and maraschino cherries Viola foisted on us at every social occasion.

Eyes wide, Viola gawked at me. "Good *heavens*, Barbara, what happened to *you*? You look like you've been in a *fight*."

In a futile attempt to hide my injury, I brought my hand to my face, wincing as I touched the corner of my eye. "I fell…uh, tripped…running…in the rain."

This was true. I did fall…*after* Nancy whacked me with her umbrella. But if I said that, I'd have to say *why* I was running after Nancy, which meant explaining I'd spotted Nancy at Franny's house, and that would mean coming up with a reason Nancy was there in the first place. And clearly, that was not an option.

Swishing in, Viola set the bowl on the counter and opened the silverware drawer. "For heaven's sake, you don't have enough sense to come in out of the rain?" She selected a serving spoon and rubbed it vigorously with a towel. Then she removed the Saran Wrap, stuck in the spoon, and placed the ambrosia on the table, where it sat, unwelcome.

I spluttered. "I was…uh…my garbage can…blew into the middle of the street…"

Ruby rescued me. "Viola, you haven't met Nancy."

Dazzling in gold jewel-studded flats, white linen pants, and a red chiffon blouse, Viola glided to the table and sat next to Nancy. "I'm Viola Banks." She turned to me. "My goodness. You have a houseful, don't you, Babs?" Then she reached out and touched Topeka's head. "So, this is Justine's

## Chapter 6 ~ Dinner with Nancy

granddaughter. Well, I never…" She glanced over her shoulder. "Justine upstairs?"

I bristled, knowing perfectly well Viola had heard through the grapevine—which had undoubtedly entangled the entire Sunday School class by now—that Justine had "just taken off to who knows where and left that baby with Babs."

Mouth open, I was about to answer, when Ruby intervened. "No," she said flatly.

Viola sat back and crossed her arms. "You've been wanting another baby, Babs, and it looks like you've got one. Have you told your kids?" She snickered.

"Yes," I said, furious. How could Viola joke about Anne wanting a baby?

Viola pushed her glasses up on her nose. "I bet Tom was fit to be tied."

"Tom was just here," I said, coolly.

Ruby stood up. "Said he'd do anything he could to help."

Viola ran her hand across the table, hoping for a crumb to brush away, biding her time, no doubt, till she could unearth some morsel of news to broadcast later. But the table was spotless, and we were speechless. I glanced at the cigar box on the refrigerator, feeling smug and superior about the "whole story" being within Viola's reach. If she only knew…

Ruby scooted her chair under the table. "Think I'll get going before it rains again."

"No need to rush off," Viola said. "I just got here."

"Actually," Ruby said, "I was hoping you'd come with me. I'd like you to take a look at some of the things that were donated for the yard sale. Give me an idea on prices."

"Now?" Viola asked. "We were just getting to know each other." She smiled at Nancy.

"True," Ruby said, "but no one has a better eye for quality than you." She nodded at the window. "And the weather's still chancy. We should go now, so we don't ruin our hair."

Ruby—what a genius. As much as Viola craved information, she valued her sense of superiority even more.

"Thanks for coming, Viola," I said, tapping her bowl. "I'll bring your dish on Sunday."

Viola gave the ambrosia a parting stir. "Hope you enjoy it, Nancy. It's my specialty."

"I'm sure I will," Nancy said. "Perfect dessert for a hot day."

I followed the ladies to the living room. "Thank you," I whispered to Ruby and closed the door behind them.

Returning to the kitchen, I snatched the crumpled Saran Wrap from the counter, resealed the ambrosia and stuck it on the bottom shelf of the refrigerator. Nancy had shifted Topeka into the crook of her arm and was rocking her gently.

"You're not as rusty with babies as you think," I said. "You've got her to sleep again. I'll put her in the crib, and we can sit in the living room."

Nancy handed the baby to me. "May I use the phone? I need to call my husband. Let him know I'm staying the night. I'll pay for the call."

"No need," I said, pointing to the phone.

I took Topeka upstairs and put her in the crib. As I left the room, I caught a glimpse of myself in the mirror over the dresser. No wonder Viola had been shocked. My face looked worse than I thought—scraped from eye to chin, swollen, and turning a deep shade of eggplant purple. Stopping by the bathroom, I treated the wound with hydrogen peroxide and Neosporin, swallowed an aspirin, and tottered downstairs, still favoring my bad knee.

Nancy was admiring the photos on the wall above my piano. "You have a lovely family. Ruby said both your children are here in town?"

"Uh-huh."

She pointed at my wedding photo. "And this is you and your husband?"

"Harry. Died of a heart attack."

"I'm sorry," Nancy said. "I know you must miss him."

"Some days more than others," I said, sitting on the sofa. "I hate that he never got to meet his grandsons. He was such a kid himself. He would've loved playing with them."

She joined me. "Will—my husband—was a widower with two sons when we got married. They were always outside playing ball or…" She stopped abruptly. "Has your life ended up like you thought it would?"

Taken off guard, I fluffed a throw pillow while I thought. "In some ways. I wanted to get married and have children, and I did. I didn't really want to live *here* the rest of my life, but it was the right thing to do. What about you?"

"No," she said, staring at the floor. "It's not that I think about Clarissa all the time, but you know how it is. You think you've finally forgotten…and then all of a sudden something happens, and the memories—"

"Are all back in your lap," I said.

"*Yes.*"

## Chapter 6 ~ Dinner with Nancy

Poor frail Nancy, a forlorn figure in a borrowed Minnie Mouse t-shirt—another casualty of Hank and Clarissa, who never one time stopped to think how changing the course of their own lives would throw so many others off track.

"If you want to talk about it," I said, "the evening's young. Hopefully, we won't have any more company."

"I haven't told the story in so long," Nancy said. "I don't know where to start."

Turning sideways, I nestled into the corner of the sofa. "Well…I know Hank and Franny were from Richmond. I found their wedding announcement. How did they end up in Florida?"

"That's easy," Nancy said. "Franklin Roosevelt."

# Chapter 7

## Clarissa's Story
### Jacksonville, Florida
### September 1979

As far as Nancy was concerned, Wall Street was responsible for breaking up her family. She was convinced the stock market crash on October 29, 1929, had triggered a chain of events that led inevitably to Clarissa's death on Highway 90 seven years later. The economy failed. The Depression deepened. Franklin Roosevelt established the Federal Emergency Relief Administration, which bought 15,000 acres at Cherry Lake, Florida, to relocate families trying to eke out a living in crowded cities. Hank and Franny Merrier, hoping to better themselves, moved there from Richmond, Virginia, and settled down next door to Cab and Clarissa Moore.

"And the rest, as they say, is history," Nancy said.

Only Clarissa was homegrown. Brought up in Madison, she stopped caring for small town life while still in her teens and began dreaming of a way out. Enter Jon-Cabot Moore, who drifted into town and asked for work at the first store he came to. 'No jobs here,' he was told. 'Try the Murphy farm.' He might as well have ridden in on a white horse. He was the closest thing to Prince Charming Clarissa had ever seen. A whirlwind courtship began. Smitten with her, Cab made promises he could not possibly keep, including someday taking her out of Madison.

From the moment they said, 'I do,' Cab did everything he could to make Clarissa happy. No wish—within his limited means to grant—was ever denied. She had a devoted husband, comfortable home, beautiful daughter, and still she wanted more.

When construction crews arrived in nearby Cherry Lake, Clarissa began pestering Cab about living there. Eventually, he applied and was accepted.

Yearning for peace, he moved his family into a neat little bungalow—less than 10 miles from the Murphy family farm, but still 'away from home.' The community had everything Clarissa wanted. The houses were new, not like the 'old' ones in Madison. 'For pity's sake,' she once observed, 'some of the houses in Madison have been around since the Civil War.' Even better, she was now rubbing shoulders with interesting people from cities like Jacksonville, Tampa, and Miami.

Women who had known luxury she had only dreamed of were happy to relive their pasts, regaling her with stories of cotillions, tea with the governor, moonlight strolls in Charleston, vacations in Boston. The woman Clarissa most envied was Franny Merrier, who, though her family fortune was lost, remained unbowed. Like the 'lady of the manor' in hiding during a peasant revolt, Franny never stopped believing her reverses were temporary. Dignity intact, she had surrounded herself with remnants of her Richmond life—fine bone china, brocade throw pillows, Tiffany lamps, a cherry headboard with winged cherubs carved at the corners.

"I thought Franny was stuck up," Nancy said. "Clarissa thought she hung the moon."

The couples became friends 'practically overnight.' Hank and Cab worked construction together and both enjoyed fishing when time allowed. Clarissa taught Franny to garden. Franny instructed Clarissa in the social graces. Ivy Leigh and Justine, both toddlers, bonded from their first meeting.

Nancy paused. "Everything would've been fine if it hadn't been for that auditorium. That was the beginning of the end."

"What do you mean?" I asked.

Cherry Lake was a fully functioning little community, she explained, with every convenience. The only amenity lacking was entertainment. So, they built an auditorium.

"It was the pride of the town," Nancy said. "Ella Fitzgerald performed there once."

"No kidding. I had no idea."

"Entertainment was good for morale. Somewhere along the line it was decided the town should produce their *own* plays. And of course, my sister thought she was destined for the stage."

"I saw a playbill with her name on it," I said, "and Hank's. I didn't recognize the play."

Her eyes grew wide. "*Abie's Irish Rose*?"

"That's it," I said.

## Chapter 7 ~ Clarissa's Story

She reached for her tea glass. "I'm surprised Franny didn't burn that."

"She left a whole box of mementos," I said. "I only got it today. Want to see—?"

But Nancy was lost in her memories. "It's so ironic."

"What?"

"That play—such a harmless little story…about a Jewish boy who secretly marries an Irish girl, because they knew their fathers wouldn't approve."

"Clarissa and Hank played the couple?"

She nodded. "It's not like it was *A Streetcar Named Desire* or anything. Nothing steamy about it. They didn't even kiss on stage. But it still put ideas in Clarissa's head."

"Did she think she could make a living as an actress?"

"I don't know. But she threw herself into that play. Always had the script with her. She'd show up at my house wanting me to 'run lines' with her. And she *loved* rehearsing."

"A break from daily life, I guess."

"Maybe. In the beginning. But it was mostly being with Hank. Away from their families. He had a kind of charisma Cab didn't have. Hank was cultured—a true Southern gentleman. Cab was a rough old cotton farmer from Texas."

Though theatre critics hated *Abie's Irish Rose,* Cherry Lake audiences loved the heartwarming story with its happy ending. Nancy summarized the plot. Act One: Abie brings Rosemary home and introduces her as "Rosie." His father, not knowing they're married, plans a wedding. Act Two: Rosemary's father arrives for the ceremony. Abie's father learns Rosemary is Irish. Rosemary's father learns Abie is Jewish. Furious, both fathers refuse to bless the marriage. Act Three: Rosemary has given birth to twins—a son and daughter. The boy is named after Rosemary's father; the girl after Abie's mother. The estranged fathers' cold hearts melt.

"And they all live happily ever after," Nancy said. "It didn't help that the heroine's maiden name was 'Murphy' like ours. Clarissa thought it was a sign."

"A sign of what?"

"That an 'impossible marriage' could work. That's what she wrote in the note she left."

Topeka began to cry. I'd almost forgotten her. I hopped up. "You can't be serious."

She nodded. "I still have the note."

"Did she say where they were going?" I asked, backing toward the stairs.

"No. Only that they were going to 'start over'…where no one knew them. She asked me to help Cab take care of Ivy Leigh. I never got much of a chance."

"Because Cab and Franny turned to each other?" I asked, hand on the banister.

"Uh-huh. I would've taken Ivy Leigh in a minute, but Cab had already lost his wife. I couldn't take his daughter. And the little girls were so close. I couldn't separate them."

The baby cried again. "Be right back," I said and hurried up the stairs.

The moment Topeka saw me, she grinned. Lifting her up, I pressed my cheek to her forehead. The fever was gone. I changed her diaper, and we went downstairs. Nancy was standing at the window, peering in the direction of Franny's house.

"Such a beautiful home," she said. "Clarissa would've loved knowing Ivy Leigh grew up there." She turned to face me. "Even if I *can* find her, do you think she'll want anything to do with me? We're strangers."

"I couldn't say. We haven't seen each other since we were teenagers. But you've got nothing to lose by trying. Come to the kitchen. I'll show you the box Franny left for me."

She held out her arms. "Could I hold the baby again?"

"Of course." I handed Topeka to her.

"Come to Aunt Nancy," she cooed.

*Aunt Nancy*, I thought, leading the way to the kitchen. Nancy was Topeka's grandmother's…stepsister's…aunt—a flimsy connection, but better than nothing, and a tenuous beginning to the 'family reunion' she had been hoping for. Who was I to discourage her?

Nancy sat at the table. I prepared a bottle, handed it to her, and took Franny's box from the top of the refrigerator. "I just got this today," I said, sitting next to her, "from Franny's lawyer. Maybe if we look through it together, we could both get some answers."

The sun went down, rain still falling. Thunder rumbled in the distance. Topeka, cradled in Nancy's arm, ate contentedly. I placed the box on the table and lifted out the items one by one, holding them up for Nancy to see.

"Oh, yes, I remember," she would say, or "No idea," until finally, when I displayed a tattered black and white photo, she gasped. "I've been looking for *that* for years."

## Chapter 7 ~ Clarissa's Story

Handing the baby to me, she took the picture and gazed at the gathering of people, some sitting, some standing, in front of a two-storied farmhouse, paint peeling from a century of weathering the blistering Florida sun. Bearded men with sweat-stained hats in hand, women with babies on their laps, ragged boys with suspenders drooping off their shoulders, prim girls with crooked bangs and ruffled collars, all stared into the camera that captured this moment, preserving their memory.

"Who are they?" I asked.

Her eyes lingered on the image. "My family. My mother, grandmother"—she pointed out each one in turn—"Uncle Rufus. Why did Franny have *this*? It wasn't hers."

"Maybe Clarissa had it. She wouldn't have taken it with her when she ran off with Hank. Franny must've found it after she married Cab and moved in with him."

"But why would she *keep* this? It meant nothing to her."

"Maybe she saved it for Ivy Leigh. Apparently, she always meant to tell both girls the truth, but never got up the nerve. That's what she said in the note she left. Want to read it?"

She nodded. "I do."

"I'll put Topeka down for the night," I said, standing, "and get the note from my room."

Nancy got up and kissed the baby's forehead. "Night-night, sweet girl. See you in the morning."

I put Topeka to bed and brought Franny's note downstairs. Nancy read it twice and added it to the other sacred relics on the table. Then we shuffled through them, volleying questions, interrupting each other so often we sabotaged the process.

"This isn't getting us anywhere," Nancy said. "At this rate we'll be here all night."

We started over, arranging the items in a rudimentary timeline like detectives in an incident room.

Teacher-like, Nancy proceeded through the artifacts, vestiges of ordinary people, who would not have imagined their lives would captivate strangers in following centuries. I felt like an archeologist, crouched over the ruins of an ancient city, brushing soil from chalk-white bones.

A serene storyteller with honeyed voice, Nancy told of growing up with Clarissa, her narrative so seamless, it sounded rehearsed. How often—folding clothes or pulling weeds—had Nancy relived these events, grieved over the lost years, lamented the sister who had strayed? She told of quiet childhood days with a loving, hardworking father and a distant, passive mother, who fulfilled the duties of 'farm wife,' but never 'had her heart in it.' Two daughters and a son completed the family circle. As eldest sister, Nancy was her mother's 'right arm,' especially after the death of the only son.

"Clarissa had always been Mama's favorite," Nancy said, "but she doted on her even more after my brother died."

Nancy described Clarissa's growing unrest with 'farm life' and subsequent marriage to Cab, which was supposed to fix everything, but didn't. We made our way through Franny's keepsakes, arriving at Hank's postcard from Sweetwater, Texas, saying the repentant couple was coming home.

Nancy read and re-read Hank's message. "They were on their way *back*. We never knew. Do you think Franny told my mother? That would've made all the difference in the world."

"I don't know."

She returned the postcard to its place in the timeline. "Well…even if nothing else comes from this trip, at least I know Clarissa was coming home. That says something."

*It says nothing*, I thought. *We only know Hank wanted to come back.*

She drifted into silence. I waited, then picked up the photo of Cab and Franny's wedding, exactly as Ivy Leigh had described it to me all those years ago—Franny in skirt, white blouse, orchid corsage; Cab in plain suit, striped tie.

"Were you at Cab and Franny's wedding?" I asked.

"Yes. At the Wardlaw-Smith house. Did you see it when you were in Madison?"

"I did. I'd love to see inside sometime."

"They wanted Ivy Leigh and Justine at the ceremony." She closed her eyes. "The three of us stood in as bridesmaids—Justine in my arms, Ivy Leigh holding my hand."

"What was that like…watching your brother-in-law marry someone else?"

She shrugged. "To me…it was sadder than the funeral."

"Why? Because…you didn't like Franny?"

"Not that. Because we all knew why we were there. It wasn't for *love*. It was just something that had to be done." She took the photo. "Cab kept

## Chapter 7 ~ Clarissa's Story

wiping away tears, and Franny"—she bit her lip—"Franny's face was ashen. I've never seen such grief."

"How long did they stay in Cherry Lake before they moved to Madison?"

"Only a few weeks. It was too hard on them…being in the house where Clarissa had lived. They found a little place on Washington Street. We gave Cab a job on our farm."

"And they made ends meet that way?"

"No. We couldn't pay Cab enough for them to live on. Eventually, Franny had to go to work, too. I watched the girls for her."

My mouth dropped open. "Franny told me she *never* worked outside her home. That's why she was against Ivy Leigh going to business college. She said it wasn't proper for ladies—"

"I'm not surprised. I think that's another reason she never came back to Madison. There might be one person left who knew she had a job at Wilson and White's."

"What's that?" I asked.

"Little tailor shop downtown. Not there anymore."

My mind rebelled against picturing Franny in that setting, perhaps because I had often seen my own mother hunched over her Singer sewing machine, pudgy hands feeding cloth under a whirring needle, stitching a seam, snipping off thread, tossing it on the floor to land on bits of discarded cloth, her "sewing room" piled high with McCall patterns, bolts of hideous-hued bargain material, "finished" garments lined up on hangers on a metal pipe my father had suspended from the ceiling by lengths of clothesline at each end. My mother called all this chaos "sewing for the public." Franny? Doing that?

I frowned. "She didn't do that for long."

"Years." Nancy said, half-smiling, almost smug. "In fact, yesterday you were right across the street from where Franny used to work."

"*What*?" Leaning in, I bumped the table, jostling the photos.

"When you were at Smith's Drug Store yesterday, you were across the street from where Wilson & White's used to be."

Deflated, I sank back in my chair. "I wish I'd known. I would've paid attention."

"It's not like you were in Washington and missed the Lincoln monument. The building's vacant. Come back to Madison, and I'll take you inside. I know the owner."

"Really? I could go in?"

Nancy began gathering the photos. "Pick a day to visit, I'll take you on a historic tour of all the places Franny used to haunt…not that she went out all that much."

"She didn't go out much when she lived here either."

Nancy yawned and scooted back from the table. "It's late. Could we finish this in the morning?"

"Sure. I've had enough for one day, too."

We left our timeline on the table and went upstairs. After we checked on Topeka, I showed Nancy to Tom's old room. Then I got ready for bed, turned off the lamp, and lay back, grateful the strange day was finally over.

Eyes shut, I journeyed back in time to the tailor shop on SW Range Street. Entering, I stood at a heavy oak counter and peeked through the open curtain separating the store from the workroom. There, poised at a sewing machine was Franny, her fine features placid, inscrutable, scarf tied around her head, shoulders as erect as a concert pianist at a Steinway; the former debutante, once a delicate belle of Richmond society, now a grimly determined young wife wed to a family friend, stepmother to his child—the daughter of the woman who had stolen her husband.

Much as I respected Franny, I admired her even more now—the choices she had made to spare two little girls from the consequences of their parents' sins.

My drowsy mind faded back to the day the Moores moved in. I was standing on our porch, calling my brothers to lunch, when a moving van pulled up to the curb across the street. I slipped down the steps and stood on the sidewalk as burly men unloaded crates and furniture. Out came a Persian rug, brocade sofa, Tiffany lamps, boxes labelled "Books" and "China" and "Linen." And then—wonder of wonders—a car arrived, and two girls about my age got out of the back seat. Could it be? Someone on our street besides boys and old people?

Now dreaming, I peered closer at little Justine. She was holding a beautiful doll. I started toward them, drew nearer, realized the doll was a baby. *I have a baby sister, too,* I said. *What's her name?* Justine turned her around. *Topeka.*

My eyes popped open. Sunlight was pouring in. Sitting up, I swung my feet onto the floor, rubbed my swollen knee, and scrambled down the hall. The crib was empty. Still barefoot, I hurried down the stairs and into the kitchen.

## Chapter 7 ~ Clarissa's Story

Nancy, wearing my apron, hummed as she turned bacon in a frying pan. The coffee was perking. A plate of toast, butter dish, and preserves waited on the table. In the swing facing the window, Topeka gazed out at the blue-skied day.

"Isn't this a happy scene?" I said, straightening my pajamas.

"Hope you don't mind," Nancy said. "Farm wives get up early. Far as we're concerned, by the time the sun's up, the day's half gone. I fed Topeka."

Stepping in front of the baby, I bent down to greet her. "Good morning."

She answered with a big gummy grin.

Nancy spoke over her shoulder. "I left all the photos on the table. You'll have to make a space to sit."

After breakfast I called Ruby and asked her to watch Topeka while I took Nancy to Franny's. When we reached the driveway, Nancy opened her car door so the sun could finish drying her seats. Then, side by side, we walked up the wide porch steps. I unlocked the door. Once inside, Nancy stood still, studying the room. Then she eased forward across the Persian rug and sank onto the sofa. When she spotted the portrait of Ivy Leigh and Justine over the mantle, she hurried to the fireplace. Reaching up, she touched the corner of the wide gold frame.

"Beautiful," she said. "They didn't wear dresses like *that* when they lived in Madison."

"Cab did well in the insurance business," I said. "Had his own agency."

"Do you think we'll ever find the girls?" Nancy whispered. "Either one of them?"

"We have to. This house belongs to Ivy Leigh, and Topeka belongs to—"

We both jumped when the phone rang. I limped to the kitchen to answer and managed to have the presence of mind to say: "Moore residence."

The voice on the other end was brusque, all-business. "To whom am I speaking?"

Irked by the interruption, I replied in kind. "To whom am *I* speaking?"

She cleared her throat. "This is Clara Simpkins with Child Protective Services. I'm trying to locate a Mrs. Justine Cribbs. This is the contact number she left. Is this her mother?"

Sweat beaded on my nose. "No…I'm a neighbor…across the street."

"Is Mrs. Cribbs there? We have an appointment this Friday. I need to reschedule."

Frantic, I waved at Nancy, motioning her to join me. "She's not here at the moment. May I take a message?" I jerked open the drawer where Franny kept a pad and pencil. "What was your name again?"

"Simpkins. When do you expect her?"

"I'm not sure. She's...doing some errands. I could take a message," I repeated.

Clara Simpkins paused. I could almost hear her forehead furrowing. "Is her mother there?" Papers rustled. "A...Mrs. Moore?"

"No..." I said, leaving it at that. I scribbled 'Child Protective Services' on the notepad. Nancy leaned in to read, and wrote back, 'Get her number.'

"May I have your number?" I asked, voice quivering.

Clara supplied it. "I need to speak to Justine as soon as possible. We have a follow-up appointment this Friday, and I need to move back the time an hour. I have to confirm today."

I leaned against the counter. "I'll tell her. Thank you for calling." But I was not off the hook yet.

"And what is *your* name?" Clara Simpkins asked.

"Babs...uh...Barbara...Allgrove. I grew up with Justine," I said, as if this mattered.

"Hmm," Clara Simpkins said. "They arrived safely?"

"Yes," I said. This at least was true.

Either I finally exhausted Clara Simpkins' patience, or the minutes she had allotted for this particular task had run out. Finally, mercifully, she dismissed me after asking where she could reach *me* "in the future."

I gave her my number and hung up, heaving a sigh. "Mercy. I feel like I've just been caught planning a robbery."

"Who was it?"

"Clara Simpkins." I imitated her brittle voice. "She has an appointment with Justine on Friday and needs to re-schedule."

"Why didn't you tell her Justine is missing? She might have given us a clue."

"I couldn't do that. Justine might still be on probation or something. I don't know how these things work. Could they still take Topeka away from us? I mean...away from Justine."

"I don't know." Nancy ripped the paper from the notepad. My *sister* and her *mess*...the gift that just *keeps on giving*."

I took the paper. "At least we're making progress."

"Oh...and how's that?" she sneered.

"Now we know Justine's last name."

# Chapter 8

# Detective Allgrove
### Jacksonville, Florida
### September 1979

"All we have to do now is call Tom," I said. "He'll call Bobby and—"

"Who's Bobby?" Nancy asked, still sullen.

"His friend on the police department." I squeezed her arm. "He can call Bobby, tell him Justine's name is *Cribbs*, and then—"

Nancy wagged her head as she strode to the door. "No. Not today."

"What do you mean?"

She turned and glared at me. "I'm going home before Clara what's-her-name calls the authorities and someone bangs on your door to take that baby."

"No one is going to take her."

"You don't know that. And as much as I'd like to think I'm her 'aunt,' I'm *not*."

"Nancy," I pleaded as she stormed down the porch steps. "Wait."

Just when things were improving, my sidekick in this great adventure was bailing on me. She paused. "Is your house locked? I need my keys."

I kept pace with her as she stepped off the curb. "Couldn't you stay one more day?" I eyed her Minnie Mouse shirt. "We could run to Stein Mart and get you some clothes."

Taking a stand in the middle of Lomax, she planted her hands on her tiny waist and stared me down. "You've only been involved in this sordid story for twenty-four hours." She dug a slim finger into her flat chest. "I've been living with it for a long time, and believe me, the new has *worn off*."

A car turning off Riverside blared its horn. I gripped Nancy's elbow and tugged her the rest of the way. "Come inside. I'll call Tom and—"

"No. I'm going home." She pulled loose. "I won't be here when the only tie I have to my sister is yanked away from me. I won't lose someone else I love." She began to cry.

I placed a tentative hand on her shoulder. "I'm sorry, Nancy. But if you'll wait—"

She was inconsolable.

"You don't know what it's like," she said. "You grew up in this beautiful house with a happy family. *Your* little brother didn't die. *Your* sister didn't run away without a word. I bet you talk to *your* sister every *week*."

Her words stung. Truth was I'd let whole months go by without calling Janie.

Nancy stormed into my house, snatched up her purse, and was out the door in two minutes flat. Braving the heat, I waited on my porch. The least I could do was wave goodbye.

Slamming the door of her little red car, she backed out of Franny's driveway and putted down the street. Slowing, she took a last look at Ruby's house, picturing Topeka inside, I supposed, and then was out of sight.

Smarting from Nancy's words, I headed to the kitchen. I hung Franny's keys on the pegboard and dialed Janie's number. The phone rang three times.

Then: "Hello?"

"Hey, Sweet Pea," I said, using her nickname. "What are you up to?"

"Babsy? I don't believe it. I was just thinking about you. I *almost* called you on Labor Day, but then I remembered you always have people over and I didn't want to bother you."

Guilt shot through me. "You can call whenever you want. You know that."

"Oh, sure. I just thought twice," she said, laughing "...in case you were busy with a centerpiece. I know how you hate to be bothered when you're arranging pinecones."

She meant it as a joke, but all the recent misery caught up with me. I failed at choking back a lump in my throat.

My voice quavered. "You're my little sister...if you *ever* need me..."

"Babsy?" Janie asked, suddenly serious. "What in the world is the matter?"

*Where to start?*

"Franny died."

## Chapter 8 ~ Detective Allgrove

Her concern was genuine. "Oh…I'm sorry. I know how much you loved her."

"That's not all," I said, drawing in a lungful of air. "Do you have time to talk?"

For the first time in years I was going to pour out my heart in honest-to-goodness, gut-wrenching conversation with my sister. Somewhere along the line our relationship had turned to a surface one—polite updates that could be shared with an acquaintance or even a stranger. That wasn't Janie's fault. It was mine. I used to justify the void between us by telling myself, *We're so far apart in age. My children are grown. I'm a grandmother. Janie still has a son in high school, two daughters in elementary school.*

But those weren't the real reasons I had distanced myself from Janie. The truth was, she was so much like our mother—too laid back, cluttered. The last time I'd stayed in her piled-up house, I'd vowed never to return.

She didn't have the means to visit me, so we stayed in our own worlds, sending Christmas cards, birthday wishes to each other's kids, but we weren't close. There was no good reason. Janie had never wounded me the way Clarissa hurt Nancy.

"Take as long as you need," Janie said. "The kids are in school. I have all day."

"I can't talk long. I have to get Topeka. I just wanted to—"

"Did you say…Topeka?"

Starting at the beginning, I recounted the events that had led to my call. By the end she was sniffling, too.

"Mama would've been so proud," she said.

"What do you mean?"

"That the house is still taking in people who need help. She always found room for one more. You remember…"

I gazed around my mother's kitchen, picturing the scratched, crayon-smudged table where Janie and I had sat with our brothers…and Ivy Leigh and Justine…to inhale a hodgepodge of leftovers, stale bread, bruised fruit, and cheap cookies from the A&P.

"I remember," I said.

"Do you want me to come help?" Janie asked, mother-like. "I could leave the kids with Phil for a few days."

A fresh gush of tears followed. "No. Thank you. Not just yet. But I may need to take you up on your offer later. Depends on how long I have to look for Ivy Leigh."

We promised to stay in touch and made tentative plans for Christmas, which we hadn't done in years. I hung up and phoned Ruby to tell her I'd be over in a few minutes and then called Tom. Though his secretary usually took a message, which might or might not result in a return call, today she put me straight through. I braced myself. I hated calling Tom at the office—it meant speaking to his 'business alter ego.'

"Mother," he answered in a voice an octave lower than usual.

"Mr. Allgrove," I mimicked.

He snickered and changed his tone. "What's up?"

"I found out Justine's last name."

"Justine?" he asked, voice muffled, which meant the receiver was wedged between his shoulder and ear, so he could keep his hands...and mind...free for more pressing matters, relegating me to 'unfortunate, but manageable distraction' status.

"The lady who left the baby at my house. Topeka. Remember? You were going to call Bobby, so we could—"

"Oh, right. Right. To-PEK-a. How'd you find out the woman's name?"

I knew better than to mention Clara Simpkins or Tom would warn me of my imminent arrest for kidnapping.

"At Franny's house. I did a little detective work." True enough.

"What's the name?"

"Cribbs."

"One 'b' or two?"

"I don't know. Does it matter?"

He huffed. "You just saw the name, and you don't remember how it was spelled?"

"I can't talk right now, Tom. Just call me back after you've talked to Bobby."

"May take a while. He's working today. But that's good. He can check the jail."

"*Jail*? Why would he check the jail?"

"Do me a favor," he said, ignoring my objection. "Call Anne and have her check with her hospital contacts. She's got to know people at every hospital in this town."

Hospital?" I asked. "Why?"

"First two steps locating a missing person. Check the jail and check the hospitals."

"You watch too much *Hawaii Five-0*."

## Chapter 8 ~ Detective Allgrove

"Common knowledge," he said. "You don't know what happened after that woman—"

"Would you stop calling her 'that woman'?"

"All right," he said, "...after *Justine* left your house. She could've been mugged or been hit by a car."

Mercifully, there was a knock at the door, giving me a good excuse to hang up.

"Someone's here. Talk to you later."

I peeked out the kitchen window. Viola Banks' powder-blue yacht-sized Cadillac was by the curb. Determined to head her off at the pass, I made a beeline for the door and wrapped my fingers around the knob as it began to turn. I felt like I was acting out a scene from the Twilight Zone, an alien outside the door, threatening the house. Bracing myself, I opened the door, wincing as a blast of Revlon *Charley* gusted in. I leaned into the doorframe to block the opening, trying to appear nonchalant as I said, "Sorry I can't invite you in…"

"Hold these," she said, whipping off her oversized purple sunglasses. "I switched purses this morning, and I don't know if I put my glasses in here." She rummaged through her orange macramé purse. "If they're not, I'll *have* to go home. I can't see the broad side of a barn without them, much less read my list."

"List?"

Triumphant, she drew out a leopard-print glasses case. "Thank goodness. I didn't want to put you off while I went home and then came back. I know you have company."

"I'm sorry, Viola. I have no idea what you're talking about."

"Hold this," she said, handing over her purse. She removed her rhinestone-studded glasses from the case and held them up to the light. "Your skinny friend from Monticello."

"Her name is Nancy," I said. "And she's not from Monticello. She's from Madison. I don't mean her. I *mean* I don't understand what *you* mean by a list."

She shoved the case into her purse, nearly knocking it from my hands. Then she blew her hot breath on her glasses and buffed them on the hem of her paisley blouse. "The To-Do list for the yard sale. We said we'd get started after the funeral."

"We didn't say *today*."

She settled her glasses on her nose. "I was thinking the same thing, what with that baby being here and all. But then I thought…your friend…what was her name? Nancy? ...could keep the baby while we work. It's a perfect solution right here under our noses."

"That won't work," I said, shaking my head. "She left."

Her eyebrows shot up. "Justine came back and got her? *When*?"

"No. The baby's still here. Nancy left. You just missed her."

She tapped her index finger on her glossy red lips. "Hmm. Well...I *could* go through Franny's house by myself, if you'll let me in." She took back her purse and sunglasses. "Franny said she'd lay out her donations on the bed in the guest room. I'm sure I can find them."

I shook my head again. "You can't go through her house before the girls do."

All these years later and we were still calling Ivy Leigh and Justine 'the girls.'

"When will *that* be?" she asked, thrusting out her chin.

"How should I know? I don't know where either one of them is...not at the moment."

She bristled. "Would Your Majesty at *least* give me *permission* to make sure the folding tables are still in the storage shed in the backyard?"

I was in no mood to argue. "Of course. I'll walk over with you." I joined her on the porch. "I'll have to find the key to the shed."

"What about the baby?" Viola asked. "Is she still asleep at this hour?"

"No. She's with Ruby," I said over my shoulder as I marched down the porch steps.

Viola followed. "You're going to have to make better arrangements for a babysitter. With that arthritis in her knees, Ruby does *not* need to be chasing around after a child."

I picked up my pace, walking two steps ahead of her across the street.

We reached Franny's porch and climbed the steps. The moment I stuck the key in the lock the phone rang. My stomach lurched. What if Clara Simpkins was calling back? Viola would love nothing more than eavesdropping on a conversation with Justine's case worker.

"Why don't you go around to the backyard?" I said. "I'll meet you there with the key."

She motioned me forward. "Get the phone. I have to go to the bathroom anyway."

She followed me in and headed down the hall, while I hurried to the phone.

"Hello," I said, breathless.

## Chapter 8 ~ Detective Allgrove

"Is this the residence of Franny Moore?"

This was another all-business female caller, but not Clara Simpkins.

"Yes," I said.

"May I speak to her?"

"Who's calling?" I asked, remembering Ruby's warning not to give out information after someone has died, because 'crooks read obituaries and then rob vacant houses.'

"This is Jennifer Belden at St. Vincent's Hospital. We've admitted a Justine Cribbs to ICU. We're trying to locate family for information about her medical history. She's in and out of consciousness and can't respond to questions."

My knees nearly gave way. "*What*? What happened?"

"She passed out on the street. Rescue brought her to the ER. We found a key to a bus locker in her pocket. The police found her suitcase. This number was on the ID tag. Are you at 729 Lomax?"

"Yes. It's her mother's home."

"Are you a relative?"

"No. Friend."

I heard Viola open the bathroom door. She would be waltzing in any minute.

"In that case, are you aware of any of Mrs. Cribbs' medical history?" she asked. "Medications she might be taking?"

I was glad I'd thought twice about throwing away the plastic sandwich bag full of Justine's medications. "She had a backpack with her. A bag of prescription pills were inside. None of them are in bottles, but I'm sure someone there can identify them."

"Could you bring those to us?"

Before I answered more questions, I had to know if Viola was listening. Crossing the black-and-white linoleum floor, I stretched the phone cord to its full length and peeked into the living room. Viola was nowhere to be seen.

"Sure," I said in a hushed tone. "Just tell me where."

She gave instructions. "One more thing. Do you have contact information for a relative in Kansas?"

"Kansas? No. Why?"

"*Topeka* is the only word we've been able to make out. We thought there might be some significance."

"Topeka is her granddaughter," I said. "Could I see Justine? Tell her the baby's okay?"

"After she's stable and in a regular room. For now, it's family only."

*Family only.*

The image of Hank Merrier, ballcap over his heart, flashed into my mind.

I turned around and retraced my steps. Hovering near the pantry as far from the living room as I could get, I pressed the receiver to my lips, cupped my hand to my face, and spoke in a hoarse whisper.

"Her father lives in Madison. I don't have a phone number, but I think I could find him."

"How long will that take?"

"I can go today."

Jennifer Belden and I shared contact information, and I hung up only seconds before Viola strolled into the kitchen, a cardboard box labeled "Yard Sale" in her arms.

She set the box on the counter. "Who was that?"

"Someone who didn't know Franny had died."

Reaching into the box, she lifted out a drab olive vase with white ceramic flowers winding up and around the sides. She turned it upside down and read the trademark.

"Roseville pottery," she said. "This is worth hundreds of dollars."

I'm not sure why I started crying. It might have been because I was standing in the very spot where Franny had died in my arms or because the only word Justine could say was 'Topeka,' or because Nancy had left broken-hearted.

But I couldn't articulate any of that to Viola when she heard me sobbing and asked what was wrong. To my surprise, she set down the vase and put her arms around me.

"I'm sorry, Barbara. I shouldn't have tried to hurry you into this." She stood back and gently brushed away my tears. "Come on. Let me take you home. We'll do this another day."

Within an hour, I had arranged for Anne to take care of Topeka, told Ruby I was leaving, and packed a bag. On my way out of town, I delivered the sandwich bag holding Justine's assortment of pills to the hospital. Then I turned onto Stockton Street and headed to I-10.

I was going back to Madison to find Hank Merrier.

Somebody had to put this fractured family back together, and it might as well be me.

# Chapter 9

# Finding Mr. Merrier
### Madison, Florida
### September 1979

Leaving Jacksonville, I cruised west on I-10 through miles of tall pines. The straight stretch of road was short on scenery, but perfect for letting my mind wander, conjuring up the heartwarming scene that would take place when I found Hank Merrier.

He would remember me from the funeral. I would ask if we could talk and suggest he sit down. I would reveal his long-lost daughter was clinging to life, and, if we left now, he could see her in an hour and a half.

But where to start the search? The only place I knew to look was the cemetery, and I knew *that* only second-hand from the conversation I had overheard when Ruby and I had lunch at Smith's Drug Store.

*What with his trailer bein' only a stone's throw from the cemetery.*

How hard could it be to find a "trailer at the edge of the cemetery"? But I wasn't sure where the cemetery was. I hadn't paid attention on the way to Franny's funeral. Harry had always told me to stop at a fire station when I needed directions. But where was the fire station? And in a town the size of Madison didn't everyone know where everyone else lived? Couldn't I ask *anyone*? But would that be like throwing a rock in a pond? Would word ripple through town to Hank? Did he want to be found?

There was only *one* person in Madison who could help me. And that was Nancy Crisp.

I was all the way to the Suwannee River before I figured this out. Instead of asking about Hank, I could find out where the Crisp farm was. From what Nancy said, the family and the farm were icons in Madison County.

But had Nancy really had enough of the 'sordid story' she had lived with for so long? I pictured myself tapping on her door. 'I found Justine. Help me find Hank.' Would she shake her head and point me back to I-10?

The farther I drove, the worse I imagined the outcome to be.

On the outskirts of Madison, I stopped at a hardware store. The bell on the door jingled as I entered. Everyone—from the portly man behind the counter to the middle-aged couple shopping for shovels on Aisle 2—turned to scrutinize me. I read the looks on their faces.

*Who's that? She's not from around here.*

*That little gal wouldn't know a crescent wrench from a can opener.*

I approached the counter. "Can you please tell me the way to the Crisp farm?"

The manager hitched his thumb under the strap of his overalls. "You mean the Murphy farm, don't you?"

"Yes." I shot him a Charlie Brown grin.

He reviewed the route. I restated the directions and thanked him. I had one foot out the door when he called after me.

"You're that lady from Jacksonville, aren't you? The one here for Franny's funeral?"

"Yes," I said, suddenly vulnerable. "How did you know that?"

He rubbed the stubble on his chin. "I was eatin' lunch with the missus the day your friend saved old Donaldson from chokin' to death. Impressive."

Listening in, the shopper, toting his shiny shovel like a warrior's lance, ambled over. His wife, doe-eyed, her gray hair tucked into a bun at the base of her neck, sidled up next to her man.

"I'd like to meet *her*," she said. "She didn't come with you this trip?"

"No, ma'am. She's busy. Church yard sale," I said, knowing this would please her.

Wouldn't they love to know what Ruby was really doing—helping my daughter with Justine's granddaughter? What a story that would make.

She slipped her arm through her husband's. "I've told Buster we need to get over to Tallahassee to the Red Cross and take a CPR class. You just never know…"

Buster, frayed checked shirt buttoned all the way to the top, hefted the shovel onto the counter. "If it's my time to go, it's my time to go. I don't need no class."

She slapped his arm with the back of her hand. "But what if it's not *my* time to go?"

## Chapter 9 ~ Finding Mr. Merrier

"Now don't start that again," Buster chided. "I ain't—" I slipped out the door.

Backing onto Duval Avenue, I drove north to Highway 90, "the first stoplight," turned right, and traveled east till 90 joined State Road 6. Once I "forked to the left," I found myself in another world—lush, rolling hills, cows grazing, fields, farmhouses.

Two miles out I located the white fence I'd been told about and followed it till I reached the "Murphy Farm" sign. Leaving the highway, I bumped along the rutted dirt road feeling like Laura Ingalls in search of the Big Woods.

And there was the house the Murphys built—two stories, white, dark green shutters, gabled roof. Three wide steps led to a porch the length of the house. Six brown wicker hanging baskets draped with variegated ivy swung gently in the breeze.

My first thought was *why* Clarissa would have wanted to leave *here*—as near heaven as anyone could want.

My second thought was why Nancy Crisp, tea glass in hand, was sitting on the porch swing, as if expecting me to show up.

I parked behind the now familiar red Beetle and stepped out into the quiet country air. The house was so far off the road, so far from town, the silence invited me to stand still, breathe in, quiet my raw nerves.

"Come on up," Nancy said with an air of resignation.

I had received warmer welcomes at K-Mart. She was in no mood for a visit…or in no mood for *me*. I wasn't sure which. Stepping off the gravel drive, I crossed the grass. Maybe a casual, offhand greeting would soften that flinty expression.

"Waiting on *me*?" I chirped, climbing the steps.

"Where's Topeka?" she asked flatly.

"Kan—"

"Don't you *dare* say 'Kansas.'"

She kept swinging. I stood at attention, studying the surroundings. There were half a dozen outbuildings of various sizes. Nearest to the house was a workshop made of cedar. A rusty metal sign over the door read: *Gwilym's Gadgets*.

Chastened, I answered simply. "She's at my house with Anne. I asked her to take a couple of days off to keep the baby. She said she would… however long it takes."

"To do what?"

"Find Hank." I straightened my shoulders, the moment calling for good posture.

Nancy stopped swinging and picked up a stack of mail lying next to her, shifting it to her lap. A yellow postcard fluttered to the floor. "Hank will be here any minute. I'll introduce you."

I bent to pick up the card. "*What?*"

"My husband's gone to get him." She patted the place next to her, inviting me to sit.

"Are they friends?" I asked, handing over the card.

She laughed. "I wouldn't say that."

I backed up to the swing and eased down into the empty spot. "When did your—?"

Nancy pushed off with her foot. I toppled backward. My feet shot up, my toes at eye-level. I gripped the arm of the swing, trying to get my balance. She did not seem to notice I was tottering precariously as we lurched back and forth.

"I was such a mess when I got home," she said. "Will got tired of my moping around."

Gripping the armrest, I managed to right myself and scoot back. "Who's…Will?"

"My husband."

I was seated, but my toes didn't reach the floor, leaving Nancy in charge of swaying us back and forth. Feet dangling, I was at her mercy and getting nauseated.

"Then who's Gwilym?" I asked, holding on.

"Will is short for Gwilym. When I told him about Topeka, he said"—she imitated his gruff tone—'If all the baby needs is a relative, I can do something about that,' and he left."

"To find *Hank*? How long will that take?"

"There's not that many places he could be. He doesn't have a car. Want some tea?" she asked, displaying her glass.

"No. But could we stop swinging? I haven't eaten all day, and I'm getting sick."

She planted both feet on the floor. We jerked to a stop. "Shouldn't you be at home looking for Justine?"

My turn to have the upper hand. "I found her."

She jerked sideways, crooking her leg onto the seat. "*Where?*"

## Chapter 9 ~ Finding Mr. Merrier

I told her about the call from the hospital, ending with: "When the nurse said 'Topeka' was the only word Justine could say, I knew I had to do *something*."

Her face softened. "Is...she...dying?"

"I don't know, but while she's in ICU, they won't let anyone see her except a relative. And there's only one left...even if Justine doesn't know he exists."

As if on cue, a gold pickup truck turned onto the drive. I scooted off the swing and walked down the steps behind Nancy. Two men were in the cab. Behind them, a Doberman, paws on the wheel well, ears perked up, barked a greeting.

Caesar remembered me. At least *somebody* was glad to see me.

The truck stopped. Hank, wearing frayed khaki pants and a faded red plaid shirt, climbed out and walked around to lower the truck gate so the dog could hop down. Caesar bounded toward me and sat on his haunches.

"Hello, boy," I said, rubbing his head. "Where's your baby?"

Hank pulled the ragged toy from his pocket and handed it over. I heaved it in the direction of a massive camellia bush, and Caesar galloped away.

Nancy spoke to her husband. "You won't believe it, Will, but this is Barbara."

Will, squarely built, his curly red hair streaked with gray, held out his hand. "Well, that saves us a step. I'm Will Crisp."

I shook his hand. "I love your truck. It's an antique, isn't it?"

"International Harvester Golden Jubilee Edition. '57. Nan says you've met Hank?"

Caesar loped back and dropped his toy at my feet. I threw it again. "At the cemetery." I turned to Hank. "How are—?"

"Is it true?" Hank asked, his voice stuck in his throat. "You saw Justine? My little girl is a *grandmother*?"

"A dozen times over," I said. "Well...nearly. I think...I can't remember."

I stood there, sweat running down my back, eyes darting from Hank to Nancy to Will. The poignant scene I had crafted had been edited out, dropped on the cutting room floor. Nancy had upstaged me...left me with only one line.

Before I could even open my mouth, Will took Nancy's hand and stepped toward the house. "Let's go inside," he said, motioning us to follow, "and we'll talk about what to do next."

Rooted in place, Nancy tugged on Will as he tried to walk away. She leaned close to whisper in his ear.

Hank's eyes were still riveted on me. "So…Justine left a baby at your—?"

"*What?*" Will whirled around. "You *found* Justine?"

Hank went pale. I thought he would faint. Caesar pranced back and deposited his soggy toy in the haphazard circle we had formed.

"I didn't find her," I said. "The hospital called. She's in ICU. They asked if she had any relatives. I said I knew where her father was, and I would try—"

"Well, there you go," Will said. "You two can head right back to Jacksonville."

Hank blinked as if he'd just emerged from a cave. "I have to go back to my place first. I didn't plan to be gone long, much less leave town. I didn't even lock the door."

"We'll go over and lock up," Nancy said. "And take care of things while you're gone." Hank laid his hand on the dog's head. "What about Caesar?"

"Leave him here," Will said. "We've got plenty of room."

"I can't…" Hank said. "We've never been away from each other."

And then—though after my mother's ancient poodle Angel died, I vowed *never* to have a dog in my house ever again—I heard myself say:

"Bring him."

Nancy gasped and surprised us all by throwing her arms around Hank and begging him to bring Topeka back, promising there was room for both of them upstairs.

"We'll take care of her till Justine gets out of the hospital," she said. "We'll go to Valdosta and get a crib, won't we, Will?"

Will gave her a blank stare. "We can talk about that later."

Hank rubbed the back of his neck. "What about clothes?"

"We'll find some when we get there," I said remembering the garage sale items in Ruby's house. I turned to Nancy. "Could I get a sandwich or something?"

"Sure," she said. "And I'll get that tea now."

We entered her spacious, high-ceilinged living room. The wood floor was worn, but gleaming. To my right was a pastel-flowered sofa, unfinished afghan tossed over the back, a skein of burnt orange yarn and crochet needle perched on the arm. Family pictures from this century and last were arranged over a black upright piano with yellowing keys. Without hitting a note, I knew it was out of tune. Ahead was a long dining table, newspaper and coffee

## Chapter 9 ~ Finding Mr. Merrier

mug at one end, checkbook and bills at the other. A white ceramic bowl of plastic grapes sat on a ruffled doily in the center.

Nancy called out from the kitchen. "Ham and cheese okay?"

"Perfect," I said, leaning in to examine the photos on the wall. If there had been time to spare, I would have asked Nancy who they were—these severe-looking people in shabby clothes.

"Mayonnaise or mustard?" she asked.

"Mayonnaise," I said, walking to the kitchen, which smelled of Pine-Sol. "This is a lovely house, Nancy."

"You'll have to come back when you can stay longer," she said. Her hand trembled as she placed a lettuce leaf on top of the cheese. She finished with a slice of white bread and cut the sandwich diagonally.

I stepped nearer. "Are you okay?"

She opened a drawer and pulled out a box of sandwich bags. "Uh-huh. I just can't believe you found Justine so soon." She tucked the sandwich inside a plastic bag. "Want me to put this in a lunch sack?"

"No. That's fine."

She handed me the sandwich. "When do you think you'll bring the baby here?"

*Never,* I thought, but didn't say so. "No way to know. I couldn't take Topeka out of town without asking Justine, and it may be awhile before she wakes up."

Nancy took a quart jar from the dish drainer, filled it with ice, and poured tea from a yellow plastic pitcher. "I guess you're right." She screwed a lid onto the jar, wrapped a paper towel around it, and presented it to me. "When Justine says it's okay, you know you can bring Topeka *anytime.*"

Will yelled from the front door. "You girls about done talking?"

I was relieved to be spared from this awkward conversation. "I better go."

We walked back through the living room and down the porch steps. Will stood by my open car door like a valet. Hank waited, Caesar at his side.

I balanced the sandwich on top of the jar and hugged Nancy with one arm. "Even if I can't come back anytime soon, you're always welcome at my house."

"Thank you," Nancy said, with an eye on her husband. "Have a good trip."

Hank opened the rear door. Caesar leaped in. Hank waved at Nancy and got in the passenger seat. I slid behind the wheel, put my lunch on the seat, and turned the key in the ignition. Nothing. Not a rattle. Only a click.

Will rolled his eyes. Hank, Caesar, and I got out. The men popped the hood and stood over the engine like surgeons over a dying patient. I remained a safe distance away. After a few mumbled exchanges, Will turned to me and ran through a checklist of car behaviors. I admitted the car had been "sluggish," lately, but it had always been temperamental, so I hadn't been concerned. Will ordered me back to the helm to try the lights. I obeyed. He rejoined Hank in front of the car. Caesar, seeing me resume *my* place, hopped in next to me.

Hank circled around to the passenger door. "It's not the battery. Lights are fine."

Will came to the driver side and gripped the top of my door. "Got a lug wrench?"

"I don't know," I said, feeling foolish.

He strode to the garage and returned with a short metal pipe. He waved it like a baton to direct Hank back to the engine. Again they disappeared behind the hood. I heard tapping. Then Will yelled at me to "try again."

I turned the key without result.

Will closed the hood. Hank returned to Caesar's door and snapped his fingers, motioning him out. Caesar bounded down and I got out to face Mr. Crisp, who sighed volubly as he scraped the back of his hand across his forehead.

"Must be the starter," Will said. "You'll have to leave the car here. I know a good mechanic. He's honest, and he'll give you a fair price. There'll be a charge for towing."

"How am I supposed to get home?" I asked.

"You'll have to take Nancy's car," Will said. He turned to Nancy. "Get your keys."

I blinked, pointing my thumb. "Hank's pretty tall…and the dog is *way* too big for *that* back seat."

"You're not going far," Will said. "Not like you're driving to California or something."

Glancing at Hank and then Nancy, I read the same silent pleading in their eyes. I couldn't refuse. By then, I'd had enough of Will Crisp anyway. I would have hitchhiked to Jacksonville if it meant putting distance between me and him.

## Chapter 9 ~ Finding Mr. Merrier

No wonder Nancy was so skittish…after a lifetime with this grouch.

"Okay," I said. "If you're sure it's all right."

Hank ambled to the Volkswagen and opened the door. He pushed the seat back forward so Caesar could clamber in. Then he righted the seat, and eased down, angling his long legs into place. Will fetched my lunch and purse from my car and handed it through the open door as I assumed command of the Beetle.

"I need the car seat, too," I said. "You'll have to take it out of the back seat."

Hank got out to help.

Nancy stepped forward with the keys. "It's a standard transmission. Can you drive a stick?"

"Oh, yeah," I said, passing the quart jar to Hank. "My dad taught me. Call me after you hear from the mechanic, okay?"

She nodded. "Don't worry. I'll take care of your car."

The men returned with the car seat. In no way would it fit in back with Caesar, so everything was taken from the "trunk" in order to stow the car seat there. I felt like I was heading for the Oregon Trail.

I revved up the Beetle, put it in first, and eased off the clutch. Away we went down the driveway to State Road 6, I-10, and home.

I turned to Hank. "Your knees are nearly up to your chin. Can you scoot your seat back?"

"Don't worry about me," he said. "I rode the rails during the Depression. This is luxury compared to that."

Caesar stuck his head between us and barked for joy at the open road. Apparently, he did not get away from the trailer by the cemetery very often.

I handed Hank the sandwich. "Could you unwrap this? I got too much going on here with the stick, but once I get this thing into $4^{th}$, I have to eat."

Hank set the jar on the floor, snug between his feet, took out half the sandwich and handed it over. "I always dreamed of finding Justine," he said, "but never like *this*."

"If there's one thing I've learned in the last few days, it's not to be surprised at anything."

"I can see that." He pointed at my bruised face. "How'd that happen?"

"Nancy's umbrella."

"*Nancy* took a swing at you?" He laughed.

"No, it was an accident." I studied the sandwich. "Tell me…has Will always been so…?"

"Cranky? Yeah. Whole family is. They pass down a sour disposition from one generation to the next. There's always been a cloud of gloom over that beautiful house."

"Was it always that way, or only after Clarissa left?" I took a bite.

"Which time do you mean? When she married Cab, or when she left with me?"

I gulped, nearly choking. "I'm sorry, Hank. I didn't mean that."

"No need to apologize," he said. "I'm sure you know most of the story by now, and as much trouble as this family has caused you, you deserve to know the rest."

"I don't mean to pry," I said.

Though I did.

# Chapter 10

# Hank's Story
### I-10 East
### September 1979

"Where do you want me to start?" Hank asked.

"Richmond," I said, offering Caesar the last bite of half-sandwich. He wolfed it down and gave my hand a cursory lick. "Could I have a drink?"

Hank lifted the quart jar, unscrewed the lid, and passed it to me. "How much did Franny tell you about Richmond?"

"Not much." I took a swig and handed back the jar, which he held on his knee. "Only that she grew up there...and her family was wealthy."

"That's *all*?"

When I heard the anguish in his voice, I added: "A little about school, parties, friends."

A semi roared by. The little car shuddered. It was one thing to compete for road space in a Buick. It was quite another to hold your own against a 40-ton truck when you were driving what amounted to a roller skate.

"I didn't expect her to forgive me," he said, "but I always hoped there was one small memory...of me...somewhere in her heart."

"There was more than that," I said. "She kept a whole box full of memories hidden away. Pictures, your wedding invitation, the—"

"*Our* wedding invitation—you mean hers and *mine*?"

"Uh-huh." To prove this, I quoted: "Mr. and Mrs. Eldert Hibbs...Eldert, right?"

"Yes. That's it."

"...request the honor of your presence at the marriage of their daughter Francesca Elizabeth to Mr. Henry Fitzsimmons Merrier IV. 'Fitzsimmons'? Seriously?"

"The IV," he said with a trace of a smile. "No one's called me Henry in years."

His head drooped. I peeked at him—eyes squeezed shut, chest heaving, as his tired heart struggled to contain the flood of emotions threatening to spill. I waited, hoping he would breach the silence—awkward, sacred—hovering between us. Caesar, sensing his master's distress, laid his head on Hank's shoulder. And in that excruciating moment, what should I notice but the water, dripping down the sides of the jar, was leaving a ring on his pants leg? I reached over and took the tea, a small gesture, but the best I could do at the moment.

"Here," I said. "Let me have that. It's getting your clothes wet."

Hank pointed at an exit sign. "Pull off here. Let's let Caesar out for a while."

The troublesome jar gripped in my left hand, I veered off the interstate, pulled into a gas station, and headed to the side of the building to park. Hank had his door open before I turned off the engine.

"I'm gonna get a bag of chips," he said. "Do you want anything?"

"No. I'm fine."

"Take Caesar for a walk?"

"Sure," I said. "He won't run off, will he?"

Hank shook his head and disappeared into the gas station.

Stepping from the car, I poured the tea in the gutter and put the jar on the floor of the back seat.

"Mark my word," I said to Caesar, "Nancy will ask for that jar the next time I see her."

I leaned the seat forward so he could lumber out. He trotted to the nearest patch of grass to acquaint himself and leave his mark. When he returned, I fed him the rest of the sandwich, minus the lettuce, and we settled into our places again.

Hank returned with a bag of Fritos and can of Dr. Pepper and joined us in the car. "Did Caesar take care of business?"

"Yes," I said, jiggling the gear shift into reverse. "I fed him the rest of the sandwich."

"You didn't have to do that."

## Chapter 10 ~ Hank's Story

"He needs it more than I do," I said. "When we get to Jacksonville, I'll stop at Winn-Dixie and get some dog food."

Hank popped the can and held it between his knees. Then he tore open the bag. "I hate putting you out like this."

"You're not putting me out. That's why I came—to find *you*." I eased back onto the interstate. "I planned on looking for you for a couple of days. But here you are. I still can't believe you're in the car with me."

"Or that we're in *this* car." He patted the dash.

When we both laughed, the years fell away from him and the dull pain lurking behind his eyes vanished. I got a glimpse of the young man Franny had fallen in love with.

I understood. Even worn down by life, Hank was handsome and charming.

He swallowed a mouthful of Fritos and sipped his Dr. Pepper. "So...tell me about this box. I guess you found it after Franny died?"

"No. Her lawyer had it. I'm her executor."

He licked salt from his fingertips. "You? Not one of the girls?"

"Neither one of them has been home in years, until Justine showed up out of the blue."

"Why? I mean...what happened?"

"It's a long, sad story," I said, glancing in the rearview mirror. "I'm not sure you want to hear it right now."

"After being in the dark all these years, I have a right to know about my own daughter."

This was *not* a story I wanted to tell. It would take from here to Macclenny to explain how the Moores had gone wrong. Starting with how Franny had always favored Justine over Ivy Leigh. How once the girls became teenagers, and boys started flocking around, Franny scared off even the *nice* ones. How J. Michael Ford came to town and met Ivy Leigh in the restaurant where she worked as a waitress. How she introduced him to me and Justine, and all three of us fell for him. And how in the end it was Justine he eloped with.

But I told the story anyway. Hank was more starved for information than I was and had more of a stake in finding out the truth.

"Franny blamed Ivy Leigh for Justine running off," I concluded. "I'll never forget that conversation. She said if Ivy Leigh hadn't brought 'that Ford man' into the house, Justine would be going to Vassar instead of 'married to that conman, holed up in some fleabag motel.'"

"Vassar?" Hank asked.

I shook my head. "Franny always exaggerated where Justine was concerned. She couldn't have gotten into Vassar if her life depended on it. She"—I almost said, 'wasn't the sharpest pencil in the box,' but caught myself—"never cared about school very much."

Hank sighed. "My poor Jussie. I always hoped she would try to find me once she was old enough, but I guess Franny turned her against me."

I rubbed the space between my eyes. "Uh…that's not it."

He closed the bag of chips and put it on the floor. "What do you mean?"

"Justine didn't know. None of us knew…" I couldn't bring myself to finish the sentence.

"Knew what?"

"From the day they moved in…we knew them only as the 'Moore family.' That's it. No one *ever* said there had been other marriages or other parents."

"Everyone thought Cab was Justine's father?" he asked.

"Franny never said otherwise. When my mother found out Franny had grown up in Richmond, she asked how they ended up in Florida. And Franny said, 'we moved here during the Depression.' Now I know 'we' meant you and her…not her and Cab."

He spoke, barely above a whisper. "All this time…Justine never knew I was her father. Maybe she *would've* looked for me…if she'd known."

"Maybe."

Mile after mile we rode in silence, little engine putting, grown-up cars whizzing by, pickup trucks looking down their noses at us. The only sounds came from Caesar, stretched out the best he could, whining in his sleep, legs jerking as he dreamed of running in open fields.

*Well, Babs,* I said to myself, *you went back to Madison and found Hank. Now what?*

What do you say to someone who's just learned his own child never knew he existed?

I was on the verge of saying, *Hot for this time of year,* when Hank finally spoke.

"Think we should turn around and go back?"

"Why would we?"

He crushed the empty can in his hand. "It may do Jussie more harm than good…to find out Cab wasn't her father. I'm sure he was good to her. That's the kind of man he was."

## Chapter 10 ~ Hank's Story

I nodded. "Everyone loved Cab."

"Why tell her the truth? After all these years? What *good* would it do?"

"*What good would it do*? She needs you. And you need her. You have a *right* to know the child who was kept from you and to be part of her life…make her part of yours."

"I don't have a life."

"My point exactly. After you've seen Justine, if you want to go home, I'll take you there myself. But I'm telling you, once you hold Topeka, you won't want to let go of her. Trust me on that. Now," I said, trying to sound stern, "you were going to tell me about Richmond."

"Well," he said, "you'd never know by looking at me now, but my father was a banker."

His mother, he went on to explain, was a respected matron of Richmond society, his childhood as perfect as anyone could want. The Merriers lived in a grand house on Monument Avenue with a maid, a cook, a gardener, and a nanny.

"After three daughters," Hank said, "my mother was desperate for a son to follow in my father's footsteps, so everyone was relieved when the 'heir to the family fortune' was born."

"Henry Fitzsimmons Merrier IV," I said. "I can't picture you as a banker's son."

"Neither could I. My mother wanted me to be a Little Lord Fauntleroy. But I was more of a Tom Sawyer. I drove her crazy when I was a kid. Shinnying up trees, digging holes in the backyard, always dirty."

"Sounds like my brothers," I said, gripping the wheel as another semi roared past.

"I locked horns with her most of my life. The one thing I didn't argue about was when she told me she'd found the perfect girl for me to marry."

"Franny."

He nodded. "Of course, Mother never called her anything but 'Francesca.'"

"So, Franny was your Becky Thatcher," I said, grinning.

"Yeah, you could say that."

"Love at first sight?"

"Was for me." Hank rubbed his leg. "Maybe we could pull off in another half an hour or so? Need to stretch my knee. Never been the same since the wreck."

"There's a rest stop not far ahead." The same one Ruby and I had stopped at...only a few days ago? "So...how old were you when you got married?" I asked.

Franny was 18; he a year older.

"Franny's mother tried to talk her out of marrying me," Hank said. "By then, it was three years since the Depression had started, and my father was in financial ruin."

"Wasn't everybody?"

"Not Franny's family. We were never sure how they managed to keep up their lifestyle, but there were rumors her father's business associates were a little shady."

*What else did I not know about Franny?*

We pulled into the rest area. Hank and Caesar took off down the sidewalk. I went inside to the bathroom and then ambled around the welcome center, staring idly at the rack of travel brochures, eavesdropping on tourists chatting about St. Augustine and Disney World.

Wishing my life could be as simple as theirs.

Back at the car, I found Hank behind the wheel. I climbed in the passenger seat.

"Mind if I drive?" he asked. "Easier to talk if I can do something else at the same time."

"Help yourself," I said. "I could use the break."

Easing onto the interstate, Hank fixed his eyes on the road. Then words poured out, as if a crack in a dam had breached, stone giving way to a splendid flood.

"Bad as the Depression was," Hank began, "it gave me the chance I'd always wanted. To leave home and start over somewhere else as myself instead of 'Henry Merrier's boy.'"

Franny, he explained, had an uncle, "the black sheep of the family," who had moved south and ended up in Cherry Lake, Florida.

"He invited us there," Hank said. "Franny's mother frowned on it, said 'no good would come of it.' But we went anyway."

"I guess she enjoyed saying, 'I told you so'?"

"Never saw her again. After the accident, no one in Richmond wanted a thing to do with me...even my own family...whether I was crippled or not."

"I'm sorry," I said.

He paused and then began again in a voice so soft I could hardly make out the words. "I was bringing her back, you know, when the accident

## Chapter 10 ~ Hank's Story

happened. The guilt was too much for me...especially what we'd done to our little girls."

"I know. I found the postcard you sent from Sweetwater, Texas."

He turned to me so suddenly the car veered onto the shoulder of the road. We skidded into the dirt. He yanked the wheel back. We lurched into our lane, crossing the center line. A Chevy station wagon, passing on our left, blared its horn and swerved to miss us.

Gripping my seat with one hand and the dashboard with the other, I squeaked out: "Pull off at the next exit. I better drive the rest of the way."

He did not argue. We left the interstate again. He pulled onto the side of the road, and we switched places.

"Sorry," Hank said, closing his door.

"My fault," I said. "I shouldn't have sprung that on you...with no warning."

"I always wondered if she got that card...if she knew I was coming back. I thought it got lost. And that's why she never tried to find me."

Creeping onto the onramp, I waited till the coast was clear before I eased back into traffic.

"All right," I said. "We're going to keep driving till we get home." I shifted into 4$^{th}$ and settled back. Hank's face was gray. I had to ease him back into talking again. "I know how the four of you got to be friends. And about the play you and Clarissa were in. So, start there?"

"I won't make excuses," he said. "Except to say it was a bad combination of circumstances and personalities...me and Clarissa..." He sighed. "And the silly idea there's such a thing as a soulmate, and we were made for each other."

When the idea to run away and "start over" first occurred to them, Hank could not recall. But once they admitted the possibility, they came up with any number of satisfactory excuses for their decision. Times were hard. They needed to seize joy where they could find it. His marriage to Franny had been 'suitable.' Hers to Cab had been a way out of her parents' house. Cab was a good father who was perfectly capable of raising Ivy Leigh on his own. Franny was independent and resourceful. The two left behind would help each other through the rough spots.

Plans were made, notes left. The couple escaped by night and drove west, hearts soaring, heads spinning with outlandish dreams, resplendent visions of new places, better opportunities, dining, dancing, and maybe someday seeing New York, London.

The Depression couldn't last forever.

"They say you don't know someone till you live with them," Hank said. "If ever there was a true statement, that's it. In the bright light of day, Clarissa…was…well, let's just say I admired Cab for his patience with her."

After one fight too many over where to eat, where to stay for the night, a flat tire, and too many miles between gas stations and greasy spoon cafes, Hank had had enough.

"One morning," he said, "after we had slept in the car again, I glanced over at Clarissa. She was upset…again…and nudged up against her door to get as far away from me as possible."

"What was she mad about?"

"She forgot to pack a coat. Never stopped to think fall…and winter… were coming. She wanted to go shopping. I said we'd find a thrift store. That did it. She was furious."

"Franny wouldn't have forgotten to pack a coat," I said.

He shook his head. "Nope. I looked at Clarissa, face all screwed up, crying. I thought how…back home…Franny was putting breakfast on the table."

"Prodigal Son moment?"

"Exactly what it was. I didn't say a word. Just started the car and turned east."

"What did Clarissa say?"

"She straightened up, sniffled a little, and said, 'Are you going to find a store?' I didn't even look at her. I said no and that she had a perfectly good coat at home. We're going back."

"How did she take it?"

"Tried every trick in the book to get me to change my mind. Apologized. Cried. The more she talked, the faster I drove."

They stopped in Sweetwater, Texas, for gas. While Clarissa was in the bathroom, Hank bought a postcard and dashed off a quick note to Franny. He begged the storeowner's wife to mail it for him. She promised she would. They got back on the road.

Four hours later, they got stuck behind a rattle-trap farm truck, piled high with hay, creeping along. Clarissa kept badgering him about giving her another chance, complaining she was hungry, begging him to find a cheap motel where they could sleep in a bed for a change.

"I was as tired and hungry as she was," Hank said. "All of a sudden, that rusty truck in front of me became a symbol of everything that was wrong

## Chapter 10 ~ Hank's Story

with my sorry life. I stomped on the gas, jerked the wheel, and pulled into the other lane, right in the path of an oncoming car."

Both cars swerved left, passenger doors slamming into each other, propelling Hank and Clarissa into a ditch.

Hank stared out his window. "I don't remember anything after that, except waking up in the hospital. I'd been unconscious for days. They told me Clarissa was dead."

My stomach churned. "The other driver?"

"Hurt, but not as bad as me. No one was in the car with him. Thank God. At least I don't have that on my conscience."

No seatbelts in those days, Hank reminded me, so his injuries were severe and excruciating. In constant pain from broken ribs, a ruptured spleen, dislocated shoulder, he was laid up for weeks. His leg, which took the brunt of the impact, was the worst.

"I hardly remember those first few days, but I came out of it enough to tell them where we were from. They contacted Clarissa's family, shipped her body back for burial. I guess they contacted my family, but no one came."

After weeks of recovery and rehabilitation, he was released.

"I was too far from home to think about going back. How could I? I didn't have two nickels to rub together. I decided to hit the road, get what work I could, and send the money home to Franny. Maybe she'd let me come back someday."

The rest of Hank's story—riding the rails during the Depression—I had heard before from men my father knew or strangers in our boarding house. From 1929 till World War II broke out, hundreds of thousands of despairing people hopped freight trains and headed to work sites like the Grand Coulee Dam or followed the harvest to pick strawberries, apples, beans, and potatoes. A great mix of humanity—from college students who could no longer pay tuition to farm kids who never made it past $8^{th}$ grade—answered the mournful call of the train whistle and lived as hobos.

"If I'd had two good legs," he said, "I could've gotten a good job with the CCC, but with my limp…I couldn't hide…I ended up being a fruit tramp…a picker following the harvest."

In some ways, Hank said, those were the best years of his life. He saw a lot of beautiful country he never would've seen otherwise and became part of a community—rag-tag as it was.

"I never could've got on those trains if my buddies hadn't given me a hand up. There's a science to it, you know—timing your jump while the train is pulling out of the yard." He demonstrated. "Get one handhold and start running. Then grab on with two hands and hoist yourself up. But for me...my buddies had to grab me by the seat of the pants and pull me in."

His weathered face softened into a smile. He was back in the trainyard and took me with him. I could almost hear the click-clack of the tracks as we ran to catch the train "before crew change" or we would miss our chance.

"And my buddies said I helped them, too, because of me being crippled. We got better handouts at farmhouses when good-hearted women saw how bad off I was."

He explained the procedure of asking for food at a back door. "Sometimes you'd get a 'lump.' That was a sack to take along. A 'knee shaker' was a tray of sandwiches you could eat on the porch. But when you managed a 'sit down,' coming in to eat with the family...that was Heaven...for a while."

Finally, he got tired of sleeping in hobo camps—nicknamed "the jungle"—set up outside towns, always worrying if his shoes would be stolen in the middle of the night.

"And running from railroad detectives," he added. "That was the worst. Because if one of us was going to be nabbed, it was me. I couldn't outrun anyone else. The last time I got caught and driven out of town and dumped on the highway, I decided I'd had enough."

The Salvation Army helped him get back home. But when he arrived in Madison, he found Franny had divorced him, married Cab, and taken Justine to live in Jacksonville.

"Could she do that?"

"Simpler than you think," Hank said. "With plenty of advice from her father...and mine. All she had to do was provide proof she'd tried to find me."

"How do know all this?"

"Titus Dove. Fellow Cab and I worked with in Cherry Lake. He was the one I sent my money to while I was gone. He told me." He pointed at the Jacksonville City Limits sign. "Well, look at that. We're here."

Never before or since have I been as exhausted as I was when we finally turned onto Lomax Street that evening.

"This your house?" Hank asked, peering through the windshield. "It's nice."

"No. My neighbor Ruby. She'll keep Caesar here while we go to the hospital. She used to have a St. Bernard, so she won't mind."

## Chapter 10 ~ Hank's Story

I parked the Volkswagen on the street in front of Ruby's house. Caesar hopped out and ran to the nearest shrub while I knocked on Ruby's door.

"Back already?" she asked. "You said you'd be gone a couple of days."

I pointed over my shoulder at Hank, strolling around the yard. "I found him. And he wouldn't leave the dog behind. Could you keep him here while we go to the hospital?"

Ruby didn't even flinch. After years of having me spring harebrained ideas on her, she was ready at a moment's notice to bail me out. She stood aside to let us in.

We invaded Ruby's house. She introduced herself to Hank and asked if we'd had supper.

"No," I said. "Hank wants to get straight to the hospital. But…when we come back?"

She patted Caesar. "Fine. In the meantime, I'll see what I can find for this guy." She cooed to him. "You're a sweet boy, aren't you?" His whole backside wriggled as he wagged his stubby tail.

"One more thing," I said. "Could we borrow your car? I can't bear the thought of getting back into that Volkswagen."

Hank and I got in Ruby's Volvo and backed onto Lomax.

"Which one is Franny's house?" he asked.

I pointed as we drove by. "That one. I'll take you inside tomorrow…if you want."

He lapsed into silence. I resolved not to disturb him with questions or badger him with instructions about hospital visitation. Instead, I let him savor the reunion he had dreamed of…no doubt…as he lay recovering in the hospital, sleeping in a freight car, dozing in his trailer by the cemetery. How I wished the strangers who had given him a hand-up or handout could see him now, know their kindness had kept him alive. Above all, I wished I could wave a magic wand and peek in the rearview mirror to find Franny smiling at me from the backseat.

We arrived at St. Vincent's. Up, up, up the parking garage ramp we rode till finally we found a place to park. Hank opened the door, got out, and stretched his legs.

"Whew," he said, rubbing his knee. "It sure was a long trip to see my girl."

"It just seems that way, because we've had such a hard day. But we really aren't that far from the hospital."

He walked around the car, and we started toward the elevator.

"I meant," he said, "a long way from Sweetwater, Texas."

# Chapter 11

## Open for Business
### Jacksonville, Florida
### September 1979

"She's *beautiful*," Hank said, emerging from the ICU, a surgical mask dangling from his fingers. "Even with all those wires and tubes…I'd know my Jussie anywhere."

He sounded like a father cooing over a newborn in a nursery.

"What's the mask for?" I asked.

"She has some kind of infection. They're running more tests in the morning. I'm going to stay here tonight. It's about time I started acting like a father."

"Is she awake?" I asked.

"No."

"Well…don't you think it would be better to come with me and—?"

He gazed at me through bloodshot eyes. "I've missed her *whole* life. I can't just waltz out of here and *leave* her alone *again*."

"But she doesn't even know you're here."

He hung his head. "The nurse told me to talk to her…that Jussie could hear my voice, but my own daughter doesn't *know* my voice. How pathetic is that?"

"She'll know soon enough." I put my arm through his. "I'll bring you back in the morning. You should get back to Caesar."

"I suppose you're right. Don't want him to think I've left him in a strange place."

He followed me into the hall, and we studied the signs that pointed the way out.

"The exit is this way," I said, pointing right. "We'll have a nice supper, get some rest, and start over tomorrow."

He squeezed my hand. "You don't know how much I appreciate all you've done for me."

I have never been able to explain it, even to myself, but on that long walk out of the hospital, the storm, which had been battering me since Franny died, mysteriously blew itself out. My plans were shipwrecked all right, but in a Swiss Family Robinson way. I wasn't at the destination I'd charted but was safe…and I'd brought Hank with me. Pressing the "Up" button, I glanced at him, the stranded soul I'd rescued. All these years, while Franny lived the good life, he had been limping around Madison, doing odd jobs, going home to a dingy trailer.

Back in the car, Hank buckled his seat belt. "Where's the baby?"

"With my daughter."

"Could I see her tomorrow?"

"I'll pick her up in the morning after I drop you off here."

We gathered around Ruby's table and recounted the day's events over chicken and broccoli. Caesar lay at Hank's feet and snoozed contentedly. No telling how much or how well Ruby had fed him before we arrived. As usual, she was the perfect hostess.

After supper, Hank hopped up and cleared the table, despite Ruby's protests. Then he took Caesar outside while I helped with the dishes. Elbow to elbow at the sink, we watched Hank through the window.

"What's the plan now?" Ruby asked, handing me a plate to dry.

"I'll take Hank back and forth to the hospital. Bring Topeka home. I don't want Anne to miss any more work. She'll have to take off again when I leave to find Ivy Leigh."

"What will you do about Franny's house in the meantime?"

"Keep it nice for a realtor, I guess. I doubt Ivy Leigh will want to move in. She's had a life all these years…somewhere."

Ruby rinsed the casserole dish. "And all you have to do is find out where."

I took the dish and dried it. "Plus tell her Franny wasn't her mother. There's that."

Hank led Caesar through the back door.

"Ready to go?" I asked, laying down the towel.

"If y'all are done," he said.

## Chapter 11 ~ Open for Business

Removing her rubber gloves, Ruby held out her hand to him. "We're glad you're here, Hank. If I can help in any way…"

When Hank took her hand, he blushed. "Thank you, Miss Ruby."

"Just Ruby," she said.

I interrupted. "Are there any men's pajamas in the yard sale stuff? I didn't give Hank time to pack."

"No," she said, "but I have some of Jack's."

"Your husband?" Hank asked.

"Passed away last year," she said. "Be right back."

Ruby returned with two pairs of pajamas and two shirts. Hank thanked her, and we drove the VW back to my house. I gave him a tour and showed him to Tom's room.

"You can take my son's room," I said. "Bathroom's down the hall. Caesar's welcome to stay inside."

"Thank you." He leaned in and gave me a tender kiss on the cheek. "Think I'll call it a day. I want to get an early start in the morning."

"Okay." I started toward my room and then turned around. "Hank. Did you want to…look through the box Franny left?"

He shook his head. "No. I need to sleep and that would keep me awake all night."

I put on my pajamas and sat on my bed. Last night Topeka and Nancy were here. Now *they* were gone, and Hank was here. Tomorrow Topeka would come back. When Justine got well…if she did…she would move in, too.

Turning out the light, I lay back in the same room where my mother once slept. My childish voice echoed across the faraway years. There I stood in the doorway, a petulant 13-year-old, whining about my "lack of privacy" while my mother tried to get some much-needed rest before another hectic day.

*I can never get in the bathroom,* I said. *The boarders go first and then the boys. There's never any hot water left for me. How am I supposed to wash my hair and look decent tomorrow?*

*Get up early,* she mumbled. *Wash your hair in the morning.*

*The boys will be in the bathroom getting ready for school.* My voice rose with each complaint. *I never have a moment's privacy. I have a baby for a roommate. I can't have friends over because the house is always a mess. Why do we have to have all these people here all the time? Some of them don't even pay.*

She rolled over and snuggled up to my father.

*People are more important than houses.*

Her words caved in on me like debris from a collapsing building, the memory so jarring I opened my eyes to dispel it. I thought of Hank down the hall, Justine in the hospital, Topeka.

*People are more important than houses.*

The next morning the scent of bacon woke me. I came downstairs to find Hank at the kitchen table, newspaper spread out, coffee mug full. He was pressed and dressed, smelling of Dial soap, and wearing one of Jack's shirts.

He stood when I entered. "Coffee?"

"Yes, thank you."

"How do you like your eggs?"

"Scrambled."

He had clearly acquainted himself with the kitchen before I woke up. He knew where everything was. Culinary poetry in motion, he whipped up eggs, popped bread in the toaster, and set a perfect breakfast in front me in moments.

"Were you a chef or something?" I asked, forkful of eggs poised at my lips.

"Short order cook at a truck stop in Wisconsin...long time ago."

How many sides were there to this man?

After breakfast, we compressed ourselves into the Volkswagen again.

Hank groaned as he shifted his bad knee into place and reminded me to call Nancy about my car. I dropped him off at the hospital and drove to Anne's to pick up Topeka.

Anne placed the baby in my arms and then pressed her cheek to Topeka's forehead. "No fever or congestion. If you need anyone to watch her again, please call."

"I will." The longing in her eyes broke my heart.

Anne gathered up both of us in her arms. "One more hug." Her voice broke. "I hate to see her go." She stepped back. "Sorry. Didn't mean to get all emotional. I'm going to miss her."

On my way, I stewed over the injustice of the situation. Topeka's mother, who had *no* trouble having babies, had cast aside this child in favor of some useless boyfriend, while my daughter had wept over saying goodbye to a stranger's child.

I found Hank in the ICU waiting room. His face lit up when he saw us. Sitting next to him, I placed Topeka in his arms.

## Chapter 11 ~ Open for Business

"Meet your great-granddaughter," I said.

He gazed at her. "Boy, does this take me back to when Justine was a baby. She looked just like this. It's like a chance to start over. Turn back the clock."

"How's Justine?" I asked.

"Still the same. They know what's wrong. Encephalitis."

"How'd she get *that*?"

"Mosquito bite. They told me the name of the virus, but I can't remember it. They said if she hadn't been near a hospital when she collapsed, she would've died."

He drew Topeka close and pressed her little pink cheek against his weathered face. She rested in his embrace, as if she knew he needed to love her. We stayed with Hank till the nurse said he could visit Justine again.

Then I brought Topeka home, settled her in the swing in the kitchen, and called Nancy to check on my car.

"Maybe tomorrow," she said. "How's Topeka?"

"Fine."

"I can't wait to see her when you come pick up your car."

I couldn't believe what she was saying. "I probably won't bring her. That would be a hard trip, since I'm just going to pick up the car and turn around and come right back."

"I thought you could leave her a few days…while Justine's in the hospital. I'm her aunt."

"I can't. When Justine wakes up, the first thing she'll do is ask for that baby. I can't say I don't have her. Besides—"

"Why would she ask to see her? She walked off and left her."

The phone almost sizzled in my hand. "She's still her legal guardian, and I—"

"Never mind. I'll call you when the car's ready."

She hung up. I pondered the irony. Topeka's mother had given her to Justine, who had also abandoned her. But in the last hour I'd deprived not one, but two women of the pleasure of keeping her for a few precious hours.

For the next three days we lived in a comfortable rhythm, delivering Hank to the hospital each morning, picking him up in the afternoon. We passed our evenings poring over photos, quizzing each other, piecing our stories together. Though dreams of Franny's house still tugged at me, I concentrated on taking care of Hank and Topeka. As a result, they were both thriving. The little child, deprived for too long, had come home—not to a house, but to Hank, as if an invisible strand joining them had stretched, twisted but unbroken, through all the years of mistakes and detours.

On the fourth day, I dropped off Hank at the hospital and drove home. I had just wrangled Topeka out of the Volkswagen and unlocked the back door when the phone started ringing.

"Hello?"

It was Hank…desperate. "Could you come back?"

My stomach flipped over. "Don't tell me Justine is—"

"She *woke up* while I was by her bed. She asked who I *was*."

Topeka, balanced on my hip, was grabbing at the phone cord. "What did you tell her?"

"That I was an old friend of her mother's."

"Oh, brother," I said, failing to stifle my rising panic.

"They're moving her to a regular room. The nurse said she's been asking for the baby. Can you bring her? And help me tell Justine…who I am?"

There was nothing to do but go back. I changed Topeka's diaper and fixed a bottle. As we hurtled toward St. Vincent's, I rehearsed introducing Hank to Justine, still wondering, as I parked the car, what in the world I would say. Topeka and I charged back to the ICU only to find neither Hank nor Justine there. A staff member gave me Justine's new room number, and we meandered around the hospital till I found the right elevator. When we reached Justine's floor, I peered right and left, and spotted Hank lingering in the hall. He rushed toward us.

"They just got her moved in," he said. "She's through the worst of it."

I handed over the baby. "Here. Hold her while I find out what's going on."

Approaching the nurses' station, I introduced myself as Justine's "neighbor" and explained I had brought her granddaughter to visit. I pointed at Hank and described him as Justine's estranged father—recently found—and asked if and when it was safe to tell the patient.

The nurse gave permission for Topeka to visit but added Justine shouldn't hold her.

"As for her father," she said, "give Mrs. Cribbs till tomorrow before you say anything that might upset her. She's still very weak."

I returned to Hank, took Topeka, and outlined the plan. Then we entered Justine's room. She was lying on her back, gazing out the window.

I inched forward. "Justine."

## Chapter 11 ~ Open for Business

She turned toward me, her face brightening, and held out her hands. "Toppy."

"The nurse said you could see her...but not hold her...till you're stronger."

Justine lowered her arms. Hank, silent, lingered at the door, while I took the chair nearest the bed. I set the diaper bag on the floor and held Topeka in the crook of my arm, facing Justine, so she could see her.

"I understand," Justine said, admiring her granddaughter. "She's a sight for sore eyes. I knew you'd take care of her...till I got back."

"Till you got back?"

"Yes."

Somewhere deep within me, a rising wave of anger began to crest. Here, flat on her back, was a poor woman, who, though gravely ill, had journeyed hundreds of miles to leave a helpless child in a good home. I should have admired her, pitied her at least. But I didn't. I resented her for mishandling her life, breaking her mother's heart, being absent for years. She had a rag-tag bunch of irresponsible offspring and a dozen grandkids. Why should I tear this sweet baby from the loving arms of my childless daughter and hand her over to this woman?

"*When*...exactly was that going to be?"

My voice was sharper than I intended, but sitting there, Topeka in my lap, Justine—who had abandoned her—within lecturing distance, the strain of the last few days got the best of me.

Justine hesitated. "After I got my suitcase. I couldn't carry everything to Mother's house, so I left it in a locker at the bus station." She glanced at Hank but did not ask who he was. "I was going get a ride back to the bus station later, but...when I found out Mother was dead...I got confused. I was so sick. I didn't know what I was doing...really."

"I read the note you left, Justine. You weren't coming back."

Behind me Hank cleared his throat. "That's enough, Barbara."

Justine's head drooped. "Okay. I *was* going to leave her with Mother. Not you. But sitting there in your living room...I remembered...your mother never turned anyone away. I thought if you were anything like her, you'd take in my Toppy."

"A child is not a stray puppy. You can't leave one in a basket on a doorstep."

Topeka, sensing my temper, began to squirm and whimper.

Hank edged closer. "*Barbara...I said that's enough.*"

Justine pointed at Hank. "Who's he? Is he from the neighborhood or something?"

Glancing over my shoulder, I wagged my head at Hank to warn him off. I wasn't finished with Justine, not by a long shot. "Family friend. I'll get to him in a minute."

What little color was in Justine's face had drained out. She broke out in a cold sweat. "Okay. But stop yelling. You're scaring Toppy."

Shifting Topeka to my shoulder, I lowered my voice, but not my intensity.

"I keep coming back to the note," I said. "You told Franny if she didn't want the baby to turn her over to *social services*. Does that sound like you were 'coming back'?"

Justine wailed. "You don't know what I've been through."

When she broke down, so did Topeka.

Hank stormed forward and spoke in a voice that shook the walls. "That's *enough*. I won't stand by and let you talk to my daughter this way." He took Topeka from me.

Silence avalanched over the room, burying us all. Topeka, safe in Hank's arms, stopped crying. Justine stared wide-eyed at him. Clamping both hands over my mouth—too late—I sank back in the chair. The room was spinning. *What* had I done?

Justine wiped her face with the back of her hand. "What do you mean... daughter?"

Light-headed, I bent over double, face buried in my hands, head on my knees, trying to gather my wits.

Hank picked up the diaper bag. "I'm taking the baby out of here. Barbara will explain. We'll be down the hall...if you want to talk. But *this* is going to stop."

I heard the door close. Sitting up, I opened my eyes and tried to focus. "I'm sorry, Justine. I don't know what came over me. Everything's been such a mess since Franny died."

She lifted the plastic pitcher from the tray near her bed and poured water into a Styrofoam cup. "Want a drink?"

Standing, I tottered to her bedside. I downed the water and handed back the cup.

"Please forgive me. That came out of nowhere. I've been practicing... how I'd tell you. But I never pictured it like this. Poor Topeka." I sighed.

"Poor *you*."

## Chapter 11 ~ Open for Business

"Never mind all that. Tell me what that man meant...calling me his daughter."

I drew the chair closer to the bed and sank down. "It's true. Your mom left a note."

Over the next half hour, I sat close to Justine, speaking in hushed tones like I used to when I spent the night at her house, and we kept whispering after Franny had warned us to stop talking and go to sleep.

Starting with the funeral, I described seeing Hank, pursuing him after the service, and Ruby's informing me he was Franny's first husband.

Justine folded back the bedsheet over her ample stomach. "First *husband*? No. That's not true. Mother would have told me."

"That's what I thought," I said, sticking to the story. "But then we met Nancy Crisp, but she left the restaurant before we could talk, because Mr. Donaldson choked and—"

"Who's Mr. Donaldson?"

"It doesn't matter. I need to tell you who Clarissa is. First, I heard two men talking about her, and then after Nancy left, she went to my car and left a photo of her...I have it at home—"

Justine grabbed my hand. "Babs. You're not making any sense. Start at the beginning."

So back I went to Richmond and Hank and Franny's wedding.

Justine grew quiet and stared at me. "Richmond. I can explain that. I *was* born there, but that's because my parents were on vacation. Mother went into labor early."

"No," I said. "That's not true. I mean, she might have gone into labor early, but they weren't on vacation. They *lived* there."

She eased up onto her elbow. "So...you're saying I was born in Virginia because she lived there when she was married to that guy down the hall?"

"Yes."

"No, Babs, you're confused. My birth certificate says 'Moore.' I have it."

"You got a new birth certificate when you were adopted."

She sank back on the pillow. "I wasn't *adopted*."

"You both were," I said. "After Cab and Franny got married, he adopted you and Franny adopted Ivy Leigh. Mumsie Murphy paid for it after you moved to Jacksonville."

"Mumsie? My dad's aunt? What's she got to do with anything?"

"She wasn't your dad's aunt. She was his mother-in-law. At least she *was* till Clarissa—"

She rolled her eyes. "*Who's Clarissa?*"

"Ivy Leigh's mother. Cab…your dad…was married to her first."

She squeezed her eyes shut. "No. That's not true. I don't care what anybody—"

I spoke louder, trying to talk over her. "Their family…the Moores…were already in Florida when you and your parents moved from Richmond during the Depression."

She pushed her hair out of her eyes. "You're saying Ivy Leigh was not my *sister*, and Cab was not my father? You expect me to believe that?"

"It's true. I've got a whole box of stuff"—I jabbed my finger in the direction of my house—"that will prove everything. Franny left the box with her lawyer…and the note."

A cheery hospital aide interrupted us with lunch. "Here we are." She set the food on the rolling bedside table and scooted it into position, and then chirped to me, "Can you sit her up a little? The control is right over there."

I found the button and raised the bed. Justine said nothing, staring blankly at the tray.

"Is everything all right?" the aide asked.

"Yes. Thank you," I said, standing to unwrap the silverware. "She's just tired."

"Let me know if you need anything else," she said, and left us alone.

"This looks good," I said, lying about the meatloaf. "Want me to help you?" Dipping the fork into the mashed potatoes, I held it to Justine's lips. She took a bite and swallowed.

"Go on," she said.

"With lunch or the story?"

"Both."

The simple act of helping Justine eat—buttering her bread, skewering green beans—gave me opportunity to atone for my temper. Our eyes focused on the food rather than each other kept Justine from interrupting and allowed me to finish the story.

"Ready for pie?" I asked.

"No."

"Are you…okay?"

"Not sure. This would be hard to take even if I felt good, which I *don't*." Taking a step back, I eased onto the chair. "Is there anything I can do?"

"Yeah," she said, wiping her mouth. "Go get Topeka."

"Hank, too?"

## Chapter 11 ~ Open for Business

"No. Not yet."

I hurried down the hall and found Hank and Topeka in a waiting room by the elevator. Nestled in the corner of a gray vinyl sofa, they were both dozing—Hank, upright, head bowed on his chest, baby cradled in his arm.

I tapped his knee. He opened his eyes. "Everything okay?"

"Justine wants me to bring Topeka," I said, easing her from his arm.

He grabbed the diaper bag and hopped up. "Let's go."

"Just…the baby. Justine needs a little more time."

His face fell. "It can't be easy…finding out you're not who you thought you were."

I shrugged. "It's a lot to take in. Knocked me flat, and I'm just a bystander."

"It's my own fault. I sprang it on her too soon. I never should've blurted it out like that."

"No, it's my fault," I said. "You wouldn't have done it if I hadn't been badgering her."

"Doesn't matter," he said. "At least we know she's going to be all right. Go on now. Take the baby. I'll wait here."

Heartsick, I returned to Justine's room and sat by her bed. Tears falling, she reached out and touched Topeka's cheek. Hank was right. This was a good first step. Justine was alive and well. Topeka's guardian had returned. Our bases were covered.

But I was far from satisfied. I had hoped for a much different scene when Hank and Justine met, pictured them embracing, while the theme from *Gone with the Wind*…Dah, DAH, dah, dah…swelled forth from the orchestra in my mind. We were, after all, in a place of healing, where open wounds could be stitched. If only Justine would listen to Hank's story, she would savor every word, as I had. Another bridge would be crossed. But not today. I said goodbye and went back to Hank. We were almost home before either of us could decide what to say.

Hank breeched the silence. "I'm not going back unless Justine asks to see me. In the meantime, I still have Topeka."

I patted his knee. "Justine will come around…after she has time to think."

We trudged in and took refuge in the living room. Hank laid Topeka beside him on the sofa. I made coffee and sat across from them. Caesar lay next to my chair. I was weighing what to say…if anything…when the doorbell rang.

Caesar's ears perked up as he sprang to attention.

Before I could move, Tom swung the door wide—"I heard your friend was—"

With a mighty bark, Caesar lunged toward the would-be intruder.

Tom stumbled back. Still gripping the doorknob, he wedged himself between the frame and the door, shielding himself from attack.

Hank rose majestically, voice booming. "Caesar. Sit."

The dog plopped down, still eyeing my son.

Easing the door open, Tom stepped in. "*Whose dog is that?*"

Hank approached and took Caesar by the collar. "Mine. We've been here long enough he feels protective of Barbara." He extended his hand. "I'm Hank Merrier."

"Tom Allgrove. Barbara's *son*." He frowned at me. "Mother. Is everything all right?"

"Fine," I said, lamenting this unnecessary complication. "Why aren't you at work?"

Hank took Caesar with him to the sofa. The dog sat, but kept his eyes trained on Tom.

Still wary, Tom surveyed the room. "Anne called and brought me up to date. I thought I'd come by and see how things are."

"Uh..." I stalled. "We're all right." I hovered near the door, ready to shoo him out.

Hank spoke up. "Your mother invited me to stay while my daughter is in the hospital. I hope you don't object."

Tom wagged his hand. "No problem." He turned to me. "Mom, could I talk to you for a minute? *Outside?*"

I almost refused but decided to deal with Tom now. He was not going to like what he was about to hear, and we might as well get it over with.

"Go ahead," Hank said. "I'll keep an eye on the baby."

Tom stepped aside to let me go ahead of him, then closed the door and followed me down the porch steps.

"Should you leave that baby alone with him?" Tom asked. "He looks kind of shady."

"He's her great-grandfather."

"And another thing," he said, pointing his thumb in the direction of the Volkswagen. "What is this junk heap doing in your driveway? And *where* is your Buick?"

"It's a long story," I said, turning right onto the sidewalk.

## Chapter 11 ~ Open for Business

Tom lagged behind. "What in the world are you doing?"

"Going to the park. Remember how we used to go there when you were little?"

"No. I mean yes, I remember the park. What I *meant* was, what are you doing with all these people in your house?"

"I don't know. Just taking one day at a time."

When we turned right onto Riverside Avenue, I quit talking altogether. I knew perfectly well Tom had practiced a lecture on his way over and was now hopelessly off kilter. He was so flummoxed, I almost felt sorry for him.

We reached the corner where we could cross the street to the park.

"Now," I ventured, studying the traffic, "what was it you wanted to talk to me about?"

"Well, for one thing...what's that Doberman doing in your house?"

"Hank wouldn't come without him," I said matter-of-factly, as if this were the most logical explanation in the world.

"And that's another thing," he said. "Why can't these people stay in Franny's house? They're *her* relatives. Anne said that guy was Franny's first husband? Is that *true*?"

When traffic cleared, I stepped off the curb. Tom, father-like, held my hand as we crossed the street.

"Yes. It's true," I said. "Franny was married to Hank. He hasn't asked to see her house. I don't blame him. Do you?"

"It doesn't matter if he wants to see the house or not. That's beside the point. You *have* to get them out of *your* house."

Entering the park, I made a beeline for the nearest stone bench and sat down. "You keep saying that, Tom, but seriously, do you have any business telling me what to do with *my* house?"

"I'm not trying to tell you what to do," he said. "It's not that. It's *Anne*."

I squinted at him, silhouetted against the afternoon sun. "What do you mean?"

He sat next to me and leaned forward, elbows resting on his knees. Gone was the executive. In his place was the little boy who used to come to me with some childish fear.

"Scott's leaving next week," Tom said, his voice quiet. "For three weeks at the company office in Beijing. Anne's going to ask if she can move in with you while he's gone."

"She's never been afraid to stay by herself before. Why—?"

He turned to face me. "So she can stay with the *baby*. She's getting too attached, Mom. The longer those people stay, the more hurt she'll be when they leave. Can't you see that?"

"Yes," I said. "I *have* seen it. But I can't just pitch them all out onto the street."

"Why can't they all go back to where this guy came from? Madison, is it?"

"Because he lives in a trailer. There isn't room for all of them."

"Why can't they move into Franny's house? It's just sitting there empty."

"Because the house didn't belong to her. That's why."

"*What?*"

"It takes too long to explain. Don't you have to get back to work?"

"I'll take as much time as I need to if it will keep my sister from being hurt again."

So, I told him the whole story, and for the first time since he left for college, he actually listened to every word I said.

"My hands are tied till I find Ivy Leigh," I said. "And I have no idea where she is."

"Have you asked Justine?"

"Well, no. She took off the minute she got here, and then she was unconscious."

"She's awake now. *Ask* her. She may know exactly where her sister is."

Standing, he held out his hand, which I took in mine. We started toward the entrance.

"I'd be surprised if they stayed in touch," I said. "I'll never forget the argument they had with Franny the day they left home. All three of them were furious."

"Just because they broke contact with their mother doesn't mean they stayed mad at each other all these years. You won't know till you ask."

We crossed Riverside. Tom's keen mind was already racing ahead, outlining strategy. I listened, delighted to share the burden I'd been carrying. I was feeling downright hopeful…until we turned on the corner of my street.

Tom noticed first. "Where's the Volkswagen?"

My heart sank. "Hurry."

Tom sprinted ahead and entered the house. No barking from Caesar. I clambered up the porch steps and through the door. I could hear Tom moving around upstairs. I rushed into the kitchen. Back into the living room. No one was there.

Tom came down the stairs. "They're gone."

# Chapter 12

# In Search of Ivy Leigh
### Jacksonville, Florida
### September-October 1979

Lunging for the sofa, I snatched up throw pillows and flung them onto the floor.

"Where's my purse? It was here a minute ago," I said.

Tom stooped to pick up a pillow. "Why do you need your purse?"

"So I can go after *Hank*." I straightened up and planted both hands on top of my head.

"Think. Think. Where did I put it?"

"You don't know where he is. Maybe he's just walking the dog."

Skirting the coffee table, I headed for the kitchen. "No. No. He's taken the baby and gone home. He was so upset over Justine. He said, 'At least I have Topeka.' That's what he said."

Tom followed and stood in the kitchen door as I ricocheted from the table to the door and back to the table again. I pulled out the chairs. Empty.

"Don't panic," Tom said. "You don't *know* he took the baby."

"Of course he did. *She's* gone. *He's* gone. The *dog's* gone. There's no other explanation." I dragged a chair across the floor and stood on it to check the top of the refrigerator. "You're the one who said he looked shady. Remember?"

"Get down from there. You've *never* put your purse on top of the refrigerator."

"*What's with that family?*" I said, shoving the Betty Crocker cookbook to one side. "As soon as I get two of them together, the other one takes off. They're always leaving each other."

He tugged on my hand. "Come on. You're gonna fall. You need to sit down."

I stepped off the chair. "I'm not *sitting down*. If I find my purse and leave now—"

"You don't have a car," he said.

I held out my hand. "Give me your keys."

"I'm not giving you my keys. We were at the park for a good hour. If he left right after we did, he's already in Baker County…*if* he left at all. And you don't know that he did."

He was infuriatingly calm.

"Fine," I said. "I'll borrow Ruby's car."

Brushing past, I stormed to the front door and jerked it open.

There was Ruby, hand raised to knock, with Topeka snuggled on her shoulder.

"Oh, thank Heaven," I said, taking the baby. "We had no idea where she was."

"I saw you walk by," Ruby said. "Thought I'd bring her home. I have to get to the bank."

"I've never been so relieved." I gave way to sobbing. "What would I have said to Anne?"

"You mean *Justine*?" Ruby asked.

"Yes. Justine," I said.

I stepped back to let her in and then retreated to my favorite chair.

"Hank said he left a note," Ruby said. "Didn't you find it?"

"No. Where'd he go?"

"To pick up your car. Nancy called and said it was ready. He wanted it to be a little surprise…pay you back for all you've done for him."

Still trembling, I held the baby close. I wondered if she could feel my heart pounding.

"I didn't even *think* to look for a note. When I saw the car was gone, I panicked."

"Hello, Tom," Ruby said. "Didn't mean to ignore you."

"No problem," he said. "I was just leaving." Bending down, he kissed my cheek. "Take my advice and stay home the rest of the day. Then tomorrow go see Justine and ask her."

"I will."

"Ask her what?" Ruby said.

## Chapter 12 ~ In Search of Ivy Leigh

"If she knows where Ivy Leigh is," I said, watching Tom close the door behind him.

"That would make things easier, wouldn't it?" Ruby said. "I've got to get going."

Left alone, I sat for a long time snuggling Topeka. How could I love her so much after only a few days? Why had I jumped to the conclusion Hank had taken her?

And why had my first thought been of Anne and not Justine?

"I've got to hold of myself," I said. "There's too much to do for me to fall apart now."

Hank called later that evening. He had the car but planned to spend the night at home packing before coming back. To think: all the while I pictured him speeding away with a stolen baby, he had been doing me a favor, as well as sparing me another encounter with Nancy Crisp. And I'd be so glad to have my car back. I'd had enough of that Volkswagen. From the moment I laid eyes on it, my life had been bedlam.

The next morning Topeka and I waltzed into Justine's room while she was finishing breakfast. Some kind soul had gone to the trouble of making her presentable. Her unruly hair had been brushed, and she was wearing a clean hospital gown.

Justine pushed the tray away and reached out. I laid Topeka in her arms. Tears spilling, she pressed her face against the baby's cheek. I stepped to the window and kept quiet, letting her savor the moment.

"Sweet girl. Sweet girl." She sighed contentedly. "Thank you, Babs, for taking such good care of her. She looks *so* much better than when we first…"

She broke off, possibly afraid of another tirade from me.

"You're welcome," I said, turning around. "I had a lot of help. Everybody loves her."

If she only knew what I meant by that.

She eased Topeka onto her lap, resting the baby's head on her knees, and tucked her finger under Topeka's chin. "Give Grammy a smile," she cooed.

Topeka complied.

I was getting antsy. "Nice view," I said. "It's a beautiful day. Maybe fall is almost here."

"You should see fall in West Virginia," Justine said, eyes glued to the baby's face. "So beautiful and cool. I'll miss that."

*Ask her.* Tom's instructions throbbed in my brain. *West Virginia. A starting point.*

"Have you lived in West Virginia a long—?"

But by then Justine was too busy playing Patty-cake to pay attention to me. "…ro-o-oll it…and pa-a-at it…and mark it with a 'T' and put it in the oven for Toppy and me."

"She loves Patty-cake," I said.

"Yes, hers does. Yes, hers does," Justine chirped, still clapping Topeka's hands. "Don't you, sweet girl? Don't you wo-o-o-ve pwaying Patty-cake wif Gwammy? Yes, hers does."

*Try again.* "Do your kids live near you?"

"Oh, no. They're all over the place. I've got four grandkids I haven't seen in over a year."

"Sorry to hear that," I said. "Do you ever hear from them?"

"Not as much as I wish I did."

*Time to get to the point.* "What about Ivy Leigh?" I stepped around the foot of the bed. "Are you in touch with her…at all? I know you parted on bad terms."

By now she had given up Patty-cake in favor of Peek-a-boo and had her hands over her face, muffling her voice. "You know Ivy Leigh." Hands open. "Peek-a-boo." Hands closed. "She's not one to"—hands open—"Peek-a-boo. Hold a grudge."

"Franny had no idea where she was, so I just wondered if you—"

"Did you bring a bottle?" Justine asked. "I think she's hungry."

I pulled a bottle from the diaper bag. "Never leave home without one."

She nestled the baby in her arm to feed her, and the room grew quiet. Maybe now we could get somewhere. I waited, hopeful.

"I've missed this," Justine said.

"Are you in touch with Ivy Leigh? Franny had no idea where she was, so I assumed—"

She turned to me, eyes wide. I'd struck a nerve. "Ivy Leigh *tried* to get in touch with Mother. Now *there* was a woman who could hold a grudge. She never forgave Ivy Leigh for me leaving home. And it just *wasn't* true."

"She should've blamed J. Michael Ford," I said. "He nearly ruined all three of us."

"You got that right. She said if it hadn't been for Ivy Leigh bringing him home, I never would've known he was on the planet, and I would've gone to college…like that would've happened anyway. I was no good in school. You remember."

Now we were headed in the right direction.

## Chapter 12 ~ In Search of Ivy Leigh

"You realize...now, don't you," I asked, "all her anger was because of Clarissa?"

"I was thinking last night...after you left. Mother was always so hard on Ivy Leigh. Said it was because 'she was the oldest.' But that wasn't it at all, was it? Reckon it was because Ivy Leigh was that other woman's daughter?"

"I do now."

"And that other woman...Clarissa...stole...Hank. I still can't quite wrap my head around that—he's my father."

"He was on his way back," I blurted out, eager to tell the rest of his story.

"Here?" Her eyes darted to the door.

"No. After they ran off, Hank decided to come home. They were on their way when they had the accident. Clarissa was killed. He was in the hospital a long time. By the time he recovered enough to get back, your mom...and Cab...had gotten married and moved away."

She was unmoved. "I appreciate you not bringing him today."

"His decision." I was determined to press his case. "He said he wouldn't come back unless you asked for him."

"He did?" She set the bottle on the bedside table. "That's...kind."

I stayed on track. "So...tell me about Ivy Leigh. I've always wondered."

She brought Topeka to her shoulder. "She married a great guy. Marshall Ransom. Korean War vet. Wounded. That's how she met him. She volunteered in a veterans' hospital. Doesn't that sound just like her?"

"It does. So...has she been happy?"

"Do you have a burp cloth?" I gave her one. She draped it over her shoulder under Topeka's head and patted her as she talked. "I promise you...Ivy Leigh has been as happy as she deserved to be. Don't you worry about that."

"She still in Atlanta?"

"No. Marshall had a friend in North Carolina...another veteran...in some kind of trouble. I can't remember. Anyway, they moved up there to help him. And stayed. Far as I know."

"Do you know the town?" I held my breath.

"Uh-huh. Little town...called Dennisonville."

There it was. One brief conversation later, and I knew the state *and* the city where Ivy Leigh lived. I couldn't wait to tell Tom.

"Have a phone number? We should let her know about your mother."

"I s'pose we should. She'd want to know. I've got it written down somewhere at home…in case of emergency. But I never call her. It's too expensive."

"Did you ever write?"

"Me? Write letters?" She exploded with laughter. "You know me better than that."

"But surely she wrote to you?"

"Birthday card. Christmas letter. But she had a hard time keeping track of me. The men I marry never want to stay put, so I'm sure a lot of mail got lost or was returned to sender."

"Remember the address?"

"Let me think. Street starts with a 'B.' Beaumont? No. That's not it. Did you bring a blanket? It's chilly in here." I gave her one. She tucked it around Topeka and kissed the top of her head. "Ivy Leigh ended up like your mom, Babs. Running a boarding house."

"Really?"

"*Beautiful* house. She sent pictures. Three stories. Little crow's nest kind of thing"—she pointed up—"on top. I don't know what you call it. I wish I could remember that street."

"Maybe you'll think of it later when—"

She brightened. "I know the name of the *house*. Magnolia Arms."

Some indefinable joy made my heart skip. At least, that's how I recall the moment I heard "Magnolia Arms" for the first time. But that memory may be tinged with the pleasure that came later, when I walked through the door and felt at once as if I belonged.

In a place I had never been.

"Sounds lovely," I said. "I'll call information when I get home. If I can get hold of her, is there anything you want me to tell her?"

"Yeah." She shrugged. "Tell her I'm okay. And say I *promise* I'll get in touch when I know where I'll be. She won't believe you, but tell her I *really* mean it this time."

"You'll come to my house, of course. It's going to take you a while to recover."

"You sure?"

"I've got plenty of room. You know that. And I already have a crib set up for Topeka. You can sleep in the same room with her…Anne's room. My old room."

## Chapter 12 ~ In Search of Ivy Leigh

Her whole face lit up. "It'll be like old times, when I used to spend the night."

"We'll make popcorn." I paused. "Hank's there, too, for now. I want you to know that."

She cringed. "Couldn't he stay at Mother's house? It's empty."

I shook my head. "No. He wouldn't be comfortable there...in any sense of the word. You understand, don't you? Plus, he's got a big Doberman."

A slight smile graced her lips. "Mother would roll over in her grave."

*She's probably flipped over several times by now*, I thought.

"Besides that," I said, "you'll need someone to take care of you when you're released. I'm going to be busy with appointments with lawyers and realtors and I don't know who else."

"What do you mean?"

And I told her the rest of the story—how the house belonged to Ivy Leigh, and we had to find out what she planned to do with it.

"That's the beatingest thing I ever heard," Justine said. "All those years Mother was so persnickety about our home, and it wasn't even *hers*."

When a nurse came to take Justine for tests, Topeka and I went home. I couldn't believe how my luck had changed. For the first time since I'd gotten embroiled with this family's carefully guarded secrets, a problem had been easy to fix. 'Ask Justine where Ivy Leigh is,' Tom had said. And he had been *right*. I put Topeka in her swing and called information in North Carolina for the number to the Magnolia Arms. As the phone rang, I practiced what I'd say. "Ivy Leigh? This is Babs. Your old neighbor. Remember me?" No. "This is *Barbara*. Your—"

"Magnolia Arms."

"Hi," I squeaked. It didn't sound like Ivy Leigh, but what did I know? I hadn't heard her voice in so long. "This is Barbara."

"Who?"

"Barbara. Your old neighbor."

"I'm sorry," she said. "I think you have the wrong number. This is the Magnolia Arms."

"Yes. I wanted to speak to Ivy Leigh..." Thrown off balance, my mind went blank. *What was her husband's name? I'd only heard it once.* "Uh...Marshall?"

Her tone assumed a professional coolness. "May I ask who's calling?"

"Barbara...Allgrove."

"Ivy Leigh is unable to come to the phone right now. May I take a message?"

She had gone from business-like to cautious. Asking for a *number* where I could reach Ivy Leigh was off the table now. I could not play the "old friend" card, when I hadn't even known Ivy Leigh's last name.

I shook my head, furious at my own bungling.

*Message? Yeah. Her mother died. Only she wasn't her mother. And the grandmother, she thought was her great aunt, has left her the house she grew up in. Ask if she'll sign it over to her destitute sister, who's really her stepsister.*

I was so lost in what I wished I could say, I had lapsed into silence.

"Hello?" she asked. "You still here?"

"Sorry. Yes. Let me explain. Ivy Leigh and I…were in school together…and we lost touch…you know how that is…and I recently heard from *another* friend that she was the manager of a boarding house in North Carolina, and I just wanted to—" in a sudden fit of inspiration, I blurted out—"…book a room, if I could."

"I can help with that. This is Agnes Carlyle. My husband and I are the managers now."

The softened tone was good. The news was bad. The one reliable bit of information I had was that Ivy Leigh was the manager at the Magnolia Arms, but that was *wrong*. Back at Square One, I had to keep this Agnes person talking.

"Oh. Okay. I know it's late notice, but I'd like to come…next week. Is that all right?"

"If you'll hold on, I'll go to the other phone, so I can look at the register."

"Sure."

When she laid down the receiver, I heard a baby crying. I waited. Then she picked up on another line. Maybe it wasn't too late to win over Agnes Carlyle.

"I heard your baby crying," I said. "Would you like to get her…uh…him? I can wait."

"Him." She heaved a sigh of relief. "Yes, thank you. I won't be a minute." She put down the receiver again.

What next? I ran through a number of scenarios. The best option was to talk about the baby. Nothing warmed a mother's heart like answering questions about her child.

She picked up again. "Thank you for waiting. I'm juggling things today. The lady who usually helps with Denver is at a conference."

## Chapter 12 ~ In Search of Ivy Leigh

I pictured her, standing at the check-in desk, holding the baby while she paged through the guest register—the same way my mother had with my little sister Janie.

"Denver. That's nice. Family name?" I asked.

"Yes, but not my family. Denver is for the father of a good friend of mine. Now, what day would you like to come?"

"Uh...Tuesday?" I chose at random. "I've...always wanted to see the fall leaves, and I've never taken the time to do it. I thought this year I would, since Ivy Leigh has a house there."

I was warming to my story.

"It's the perfect time of year," she said. "Next week, I have only one room available. It's small and on the first floor. The upstairs rooms are all booked for a family reunion."

"That's fine," I said.

"How long will you stay?"

*As long as it takes to wheedle information out of you, because I'm pretty sure it's not going to be as easy as I thought.*

"Till the weekend?" I ventured.

"That's great," she said. I could tell she was smiling. "We'll expect you on Tuesday. Would you like me to send a brochure so you can see a picture of the house? It might have time to reach you before you leave."

"That'd be nice." After hearing Justine's description, I was dying to see a photo.

I gave her my address—the game-changer.

"Jacksonville, Florida?" she asked.

"Uh-huh."

"So when you said you were in school with Ivy Leigh, you meant elementary school—not college."

"Yes. And junior high and high school."

"You're the first Jacksonville friend to call since I've been here." Her curiosity was getting the best of her. "Ivy Leigh said she grew up there, but that's about it. I've always thought that was odd, because"—she caught herself—"well...see you next week."

"Looking forward to it."

She had no idea how much.

Later that day, Hank returned with my car. Caesar bounded in, obviously glad to be back. I gave Hank the good news that I had located Ivy

Leigh, and Justine had agreed to stay with us after she was released from the hospital.

Against Tom's advice, I asked Anne to stay with my charges while I was gone. Hank couldn't take care of Justine and Topeka by himself, and Anne's gentle presence would be a buffer while the two of them got to know each other.

Two days later, the brochure arrived. There on the front was the Magnolia Arms.

A high-pitched shingled roof topped three stories of pale gray walls. Full-paned windows framed with gleaming white casements lined the lower two floors. Smaller gabled windows circled the third. A widow's walk sat atop a splendid cupola adorned with a tall arched window. Four wide steps led up to a spacious columned porch which ran the length of the house.

Agnes had included a note.

*The man who built this house called it a monument to love. I'll tell you the story when you get here. Looking forward to meeting you. We can swap stories about our mutual friend while she's still away. That way, she can't interrupt.*

Ivy Leigh was still "away"?

No use worrying about that now. The plans were made. And from the sound of this note, Agnes Carlyle was less suspicious of me than she had been. Besides, now that I had this picture in hand, I longed to see the Magnolia Arms in person. The trip would be an ideal excuse to escape the stress I had been under for weeks. I gazed at the photo. Beyond those doors, life would be an unbroken series of calm days and dreamless nights. No more buried secrets, estranged families, missing persons, troubled pasts, broken hearts. There—life would be serene.

The following week, Tom drove me to the train station before dawn. As usual, he had to have the last word about the foolhardy course I was pursuing.

"I still don't like you staying at this place we know nothing about," he said, voice booming through the crowded terminal.

"I called the Better Business Bureau just like you said. The Magnolia Arms has a sterling reputation. And the manager is a lovely person. I feel like I know her."

He wasn't convinced. "I still think I should go along as a disinterested third party to talk to Ivy Leigh. I have a better head for business than you do."

## Chapter 12 ~ In Search of Ivy Leigh

I had seen no need to tell him Ivy Leigh wasn't even there at the moment.

"This doesn't call for a head for business. I know Ivy Leigh. Once she finds out how bad off Justine is, she'll be reasonable about the house."

"What if Ivy Leigh *needs* the money from the sale? You said her husband is disabled."

I squeezed his arm. "I won't know till I get there and talk to her."

"I could go with you, if you'll wait till the weekend."

"You can't. They only have one room available. The other rooms have been booked for months. I told you that. I can't even get into *my* room till tomorrow."

"So why are you leaving today?"

"I'll only have the room for four days. I don't want to waste one of them travelling."

"But do you have to stay in some mom-and-pop motel tonight? Isn't there a Holiday Inn or something?"

"Agnes recommended it. She knows the owners. Now stop worrying. I'm going to North Carolina. Not the moon."

He hugged me. "Call me the minute you get there."

We said goodbye, and I boarded the train. Settling by a window, I lifted a manila envelope from my tote bag and took inventory: two wills, the deed to Franny's house, the eulogy I had delivered at Franny's funeral, in case Ivy Leigh cared to read it. I had pored over Franny's papers and keepsakes so often they had lost their original fascination for me…all except one—the photo of *Cab, Clarissa, & Ivy Leigh Moore*. This was irrefutable black-and-white, 5"x7" proof of the story I would tell Ivy Leigh, the truth Franny had concealed all these years.

"I love old photos," said a red-haired lady across the aisle. "Is that your family?"

"My friend. Her mother passed away, and I'm on my way to tell her."

"I'm sorry," she said. "Is that her mother in the photo?"

"Yes," I said. "It is."

Twelve hours later, I arrived in Dennisonville and lugged my suitcase through the terminal and then outside where a single cab waited by the curb. I bent down and peeked in. The driver, about my age, was working a crossword puzzle. I tapped on the window. Newspaper in hand, he scrambled from the car.

"Sorry." He tugged on the bill of his gray newsboy cap. "I was absorbed in 13 down. Where to?"

"Whispering Pines Motor Lodge."

He unlocked the trunk and hefted in my bag. "Know right where it is." Then he opened the door to the backseat. "You're not by any chance Madge's niece, are you?"

"No," I said noting his name, *Asa Ludlow,* embroidered above his shirt pocket.

He climbed behind the wheel and started the meter. "Reason I ask is my missus told me Madge's niece was coming to town and for me to keep an eye out."

"No. Just sightseeing. I have so many friends who come north every year to look at leaves. I've always wanted to see what the fuss is about."

By now I had almost convinced myself this was the real reason for the trip.

He pulled onto the street and peered at me in the rearview mirror. "Where you from? If you don't mind me asking."

"Jacksonville, Florida."

He brightened. "I was gonna head to Florida after I retired a few years ago. Go to Disney World. Maybe down to the Keys. But couldn't make ends meet. You know how that is."

"For sure. I'm a retired school secretary."

"Would you be interested in the scenic route?"

"Why not?" I said. *How long could the scenic route be in a town this size?*

We headed to the center of town. The fading sun seeped through the oaks lining Main Street, casting shadows onto brick storefronts. A lone shopkeeper threw a white canvas over a pile of pumpkins on a wood table. Then he disappeared into his store and flipped the "Open" sign to "Closed."

I half-expected Barney Fife to be waiting at the next corner.

We turned onto Second Avenue. Asa pointed to a stately Victorian home on his right. A sign in the yard read: *Spenlow School of Music.*

"That's our latest claim to fame," he said.

"Beautiful," I said.

"And see there on the corner?" Asa nodded at a colonial-style house on his left. "George Washington slept there."

We arrived at the Whispering Pines Motor Lodge, a long red brick building, rooms numbered 1-12, white curtains at the windows, maroon

## Chapter 12 ~ In Search of Ivy Leigh

mums and variegated ivy in a planter under the picture window of the manager's office. A sign out front, neon green letters lit, read "Vacancy."

"301," I said.

Asa turned off the meter. "Huh?"

"301. Highway out of Jacksonville. Old motels like this all along the road. Like stepping back in time."

Asa got out and opened my door. "It's a classic. One reason tourists like to stay in our—"

The office door flew open. A wiry, gray-haired woman wearing a white bib apron over a yellow-flowered dress burst out and scurried toward the cab.

Asa called to her. "Hello, Gretchen. I brought you a—"

She rounded the back of the cab and grabbed Asa by the arm.

"Oh, thank Heaven you're here," she said.

"What's wrong?" Asa asked. "Is it Moe?"

"No. Ida. Her house is *on fire*. Agnes just called."

*Agnes? Carlyle.* Had to be.

Asa shook his head. "We *warned* Ida about her wiring. Did everyone get out?"

"I don't know. But I have to see for myself."

Asa pointed to me, stranded in the back seat. "What about your customer?"

Gretchen stepped back to let me out. "Sorry. I don't usually welcome people this way."

"No problem," I said. "Is this lady a friend of yours? Ida, I mean."

"Since grade school. Are you Mrs. Allgrove?"

"Yes. I have a—"

"Your room is ready." She grasped my hand in both of hers. "Could I ask you a favor?"

"Sure."

"Could you manage the desk for a while?"

"Me?"

Gretchen squeezed my hand. "My friend, Verbena, is on her way. She helps me out sometimes, like when I take my husband to the doctor. But she's at the beauty parlor. I just got off the phone with them. She's almost finished. If you'll man the counter a while, I could leave now. I hate to ask. But I feel like I know you, since we had that nice chat when you called for a reservation."

She explained all this in one breath.

"My parents owned a boarding house," I said. "I ran the front desk all the time."

Putting her arm through mine, Gretchen led me to the office. "You're like God's good angel, sent to me at exactly the right time." Asa followed us and set my suitcase inside the door. "Phone's over there," Gretchen took off her apron. "Not expecting anyone, except you. But you never know." She paused at the door. "Help yourself to anything you need."

The bell on the door jangled as she hurried out.

Asa lingered in the open door. "Just to let you know…her husband, Moe, is a little…confused sometimes, but he's harmless. If he comes in, don't—"

Gretchen called from outside. "Asa. Hurry."

"Don't worry," Asa said. "Moe never hurt anyone."

*Never hurt anyone?* Dazed, I stepped behind the counter and studied the frames displayed on the wood-paneled wall behind Gretchen's desk. Faded black-and-white photos; yellowed newspaper clippings; two high school diplomas—the Tate offspring; a recent color photo, captioned *Dennisonville High, Class of*—

The door burst open. A plump, sweet-faced woman bustled in, the pungent smell of perm solution in her wake. "I came as fast as I could. Have you—?" She stopped, squinting at me. "Where's Gretchen?"

"She left to check on the lady whose house is on fire. Asked me to stay till her friend got here. Are you Verbena?"

"I am." She closed the door. "Isn't it terrible? About Ida? Is there any news?"

"Not yet. They just left."

She plopped her purse on the counter. "If you don't mind me asking… who are you?"

"Barbara Allgrove. I just got here from—"

"Oh, you're the lady from Jacksonville. Gretchen told me someone from Florida was coming. How often do you go to the beach? Once a week? I would, if I lived there."

"Not that often…really."

She stepped behind the counter. "We can talk about it later. You must be worn out after that long trip. Let's get you checked in. Have you had supper?"

"No, I—"

"Newman's is two blocks down. You can call a cab, or walk, if you prefer. She opened the guest register and slid it toward me. "Might do you

## Chapter 12 ~ In Search of Ivy Leigh

good after you've been sitting all day." She talked to me like we had been friends for years.

I followed her to Room 8. She unlocked the door, and I set my suitcase at the foot of the double bed. She breezed past and flipped on the bathroom light. "Looks like you have plenty of towels. Want me to show you where the ice machine is?"

"No, thanks. But I think I'd feel better if I ate something. How do I call a cab?"

"I'll call one for you and ring when it gets here. Anything else?"

"I need to call my son. Let him know I'm here."

Verbena pointed to the phone on the nightstand. "Dial 9 for an outside line. There's a charge for long distance."

She closed the door. I sank onto the gold-quilted bedspread. The long trip was done. But instead of feeling exhilarated, I was wrung out, sinking into that strange, empty, morning-after-Christmas melancholy, when the bustle is over and all that's left is the mess.

I dialed Tom's number. The phone rang. I decided to say a quick hello, 'the trip was fine, I'm headed to supper.' Not: *I'm exhausted and the house I came to visit is going to burn down before I get to it.*

No answer. Relieved, I lay back and stared at the ceiling. Had I packed aspirin?

The phone rang. I bolted up.

"Ernie's here."

"Ernie?" I asked.

Verbena laughed. "The cab."

Grabbing the room key, I put on my all-weather coat and headed to the office. By the time I got to the cab, I had made up my mind. I couldn't wait any longer. I was going to the Magnolia Arms tonight.

Ernie, curly-haired, twinkle-eyed, opened the rear door. "Verbena said you're headed to Newman's?"

"Yes. Do they have take-out? I thought I'd just grab a sandwich to eat on the way."

"Where to?"

"Do you know where the Magnolia Arms is?"

"Yeah. But there's a fire two doors down. The street's blocked off."

"Could you park as close as you can? I'll walk in, if they'll let me."

We made a quick stop at Newman's, and I wolfed down a turkey sandwich as we drove through the streets of Dennisonville. Ernie leaned into the steering wheel and pointed up. "Look at that. See that glow? Looks like the sun's coming up." He whistled. "That's really something."

A police car, lights blinking, blocked our way at the corner of Belmont Drive.

Ernie rolled down his window to speak to the officer. "Okay if I drop off a fare, Bert?" He pointed over his shoulder with his thumb. "This lady needs to get to the Magnolia Arms."

Bert, a red-haired, no-nonsense cop, peeked in. "Madge's niece?"

"No," Ernie said. "I told her about the fire, but she wanted to come anyway."

"Park over there. Stay back from the barricades."

I slipped a $20 into Ernie's hand. "Could you wait? Then take me back to the motel?"

He smiled at the bill. "Sure."

We got out to survey the scene. Fire hoses, bulging with water, snaked across the road. Sympathetic neighbors still clad in work clothes or attired in pajamas and robes huddled in each other's yards, gaping spellbound at the flames in Ida's windows. Pulling my coat snugly around me, I crept along the sidewalk, hoping nobody would notice and stop me from getting closer to the fire. Easing around one group, skirting another, I picked up scattered pieces of information. *Nestor had warned Ida about the wiring. Bernard had most likely let the water boil out of the kettle again.*

Shoving my hands into my pockets, I kept walking, past one house, another, and then, to the left, there it was—the Magnolia Arms. The columned porch, wide steps, arched window, the cupola towering like a lighthouse in the black sky.

A young woman was standing in the yard. I could just make out her face in the flashing lights of the fire engines. I recognized her face from the brochure.

Agnes Carlyle. The manager of the Magnolia Arms.

# Chapter 13

## Room Assignments
### Dennisonville, North Carolina
### October 1979

Two onlookers stood between me and the Magnolia Arms: an overbearing woman, hands on plenteous hips, pontificating over the roar of the fire engines; and a perfectly coiffed lady, held captive to this speaker solely by a social obligation to be polite.

"I *told* Ida not to leave that brother of hers alone in the house. Everyone knows Ber-NARD is senile," the hefty woman said. "When he visits, we all hold our breath just waiting for disaster. I'd bet my *bottom dollar* he left grease on the stove."

The other lady, shoulders squared, hands folded, replied in a voice every bit as imposing but restrained...and withering.

"I believe it's BER-nerd, and I've told you before, Mrs. Ludlow, I'm not comfortable discussing the mental health of a man who is a total stranger to me."

*Ludlow? A relative of Asa's?*

The gentle reproof breezed right past Mrs. Ludlow.

"I bet you don't have this kind of excitement in Su-u-mp-tuh, do ya?" she asked, mocking with an affected Southern drawl. She wrapped her ample arm around her companion's shoulders and drew her close with a squeeze and a chortle.

The other woman pulled away. "Mrs. Ludlow, please. I'm not comfortable with—"

"You're not comfortable with anything, are you? Your sister Piney was the same way when she first got here, but we fixed *her*, and if you stay long enough, we'll fix you, too."

Sidestepping them to take a shortcut across the lawn, I was within inches of Agnes when another woman, pale, spare, her thin gray hair slicked back into a tight bun, swept in from the opposite direction, calling to Agnes as she ran.

Clutching a large white cat in her arms, the woman gasped out, "Agnes. We found Soapy under the bottlebrush, but I can't find little Jean Marie anywhere. Is she over here?"

My heart leaped into my throat. A child trapped in the burning house? I broke in.

"I can help," I said, looking up at Agnes—taller than I'd pictured, 5'8" at least. "When's the last time you saw the little girl?"

Agnes glanced in my direction. "Jean Marie is a Yorkie." She turned back to her friend. "Maybe she's at Rowena's. Probably went over there to visit Bruno."

Bruno, I assumed, was also a dog.

The fretting lady's voice broke. "She must be terrified. You know she can't see good any more…or hear either. If she's gone too far away…and got turned around…"

"Someone will bring her home," Agnes said. "Where's Bernard?"

At least one mystery was solved. The name was "BER-nerd."

"He's over there getting checked out by the paramedics. See?" She pointed. "They put that yellow blanket around him. Isn't that nice? Oh, Agnes, what am I going to do? The Bisbees will be here tomorrow. Where will they go?"

I peered through the dark at the rescue unit and could just make out the top of Bernard's head, a yellow blanket around his shoulders.

"We'll work that out later," Agnes said.

"Where will I stay tonight? And Bernard? You know he doesn't like to have his routine upset. What am I going to do with *him*?"

When the poor woman dissolved into tears, Agnes slipped her arm around her. "You'll both stay here, of course. Come inside." She shepherded her into the Magnolia Arms.

I was still standing there when the proper lady approached, mumbling and shaking her head as she walked. My heart warmed. A longtime friend, I assumed, sorry about her neighbor's troubles. I waited, thinking she might stop to chat, but she brushed by.

"I'm *not* supposed to be here," she said to herself. "I'm not supposed to *be* here."

## Chapter 13 ~ Room Assignments

I watched her enter the house and close the door, stranding me in the cold, dark night. I gazed at the rows of lighted windows and pictured Agnes leading her friend—undoubtedly Ida—to the kitchen. They had probably been neighbors for years and shared many a sorrow and cup of sugar. Ida and her brother would stay the night and need Agnes' attention. There would be no tour for me. Not tonight. Oh, well, I had a cab waiting. I would get a good night's sleep and start fresh tomorrow, returning when there was no crisis to be handled.

Pausing to admire the house one more time, I spotted a shadowy figure looming in the arched window of the cupola. I could not make out his features, but there was no mistaking his officious posture. Hand on the window frame, he peered down like a factory owner watching underpaid seamstresses at work. I shivered, not because of the cold, but because this was one mysterious man too many. Not that long ago, I'd spied a stranger in the Oak Ridge cemetery in Madison, and I still wasn't over the commotion that had brought into my life.

A gentle hand touched my shoulder. I jumped. Gretchen Tate was standing next to me. "Mrs. Allgrove? I thought that was you. I saw you from across the street. What're you doing here? You'll catch your death in this cold. That little coat may do for Florida, but not here."

I glanced at the window again. The man had disappeared.

"Ernie drove me," I said. "I was curious about all the excitement. I asked him to wait for me at the corner."

"Come on then," she said, taking my hand. "Let's get back to the Pines. I'll share your cab, if you don't mind."

"Of course not," I said, suddenly homesick and glad to have a friend.

Gretchen and I climbed in the backseat. Ernie started the engine and turned the heater on high. He looked at us in the rearview mirror.

"Any news on what caused the fire?" he asked, pulling away from the curb.

"Not yet," Gretchen said.

"Sorry for Ida," he said. "I'm sure she was counting on that money from the Bisbees. She'll need it more than ever now. Was anyone else supposed to stay at her place this week?"

"The Finches, I think," Gretchen said. "I could be wrong."

"For the family reunion?" I asked.

She turned to me. "Agnes told you about it?"

"Yes, when I called to make my reservation. She said she had only one room downstairs because the upstairs rooms had been reserved for this reunion. Is it a big family?"

"Unfortunately, yes," she said. "And they *all* come. Been fighting for years over the great-grandfather's will. Once a year they all show up on his birthday and fight some more."

Ernie spoke up. "It's a challenge to keep the worst ones from running into each other while they're here. Last year, two of the brothers had an all-out brawl right on Main Street. Made the paper."

"I don't understand," I said. "If they all hate each other, why do they arrange to meet?"

Gretchen shrugged. "Tradition. No one wants to be gossiped about as 'the ones who didn't show up on Granddad's birthday.' That would be disloyal. That's what they'd say."

"I saw two ladies talking in front of the Magnolia Arms. One of them was…a little heavy…very chatty, and the other was kind of prim…and proper. Are they from that family?"

Gretchen laughed. "Oh, no. That was Bridey Ludlow and Miriam Goddard. Bridey is a native, and Miriam is…well, let's just say she's visiting."

"Go ahead and say it," Ernie said, eyeing me in the rearview mirror. "Whole town knows Miriam's husband got arrested for embezzling all that money from his company."

"*Ernie*," Gretchen said, "what would Ivy Leigh say if she could hear us blabbing about the people at the Magnolia Arms? To a *visitor, no less*?"

Ernie was unrepentant. "Ivy Leigh's not here now, is she? And besides that, the story was in the Raleigh paper. It's old news by now."

"But not to Mrs. Allgrove, and she's going to meet Miriam in the morning. Here you've gone and put her in the most catawampus position." She turned to me. "How good are you at keeping a straight face? Because that's what you're gonna have to do when you meet her."

I nearly exploded with laughter, thinking, *You have no idea*. But instead, I replied: "I grew up in a boarding house. My mother drilled into me from the time I was little we were *never* to discuss our tenants with anyone. I'm good at acting like I don't know a thing."

"See?" Ernie said. "Problem solved."

Gretchen was not mollified. She put her hand on the back of the driver's seat and leaned in close. "Mark my word, Ernie Phipps. Somewhere

## Chapter 13 ~ Room Assignments

in Paris, France, Ivy Leigh just got a cold chill from she knows-not-where, and it's all because of you."

Now I knew—Ivy Leigh was in Paris.

Not wanting to cause a rift, I changed the subject. "Bridey said something about Miriam's sister. Sounded like she said 'Piney.' Is that right?"

"She meant Pinetta Fraleigh…uh…Spenlow," Gretchen said, sitting back. "She just got married to our choir director. Anyway, when Miriam's husband was arrested, she was so mortified, she asked Pinetta if she could stay here a while to get away from the news people."

"Nice she had someplace to go," I said.

*That's why she's 'not supposed to be here.'*

"If you ask me," Ernie piped up, "it's not just for 'a while,' if you know what I mean."

Gretchen shot him a sideways glance. "That's enough about us," she said and patted my knee. "Tell us about you, dear."

I said I was a widow, retired school secretary, mother, grandmother, reprised my "wanting to see the leaves" story, and left it at that. Local news obviously travelled fast, and I didn't want anyone knowing *why* I was here to see Ivy Leigh. Especially not Ernie. When he delivered us to the Whispering Pines, I tried to pay him, but he said the $20 I gave him was more than enough. Gretchen said there would be complimentary coffee and Danish in the office at 6:30 a.m., and we said goodnight.

When I got to my room, I called Anne to tell her I had arrived safely. "Would you call Tom and tell him? I don't feel like the third degree tonight."

She laughed. "I understand. I'll tell him."

"How are things there?" I asked. "Is Justine softening up any towards Hank?"

"We all sat at the table together for supper. I thought that was a good sign. Tomorrow she wants to see Franny's house. Think it's too soon for that?"

"Only Justine knows that. How's Topeka?" I asked, realizing I missed her.

"Blossoming." The lilt in Anne's voice was both good to hear, and worrying.

I said nothing about the fire, embezzlement, Bridey, or the man in the window. We said goodbye, and I went right to sleep, dreaming Bernard set fire to the lawn of the Magnolia Arms while Miriam peered down from the arched window.

The next morning I packed my suitcase and arrived at the office promptly at 6:30. Gretchen was on the phone. She waved at me and pointed to a table by the wall where a full coffee pot and tray of Danishes waited. I helped myself and sat down. From the look on her face and tone of her voice, the situation on Belmont Drive had not improved since last night.

Pen in hand, she scribbled furiously. "Yes. Yes. All right. I happened to think…has anyone called Newman's? I take Moe there to have breakfast with Bernard whenever he's in town. Maybe in his confusion, he ended up there."

When Gretchen hung up, I asked, "Is Bernard missing?"

She came from behind the counter and sat next to me. "Yes. Nowhere to be found. I'm so sorry for all this upset. This is not the way we usually welcome people to town."

"No need for apologies. The last time I saw him, he was with the paramedics."

She nodded. "He was. But by the time Ida got back from talking to Agnes, he had wandered off. He's done it before, but he always comes back…till now."

"He was gone all *night*?"

"Yes. They've looked everywhere. We're just hoping somebody took him in, or he found someplace warm to sleep."

"I should get back over there and help them look. Would you call me a cab?"

She touched my arm. "Bless your heart. You've barely been here 12 hours and already it's like you're one of us."

"I feel right at home," I said, and meant it.

She returned to the check-in desk and called a cab. Within minutes, 'my old friend' Asa was back. He put my suitcase in the trunk, while Gretchen fixed us both a coffee to-go. I paid my bill, and she hugged me again.

As Asa drove past Newman's, I scanned both sides of the street to see if I could spot Bernard. No luck. Two blocks later I spied an elderly man snoozing at a bus stop.

"Is that *him*?" I yelled.

"No," he said. "And it'd be better if you didn't scream like that. Nearly ran off the road."

## Chapter 13 ~ Room Assignments

"Sorry. I only saw the top of his head while he was sitting in the back of the rescue unit."

He went on. "Bernard is a little fella. Bald. Beak nose. Uses a wooden cane. Carved dog's head on the handle. But he may have left home without it, if he was confused."

"Okay," I said, keeping my eyes peeled as we drove. Any and every old man, with or without a cane, was a suspect. I would point out one and then another. Asa would shake his head. Too tall…too heavy…too much hair…

We drove onto Belmont Drive. Stately homes, beautiful in the bright light of day, lined the street, each home distinctive with its own special character. *This* was the image from the brochure. Fallen leaves, raked, unraked, carpeted lawns. Children toting schoolbooks dawdled on the sidewalk. A few neighbors, newspapers tucked under their arms, coffee mugs in hand, gazed and pointed at Ida's home from a respectful distance. A police car was in the driveway of the Magnolia Arms, so Asa parked at the curb. We got out and stood in the street, joining the others lamenting the ruined house.

"Poor Ida," Asa said. "That was her grandparents' house. No telling what she lost that can't ever be replaced. Pictures…furniture. She had an old Victrola. Wonder if she got it out."

"I suppose that's the least of her worries now…with her brother missing," I said.

He nodded. "You're right. Well, I got to get going. I'll take your suitcase in."

I took out my wallet to pay him. "Leave it on the porch. I don't want to go in right now, while they're busy with the police. I'll just look around till they're gone."

He touched the bill of his cap and started up the sidewalk with my suitcase.

Conscious of the neighbors' eyeing me, I strolled toward Ida's house—a smoldering wreck. I estimated a third of the home to be a complete loss. The front corner—where the kitchen had been?—had collapsed on itself, black and shattered. I thought of how deeply I would take it to heart if this happened to one of my neighbors. Walking up the driveway, I studied the white walls, black shutters, neat boxwood hedges hemmed in by scalloped stone edging. Ida was the "Franny" of Belmont. Every neighborhood—I supposed—had one home which set the standard for perfect order.

## The Moores, the Merriers

The driveway ended at a detached garage. I stopped to admire the backyard—wrought iron bench, bird feeders, birdbath, sundial, garden shed—painted white with black shutters, an exact replica of the house. I heard whining...listened...the sound came from the viburnum bushes under the rear windows. "Jean Marie?" I called. "Come here, sweetie." She whined again. I crept toward the bushes, got down on all fours, and found the Yorkie huddled underneath, wet with morning dew and shivering. I took off my coat and laid it on the ground. Then I reached in, lifted her out, and wrapped her up.

I was about to make a beeline for the Magnolia Arms when a glint of gold in the grass caught my eye. I stepped nearer the shed. At my feet was Bernard's wooden cane with a carved dog's head, exactly as Asa had described.

Shifting Jean Marie to my left arm, I opened the door to the shed and found Bernard, wrapped in the yellow blanket—thank goodness—resting his head on a bag of potting soil. I dashed across the backyard and raced down the driveway, shouting for help. A man taking his garbage can to the curb looked in my direction. I sprinted toward him.

"I found Bernard," I gasped. "He's in the shed. Get Ida. Here...take the dog."

Without question, he accepted Jean Marie and took off for the Magnolia Arms. I hurried back to Bernard, knelt on the cold concrete floor, and shook him gently. To my great relief, he opened his eyes.

"Ida?" he whispered.

"I'm Ida's friend," I said. "She sent me to find you. Can you sit up?"

He eased up onto one elbow, wincing with pain. "My hip. My hip."

Sitting next to him, I rubbed his arms to warm him.

"Help's coming," I said. "They'll be here in a minute. We'll get you inside."

"Why are you in Ida's house?" he asked.

The door swung open. A young dark-haired man rushed in, followed by a big burly policeman.

The young man knelt next to me. "I'm Nestor Carlyle." He pointed over his shoulder at the officer. "This is Chief Wilde. We'll take him now."

The policeman acknowledged me. "Ma'am."

I scooted back. Chief Wilde crouched down, put his strong hands under Bernard's arms, and told Nestor to "get his feet." Nestor spoke

## Chapter 13 ~ Room Assignments

quietly, explaining what was happening. When they lifted him, Bernard cried out again. The men carried him out of the shed. I followed.

Agnes, waiting outside with a tearful Ida, extended her hand. "I'm Agnes Carlyle. Thank you for your help. This is Ida, the sister of the man you found."

Ida threw her arms around me. "I don't know how to thank you. You saved my brother's life. How in the world did you find him?"

Agnes touched Ida's shoulder. "We'll talk about that when we get back to my place."

Ida released me, sniffed loudly, and took an embroidered hanky from her coat pocket. She wiped her eyes and then slipped her arm through mine as we walked down the driveway.

"Have we met?" Agnes asked me. "Seems like I remember you from somewhere."

"I was here last night," I said, "but we didn't meet. I'm Barbara Allgrove."

"Oh, no," Agnes said. "Nestor was going to pick you up this morning, but we lost track of the time." She sighed. "There's so much going on."

"I took a cab," I said, "so I could help you look."

Agnes led me and Ida to the Magnolia Arms. She stopped short of the sidewalk to the front porch, turning right onto the driveway. We took the back steps into the kitchen—not the grand entrance I had imagined. My letdown was short-lived. The kitchen exceeded expectation. Tall gleaming windows, crisp white curtains, African violets on the windowsill above the porcelain sink, a high ceiling, plate of muffins on a round table, the aroma of fresh coffee perking would have made me want to linger all day, if the room had not been crowded with a wide assortment of people.

The venerable lady I now knew as Miriam Goddard was at the stove, pouring steaming water into a china teapot. Another man, about Nestor's age, but sullen and disheveled, was washing dishes. Neither of them looked up when we entered.

Ida walked straight through the kitchen into the hall.

"Come with me," Agnes said. "Chief Wilde will want to talk to you. Once the ambulance gets here and takes Bernard, we can relax."

We stepped across the hall and into the parlor.

Centered on a bay window across the room was a worn brocade sofa, striped throw pillows in haphazard piles at each end. Bernard, magenta afghan around his narrow shoulders, was holding a cup in both hands, sipping something steamy. Ida, Jean Marie in her lap, patted his back. Nearby, Nestor and Chief Wilde watched, whispering to each other. Across from the sofa, two burgundy wingback chairs were drawn close to a marble-topped coffee table where a chessboard, game in progress, had been suspended. To my left was a grand piano, bench pulled out, sheet music scattered on the floor.

Chief Wilde noticed us and invited me to sit at the card table to my right. Agnes and Nestor joined us. I explained how I happened to be nosing around Ida's house, and that I recognized Bernard's cane from Asa's description.

"The shed was the first place we looked last night," Nestor said. "I guess Bernard got tired of wandering around and circled back home. We should've checked again."

"He asked me what I was doing in his house," I said. "I think that's where he thought he was. They look exactly the same."

The ambulance arrived to take Bernard to the hospital. Ida left Jean Marie sleeping on the sofa and rode along. Chief Wilde thanked me for my help and left for the station. Nestor welcomed me "officially." Then he kissed Agnes goodbye and said after he helped "set things up at Kimball Pines, he would pick up Denver." Agnes invited me to the kitchen. Glad no one was there, I sat at the table. She offered coffee and told me to help myself to a muffin. At ease for the first time since leaving home—only yesterday?—I felt suddenly exhausted.

Without warning, I started to cry. Chest tight, throat constricted, I tried to settle myself down while Agnes poured my coffee, but I failed miserably. Busy at the counter, she was chatting about the morning's events, oblivious to my declining mental state.

Clamping my hand over my mouth, I bowed my head and tried to breathe deeply, but it did no good. Random scenes kept looping through my mind like dreams I could not wake up from: Franny dying in her kitchen; the merciless sun beating down on us at her funeral; Hank, glad Franny was "back home," even if in her grave; Justine, wreaking of cigarette smoke; poor sick Topeka in that nasty sleeper; chasing Nancy through the downpour; semis bearing down on the little red Volkswagen as I drove Hank to my house; Bernard shivering on that icy concrete floor.

Sinking, I did not realize Agnes was at my side till I felt her hand on my shoulder.

## Chapter 13 ~ Room Assignments

"You're like me," she said. "Rise to the occasion when you have to, but once it's over, fall apart." She sat next to me. "Drink this. And have a muffin. Muriel made them. One bite and you'll feel better. She has magic in her fingers."

I did as she said and found she was right. I munched and sipped coffee. She reached across the table, snagged a napkin from the holder, and laid it at my plate. Then…to my surprise…she did not say a word. Just waited.

"I'm sorry," I said.

"For what?"

"Making a fool of myself." I threw up my hands. "I was so excited about coming here and the first thing I do is sit down and blubber."

She laughed. "If you had any idea how many people…including me…have sat in that very chair and done what you just did…you wouldn't be apologizing, believe me."

I wiped my nose. "I guess I'll have to take your word for it. But I'm still embarrassed."

She leaned back. "It's the house. The minute you walk in here, you feel at home. I did." Her face eased into a wry smile. "My first day…let's just say it was a lot like yours. Tell me about you. Gretchen said you grew up in a boarding house?"

"Uh-huh. It wasn't like this, though." I gazed around the kitchen. "Our house was a lot…simpler. I still live there."

"You do? That's amazing."

Why she thought it was 'amazing,' I couldn't imagine. I told her I'd married my high school sweetheart, had two children, who also lived in Jacksonville, and I'd retired from being a school secretary so I could stay home with my grandsons.

"I'm a teacher," she said. "We'll have to swap school stories later."

"Got a lot of them," I said, grinning. "Faculty meetings…"

"Don't get me started," she said, and then pushed back from the table. She stepped to the door, leaned into the hallway, and peeked left and then right. Satisfied we were alone, she returned to the table. "There's something I need to talk to you about, while we're alone."

"Okay," I said, hoping she would tell me about the mysterious man in the window.

Her face was etched with worry, her voice tentative. "I know I promised you a downstairs room, but I'm going to have to put you on the second floor instead, if that's okay."

"I don't mind."

She heaved a sigh of relief. "Thank you. You probably figured out Ida will need to stay here for now. She won't send Bernard back to where he's living till he's better, and she'll *have* to be near him. He can't manage the stairs, so they'll need the two rooms on the first floor."

"I understand. It's not a problem."

Encouraged, she went on. "You'll be in the middle room upstairs. Got a lot of history. Actually, they all do. The whole house does."

"Mine does, too. The people who have paraded in and out over the years…I could write a book. So, is that all? Moving me upstairs?"

Her face twisted into a slight frown. "Not exactly. I need to explain about"—she lowered her voice—"our other guests. It's kind of tricky."

Following her example, I spoke in a conspiratorial tone. "If you mean Miriam, don't worry. Gretchen and Ernie filled me in last night. I won't say a thing about…you know…"

"It's not just that," she said. "She's not very easy to be around. So, don't get offended."

"I've had lots of practice with moody women. Don't worry about me."

"The good news is," Agnes said, "Miriam's not in her room much during the day. Since she discovered Nestor's greenhouse, she spends a lot of time out there. She's there now."

"Miriam won't bother me in the slightest. Trust me. But didn't you say the upstairs rooms were reserved for the people coming for the reunion?"

She rolled her eyes. "They were. But with Ida and Bernard here for who knows how long, they'll have to be relocated. Ida's people, too."

"Where?"

She reached for my coffee cup and walked to the counter to refill it. "Did you notice the Spenlow School of Music on your way into town?"

"Oh, yes. Beautiful. That's one of the first places Asa pointed out."

She returned to the table with a full cup. "That belongs to Pinetta, a friend of ours. Well, she doesn't own it. She's the trustee of the property."

"Pinetta? That's Miriam's sister, right?"

"Uh-huh. It used to be called Kimball Pines, and it has enough rooms to accommodate our guests plus Ida's. I just hope it's big enough they don't kill each other before the week is out."

I stirred cream into my coffee. "Maybe it'll force them to get along."

## Chapter 13 ~ Room Assignments

"Maybe. Anyway, Nestor and Roger have gone to set things up. The rooms had already been converted to classrooms, so they're not exactly places to sleep anymore."

"Surely they can make it work for a few days. They'll still pay, right?"

She nodded. "At a reduced rate. Nestor's idea…so they won't pout. We want them back next year. Why, I don't know, but Nestor says—"

Someone kicked at the back door. A voice boomed. "AG-nes. Ag-NES."

"That'll be Bridey," Agnes said, "with a pot of chicken and rice. Just watch."

She stepped to the door and had barely opened it before Bridey Ludlow, huge pot gripped in oven-mitted hands, strode in. She pressed her wide hips against the door to close it and then marched to the stove to clunk down the pot.

"I put the chicken on to boil last night," Bridey said. "Made the rice this morning." She snatched a dishtowel from the counter and wiped her face. "Verbena's bringing black-eyed peas and broccoli cornbread. Mary Grace made her sour cream pound cake. Y'all won't go hungry."

"Thank you," Agnes said, hovering near the door, ready to usher Bridey out.

Hand aimed like a battering ram, Bridey advanced toward me. "You must be Mrs. Allgrove, that woman from Florida." She pumped my hand up and down. "It's all over town how you saved Ber-NARD. Good thing for him you were snooping around this morning."

Thanks to my long history with Viola Banks, I knew better than to defend myself. I faced Bridey with inscrutable tolerance and good will.

"'Love thy neighbor' should be our policy everywhere. Don't you think?"

Over Bridey's hefty shoulder, I saw Agnes beaming. Our friendship was sealed.

The door opened again and the 'dishwasher' I had seen earlier appeared. When he caught sight of Bridey, he backed out. Agnes eased the door closed and gave me a thumbs up.

I stood. "It was nice meeting you, Mrs. Ludlow. I can't wait to dive into that chicken and rice. It smells delicious."

She wagged her hand. "Call me Bridey. Everyone does."

"Bridey," I repeated. "Wish I had time to talk, but Agnes is taking me to the store so I can pick up a few things I forgot. Honestly, I'd forget my head if it wasn't screwed on."

Agnes opened the door. "Thank you for the chicken and rice. I'll return your—"

"I'll come back tomorrow," Bridey said, and whisked out.

"Do you really need to go to the store?" Agnes asked after she closed the door.

"No-o-o."

"Used to thinking on your feet. I like that." She returned to the table. "Would you like to see the rest of the house?"

"I sure would."

"We'll get your suitcase and take it up to your room when we go."

She led the way to the dining room. Standing in the door, she gazed wistfully around the room and told about her first night at the Magnolia Arms. She was such a good storyteller, I felt like I was living it with her.

"That was the night I met Margaret," she said, eyes beaming. "You'll love that story." She turned to face me. "This is where Nestor proposed."

"I can't wait to hear *that* story," I said.

"I have to warn you...I don't come off well. Didn't say yes till later. I had hopelessly flawed ideas about what it meant to be in love."

"Don't we all?"

I followed her to the check-in desk by the front door. She turned the guest register around and handed me a pen to sign it. She pointed to a closed door beyond the desk.

"That's where Bernard will be when he comes back. Jericho's staying in there now...well, not this minute. He's painting on the third floor, as usual." Stepping to the front door, she picked up my suitcase and headed for the stairs. "I'd let you peek in, but he'd pitch a hissy fit backwards. We've never had a tenant so dead set on privacy...not since Oliver Martin Farrell. But that's another story."

"Jericho?" I asked. "That's an unusual name."

Stopping at the foot of the stairs, she spoke low again. "Jericho Fenton. I don't think it's his real name. He spelled it 'G-e-r-i-c-a-u-l-t' when he signed in. I had to ask him how to say it."

"Famous French artist," I remarked. *J. Michael Ford's favorite. Funny the useless details you remember from a past you long to forget.*

Past the haphazard rows of old photos and faded landscapes on the staircase wall, I followed Agnes to the second floor.

"I love staircases in an old house. Do you ever picture the man who built this banister?"

## Chapter 13 ~ Room Assignments

Agnes paused when she reached the landing. "No need to 'picture' him. It was Jonas Grinstead. One of my best friends. Nestor's best man. It's his father we named Denver after."

The second floor hallway was wide and brightly lit. A blue hurricane lamp and vase of silk sunflowers sat on a dark wood table between two closed doors.

Agnes nodded at the first door. "This is Miriam's room." She pointed to the end of the hall. "We'll move Jericho in there." Opening my door, she spoke low, "You'll be a lonely little petunia in an onion patch."

Then she showed me my room—tasteful, elegant; pale gray walls, tall windows, white curtains, full bed with white quilted spread, throw pillows in shades of pearl gray and steel blue, nightstands on either side with gray ceramic lamps, white-shaded. An art print hung over the bed—Bruegel's *Peasant Wedding*. A gray-flowered overstuffed chair sat in the corner by the window. A collection of books stood in a basket on the floor. On one end of a dark brown dresser sat three urns, blue and gray; on the other end a clear vase of white silk daisies and lilies.

In front of this vase was a black and white photo in an antique gold frame. Three teenage girls in "Sunday best" stood in front of the World War I memorial sculpture, *Life*—a globe with winged figure, laurel-crowned, on top—centerpiece of Jacksonville's Memorial Park. Trying to "pose," they were, nevertheless, giggling, as a stiff spring breeze blew in from the St. Johns River, undoing all the preparations they had made. The middle girl had one arm around her sister, bent over, trying to tame her swirling hem; and the other arm around their friend, who was fixing her hair.

Justine. Ivy Leigh. And me.

Picking up the photo, I gripped it with both hands.

"I can't believe she kept this," I said, breathless. "Franny hated this picture, but Ivy Leigh got copies made for each of us, because she said this was the way we really were."

Open-mouthed, Agnes pointed at me. "You...you're *Babs*. Of course. Why didn't I make the connection? Your name is *Barbara*."

I clasped the picture to my heart. "Yes."

She folded her arms. "You didn't come here for *leaves*. You came to see Ivy Leigh."

# Chapter 14

## Meeting the Neighbors
### Dennisonville, North Carolina
### October 1979

So much for my cloak-and-dagger plans. Thanks to this photo, my cover was blown.

"Yes, I'm Babs," I said. "And you're right. I've got to talk to Ivy Leigh."

The phone rang on the first floor.

Agnes sat on the bed. "Why didn't you just *say so* in the first place?"

"She hasn't been home in almost 30 years." I leaned against the dresser. "I thought if she knew I was coming, she might refuse to see me."

Someone hurried up the stairs, taking them two at a time.

Agnes shook her head. "Ivy Leigh takes in total strangers. She's not going to refuse to see an old friend." She pointed at the picture. "Especially not *you*."

Footsteps sounded in the hall; the dishwasher appeared at the door.

"Here you are," he said, out of breath. "That was Nestor. He needs you at the school. Bring sheets and towels."

Agnes stood. "Is he still on the phone?"

"No. I said I thought you were showing the new lady around. He said not to bother you, but when you're done, would you call?"

"Babs," Agnes said, "this is Roger Merriman, our handyman. He and I grew up together. Our mothers are best friends. Roger, this is Barbara Allgrove. She's from Florida."

"Hello," I said.

Averting his eyes, he gave a quick nod, but did not reply.

Roger was a pitiful figure with a hangdog expression. His faded denim shirt, one size too large, hung off his shoulders, exaggerating his stooped posture. His hair, the color of corn flakes, was cut too close to his head by a very bad barber.

Here was a young man, old before his time—knocked down, struggling to get back on his feet. I scrutinized him. Was he the man I had seen in the window? No. Too short. And not striking or intriguing in the least.

He was more like a Lost Boy from Peter Pan.

"Thanks, Roger," Agnes said. "I'll take care of it." She turned to me. "I'll show you the third floor, and then I'll have to get to the school."

"Need some help?" I asked.

She stepped into the hall. "Sure. It's going to be all hands on deck for a while."

"When is it not?" I asked.

Roger went downstairs. I followed Agnes to the third floor.

When she reached the top step, she paused to whisper. "Wait here. Jericho doesn't like to be disturbed when he's working. Actually, he never likes to be disturbed."

I stayed put while she tiptoed down the narrow hall. There in front of the beautiful arched window I had peered at the night before was a tall, lean man, early 40s, I guessed, positioned at a large canvas on an easel. Dressed in threadbare khakis and a dingy paint-dappled shirt, paintbrush in one hand and palette in the other, he was the very image of a "starving artist," suffering over his masterpiece. When Agnes said his name, he stopped, brush poised on canvas, and bowed his head. His shoulders heaved as he sighed with profound displeasure.

This was the man who had watched from the window the night before, sneering with disdain at the commotion annoying him.

"Jericho," Agnes said with a forced lilt in her voice, "we have a new guest. I'd like to show her the view."

He huffed and turned around, his back so close to his painting he almost brushed against it. Chin tucked to his chest, he gestured toward the window with the brush, tipped with cobalt blue. Following Agnes' example, I crept down the hall. What was it about Jericho Fenton that made people feel they must tiptoe? Sidestepping the tarp beneath his feet, I approached the window and stood shoulder-to-shoulder with Agnes, gazing out at Dennisonville, my temporary home. To my right, a spiral staircase led up through the cupola. I longed to climb the stairs but knew better than to ask.

## Chapter 14 ~ *Meeting the Neighbors*

So this was where Ivy Leigh had been living—this was her view. No wonder she had no desire to return to the narrow, confined world of her mother's house.

"This used to be my room," Agnes said, turning from the window. She pointed to the arched entry leading into the hall. "The door was there." She laid her hand on the banister. "This staircase wasn't here back then. Our friend Ham built that. With my father-in-law."

Jericho cleared his throat, shifting his weight to one foot. Agnes, lost in her memories, did not notice. While she explained where the furniture had been, I looked Jericho full in the face. His penetrating eyes—sky blue—shot straight through me.

He made no effort to disguise his disdain. His smirk and arched eyebrows read: Seriously?

But I, hardened in the furnace of affliction, narrowed my eyes and stared back. *Say one word to this sweet girl, mister, and you and I are going to go at it right here, right now.*

He must have read my warning. He dropped his eyes. His grip on the palette eased. He returned his brush to the glob of cobalt blue and dabbed, impatient to send us on our way, but not daring to hurry us along.

For a moment I had a chance to glimpse the outside edges of the painting: on the right, a stretch of blue sky, white clouds, edges of the sea, sandy beach; on the left, a slate gray rock cliff rising from the shore.

Intent on my standoff with Mr. Fenton—I did not realize Agnes was repeating my name.

"Barbara?" she asked. "Barbara?"

Giving my head a quick shake, I blinked stupidly. "I'm sorry. What?"

"Would you like to come up tonight? There's a platform"—she pointed up the stairs—"where you can stand and look out the four windows. Beautiful."

"Sure," I said.

She started toward the hall. "We'll let you get back to work, Jericho."

"Thank you," he said, meaning, *It's about time.*

I almost said, 'Nice meeting you,' but decided to glower at him instead. In my years as a principal's secretary, I had perfected the "warning look," sending many a fractious youngster back to class with an icy expression which said, *Straighten up.*

Jericho met my gaze. My face sizzled like dry leaves ignited by a sunbeam streaming through a magnifying glass. Feeling my cheeks flush, I hurried past him, hoping he presumed I was angry rather than rattled.

Agnes, a few steps ahead of me, paused at the door on her right, which squeaked as she forced it open. "This is the study. If you want ever want to come up here and read or—"

Within earshot, Jericho stormed from his easel and loomed, a menacing presence, under the archway. "Don't come back in the *morning*. At this time of day the angle of sunlight is perfect, and I can't afford to lose another minute—"

Agnes gasped, wilted by his hot rush of temper. I could almost feel her deflating.

I whirled to face him. "Whose house do you think this is? Is your name on the mortgage?"

Agnes gripped my elbow. "Please don't," she whispered.

It was a frantic plea I could not ignore. I turned and followed Agnes down the stairs.

"Why do you put up with that?" I protested, but stopped squawking when Agnes pressed her finger to her lips.

When we reached the first floor, Agnes leaned in and whispered, "He pays twice what we charge for his room. I can't afford to offend him…not now, when we've lost this week's guests."

Her green eyes were swimming in tears.

"I'm sorry," I said. "I won't say another word. Promise."

"Let me call Nestor," she said, swiping at her tears, "and find out what he needs. Then we'll head that way."

She stepped behind the front desk to make the call. I headed toward the parlor and almost ran into Miriam emerging from the kitchen.

"Excuse me," I said. "I didn't mean to run you over."

"Happens all the time around here," she said, not amused. "How my sister lives here I'll never know. We weren't brought up like this."

Remembering my vow not to offend bill-paying customers, I overlooked Miriam's condescending attitude, while still reflecting that her long, thin nose and the white streak in her dyed-black hair made her look entirely too much like Cinderella's stepmother. I held back a smile.

"I'm Barbara Allgrove. I just got here this morning. You're Miriam, aren't you?"

"Yes."

## Chapter 14 ~ Meeting the Neighbors

I waited politely for her to elaborate. When she offered nothing further, I asked, "How long have you been here?"

"A week. Seems longer. I came to visit my sister, Pinetta, but then she took off for some conference or other and left me"—she swept her manicured hand in a grand gesture—"…here."

The way she said, 'here,' was bone-chilling. Uneasy, I tugged on the collar of my blouse and smoothed the hem of my sweater. One word from this well-ordered society matron and I felt the need to apologize for scuffmarks on my shoes.

"Hmm." I nodded, done with the conversation. "Well…I'm going to take another look at that beautiful piano." I did not invite her to follow.

Before I could enter the parlor, Agnes was off the phone and headed our direction. "Hello, Miriam. Did you meet Barbara?"

"Yes. I'm going to Raleigh today to see a lawyer, husband of a friend of mine."

"Okay," Agnes said with the same forced cheerfulness she'd used on Jericho.

Miriam strutted grandly up the stairs. We watched her go.

"Just in case you're wondering," I whispered, "I was nice to her. Didn't say a word."

Agnes chuckled. "Sometimes I wonder if I locked her and Jericho in a room together, which one would come out first."

"Find out what Nestor wanted?"

She started toward the kitchen. "Uh-huh. Come with me."

We went back into the kitchen and turned right, entering a small cozy room, large enough only for a desk and daybed. Agnes opened a double-door closet, lined with shelves, took out sets of sheets and towels, and handed them to me.

"God bless Pinetta," she said. "Her obsessive side used to drive me to distraction, but I'm glad for it now. Look at this."

Each shelf was labeled by item (sheets/towels) and sizes (twin, full, queen), or uses (dish, bath, hand, fingertip, guest, and daily).

"Pinetta and Miriam are sisters?"

"Uh-huh," Agnes said, counting her fingers as she checked items off her mental list.

"If we could get a look at their mother," I said, peeping over the pile in my arms, "it would probably explain everything about the daughters."

"There are five of them. One of the wealthiest families in Sumter. Pinetta doesn't talk about them much."

"Where is she, by the way? When will I meet her?"

Again Agnes stepped toward the door to peek out and make sure we were not overheard.

"To tell you the truth," she said, "going to that conference in Colorado was a last-minute decision after Miriam moved in. Pinetta and her husband are going to the Grand Canyon after that. She and her sister are not exactly…close."

Here was my chance. "Did Ivy Leigh ever talk about her sister?"

Agnes took a final stack of towels from the shelf. "Not much." She closed the closet. "Ivy Leigh never brought up her childhood. When I tried to quiz her, she'd change the subject."

I followed her to the kitchen table where we placed the supplies. She took plastic garbage bags from a bottom drawer, and we packed the linens.

"How about Ivy Leigh's parents? Did she talk about them?" I asked.

"A little about her dad." She tied up one of the bags and set it by the back door. "To tell you the truth, she talked about your mother more than anyone else."

"My mother?"

She snapped open another bag and kept packing. "Your mother was Gladdie, right?"

"Yes. Short for Gladiola."

Agnes smiled. "That's her. Ivy Leigh said Gladdie taught her everything she knew about how to have a good marriage and run a house."

"My mother?" I repeated.

"Uh-huh."

I could almost feel the floor shifting under my feet. All those years I had been admiring Franny for her spotless sink and dust-free porcelain figurines, Ivy Leigh had been watching my mother love her family and open her heart to strangers.

"Are you okay?" Agnes asked. "You went pale all of a sudden."

I pulled out a chair and sat down. "Yeah. I just…need a drink of water."

She filled a glass and set it in front of me. "Are you sure you feel like going with me? You could stay here, enjoy the morning, and—"

"No," I said, too forcefully. "I want to go." Truth was: I didn't want to be alone.

She told me to "rest a minute" while she loaded the truck.

## Chapter 14 ~ Meeting the Neighbors

"We don't need a truck," I said, trying to get hold of myself. "We don't have that much."

She picked up a bag in each hand. "Nestor took the car. It has the car seat in the back. I always drive the truck, unless Denver's with me. Since you're going, you can help with Ida's dog and cat. We'll take them to the vet on the way. Ida boards them there when she needs to."

I followed her outside. When I saw the white Ford pickup, late 1940s model, fully restored, I understood why she "always drove the truck." Beautiful. Best of all was the logo on both doors—a stately tree with Magnolia Arms printed beneath in glistening black letters.

"Need a hand up getting in?" Agnes asked, a tacit comment on my short legs.

I walked around to the passenger door. "Nope. My husband drove a truck, too."

The ride to the music school was the smoothest I had ever enjoyed. Not even Viola Banks' Cadillac could compare. As we drove, Agnes pointed out sights—houses, businesses, the city park—and told story after story about the people of Dennisonville.

"You know," she said, "you're not like one of our usual visitors. I feel like I know you."

"I feel the same way," I said. "It's been a long time since I've been this comfortable."

"You sure about that? Are you comfortable?"

"Sure. Why do you ask?"

"The photo on the dresser upset you, and then when I mentioned your mother…what Ivy Leigh said about her…that bothered you, too. Did your mom pass away recently?"

"No. It's not that."

"Then…what is it? If you don't mind if I ask."

There was no longer any need for mystery. Agnes knew who I was and why I was here. It was time I told her my story.

"I don't where to start," I said. "It's so complicated."

"Start with Ivy Leigh. She's the reason you came."

So I told her my family lived in a big old house my parents "got for a song." To make ends meet, we took in boarders. There was never enough order or privacy to suit me, but I did not know life could be different, until the Moores moved in. I was playing outside when the moving truck arrived. I watched the men unloading—brocade sofa, tasseled pillows, lamps, dresser with a mirror, ornate wooden headboard, winged cherubs carved on each post. Best of all, in the yard were two girls—one about my age, the other a little younger.

"Sounds trite," I said, "but after that day, my life was never the same."

Agnes turned onto Second Avenue. "Doesn't sound trite to me. My life was never the same after I met Ivy Leigh." She parked by the curb. "We'll pick it up there…over lunch, okay?"

We entered the music school—deserving the title mansion. Cinderella, setting her glass-slippered foot on the ballroom floor, could not have been more awestruck than I as I gazed up at the glittering chandelier overhead. To my right was a formal dining room furnished with a long table. A crystal bowl of fresh mixed flowers was centered on a dark green table runner trimmed in gold brocade. Ornate gold-framed landscapes, portraits, and timeworn family photos lined the walls. To my left, a wide archway opened on a large room with fleur-de-lis wallpaper and rows of white chairs facing a grand piano.

Agnes carted the bags to the foot of the grand staircase and called up. "We're here."

Nestor appeared at the top of the stairs. He walked down and lifted the bags. "I think we just might pull this off." He kissed Agnes on the cheek. "Hello, Mrs. Allgrove. I see you got drafted."

"Volunteered," I said.

Agnes grabbed Nestor's arm. "You're not going to believe who this is." She pointed to me. "This is Babs. Ivy Leigh's friend. The one she told us all those stories about."

Nestor grinned. "I should've known. We probably would've figured it out sooner, if we hadn't been so distracted with the reunion…and the fire."

"Have you talked to Fiona?" Agnes asked Nestor.

He started upstairs. "Uh-huh. She said Denver's asleep, and there's no rush about picking them up. She'll be ready to go when we get there."

"Who's Fiona?" I asked as we followed Nestor upstairs.

"She used to work here," Agnes said. "She was Vesper's maid. Now she's married to Ham, who used to work for us. They're going to stay here this week and take care of the guests."

When we reached the second floor, I heard singing coming down the hall—two surprisingly accomplished voices singing a duet I'd heard on Franny's record player many times.

## Chapter 14 ~ Meeting the Neighbors

"Serafina and Mary Grace came to help," Nestor said over his shoulder. "Decided to get in a little Mozart while they're here."

"That's Hoffmann," I said.

Agnes laughed. "I didn't take you for an opera buff."

"I'm not. But Franny was. Taught me more than I cared to know."

The singing stopped, and two young women joined us in the hall. They were obviously good friends but couldn't have been more different. One was tall, slender, dark-haired; the other short, plump, with mousy brown curls. Smiling, they walked toward us.

"Hello, Agnes," the plump one said. "Gretchen called and said you needed help, so I called Serafina. The whole soprano section will come if you want. Just say the word."

Nestor interrupted. "That's not necessary. If we make the beds and give the bathrooms a once-over, I think we'll be good to go."

Nestor introduced me to Serafina Rummage, pronounced Roo-MAZH. The other was a neighbor from Belmont Drive, Ida's longtime tenant, Mary Grace Dodson. The second Nestor said her name, Mary Grace thrust out her left hand, displaying a modest diamond ring.

"Soon to be 'Monroe.' I'm engaged."

I congratulated her, and we went through the 'you're-the-lady-from-Florida' conversation before we all got to work.

For the rest of the morning, I half-cleaned and half-snooped—dusting tables here, putting out towels there, and then wandering around the house, ogling the cornice boards, ceiling medallions, marble fireplaces. I could not fathom how anyone would leave all this behind.

Entering the central room on the second floor, I gave the hurriedly made bed a perfunctory straightening, and then, as a final flourish, grabbed an embroidered throw pillow from the Queen Anne chair by the window and placed it on the bed.

"Couldn't resist?" Agnes said from the door.

"This was Vesper's room, wasn't it?" I asked.

"Yes. The drapes were usually closed back then—a very pretty prison. Come to the kitchen. Lunch is ready."

"Already? I could stay here all day. Hope I didn't hold everyone up."

"Not at all. Mary Grace had a lunch date, and Serafina had to get back to her job. It's just Nestor and me. It'll be quieter that way," she said. "Believe me."

We went down a different staircase into the kitchen, another place of delights, with a high white ceiling, gleaming porcelain sink, tall windows opening onto a lush backyard with trellises and white gazebo. The table was spread end to end with food.

"Where'd this come from?" I asked.

"Best restaurant in town," Nestor said.

"Newman's?" I asked.

"No," Agnes said. "Newman's is for the working crowd and coffee drinkers. This is from the restaurant we started at the Magnolia Arms but had to move once the crowds got too big."

"You had a restaurant at the Magnolia Arms?" I asked.

How many fascinating stories could there be about a single house?

Nestor sat at the table and grabbed a baby carrot from the relish tray. "We were having financial problems and had to figure out ways to make money. That was one of them."

"Ivy Leigh did the cooking," Agnes said, sitting next to Nestor. "She was magic in the kitchen. But you know that. It was your mother who taught her to cook."

Once again, I had the uncomfortable feeling I was hearing about a total stranger, instead of the friend I grew up with. I stared, bewildered, repeating the same question I'd asked before.

"My mother?"

"Yes." She pointed to a chair. "Have a seat."

I sat across from her.

"Your mother was Gladdie, right?" Nestor asked, filling his tea glass.

"Yes," I said. "But our kitchen was full of dishes that didn't match, pots with broken handles. Franny was the one with the dream kitchen. She had whisks, zesters, a garlic press, herb scissors, crepe maker…a white marble cutting board."

All of which Franny said I could have.

Agnes laughed. "Yeah. That's what Ivy Leigh said. That's why she asked your mom to teach her to cook. Because her mother wouldn't let her touch anything."

"I'll admit," I said, feeling defensive, "Franny was…particular." I spooned chicken salad onto my plate. "But my mother never measured anything. It was a 'dab' of this and a 'pinch' of that. She never followed a recipe."

## Chapter 14 ~ Meeting the Neighbors

"And everything she cooked was delicious," Agnes said, as if she knew from experience.

"I guess you could say that. My brothers inhaled everything, but boys do that—"

The phone rang.

Nestor stood. "I'll get it. Probably Fiona wondering when we're coming."

When he left the kitchen, I seized the opportunity to change the subject, which was embarrassing and uncomfortable.

"Is Fiona your regular babysitter?" I asked, stabbing a cherry tomato.

"Yeah, but more than that. She's a good friend."

Nestor returned, his face grim. "That was Roger. He's upset. I need to go home."

"What's wrong?" Agnes asked.

Standing at the table, Nestor made a second sandwich as he explained. "A man came to the door looking for someone named Greer."

"Greer?" Agnes asked.

"Roger told him there was no one there by that name."

"He didn't let him in, did he?" Agnes asked.

Nestor shook his head. "No. Roger was convinced he was an undercover cop." He shrugged. "But you know how paranoid he is."

"Whoever the man is," I said, "I bet he's looking for—"

"Jericho," Agnes said the same time I did. "I knew that wasn't his real name."

Nestor wrapped his sandwich in a napkin. "We don't know who he was looking for. Let's don't jump to conclusions. He might've had the wrong address."

Agnes scooted away from the table. "We should all go. What if he comes back?"

"That's what Roger's worried about," Nestor said. "He said he can't be in the same house with someone wanted by the police. It'll mess up his parole. He may have a point."

"Roger was in prison?" I asked, too loud. "What for?"

Agnes stood and began clearing the table. "Not murder or anything. Mostly petty crime like shoplifting, breaking and entering. But he wouldn't stop. Finally, the judge decided jail time was the only option. After he was released, my mother asked us to take him in till he could get on his feet."

Sandwich in one hand, Nestor reached into his pocket and produced the car keys. "I'll go settle Roger down. You two finish lunch. Then you can pick up Denver and Fiona. Okay?"

"I'm too nervous to eat now," Agnes said. "We'll take lunch home and eat there."

She crossed to the counter for her purse. They exchanged keys, and Nestor left.

"Wow," I said. "The people in your house are way more interesting than the people in my house. I didn't think that was possible."

She began snapping plastic lids on dishes. "Let's see. I've got an ex-con, wife of an embezzler, shady character with an alias. What do you have?"

"Best friend's first husband I knew nothing about till—"

The doorbell rang.

Agnes frowned. "I hope people aren't showing up already. I wanted to sneak out before anyone came." She handed me the container. "Be right back. Maybe it's the mailman."

She stepped into the hall; I took over packing. She was back in under a minute, panic on her face. "It's the Bisbees."

"Who?"

"The Bisbees. They're the ones who are supposed to stay with Ida. They complain about everything. They are not going to be happy about changing their plans."

I lowered my voice. "Did you let them in?"

"No. When I saw them through the side window, I came back. I can't deal with Mr. Bisbee…not right now." She whispered, "But they parked behind me. We can't get out."

The doorbell rang again…twice.

"You have to let them in," I said. "You can't just leave them standing there."

"I know. I just hoped I could get Fiona over here before anyone arrived."

Ruby-style, I took charge. "Get your purse and come with me."

She did as I said and walked behind me to the front door. I swung it open as Mr. Bisbee, a stocky, sour-faced man, was reaching out to jab the doorbell…again.

"Hello," I said in my best pretend-cheerful voice. "You must be the Bisbees."

## Chapter 14 ~ Meeting the Neighbors

He narrowed his steely eyes. Mrs. Bisbee, thinning brown hair, gray at the roots, crooked bangs, gripped her purse in both hands and blinked, totally confused.

"Who are you?" Mr. Bisbee demanded, bushy eyebrows drawn together.

"Barbara Allgrove. The Carlyles have asked me to help out today." I was fairly singing.

Mr. Bisbee cleared his throat. "Same price we would've paid Ida, right? That's what we were told." An ogre under a bridge would have been friendlier.

I glanced over my shoulder at Agnes, who mouthed, 'Yes.'

"Yes, that's correct. And let me say we're sorry for any inconvenience this has caused you. But I'm sure you understand the extenuating circumstances."

"Inconvenience?" Mrs. Bisbee said, breathless. "Never in a million years did I ever dream I'd get to step inside this house, much less stay here."

"Don't get emotional, Mildred," Mr. Bisbee growled. "It's just a house. Four walls like anyplace else."

Waving my hand behind my back, I motioned to Agnes, who joined us. Subtly excluding Mr. Bisbee, I pivoted slightly toward his long-suffering wife.

"You know Agnes Carlyle? Ida's neighbor. They've taken in Ida and her brother."

Mrs. Bisbee extended her hand. "How is Ida? I'm sorry for her trouble."

"Thankful no one was hurt," Agnes said. "She's with her brother at the hospital."

"Agnes was just on her way to pick up her son," I said. "She's been here since early this morning. If you'll let her out, we'll bring in your luggage and I'll show you to your room."

"George," Mrs. Bisbee said, "could you move the car, please?"

He huffed and stuck his beefy hand in his pocket to fish out the keys. He stormed to the driveway.

"Come in, Mrs.—may I call you Mildred?" I asked.

"Of course."

"Come in, Mildred. And have a look around. I'll wait for your husband and help him with the luggage. You'll be staying in the Wisteria Room."

She hitched her purse over her arm. "O-o-oh," she said, gliding in.

Agnes slipped outside. "Wisteria Room? Where in the world did you get that?"

173

## The Moores, the Merriers

I shrugged. "Something my mother did. She named all our rooms. Said it gave the house some class."

"You're a genius," she said. "I'll be back as soon as I can."

"No rush. I'll give Mildred the grand tour and try to settle George down."

"I don't know what in the world we would've done without you," Agnes said.

"Go on now. We don't want Grumpy waiting too long for you to back out."

Agnes escaped. Mr. Bisbee parked in the driveway and brought in the luggage. I took the two smallest bags and guided the couple to the second floor, pointing out the features of the house I had learned myself only hours before.

Mildred was enchanted. George observed it was "a lot of money to spend on decoration that doesn't serve any useful purpose."

I led George to the downstairs study and settled him in front of the television so Mildred could unpack and enjoy the view from her room. Agnes was back within the hour. I met the lovely Fiona and gave her the lowdown on the Bisbees. Then Agnes and I drove home with Denver, content in the back seat. When we arrived at the Magnolia Arms, Agnes warned me Roger was probably waiting to see her and suggested we ease in quietly, so we could keep talking. She carried Denver. I brought the bags. The downstairs was empty; the house quiet.

"Maybe Nestor took Roger to Newman's to calm him down," she whispered. "Let's go into the parlor and close the door. I'll feed Denver and then put him down for a nap."

I set the bags on the table. "You take care of him. I'll put everything away and meet you in there."

"Thank you," Agnes said, heading from the kitchen.

She did not get far.

Footsteps on the stairs. Pounding of feet in the hall. And Miriam appeared, her voice like chalk scraping a blackboard.

"Mrs. Carlyle," Miriam said, lips white with suppressed rage. "Let me be the first to inform you. While you were out, the FBI came here looking for Roger."

# Chapter 15

# Prisoners
### Dennisonville, North Carolina
### October 1979

I stared wide-eyed, warning myself not to laugh. In the course of one brief hour, the "man at the door" had gone from being an undercover cop looking for Jericho to an FBI agent looking for Roger. What was next? The CIA looking for *me*?

"Let's not jump to conclusions," Agnes said, borrowing Nestor's advice. "That's why we came home early…to make sure everyone was all right. I'm sure—"

Miriam ignored her. "This is *not* the way I'm used to living. I"—she tapped on her top mother-of-pearl button—"lived in one of the *finest* neighborhoods in Sumter, not with jailbirds and houses burning down"—she jabbed the air in the direction of Ida's house—"and non-stop visitors coming and going all hours of the day and night." She glared at *me*.

Agnes caught my eye and eased Denver toward me. I took him and stepped into the parlor, closing the French doors behind us. I walked toward the bay window to admire the black walnut tree towering over the house. Even with the door closed, I could hear muffled voices: Agnes, calm; and Miriam, just this side of hysteria.

I turned sideways so Denver could see out. "Someday you'll climb that tree," I whispered to him. "You're one lucky little fellow to be growing up here. You're never going to want for excitement or people to love you."

Out in the hall Miriam was near shrieking. I could make out scattered phrases: 'the minute I got here' and 'no privacy.' Should I intervene? Agnes was capable, but young, and a novice at locking horns with pampered, self-

175

absorbed women twice her age. Agnes would be respectful, not only because she had been brought up that way (easy to tell), but also because she needed the rent Miriam was paying. She was having to placate this raging woman when what Miriam needed was a swift kick in those narrow hips of hers.

When the commotion stopped, I turned around. The parlor door opened. Agnes, head down, approached, wiping her eyes. I met her halfway. She took Denver and drew him close to her face. Swaying gently, she sniffled, her words catching in her throat.

"It's not fair," she said, voice breaking. "It's not fair."

"What's not fair?"

"Denver shouldn't have to live his whole life wondering…*every single day*…if there are going to be enough people in the house to pay the bills."

Putting my arm around her, I guided her to the sofa and sat next to her. "It's not always going to be this way. Things will turn around. You'll see."

She shook her head. "Miriam's leaving and wants the month's rent back. We're already in the hole because of losing the reunion people, and I can't ask Ida to pay. I *can't*."

"Well, I'm not going anywhere," I said. "And I'm paying."

"Can you stay till next year?" she asked with a little laugh.

"If I need to," I said.

She sank back. "It's times like this I wish Ivy Leigh were here. She'd know *exactly* what to do about Miriam…and Roger *and* Jericho."

"So, if she were here right now, what would she tell you to do?"

She thought a minute. "She'd tell me to put Denver down for a nap and then take one myself, and when I woke up, I'd feel better and could think my way out of this."

I stood. "Then that's what you should do."

"But we were going to talk, while it was quiet."

"There's plenty of time for that. I might take a nap myself."

But I had no intention of going to my room after I sent Agnes to hers.

I put away the food and then up the stairs I marched, lecturing myself with each step.

*Don't mess this up. You're trying to talk this woman into staying. Appeal to her sense of propriety. And don't be a smart mouth.*

I straightened my posture and knocked on Miriam's door. When she opened it, I saw an open suitcase, half-packed, on her bed.

Her tone was below freezing. "Yes?"

"I wondered if we could talk for a minute."

## Chapter 15 ~ Prisoners

No one I'd ever met expressed more with one raised eyebrow than Miriam Goddard. She was frighteningly like my high school Algebra teacher. But that old inflated sense of Southern decorum would not allow her to ignore my polite request. Even if I had come to her door asking for plum chutney, she would have felt obligated to suggest where I might find some.

She restrained a sigh. "All right, if you don't mind talking while I pack. I've already called a cab. And here in *Mayberry*," she sneered, "it doesn't take long for one to show up."

"I don't mind." I edged in, reminding myself I 'knew nothing' about her. "Going home?"

"No. Raleigh," she said, taking a symmetrically folded blue cashmere sweater from the dresser drawer. "Better chance of getting a nice hotel room. What do you want?"

I stood my ground. "To ask you to stay."

She bristled. "And why should I do that?"

"To help Agnes."

"What do you care? You only met her this morning." She lifted a photo from the nightstand and laid it face down in the suitcase before I got a good look.

I lifted my chin slightly. "We have a mutual friend."

"You'll forgive me if I don't see the significance." She swished to the closet and brought out half a dozen dresses.

Exasperated, I walked to the window and peered out, hoping to curb my temper. "Look, Miriam, it's easy for women our age to forget what it's like to be young and insecure."

"I've *never* been insecure. Pembroke women don't let circumstances dictate…"

As she droned on, my eyes fell on Ida's burned up house. Images swirled in my mind, like dead leaves blown by a stiff wind: Agnes, consoling Ida while the flames leapt from her windows; Agnes, watching quietly as Bernard was carried from the garden shed; Agnes, cleaning the music school for the tenants she could no longer host; Agnes, weeping over the loss of a month's rent from *this* woman, whose Bill Blass dusty rose silk dress with matching linen jacket lying on the bed—let alone the rest of the pile—would have paid 3 or 4 months' rent.

I don't know how long I stood there before I noticed Miriam had stopped talking. I turned from the window. As I did, I caught sight of a man in a white car across the street—sitting there, staring at the Magnolia Arms. I would have eyed him longer if I hadn't spotted Miriam crouched on the floor, worked up into such a frenzy she was hyperventilating. I hurried over, knelt down, and put my arm around her.

She was trembling. "Can't…breathe."

I helped her up and guided her to the bed. "I'll be right back."

Rushing downstairs, I dashed into the kitchen and flung open the pantry door. Thank goodness I had been the one to put the food away. I knew exactly where to find what I needed. I grabbed a brown paper lunch sack and loped upstairs to Miriam. I held the bag over her mouth and nose. Gradually, her breathing slowed. Drops of sweat beaded on her temples. I took away the bag and returned the dresses to the closet, then lifted her feet onto the bed. She sank back.

"Better?" I asked.

She gave a slight nod.

I found a quilt in the closet and covered her. Then I went to the bathroom for a cold washcloth to place over her eyes. I sat next to her. The autumn afternoon grayed into twilight.

When a car horn sounded from the street, she whispered, "That's the cab."

I jumped up, glad for an excuse to check the street again. The white car was still there.

"I'll take care of it," I said.

By the time I got downstairs, Nestor had answered the door and was telling Asa no one had called a cab.

I tapped Nestor on the shoulder. "It was Miriam, but she changed her mind."

"Just as well," Asa said. "I can get home early. Chicken and dumplings night."

Nestor closed the door. "Please tell me Miriam wasn't leaving."

"She was, but she changed her mind," I said. "Have you talked to Agnes?"

He shook his head. "Just got home. She and Denver are asleep."

I started toward the kitchen. "Come with me, and I'll fill you in."

We entered the kitchen, and I filled the teakettle. While I waited for the water to boil, I told Nestor about the last half-hour, leaving out the part about the white car…in case I was imagining things.

He shook his head. "Miriam has no idea how much she'd love it here, if she'd give herself half a chance. But she's too hurt to think straight."

## Chapter 15 ~ Prisoners

I found peppermint tea in the cabinet by the stove. "What happened to her...exactly?"

"Her husband was embezzling from his company. Had been for years. Finally got to the point he couldn't 'rob Peter to pay Paul,' as Ivy Leigh used to say. And they got him."

"Nothing like that ever happened before to a 'Pembroke woman,' I guess."

He chuckled. "You got the Pembroke woman speech, did you?"

"Yeah. I won't forget that anytime soon. Is there a tray I can use?"

He pointed to a cabinet next to the sink. Setting the tray on the table, I reached for the box of almond cookies.

"I don't suppose Miriam eats anything as mundane as cookies, does she?"

Nestor laughed. "You can try."

"I'd better get back up there," I said, picking up the tray.

I had one foot in the hall when Nestor said, "Barbara." I paused. "Is Jericho upstairs?"

"Yes. Why?"

He sighed. "Because I need to tell him he's moving upstairs. He's not going to like it, and it would be better if we could get that over with before Agnes wakes up."

Back upstairs, I set the tray on the hall table to open Miriam's door. It was so quiet, I wondered if Jericho *was* upstairs. I tiptoed to the foot of the third floor stairs...listened, heard nothing. I crept up, reached the top step, and peeked down the hall. There was Jericho—stock still, silhouetted against the arched window. Feet planted, left hand on his hip, he gripped the paintbrush in his right hand, tip pressed to his lips, face as chiseled as the rest of him. *What* was he painting? I had to find out. He had to sleep *sometime.*

I returned to Miriam's room and found her dozing. With her eyes closed, lamplight glowing on her face, she looked like a different person. I set down the tray to move the suitcase off the bed. She stirred, opened her eyes.

"I brought tea," I said.

She eased up. "Thank you."

"Have a cookie." I set the tray on her lap. "They'll tide you over till supper."

She reached for a cookie, sneaking it to her lips like some forbidden sin, gave it a quick sniff, and nibbled. A faint look of pleasure flickered on her face.

"I can't come down tonight," she said, "...not after what I said to Agnes."

This was a subject I wanted to pursue but didn't. Huddled there in wrinkled clothes, hair out of place, makeup smudged, she was pitiful—in some ways, worse off than Justine when I first met her. I took a chair from the writing desk and sat next to the bed.

"I had a friend like you," I said. "She liked things a certain way and kept people at a distance. I didn't find out till after she died, it was because she had a terrible secret."

Miriam met my eyes. "You know about me?"

I nodded.

"Agnes *promised* she wouldn't tell."

"She didn't."

Color seeped into her pale cheeks. "It was that Ludlow woman, wasn't it?"

"It was in the paper," I said, remembering Ernie's excuse.

She looked away. "That's the reason I asked Pinetta if I could come here. I thought maybe in a backwater town like this…the news…"

I almost objected…arguing Dennisonville was 'quaint,' but did not want to lose the advantage I had gained. "How did you find out about your husband?"

Nestor passed by the open door on his way upstairs to Jericho.

"The timing couldn't have possibly been worse. I was hosting the garden club, and I'd outdone myself." She sipped her tea, pinkie finger up.

Above us, Jericho's voice thundered. "I've paid you in *advance*. We had an *agreement*."

Miriam glanced toward the door. "What's that about?"

"Ida and Bernard are going to stay here a while. Nestor's asking Jericho to move up here…so they can be downstairs."

"I don't want *him* down the hall."

I got up and closed the door; the shouting went on. "Go ahead. Garden club meeting…"

Staring into the corner, she was back in Sumter, surrounded by the people who mattered.

"We had just opened the serving lines when the phone rang. Elsie…my maid…said there was a call. I slipped into the kitchen. Giles…my husband…said he'd been arrested. I said to stop joking around." She turned toward me, lip curled in disgust. "He started crying. Like a baby."

She asked the vice president to take charge and drove to the police station, arriving the same time as their lawyer. Giles was released on bail.

## Chapter 15 ~ Prisoners

"By the time we got home, the guests were gone, house empty," she said, "food put away. Eerie. I knew right then my life would never be the same."

The shouting stopped. Footsteps in the hall.

"So, what had your husband done?" I asked, mind on Nestor.

"It'd been going on for years. Started as an accident. Wrong charge to a company credit card. He let it slide. Then he started inflating expense reports. When he didn't get caught, it became an addiction...seeing what he could get away with."

"Like gambling?"

She finished her tea and scooted the tray off her lap onto the bed. "He blamed me. Blamed *me*. Said he couldn't keep up with everything I wanted."

"And he'll go to prison?"

"Eleven years. We'll lose everything. If it weren't for the money my father left me when he died, I'd have nothing."

"I'm sorry, Miriam," I said. "I can't imagine how—"

There was a knock at the door. Agnes peeked in. "Supper's ready. Actually leftovers from lunch, but there's plenty."

Miriam shook her head. "None for me...thanks."

"Be down in a minute," I said. Agnes closed the door. I walked to the window to check on the white car. It was gone. "Want me to close the curtains?"

"No. Leave them open. Thank you."

Agnes waited for me in the hall, and we walked down together.

"Is she all right?" Agnes asked. "Nestor said she hyperventilated. What brought that on?"

"Don't know, but I'm pretty sure it's happened before."

I didn't mention the white car. Agnes had enough to worry about.

Over supper, Nestor, Agnes, and I pieced together our stories, weaving events, picking up common threads, creating a finished likeness of Ivy Leigh. They were most intrigued to learn about Franny, who cast only the faintest shadow over Ivy Leigh's accounts of her past. Their most pressing question was why she had left Jacksonville without looking back. As little as I liked to relive my youthful stupidity, I obliged, dragging J. Michael Ford out of a dark corner of my mind into the light where we could examine the rift he had caused between friend and sisters, mother and daughters.

By the time we graduated from high school, Ivy Leigh and I were both desperate to escape home: she, from Franny; me, from being responsible for my siblings and our boarding house. We enrolled in business college and found part-time jobs to pay our tuition. I worked at Woolworth's, and Ivy Leigh took a job as a waitress at Marco's Pizza Parlor on Park Street. That's where she met J. Michael Ford, a would-be artist who had opened a studio in a vacated doctor's office. At 25, he was a man of the world, charming, handsome. And an experienced conman.

"Ivy Leigh never mentioned him?" I asked.

"No," Agnes said. "She told me she left Jacksonville after she graduated from high school and moved to Atlanta. She never mentioned Ford. He's the reason she left home?"

"The reason all three of us left. I was the only one who came back."

Shortly after Ivy Leigh started working at Marco's, J. Michael Ford came in for lunch. Ivy Leigh seated him and returned with a menu to find him sketching on a napkin—a flight of geese, wings spread. She filled his water glass, asked if he were an artist. He said he was more interested in mosaics and hoped to become a restorer. He was trying to earn enough money to move to Atlanta, and then work his way north to Chicago or New York. He started coming to the restaurant every day and then walking Ivy Leigh home after work.

"That's when he met Justine," I said. "Ivy Leigh wanted me to meet him, so I came to the restaurant one Saturday, and Ivy Leigh brought me to his table." I shook my head. "I should've known *right then* what kind of man he was. He flirted with me the minute she walked away."

Ford was a second-rate artist with dreams bigger than his talent. When he realized he could make a living painting portraits, he began targeting well-to-do women with money to spend on paintings of themselves or their families. He would rent a studio and advertise himself as a portrait artist. After the women he charmed got too attached, or wised up, he would disappear, leaving unfinished portraits and broken hearts behind. When he reached Jacksonville, he opened a studio in Riverside. He wandered into Marco's, where he met Ivy Leigh. She brought him to their home full of antiques and art.

"He knew he hit the jackpot," I said. "And pegged Franny as a woman who would *love* the status a 'commissioned portrait' would bring her."

"I'm surprised Ivy Leigh fell for him," Agnes said. "She's so savvy about people."

"She was only 19," I said. "And so unhappy at home. Ford looked like her way out."

"Her father didn't see through him?" Nestor asked.

## Chapter 15 ~ Prisoners

"He did, but Franny was smitten with Ford. She hadn't met anyone like him since her Richmond days. And having an artist in the family…that was the kind of match she wanted for Justine. So she hired Ford to paint her portrait, so he'd have an excuse to come to the house."

"And Justine fell for him, too?" Agnes asked.

"Yes, and so did I," I said, slumping in my chair. "I was obsessed with him from the moment I saw him. I started hanging out at his studio when I knew Ivy Leigh was at work."

We finished eating and brought Denver with us into the parlor. The three of them settled on the sofa. I sat in the wingback chair across from them to continue the story I'd never told anyone, not even my own children.

After Franny hired Ford, he was at their house twice a week. When he was there, he flirted with Justine. At the studio, he sweet-talked me, and he was still seeing Ivy Leigh every day at Marco's. Eventually, he made his move to marry into the family he could squeeze dry for the foreseeable future. He pressured Ivy Leigh about eloping. When he quizzed her once too often about finances, she got suspicious and her interest began to cool. He grew belligerent. She saw an ugly side of him she had never seen and broke it off.

"I was over the moon when I found out. At last, Ford and I were free to meet someplace other than his studio. We could tell everyone we were 'together.' But he told me we had to wait."

He explained Justine had fallen for him. If he told her 'about us,' Franny might cancel the portrait and 'we' needed the money. So I waited. When he finished the portrait, he sent me to St. Augustine to wait for him at the Columbia Restaurant.

"I took a bus, sat in the restaurant, and sipped ice water, picturing us strolling down St. George Street. He would drop down on one knee and propose."

"But he never showed up," Agnes said, Denver snuggled in her arms.

I shook my head. "I waited two hours and dragged myself back to the bus station. When I got home, the whole neighborhood was in an uproar. Ford was gone and Justine with him."

"Let me guess," Nestor said. "He left a note?"

"No. Justine did. Nothing was the same after that. Ivy Leigh blamed herself. Franny did, too. She downplayed her own role in encouraging Ford to pursue Justine. Cab called the police, but there was nothing they could do. Justine was 18, a legal adult. When I couldn't stop crying, my dad coaxed the truth from me."

The two fathers started investigating, and the truth was discovered. All the animosity that had been simmering between Franny and Ivy Leigh kept festering. One day Franny exploded. Told Ivy Leigh she wished it had been her Ford ran off with, that she wouldn't have cared if *that* had happened. Ivy Leigh packed her bags and left. That was the point where our histories intersected. Ivy Leigh moved to Atlanta and met Marshall Ransom when she volunteered in a veterans' hospital. They married and relocated to Dennisonville.

Shortly before 11:00, Agnes' eyes drooped. Her head eased onto Nestor's shoulder. He suggested we 'call it a day.' We said good night, and they went through the kitchen to their room at the back of the house. I tiptoed upstairs like a child on her way to pilfer change from her parents' wallets. The second floor doors were all closed. I paused to listen at Miriam's door and walked past mine, then glanced at the room at the end of the hall. Had Jericho moved up here while we were downstairs talking? No way to know. I kept going.

The third floor was faintly illuminated by light from the street and a half moon shining through the tall window, barely enough to see by. I kept my hand on the wall as I crept toward the space Jericho had claimed as his studio. My fingers bumped into a doorframe—the door to the study, shut tight. I shuddered. Too much like a childhood nightmare—alone in the dark with a mad fiend lurking behind a closed door. *Don't be silly*, I thought. *Nobody's in there.* Eight steps later, I eased under the archway and groped for a light switch.

When I flicked the switch, the study door flew open.

I gasped, stumbling backward toward the window.

Partly because Jericho was charging toward me, and there was no way out.

Partly because his painting was so beautiful it took my breath away.

And partly because the picture...as near as I remembered...was an exact copy of the one in J. Michael Ford's studio...a work by his favorite artist.

Jericho loomed in the archway like a dragon guarding his lair. If he could have breathed fire, I would have been a cinder on the spot.

"What are you *doing* up here?" he snarled.

I pointed at the easel, accusing. "That's *The Cliffs at Etretat* by Courbet."

His mouth fell open. "How do you know that?"

"I had a friend who was an artist." I leaned in to examine the painting, then straightened up and swept my arm in a grand gesture. "I know what this is all about. You're an art forger."

# Chapter 16

## The Walls of Jericho
### Dennisonville, North Carolina
### October 1979

How I managed that level of bravado I did not know, but the balance of power shifted in my favor. Jericho was deflated.

He signaled me to lower my voice. "It's not what you think."

"What else is there to think?" I asked. "You set up shop in a small town, pay twice what your room is worth, take over an upper floor with perfect lighting, *and* you're copying someone else's work. There's only one explanation."

He threw up his hands. "I'm not going to *sell* it." He crossed to the spiral staircase and sank down on the second step. "Believe me, forgery would be simpler."

I waited, hoping he would elaborate. But when he kept quiet, staring down at his sock feet, I stepped toward the painting for a closer look.

"It's stunning," I said. "You're very talented."

"Most people aren't that familiar with Courbet."

I turned around. "The 'friend' I mentioned…Courbet was his favorite. Plus, I live down the street from an art gallery."

"Where are you from?"

"Jacksonville, Florida."

His face eased into a smile. "Then you mean the Cummer."

"You've been?"

"Many times, but when I go, I spend as much time in the garden as I do the gallery." He stood and returned to the canvas, bending down to peer at

185

## The Moores, the Merriers

the lower right-hand corner. "I don't suppose there's room in *your* house for a renter, is there?"

"Not at the moment," I said, amused at the idea of Jericho looking for a quiet place to paint in *my* house—surrounded by Topeka, Caesar, and all. "Why do you ask?"

He straightened up, still studying the work. "In case I need to relocate."

"What you're doing is none of *my* business. I'm not going to say a word. Or are you worried about the guy looking for you this morning?"

His face fell. "What guy?"

"A man came to the door asking for someone named Greer. We thought it might be you."

He ran his hands through his hair "*How* did they find me?"

"So you *are* Greer?"

He picked up a white bedsheet from the floor and covered the painting. "Do you know if the old guy...from the burned-up house...moved into my room yet?"

"No, he's still in the hospital."

He walked to the light switch. "Good. I've got to get some sleep. Go ahead...downstairs. I'll get the light after you leave."

My glimpse at the 'real' Jericho was over—as if a stage curtain had closed for intermission. I got my pajamas and toothbrush from my room, then took a warm bath, dozing off once or twice, and went to bed. Exhausted, I fell asleep, plummeting headlong into a succession of bad dreams, the worst shortly before dawn. I was hosting a garden party at Vesper's house. Franny came to the door with a Doberman and demanded to know why I had let her house burn down. I jolted awake and sat up. The clock on the nightstand read 7:02.

Before I could get to my feet, there was a knock at my door.

"Barbara?" Agnes said. "Telephone. Your daughter."

Naturally, I assumed the worst. I grabbed my bathrobe from the foot of the bed, opened the door, and followed Agnes to the phone at the check-in desk.

"Hello?" I said, breathless.

"Mom?" Anne said. "I wanted to let you know what we're doing today, in case you called and we weren't here."

"Is everything okay?"

"Everything is *wonderful*," she said.

## Chapter 16 ~ The Walls of Jericho

I hadn't heard her sound so bubbly in a long time. She had always been cheerful and optimistic, but in the last few years, childlessness had begun to wear her down.

"Tell me," I said, masking my weariness.

"We're doing great. Topeka is so precious. Honestly, I think she gets bigger every day."

"I knew you could take care of everyone."

"Me *and* Ruby," she said with a hint of the mysterious. She lowered her voice. "She invited Hank for supper last night. He didn't come home till 11:00."

*I never saw that one coming.*

"Whatever you do, don't tell Viola."

She laughed. "I know better than that. We're all going to St. Augustine today. Packing up the stroller and heading to the fort. Lunch at the Columbia Restaurant."

I was almost on the verge of tears, not sure why. "That's a great idea."

Anne noticed the quiver in my voice. "You all right?"

"I'm fine." I choked back the lump in my throat. "I wish you could see this house. You'd love it. And you'd like Agnes."

"Have you seen Ivy Leigh yet?"

"Not yet. Have a good time today. Send me a postcard," I added, as an attempt at humor.

"I will," she said, laughing.

I hung up and turned to go upstairs. Roger appeared in the hall. Finger to his lips, he motioned me into dining room. I followed. He closed the French doors and spoke in a low tone.

"You don't know me, and I guess Agnes told you I'm an ex-con, and I'm probably crazy for asking this, but…you seem nice…and I was wondering…when my parole is up, and I can leave here…could I come to Jacksonville?" He glanced nervously at the door. "I gotta get out of here." He leaned in to whisper. That Mr. Fenton wants me to steal something for him. But I *can't*. I *can't* go back to jail."

Poor Roger exhaled all this in one breath, then hung his head.

He was sunk in such despair, I couldn't dash his last hope. But there was absolutely no way in the world I was going to add *him* to the assembly already in my house.

I squeezed his arm. "I can't make any promises, but we'll talk later, okay?"

187

He nodded. "Don't tell Agnes about Fenton. She's got enough on her mind."

"It'll be between us. I promise. In the meantime…try to stay away from him."

"Nestor asked me to go to the music school to help with the guests. That'll keep me away all day." He headed toward the door. "You'll think about letting me come to Jacksonville?"

"I'll think about it."

By now, my head was throbbing. I went upstairs to get dressed. When I left my room, I tapped on Miriam's door and opened it. No sign of her. Bed made. Suitcase gone. Sick at heart, I hurried to the kitchen.

There was Miriam, washing dishes, chatting with Agnes, who had Denver in her arms.

At the table…Jericho was hunched over a bowl of Wheaties.

Where were the finicky society matron and tortured artist I had talked to only yesterday? These two were chatty, pleasant, and did mundane things like eat cereal.

Agnes greeted me. "Everything okay at home?"

Hopelessly muddled, I could not make out what she was asking. "Home?"

"Your phone call," she said. "Everything all right?"

"Oh…yeah. They're going on a little day trip, and my daughter didn't want me to worry if I called and they didn't answer."

"Coffee?" Agnes asked.

I nodded and sat across from Jericho, who caught my eye and winked. Agnes handed Denver to me while she filled my cup. When she came back to the table, she asked if I could do her a favor.

Returning Denver to her, I reached for the cream. "Sure. What do you need?"

"Bernard is going to be released from the hospital this morning. I need to pick him up and bring him and Ida home. Could you watch Denver for a couple of hours?"

"Of course."

Miriam drained the water from the sink. Dishtowel in hand, she walked to the table. "Anything else I can do before I go?"

"No, thank you," Agnes said. "Roger should be ready in a minute."

Miriam turned to me. "How are you, Barbara?"

I *wanted* to say, 'Who are you and what have you done with Miriam?' But instead I asked if Roger was driving her to the train station.

## Chapter 16 ~ The Walls of Jericho

"No. Music school," she said. "I offered to welcome the people coming for the reunion. It's the *one* thing I do well…etiquette." She said this as if admitting a character flaw.

Meanwhile, Jericho, who 'never ate with the rest of them,' was still intent on his cereal bowl, sipping one spoonful of milk at a time.

I was failing miserably at camouflaging my confusion…my bloodshot eyes darting from Agnes to Miriam to Jericho, and back.

Agnes noticed and bailed me out.

"Miriam came down early while Nestor and I were having breakfast. She volunteered to help at Kimball Pines…I mean, the music school…so I could go to the hospital."

"Where's Nestor?" I asked.

"Teaching. Community college in Bellport. We teach on different days so one of us can be home with Denver."

Jericho stood and took his bowl to the sink. He stopped on his way to the door. "Thank you for breakfast. I'm going back to work."

"Sure," Agnes said. "And…thank you for letting Bernard have your room."

He gave a quick nod and was gone.

"Be right back," Miriam said. "I'm going to get my coat."

Agnes waited till we heard Miriam's footsteps on the stairs and then said, "Breakfast?"

"*Breakfast?*" I crossed my arms on the table. "Is that all you have to say? *What's* going on? Who *are* those people?"

She tiptoed to the hall door and peeped out. Then sat next to me. "I was going to ask you the same question. What in the *world* did you say to them last night?"

Wide-eyed, I lifted my shoulders. "You got me."

"Whatever it was, *thank you.* I feel like I'm in a different house." She stood up. "Help yourself to breakfast. I'm going to put Denver in his crib. I'll tell you when I'm leaving."

"Okay," I said, eyeing the muffins on the table.

"Maybe we can get back to normal today," she chirped.

"You have a 'normal'?" I asked.

She laughed. "Good point."

Agnes disappeared into her room. Miriam returned with her coat over her arm.

"Is Roger out at the car?" she asked.

"No. He hasn't come up yet."

She walked to the sink and gazed out the window. "Thank you for helping me last night." She pinched a dead leaf off an African violet on the windowsill. "You knew exactly what to do."

The basement door opened. Roger entered. "Ready, ma'am?" he asked Miriam.

She put on her coat and waved at me as she followed him out the door. Agnes came back and took the truck keys from the pegboard by the pantry. She went over the baby's schedule, showed me his bottles in the refrigerator, and left.

Alone downstairs, I lingered over breakfast in Ivy Leigh's kitchen—a comfortable mix of worn-out and new, order and hodge-podge—and thought about the friend I had not seen since she was 19. I had learned from being in her house and talking to the Carlyles what kind of woman Ivy Leigh was—exactly the same as when I knew her. She was always the one who brought me and Justine back to earth when we were hysterical about some teenage heartache. She was our anchor. Her father's daughter. Level-headed. Responsible. Respectful—even to the mother she could never please.

Staring idly at the door, I pictured her coming in, finding me here. After we laughed and hugged, we would talk about 'how long it had been,' and she would ask why in the world I was here, and I would say…

The phone rang. On the wall by the back door…exactly like my mother's kitchen.

"Hello?" I answered.

There was a pause. Then a kind, deep voice: "Is this the Magnolia Arms?"

"Sorry. I should've said. I'm keeping the baby while Agnes is out. May I help you?"

"This is Torbert Hampton. My wife Ivy Leigh used to be the manager there."

*Torbert. Were they back from Paris?*

"Agnes mentioned you last night," I said, trying to keep my voice even.

"Could you give Agnes a message? Be careful. Ivy Leigh doesn't want to upset her."

"Something wrong?"

"Everything's fine now," he said. "On the flight home, Ivy Leigh wasn't feeling well. As soon as we landed, I insisted on her going to the hospital. Turns out it was her appendix."

## Chapter 16 ~ The Walls of Jericho

My heart sank. "Is she okay?"

"She's fine now. Just came out of surgery. But it's going to be a few days before we're on the road. Tell Agnes everything is fine. She's such a worrywart."

"I will. Tell Ivy Leigh...your wife...I'm...looking forward to meeting her."

Somehow I managed to have enough presence of mind to remember I was a "stranger" and would only be politely interested in Ivy Leigh's health. Now was not the time to bring up why I was here waiting for her.

"Thank you," he said. "I'll call when I have a better idea of when we'll be there."

"Do you want to leave a number where you can be reached?" I asked.

"When we get to a motel." He paused. "Is everything okay there?"

"Not right at the moment."

"May I ask why? I don't want Ivy Leigh to be blindsided when we get there."

I told him about the fire and how we rushed to transform the music school to an inn.

"Hmm," he said. "Sounds like you came at exactly the right time. What's your name?"

"Barbara."

He hesitated, waiting for a last name, but I didn't offer one.

"Nice talking to you, Barbara. Take care of Agnes for us."

I hung up and surveyed the kitchen where Ivy Leigh had gone about the business of living. I pictured her, listening to broken people explain in hushed tones why they had come here. Unlike me, she had not fretted about fine china or art prints. Though unjustly accused of "corrupting" Justine, she had not become bitter. She had turned her sorrow inside out, offered her heart, stretched out her hands. Her life was rich with intangible wealth. She wouldn't think twice about helping Justine. I was certain. Only one hurdle remained: revealing Franny was not her mother and introducing Clarissa.

Still musing, I was pouring another cup of coffee when Bridey Ludlow pounded on the back door and pushed through with yet another unsolicited food offering. This time it was a long Pyrex baking dish cradled in a threadbare dishtowel.

"Morning," she said, whisking toward the stove to deposit the dish. "I heard Ber-NARD was coming home today, so I thought y'all could use a little dessert. I make a *mean* cobbler, and I still had some frozen peaches left from summer before last."

Bridey tugged at the towel to unstick it from the dish where the cobbler had boiled over and drizzled juice down the sides. The crust, dark brown, was burnt at the edges.

"Thank you," I said, meaning anything but.

She got the towel unstuck, rolled it up, and tucked it under her arm. She spied the pot she had brought yesterday on the stove. Tilting it, she peeked inside and whistled. "You made short work of that." She proceeded to the refrigerator and swung open the door. "You mean to tell me y'all polished off *all* that chicken and rice in just one day?"

"I don't know," I said. "Supper kind of got waylaid last night." I kept quiet about Miriam's panic attack and the stranger looking for Jericho. I also left out the part about eating the leftovers from Muriel's restaurant. What happened to the chicken and rice I could only guess.

"Well," she said, slamming the refrigerator, "just let me know if you need anything else." She took the towel from under her arm and wiped her face. "When will they be home?"

"No way to tell. You know how long hospital paperwork can take."

She nabbed the last muffin. "Shame about the reunion and them losing all that money. I really shouldn't say…but they're barely keeping up with their bills. And don't even *get* me started on property taxes on a house like this. Much less the repairs."

I started to object but did not want to encourage her to keep talking, so began clearing the dishes instead. When I removed the muffin plate, Bridey licked her index finger and dabbed at the crumbs on the table, snagging every last one.

Retreating to the sink, I stared out the kitchen window and racked my brain for harmless topics of conversation. I spied the newspaper on the driveway.

"Looks like no one got the paper in. Would you mind—?"

But she wasn't listening.

"Of course, if Agnes could ever finish that *book* of hers…" Bridey chuckled. "But if you ask me, that's a pipe dream. *Who* in the wide world wants to read a long drawn out story about some old house and everyone who's lived there, world without end?" She laughed again.

Hands submerged in suds, I glanced over my shoulder. "Agnes is writing a book?"

Bridey stepped to the hall and peered both ways. "Yeah. Starting way back with the house that used to be here…torn down a long time ago…going

## Chapter 16 ~ The Walls of Jericho

straight through to..." She rejoined me at the sink and leaned close to whisper. "Where's that snooty woman?"

"Who?" I asked, though I knew she meant Miriam.

"Miss High and Mighty from Suh-uh-mm-tuh." She wagged her plump, dimpled hand in an affected Southern belle gesture.

"Helping at the music school," I said.

Bridey would have been less surprised if I had slapped her with the wet dishcloth.

"How'd she get there?" she demanded. "With Agnes?"

"Roger."

"She got in the same car with that *jailbird*? I can't *believe* it." She settled her wide backside against the counter. "Somebody like her? But then...her husband is a jailbird, too." She slapped her thigh and guffawed, bent over double.

By then I'd had enough. I drained the water from the sink and dried my hands. "Thank you for the cobbler," I said. "I'll tell Agnes you came by."

"Oh..." she said, miffed at my dismissal. "Maybe I'll drop by the music school on my way home and see if *they* need any help."

"I'll walk you out," I said, opening the back door. "I want to get the paper."

She snatched her pot from the stove, dropped in the dishtowel and strode past, mumbling words I couldn't quite make out. I followed her down the driveway and waited for her to back out, giving her a final wave as she drove away.

And then I spotted him. The man in the white car was back.

Day before yesterday, I might have thought twice about accosting a stranger, but only last night, Agnes had recounted how Ivy Leigh confronted Olympia Pillburn in this very driveway and demanded to know why she wanted to destroy the Magnolia Arms. Further: my wounds, reopened from reliving the sins of J. Michael Ford, were still smarting. Beyond that: I now knew this house was sheltering three shattered souls—Miriam, Roger, and Jericho—and soon poor Bernard and Ida would be joining them. Add: an innocent child was asleep inside and within seconds I had worked myself up into a tizzy.

Thinking too much and not at all, I drew myself up to my full 5'2" and stormed across the street to the car. I rapped on the driver's window and then stood back, hands on my hips.

Unperturbed, he rolled down the window and squinted at me. "Yes?"

He was as near a real-life Sam Spade as I had ever seen: strong square jaw, Roman nose, black hair, parted razor-straight, slicked down.

"You were here yesterday," I said. "And now you're back. May I ask why?"

He puckered thin lips; his voice was flat. "Not your house. What's it to you?"

"How do you know it's not my house?"

He took a small spiral notebook from the seat and flipped through it. "You only got here yesterday." He took a stubby pencil from behind his ear. "Want to tell me your name?"

Planting my hands on my knees, I bent down for a closer look. "What's *your* name?"

"Smith." He shot me a crooked Clark Gable grin.

"Uh-huh," I said. "Tell me what you want. Otherwise, I'm going to call the police. I may have only gotten here yesterday, but I know a man on the local force."

"You mean Bert." He pointed his thumb over his shoulder. "Met him last night when he was directing traffic during that fire…talked to him about your so-called 'painter.'"

That rattled me, but I stayed on course. "Look, Mr. 'Smith,' I'm just trying to help out while I'm here. I'll answer your questions, if I can."

"Pretty simple, really." He draped his arm over the steering wheel. "My employer needs Mr. Greer to come back and settle their old man's estate. Everything's on hold till he"—jerking his head in the direction of the house—"signs on the dotted line, as the saying goes."

"Estate?" I asked.

He rolled his eyes. "You don't know so much after all, do you, lady?"

Thinking of Denver, I backed away. "Will you leave now? You're upsetting everyone."

By which I meant *me*.

"Free country." He reached into his shirt pocket and pulled out a business card. "If your guy decides he wants to talk," he said, holding out the card, "have him call me."

He rolled up his window.

Crossing the street, I grabbed the newspaper, and read the card as I hurried up the driveway. *Thorne Investigations.* When I came through the door, I heard Denver crying. I went to his room, changed his diaper, and carried him to the kitchen, where I found Jericho waiting.

## Chapter 16 ~ The Walls of Jericho

"What does he want?" Jericho asked.

"Hungry," I said.

"Not the baby. The guy in the car." He stepped past me and locked the back door.

Juggling Denver in one arm, I took a bottle from the refrigerator and stuck it in the warmer. "He said his employer needs 'Mr. Greer to come back and settle the old man's estate.'"

Jericho leaned against the door. "She can hound me all she wants. I'm not going home till I get back what she stole from my dad's house."

He said this more to himself than to me.

"*Who's* hounding you?" I asked, rocking Denver to soothe him.

"My sister...*stepsister*, she would want me to say." He walked to the table and sank onto a chair, and then surprised me by opening his arms. "Let me hold him till the bottle's ready."

"You sure?"

"I have two girls of my own."

*Jericho was a father?*

I did as he asked. Sure enough, he handled Denver with ease. I poured the last cup of coffee and set it in front of him. "Cream and sugar?"

He shook his head. "Black."

*Like his mood*, I thought, and sat next to him. "So...your stepsister...."

"Lorraine."

"She's after you about your father's estate? That's what this is all about?"

"It's mostly about our family business."

"What do you do?" I asked.

"Make chocolate."

"You make *candy* for a living?"

I tried to picture the sullen Mr. Fenton...Greer...in a red-and-white striped apron and tall white hat, stirring a stainless steel pot of melted chocolate...but could not do it.

"More than 30 years," he said, eyes resting on Denver. "My dad and his Army buddy, Sam Wilson, dreamed up the idea while they were stationed in France."

Jericho settled into his story, describing his father Ike as a man 'passionate about three things—his family, his company, and his art.' A child of the Depression, Ike was brought up in the 'school of hard knocks,' and as a teenager, worked odd jobs to help support his family. But whenever he got the chance, he was drawing on any scrap of paper he could find—margins of his schoolwork, napkins, envelopes. When he came home from World War II, grateful to be alive, he determined to keep up with his art and began investing in the proper tools.

"He thought if he was his own boss, he'd have more time to paint," Jericho said. "It didn't turn out that way, of course." He pointed at the counter. "Bottle's ready."

I handed the bottle to Jericho and scooted up to the table.

"So he and Sam went into business together," I said, "after the war?"

He nodded. "It was a perfect partnership. Sam was from a wealthy family, so he had money to invest, and my dad had a head for business. He and Sarah built it from the ground up."

They called their business *Sarah's Sweets* and eventually had a dozen employees. They and their daughter Lorraine lived in a lovely home. Ike set up a studio on the second floor and went to work on his 'masterpiece,' copying *The Cliffs at Etretat* from an art book he brought back from France—another 'foxhole promise' he made himself. And then, Sarah died unexpectedly of pneumonia in her 30's. Jericho's mother, Rose, was Sarah's best friend and had been working in the factory since it opened. When Sarah died, Ike asked Rose to become his housekeeper and look after his daughter.

Jericho set down the bottle and eased Denver onto his shoulder, patting him gently.

"Mom was a war widow, supporting a five-year-old son," he said. "So the extra money was a godsend. She'd leave work at 3:00, pick me up from kindergarten, and we'd head to Dad's house to be there when Lorraine came home from school."

"And how old was Lorraine?"

"Thirteen. Mom would help with her homework, fix supper, do some cleaning, till Dad got off work. Then we'd all eat supper together, and Mom and I would go home."

"That must have been such a relief for Ike," I said. "Having a woman in the house."

"It was. And they gradually grew to love each other. They waited a year after Sarah died before they got married. That seemed appropriate. But not to Lorraine. She did not want another mother and never accepted my mom."

Denver rewarded Jericho's efforts with an impressive burp. Jericho resettled the baby in the crook of his arm.

"But you loved Ike," I said.

## Chapter 16 ~ The Walls of Jericho

"He was the only father I ever knew. And he was a great dad. He's the one who taught me to paint *and* taught me how to run the company. I couldn't have had a better father."

I leaned back in my chair. "So...how does the painting fit into all this?"

His anguished look told me this was not a story he wanted to relive, but he continued.

The Greer family muddled through Lorraine's tumultuous teen years. Ike, never losing hope he could win back his daughter's heart, gave in to her every wish. Rose, for love of her husband, went along, reminding herself one day Lorraine would be on her own. And after Lorraine graduated and left for college, their lives settled into a simpler routine...for a while. The reprieve was short-lived. During her sophomore year, Lorraine met the wealthy Fred Hunt, who proposed. Rather than reasoning with her, Ike went along with the idea, hoping a lavish wedding might finally mend his relationship with his daughter.

But after Lorraine accepted his generosity, she moved to Bleakridge with her husband and remained estranged from Ike. She began living the life of privilege she had always dreamed of, racking up a mountain of debt while "keeping up with the Joneses."

"Her husband bailed out on her a couple of years ago," Jericho said. "I don't know all the details, but she's not living as well as she used to. I heard they're in court all the time about alimony. That's why she wants to get her hands on the company. She needs the money."

"So Sam's minding the store while you're here?"

"No. Sam's what you call a 'silent partner.' He diversified. Moved to New York. Our business is only one of many he owns a share in."

"Oh, so your mom's running things?" I asked.

"No. My wife Claire. Mom died a year ago."

"Did Lorraine come home for her funeral...at least?"

"Oh, she came home all right." He peered at Denver. "I think he can go to bed now."

I stood and took the sleeping baby. Jericho glanced up. There were tears in his eyes. I took Denver to his room and lingered so Jericho could have some time alone. When I returned to the kitchen, he was staring out the window.

"Is he still there?" I asked. "Thorne?"

He nodded. "Let's sit somewhere else...away from the window."

I followed him into the parlor, and we sat on the sofa. He leaned forward, propping his elbows on his knees, and stared idly at the chess game on the coffee table. I nudged him back toward his story.

"Did your mother die suddenly or had she been sick?" I asked.

"Car wreck. Drunk driver. My dad never recovered. Losing *two* wives. But he was thrilled when Lorraine came home."

Lorraine became a fixture in their lives, visiting regularly, bringing her two sons Ike barely knew, quizzing him about the business, asking when he was going to retire and start living "the good life," trying to whet his appetite by inviting him to their condo in Myrtle Beach.

"You think she was trying to get him to sell out even then?" I asked. "To get her share?"

"I do now. But Dad was *so* happy to have her back, I kept quiet." He moved a pawn. "But eventually, Dad got suspicious. I don't know why. But one day out of the blue, he told me it was time to 'let go.' He sold me his interest in the business, but he never told Lorraine."

He drifted into silence, wrestling with his memories. I waited, watching, hardly believing this was the same man who had scared the living daylights out of me only last night. That gruff exterior was only a façade masking his grief.

"When did Lorraine find out what your dad had done?" I asked.

He turned to me. "The day after his funeral. She wanted to get her belongings from his house…childhood photos, things like that. So I took her over. We went into his study, and she stared at the painting over his desk, actually got tears in her eyes. I'd never seen her like that."

"That had to make you feel better. Some sign of warmth."

"She said her mom had always loved the painting. I said my mom loved it, too. I honestly thought we were connecting."

"That would've made your dad so happy. Parents love it when their children are close to each other."

He hung his head. "I know. I thought the same thing. Then she sat behind his desk, propped her arms on the armrests and said, 'Now what are we going to do about the business?' I said we'd just put Dad in the ground, and it wasn't the right time to talk about it."

"You think she suspected something…when you stalled?" I asked.

"Maybe. She said, 'I need to know, John. I have to prepare myself if I need to move here to help.' So I told her she didn't need to worry. Dad had turned over the business to me. Sam and I were partners now."

## Chapter 16 ~ The Walls of Jericho

I scooted to the edge of the sofa. "What did she *say*?"

"She didn't *say* anything for a long time. She was perfectly calm. Then she said, 'I see.' I told her I'd explain everything tomorrow after we'd had a good night's sleep and that we should go back to my house. But she said she needed some time alone."

"You didn't leave her there…by herself…in your dad's house?" I asked.

He sank back. "I know. I've regretted it a thousand times. But I couldn't kick her out. Half the house belongs to *her*. I never dreamed she'd leave that night or that she'd take the one thing that meant the most to me."

"Your dad's painting."

He nodded. "I don't know how she got it down off the wall by herself. Left the frame on the floor. Took off with the canvas. I thought at first it was just shock over losing Dad."

"Shock over losing the *business*," I interjected.

"For Dad's sake, I gave her the benefit of the doubt. I waited before I called to ask if we could work something out about the painting. I even offered to buy it."

"What'd she say to that?"

"She said it was priceless"—he mocked her tone—"a 'childhood memory,' but she was willing to let it go in exchange for her fair share of the business *her* parents built. She only wanted what was coming to her."

"I'd like to give her what's coming to her," I grumbled.

He smiled. "I wish you could. The court costs are eating up my dad's inheritance. And he wouldn't have wanted that. I decided to put a stop to it."

I began to surmise what Jericho was plotting.

"So, you're painting a copy," I said, "and you came here to hide out till you're finished."

"I couldn't paint *and* run the business, much less put up with the constant phone calls from Lorraine, so I left."

"Why here?" I asked.

"Sam recommended it. He stayed here a couple of years ago, after his wife died."

I kept prying. "And once you're finished painting?"

"I…can't say. If things go sideways, and you're all questioned, I want everyone to be able to say in all honesty they had no idea what I was up to."

"You mean…when we're interrogated after Roger's caught breaking and entering."

He sat bolt upright. "He *told* you?"

"Yes, he told me. Because he's scared to death. And I don't blame him. Have you thought about what will happen to him if he gets caught breaking into her house?"

"We're not breaking into her *house*. The painting's in her garage. And it's detached. That makes matters a *whole* lot simpler."

"How do *you* know where the painting is?" I asked.

"I hired someone to do a little reconnaissance. Once I found out the painting wasn't in her house, I came up with the idea of switching them."

I turned to face him. "But it's still against the law to break into her garage. That's her property, too."

"But the painting's *not*. And the will doesn't say *who* it should go to."

"You honestly think you can get away with this?" I asked.

"It's entirely workable. Once I finish, Roger and I will drive to Lorraine's, get into the garage, switch the canvases, and be on our way in minutes. She'll never know the difference. I've thought through it a thousand times."

"You can 'think through it' a thousand more times, and it'll *still* be a *dumb* idea."

That was one step too far. The old Jericho, like a sleepy snake, reared his head. "Easy for *you* to say. It's not *your* father's legacy being trashed."

I lowered my voice. "I understand…but you *can't* involve Roger. And you really shouldn't put yourself at risk. Think about your wife. Your daughters. What if you're arrested?"

He met my gaze. "You have a better idea?"

I sat back. "Knock on Lorraine's door. Tell her what you told me. Court costs are hurting both of you. And for your dad's sake, you want to make amends. You made a copy of the painting for her…as a peace offering."

"She won't fall for that. And anyway, she won't talk to me."

"Send someone else. A mediator."

"Like who?"

"Me," I said.

# Chapter 17

## On the Road Again
### Dennisonville, North Carolina
### October 1979

Jericho's mouth dropped open. "You? No. You don't know Lorraine. She'd eat you for breakfast in one gulp."

I stiffened. "You don't know *me*. I've tangled with women like Lorraine my whole life, and I know precisely—"

"I appreciate the offer," he said, "but—"

"But *nothing*. I've spent more than a month meddling in the business of a family that isn't even mine," I said in my best no-nonsense voice. "That's why I'm *here*."

And I told Jericho my story, ending with my hopes for settling Hank and Justine into a home of their own, and adding I *still* had to tell Ivy Leigh Franny wasn't her mother and…didn't he agree dealing with Lorraine would be "a piece of cake" compared to all that?

He yielded, softening his tone. "When's Ivy Leigh going to be here?"

"She's recovering from surgery, so not for a few days. If you'll finish your painting and tell me where Lorraine lives…I can be there and back before Ivy Leigh gets here."

He shook his head. "It's impossible."

"I thought it was impossible to find Justine and Ivy Leigh, but I did."

"Can't argue with that." He stood and started toward the hall. "I'm going to get back to work." He paused, hand on the doorframe. "If Agnes needs help when they get back from the hospital, come get me."

I said I would. Then I put Denver in his crib. When I came back through the kitchen, I caught a whiff of the cobbler. I walked to the stove and wrinkled my nose at the dish. Bridey's voice came back to me, mixed with the scent of cinnamon and burnt crust.

*If Agnes could finish that book of hers...*

What book? And where was it?

Not even I would be brazen enough to snoop in the bedroom, but what if the book were in the office—door open—right over there? I had already been in there…yesterday…helping Agnes pack linens for the music school. Peering over my shoulder, I eyed the typewriter on the desk, paper rolled into the carriage. I tiptoed into the office, as if I were being watched, and surveyed the stack of typewritten pages. I lifted the top sheet and read:

*His dreams of Margaret shattered, Jonas finished building the Magnolia Arms and made plans to leave town and start over somewhere else. He could not leave the house empty indefinitely. He offered the house to Abel Sutton, who had helped with the project from the beginning. All Abel had to do was maintain the house, pay the bills, and…*

Still clutching the page, I pulled out the chair and sat down. Then I lifted the hefty stack of paper and started reading, getting so lost in the story I did not hear Agnes bring Bernard and Ida through the front door ninety minutes later.

Agnes entered the kitchen from the hall. "There you are," she said, skirting the table to make her way to the office. "You found my book. What do you think?"

"I couldn't put it down. How's Bernard?"

"Okay physically, but very disoriented. Ida got him settled and walked down to her house to look around. I feel so sorry for her." She set her purse on the desk. "How's Denver?"

"Fine. We fed him right after you left. He's been asleep ever since."

"We?" Agnes asked.

"Me and Jericho. And by the way, he said to come get him if you need help with—"

"Jericho?"

I returned the papers to the desk. "He saw me go across the street to talk to Mr. Thorne, and he was waiting for me when—"

"Talk to who?" she asked as she walked to the stove and stared at the cobbler.

## Chapter 17 ~ On the Road Again

"The mystery man from yesterday. I saw his car across the street last night, and when it was still there this morning, I kind of lost it. Marched right over to find out what he wanted."

She stepped to the window to look out. "So, *is* Jericho the man he's looking for?"

"Yeah. Well, John Greer."

She pulled a trashcan from under the sink and set it in front of the stove. Then she took a large serving spoon from the drawer, picked up the cobbler, and began scraping it into the trash.

"John Greer," she repeated. "Did you find out anything?"

"He's on the run from his sister." We heard Denver cry. "Want me to get the baby?"

"No. I'd rather get him than do this." She set the dish on the stove. "I'm not going to be able to scrape this off anyway. We'll have to soak it…as usual."

The pungent smell of warm peaches drifted up from the trashcan.

"I'll take this out," I said. "We don't want to smell that the rest of the day."

She thanked me and started toward her bedroom door. "Warm up a bottle for me?"

I took a bottle from the fridge and set it in the warmer. Then I took the trash outside. When I came back, I found Agnes at the table with Denver. I made a fresh pot of coffee. While we waited on the coffee to perk and the bottle to warm, we compared notes.

Bernard was going to be fine, she said, but the incident had been a wake-up call for Ida.

"She's been a landlady a long time," Agnes said. "And she said she can't worry about that house any longer. When she takes Bernard home, she's going to find an apartment close by."

"Probably for the best," I said. "It's going to take a long time to make all those repairs."

"I don't blame her for not wanting to deal with it," Agnes said. She glanced around the room. "This house was damaged in an ice storm, and it took us forever to get everything fixed."

I checked on the bottle and handed it to her. "Will you be sad to see her go?"

"I haven't known her that long, but I'm going to hate to break the news to Ivy Leigh."

"Uh…about Ivy Leigh," I said, sitting next to her. "Mr. Hampton called."

Her face brightened. "Torbert? They're back?"

"Back in the states, but it's going to be a few days before they get here. He said not to worry, but…" I told her about the surgery, ending with: "So, I need to stay a few more days, if that's okay. Makes no sense to leave before I've seen Ivy Leigh."

She looked relieved. "Of course, you can stay."

The back door flew open, and Miriam, with Roger close on her heels, bustled in.

"He's back," she said, face taut with rage. "That man that was here yesterday. Roger recognized him. He's standing by his car, ogling *this* house. I'm going to call the police."

She moved toward the phone. Roger blocked her way.

"*No.*" He sounded desperate. "You can't do that." He appealed to Agnes. "Somebody has to go up there"—he jabbed his finger at the ceiling—"and get some answers from Jericho."

Miriam planted her hands on her narrow hips. "It doesn't matter *who* Jericho is. That man outside has *no right* to frighten decent law-abiding citizens. He's trespassing. And I, for one—"

"I've already talked to him *and* Jericho," I said. "Everybody just calm down, and I'll tell you the whole story."

Miriam, only slightly miffed, took off her coat. "I need tea," she said and put water on to boil. Then she took a china cup and saucer from the cabinet and stationed herself by the stove.

Roger hung the car keys on the pegboard, pulled out a chair, and sat down.

Agnes shifted Denver to her shoulder. "Go ahead. We're all ears."

I repeated Jericho's story. Miriam brought her tea to the table and listened politely, pinky finger raised as she sipped. Agnes hung on every word, interrupting often with questions. Roger, already on edge, jiggled his knee nervously, his face creased with worry.

I wrapped up the story with Jericho's foolhardy plan to switch the paintings, adding I had tried to talk him out of it by volunteering to act as mediator between him and Lorraine.

Miriam interrupted. "I doubt you'll make much headway with her. If the painting is on the floor of the garage, it has no value to her. She only wants it as a bargaining chip."

"She's holding it hostage," Agnes said.

## Chapter 17 ~ On the Road Again

"It's never simple," Miriam went on, "transferring ownership of a family company. "It's a shame Ike didn't act sooner." She set her cup and saucer on the table. "This whole unfortunate situation could've been avoided with a trust-owned life insurance policy."

Roger's knee stopped jiggling. "Huh?"

"A what?" Agnes asked.

"Trust-owned life insurance policy," Miriam repeated. "It equalizes the asset among the people inheriting it, while preserving the asset for the person using it."

"How do you know *that*?" I asked.

"My father had no sons, so he chose me, the oldest daughter, to learn about his business. Sent me to law school." She stood and took her cup to the sink. "I practiced for a few years till I got married and got busy with…well"— she lifted her china cup—"things like this."

The back door opened, and Ida slipped in, cheeks wet with tears. Nestor followed.

"I saw Ida on her porch when I pulled onto the street," Nestor said, trying to sound casual. "I brought her home for lunch."

He zeroed in on Agnes. She handed off Denver to me and met them at the door.

"We were just talking about that," Agnes said, putting her arm around Ida. "I had no idea you were still at your house. I should have checked on you."

Ida tried to speak, but all she could manage was a sniffle and a little wave of her hand. Nestor and Agnes guided her to the table. Miriam, without being asked, brought a glass of water.

Roger headed to the cabinet and took out dinner plates. "We'll need to eat in the dining room now that there are"—he scanned the crowd, lips moving as he counted—"seven of us…counting Bernard."

"Eight," I said. "You're forgetting Jericho."

"No," Roger said, plates in hand, "I'm not forgetting him. He never eats lunch with us."

"He is today," I said, and headed upstairs, where I found Jericho, sitting cross-legged on the floor, studying his canvas. "Lunch," I said. He ignored me. "You might as well come down. Your cover's blown, and you should be in on the discussion."

He finally looked up. "Discussion about what?"

"Miriam was a *lawyer*. I think she can help you. And you can't hide out here forever."

He got to his feet. "Don't need to," he said, nodding at the painting. "I'm finished."

While he cleaned his brushes and sealed his paints, I admired the finished work. I was no expert, but as a copy of Courbet's cliffs, sky, clouds, lone boat on the shore, this painting was exactly right.

Stepping closer, I peered at the lower right corner and read the signature: 'I.F. Greer.'

"I.F." I asked?"

"Isaac Fenton," Jericho said. "Family name. That's why I used it as an alias. Not the smartest thing I ever did. That's probably how they found me."

He followed me downstairs and into the kitchen, where we fell into rhythm with the others, ferrying lunch to the dining room. Then we gathered in the high-ceilinged room—raspberry pink walls, wide white enamel baseboards, dark green carpet printed with small red rosebuds—and took our places, three on either side of the table, Nestor and I at opposite ends.

As I was pulling out my chair, Bernard demanded to know who I was.

"That's Barbara," Ida said. "She's the one who found you."

"Found me?" he asked.

"After the fire," Ida said. "You were lost."

His face was blank. Then he surveyed the others. "Where's Ivy Leigh?"

"She got married," Ida said in the same soothing tone. "She's on her honeymoon."

"With Marshall," he said.

"No. Marshall died."

Bernard was genuinely surprised. "When?"

Ida placed a napkin in Bernard's lap. "Several years ago. We went to the funeral."

"Whose house is this?" he asked.

"It was Ivy Leigh's, but Nestor and Agnes live here now."

His eyes flitted from person to person as he tried desperately to make sense of what she was saying. He gave up and straightened his silverware. "Do we have cranberry juice?"

"No," Ida said. "I'll go to the store later. What do you want on your sandwich?"

"Mustard," he said.

## Chapter 17 ~ On the Road Again

I passed the jar to Ida. She thanked me, and we all politely overlooked the obvious.

Attention shifted to Jericho. While we ate, he spoke, halting at first, and then with abandon, as if a sealed fountain had been unstopped to let water spring up, flow out. I only half-listened as I perused his audience. Night before last, they had been strangers to me. We had met on the sidewalk, our faces illuminated only by streetlights and the fire consuming Ida's house. I had sized them up and formed firm impressions…half of them wrong.

I glanced at Ida on my right. Two nights ago, I had pegged her as frail, as she wept over her house. Today, still teary, she had resolved to give up her home for love of her brother. Poor Bernard sat next to her, lost in his own failing mind. What kind of man had he once been? To his right was Roger, trying to scramble up out of the morass of his past. At the head of the table, Nestor cradled Denver in his arm. Last night, he spoke of my friend Ivy Leigh with a depth of feeling almost reverential.

Agnes was on his right. My first impression of her had been spot-on. She and I had eased into friendship which would last a lifetime. Some things you just knew. Next to her, Miriam, prim as if she had been lunching with the governor, delicately cut a deviled egg in half and drew it majestically to her lips. Jericho sat between us. I had labeled him a 'tortured artist,' then a forger. But his furtive behavior had not sprung from a mere passion for paint, but from desperation to preserve his father's legacy—an act of love, noble, though misguided.

My mental flight landed me at *my* reason for being here. Like Jericho, I was trying to resolve the problems left behind by a well-meaning parent, who chose to avoid conflict rather than face it. Lost in thought, I was picking up on only scattered snatches of conversation.

"—lost my mother when I was a little boy—"

"—think what would happen if you got caught. Your sister—"

"—some things you treasure because—"

Bernard, using his knife to corral English peas into a pile on his plate, turned to Ida.

"I should call Dougan," he said.

Everyone stopped talking to focus on Bernard.

"Why's that?" Ida asked, placing a tender hand on his shoulder.

"He's got that art gallery. Can't remember the street. He could ask this boy's sister"—he pointed his knife at Jericho—"if he could show the painting in an exhibit."

"Like an art show?" I asked him.

He laid the knife on the edge of his plate. "Sounds to me like this woman would *love* to see that painting in a showing…gold plate on the wall…" He ran his fingers through the air over an imaginary plaque. "On loan from the collection of…" He peered at Jericho to fill in the name.

"Lorraine Hunt," Jericho supplied.

"Lorraine *Hunt*," Bernard repeated, turning to Ida. "Give this boy Dougan's number. I don't remember it. Do you?"

"I could look it up," Ida said.

Planting his hands on the table, Bernard eased himself up. "Dougan owes me a favor. I'll ask him about a showing." He winked at Jericho. "He's always on the lookout for new talent."

He ambled out into the hall. Ida followed him and then paused at the door.

She lowered her voice. "Dougan's been dead for eleven years."

Silence fell. One by one, we stood. And in those hazy moments when Agnes began clearing the table, and Roger and Nestor discussed a trip to the hardware store, and Miriam told Jericho she was sorry for his trouble, an inspired plan—like time-lapsed photos—sprang fully grown in my mind, as clear as if I were watching the scenes flicker by on the black-and-white photo of London on the opposite wall. Roger, driving Miriam and me in the truck…no, the Buick to give the proper impression…on our way to outwit Lorraine.

I told Agnes I thought it was time I did some sightseeing…have Asa Ludlow take me on his tour of Dennisonville. She agreed and called him for me. When he arrived, I climbed in, handed him a $20 bill, and asked him to drive me around till that amount ran out. There was no need to talk. Asa drove, spouting off a practiced lecture. The first few minutes, I responded with 'uh-huh,' and 'oh, really?' till he was convinced I was listening and then sank into myself to think. By the time we returned, I had created the perfect plan.

That night, after I helped Agnes with the supper dishes, I slipped down the hall to the check-in desk to call Anne. They were all tired, she said, after their day in St. Augustine, but everyone was happy and getting along.

"You won't believe it, Mom," she said, lowering her voice. "But when we were walking down St. George Street, I saw Ruby and Hank holding hands."

"Are you serious?" I asked.

"It was so adorable."

## Chapter 17 ~ On the Road Again

Unsure how I felt about this news, I changed the subject. "How's Justine?"

"We had to take it slow, so she wouldn't get worn out. But the exercise did her good. I talked to her about taking better care of herself. We're going to start working on that tomorrow."

"Somebody needed to have that conversation with her. I couldn't have done it."

"It came up naturally, and she didn't argue. She said being that sick was a wake-up call for her. Made her think about what would happen to Topeka if she wasn't around."

"Hadn't even thought about that," I said. "Franny was her back-up plan, and she's gone. Hank would be willing, but he can't raise a baby in that trailer."

"I told her we'd talk about it when you get back. When are you coming home?"

"That's why I'm calling," I began and then summed up the situation in as few words as possible. "I need to wait a few more days to see Ivy Leigh. Can you stay a while longer?"

She did not hesitate. "Not a problem. Between Ruby and me, we're managing."

We said goodbye, and I wandered toward the parlor. As I drew closer, I heard the piano. Coming nearer, I made out a reedy soprano voice, "I'll be loving you…always. With a love that's true…always." I stopped just outside the door and peeked in. Ida was singing; Miriam accompanying—another hidden talent. Nestor and Agnes were on the sofa. She was cooing over Denver in her lap, while Nestor studied the chessboard on the coffee table, locked in mortal combat with Jericho in the chair across from him. At the table in the corner, Bernard dozed over an open book.

"That's the way it was when I first got here."

Startled, I turned to find Roger snapping off the light as he came from the kitchen.

"Peaceful…you mean?" I asked.

He studied the scene. "Yeah. I thought I'd be bored to death, but I haven't been."

"Why *did* you come here?" I asked. "Instead of going home after—"

"My mom wanted me to, but my sister is ashamed of me. She's married to a minister, and it looks bad…ex-con for a brother." He hung his head. "She never came to see me."

His defenses were down, so I pressed further. "Why were you...in prison?"

His head jerked up. "I didn't *murder* anybody or anything. Just a lot of misdemeanors—shoplifting, petty theft—judge got tired of giving me second chances."

"But why here...with Agnes?"

"We grew up together." He leaned his shoulder against the wall. "Our moms were best friends. So my mom asked Miss Betty for a favor. Agnes had pity on me. That's what she does."

"Good place to start over," I said.

"It was," he said. "But I still want to move to Jacksonville...where no one knows me. Mrs. Ludlow's spread it all over town...who I am...and—"

Agnes spotted us and waved us in.

"We'll talk tomorrow," I whispered.

He nodded and followed me in. I had intended to announce my plan right away but reconsidered. This was Ida's last evening with her friends, so I kept quiet, making mental notes. Bernard and Ida would leave in the morning. Nestor would drive them to the station, since Agnes was going to Bellport to teach her class. Jericho offered to go with Nestor and "help with the luggage," which I assumed was an effort to be neighborly for the first time since he had been here. That would leave Miriam, Roger, and me alone in the house—the perfect situation.

The next morning, after we said goodbye to Bernard and Ida, I called Miriam and Roger into the kitchen to outline my plan. Roger was enthusiastic from the beginning. Miriam resisted.

"What are you *thinking*?" she asked, tight-lipped. "I was married to a fraud, and now you want *me* to become one, too?"

"No. Just play a role. Like an undercover cop. Think of yourself as a character in a play."

"I think it's a great idea," Roger said.

"You would, wouldn't you?" Miriam demanded, red splotches creeping up her neck and over her jaw, turning her into a human thermometer.

"What if Jericho were your son?" I asked. "Wouldn't you want someone to help him?"

"My son would never try something like this," she said.

When she remained unmoved, I persuaded her to tutor me, so at least I would sound legitimate. She reluctantly agreed, and we moved into the parlor

## Chapter 17 ~ On the Road Again

to simulate an interview with Lorraine. We sat on the sofa. Roger sat in one of the wingback chairs and observed.

We were still rehearsing when Nestor and Jericho returned. When they entered the parlor, I clammed up. Miriam, with a sly smile, eased back in the corner of the sofa and crossed her arms. She couldn't wait to tell on me.

Jericho plopped down in the other chair. Nestor perched on the sofa arm next to me.

"What's going on here?" Nestor asked.

"Tell him," Miriam demanded. "If you're going to involve *his* home, which is also his *business, and* his reputation, he has a right to know what you're up to."

My scheme had to come out sooner or later. Now was as good a time as any.

Miriam and I would visit Lorraine. Roger would play chauffeur to give the impression of wealth. Miriam would play an art dealer, Mrs. Dougan—Bernard's old friend. Mr. Dougan was, after all, long dead, and would not mind if we borrowed the name.

"Mrs. Dougan here has her own gallery," I said, "and is planning an exhibit on 'artist soldiers' and wants to include an unknown work."

"Artist soldiers?" Nestor asked.

"Like Harvey Dunn," I said. "Harry Townsend."

At last—my misguided affection for J. Michael Ford had yielded at least one dividend. I could speak with mild confidence about art and artists.

Nestor stared in bemused silence; Jericho bowed his head. I had the feeling if they had known me longer or had not been so well brought up, they would have been less genteel, when they poked holes in my plan.

"And who will *you* be?" Nestor asked.

"The executive assistant."

"And how will you explain knowing about the painting?" Jericho asked, to stump me.

"From a friend of your mother's. Since Lorraine had nothing to do with her, she wouldn't know one name from another…or any name at all, for that matter."

Nestor said he had to check on Denver. I wasn't sure if he was feeling fatherly, or if he was about to say something he would regret and decided to bail out before he did.

He paused at the door and addressed Jericho. "You'd better tell them what happened this morning. Might change their minds about what they're planning."

"Tell us what?" I asked.

Jericho frowned. "The white car followed us to the train station."

Miriam sat straight up. "*What?*"

"Yep," Jericho said. "I guess he saw me get in the car and thought I was leaving."

"That's perfect," I said. "When we get ready to go, you and Nestor can leave in the truck and drive one direction, and we'll get in the car and head to Lorraine's. He'll follow you."

Jericho shook his head. "I can't ask you to do this."

"You're not asking," I said. "We're volunteering."

Miriam cleared her throat and smoothed her skirt over her bony knee.

"We?" Jericho asked, turning to Miriam. "This doesn't sound like something you—"

Agnes, home from school, breezed in. "Hello. Nestor said I should come in and find out what you're up to." She moved the chess board aside and sat on the coffee table.

I reviewed the plan…not deflated in the least by the objections which had been raised.

"I think it's brilliant," Agnes said, eyes dancing.

"You do?" I asked.

She grinned. "It was this kind of act that saved our house."

"How's that?" I asked.

"You remember the woman I told you about? Olympia Pillburn?" She addressed Jericho. "She was trying to take the Magnolia Arms from us…so she could tear it down. Our friend, Mr. Bridger, sent a lawyer to persuade her to be reasonable."

"A real lawyer?" Miriam asked, cutting her eyes at me. "Not a *fake* one?"

"He was for real, all right," Agnes said. "But his story wasn't *exactly* true. He told her there was a book being written…about the history of this house."

"Your book?" I asked.

"Uh-huh. And that a chapter about her brother, Bentley, was included." She shrugged. "He was the black-sheep of the family. Olympia signed over the house rather than expose her family secrets." She was beaming over the memory. "I just wish I could go with you."

## Chapter 17 ~ On the Road Again

"I don't want to involve the Magnolia Arms," I said, "in case things go wrong. We'll take Jericho's painting with us as a back-up plan. If everything falls through, we'll tell the truth and appeal to Lorraine's better nature. Try to make a trade."

"She doesn't have a better nature," Jericho said.

Nestor returned and handed Denver to Agnes. "While you're all playing 'Mission: Impossible,' I'm going to check on the guests at the music school."

Jericho stood. "I'll go with you. This is making me nervous." He looked at me. "Don't get me wrong. I appreciate what you're trying to do. I just don't see how it can work."

"I'll go, too," Roger said, standing. "I don't need hear the rest. All I have to do is drive."

After the men left, we shifted into high gear. Agnes brought a yellow legal pad and handful of pens from the office, and we put the plan on paper, outlining every eventuality, and coming up with Plans B through H, depending on Lorraine's possible reactions.

For each scene Agnes and I adlibbed, Miriam provided critiques and revisions. Once she pointed out we needed to provide legal documents for Lorraine's approval, she retreated to Agnes' office and perched at the typewriter. Agnes and I took a backseat, becoming a *de facto* administrative team, supplying her with paper and plying her with cups of tea. Miriam even called her lawyer friend to put a 'hypothetical case' before him. She emerged from the office with a loan agreement and insurance plan, adding we would need Lorraine's approval on the wording of the plaque to be displayed with the canvas.

That night, when it was finally time to go to bed, Miriam and I walked upstairs together. I paused at the door to her room.

"What changed your mind?" I asked her. "Why did you decide to help?"

She stood in her open door. "A lot of reasons. My father died not long ago, and with five daughters…you can imagine how we squabbled. I learned from that." Then she grinned. "And besides, I can't possibly let *you* go off on your own without supervision. Way too dangerous."

"Think we can pull it off?" I asked.

"No idea. I would say we need to hang together or we'll all hang separately, but that's going a bit too far, don't you think?"

I responded with a smile.

The next morning I dialed Lorraine's number and introduced myself as Miriam Dougan's executive assistant. Surprised at the sweat beading on my

213

forehead, I steadied my voice and read my speech off the legal pad. After answering a few cursory questions, I hung up and announced we had an appointment with Lorraine for the day after tomorrow.

Leaving Denver with Nestor, Agnes drove our cast of players to Raleigh to go shopping. Roger was fitted with a black suit and tie and crisp white shirt. Then Miriam directed Agnes to Talbot's, where she purchased a navy blue silk dress with matching jacket. I hoped for equal treatment, but Miriam assured me 'executive assistants' did not wear Ralph Lauren. For me she selected a pleated camel-hair skirt and white blouse. A fall-colored paisley scarf and deep brown cashmere sweater completed my costume. 'The colors will go nicely with your auburn hair,' she observed. 'You should have it colored again…soon.'

I almost objected but kept my mouth shut when Miriam whipped out an American Express card from her wallet and paid for everything.

I picked up the bag. "Thank you. I've *never* bought clothes from—"

She returned her wallet to her purse. "A little gift to remember me by."

The night before our fateful meeting with Lorraine, I got ready for bed and then peered out my window to see if…by-now…the infamous white car was still parked across the street, our Mr. Thorne on duty. But the street was empty.

I crept into bed and slept without dreaming.

The next morning we all had breakfast together. Then Nestor and Jericho got in the truck with the Magnolia Arms logo on the side and backed out of the driveway. The white car followed. Agnes was watching from the kitchen window.

"Poor guy's going to be awfully surprised when he ends up at the community college," she said. "I hope he brought money for parking. He doesn't have a sticker."

Miriam, Roger, and I dressed for the occasion. While Agnes waved from the porch, Roger, already 'in character,' opened the car doors for us. I sat in the front. Miriam climbed in the back, with just enough room to sit beside Jericho's painting.

"Where to, Mrs. Dougan?" Roger asked.

I straightened my paisley scarf and opened the Rand-McNally road atlas on my lap.

It was what executive assistants did.

# Chapter 18

# Alarms and Excursions
### Bleakridge, North Carolina
### October 1979

The one factor I had not taken into consideration was how we would pass the time on the two-hour trip to Bleakridge. The three of us were barely acquainted, had little in common, and were all painfully nervous, unsure of success and fearful of failure.

We were as quiet as ill-prepared piano students waiting for our turn at a recital. Finally, Roger spoke up. "You know, Miss Barbara, we don't really know anything about you. Why did you come to the Magnolia Arms? If you don't mind my asking."

"I've wondered that myself," Miriam said, hand draped over the edge of the canvas. "You're good at wheedling information out of people, but you've said nothing about yourself."

"I'm not all that interesting," I said, launching into my prepared biography. "I was a school secretary. I have two children, three grandsons. I still live in the same house my—"

"But why did you come here?" Roger repeated.

I'd almost lost track of my original mission. I was like a concert master who sounded a note so the instruments could tune up, and then sat down to play, only to find the orchestra was performing a different piece.

I sighed audibly. "I came to see Ivy Leigh."

"You know her?" Miriam asked. "The lady who used to run the house?"

"We grew up together. I still live across from street from her mother. I mean...I did. She passed away on Labor Day. Ivy Leigh doesn't know."

"That was over a month ago," Miriam said. "Why did it take you so long to—?"

"She left home…under bad circumstances…nearly 30 years ago."

"You had to *find* her," Miriam concluded.

"And now the first thing you're going to tell her is her mother died?" Roger asked. "That's going to be hard on both of you."

"It's worse than that," I said. "Believe me."

As gentle green hills rolled by, I retold Franny's story, beginning with her final wish that I find "her girls" and then, easing into meeting Hank at the funeral, Nancy Crisp in the restaurant, Justine on my porch, and then looping back to Cherry Lake and the car wreck that killed Clarissa.

"And then, of all things," I said, "when I finally get to the Magnolia Arms, the street's on fire, and Ivy Leigh isn't even here."

"I can't imagine," Miriam said, "what Ivy Leigh will say when she finds out about Franny. At her age? To find out her whole life she didn't really know who she was."

Roger snapped on the blinker and looked over his shoulder before changing lanes. "I think she'll be glad. It'll make sense why Franny treated her like she did."

Halfway there, we stopped for a snack and a bathroom break and arrived at Lorraine Hunt's house, five minutes to spare, at 11:25. Roger steered the car up the steep winding driveway and turned off the engine. I scrutinized the brick house—institutional shade of Dijon mustard yellow—with a bright red enamel front door.

Miriam said what I was thinking. "Oh, dear. This is *awful*."

The front of the house was obscured by untamed Confederate jasmine vines clinging to leaning trellises and the low-hanging limbs of a magnolia tree badly in need of pruning. Its gnarled roots jutted up, pushing up the sidewalk leading to the porch.

"Roger," I said, "the first thing we have to do is make sure Miriam's high heels don't get caught in one of those cracks in the sidewalk. Can you help with that?"

But he hadn't heard me. Leaning into the steering wheel, he had his eyes trained on the wooden privacy fence at the end of the driveway.

"See? Back there?" he asked. "That roof. Must be the garage Jericho talked about. The painting's in there."

I undid my seat belt. "It's not there now. She'll have it inside where we can see it."

## Chapter 18 ~ Alarms and Excursions

"Maybe." He adjusted the rearview mirror and addressed Miriam. "Stay put till I open your door, in case someone's watching." He turned to me. "You open your own door, since you're an employee like me."

"Good thinking," I said, heart warmed. He probably hadn't felt this important in years. Maybe never.

Like Daniel Boone charting the wilderness, Roger escorted us around a half-moon shaped flower bed where a life-sized red Asian goddess statue presided in the center. Clutching a leather portfolio (forgotten by a former Magnolia Arms tenant), I rang the doorbell. The maid, a demure young woman in classic black dress/white apron attire, answered. I introduced "Mrs. Dougan," who inquired where her chauffeur could wait during our appointment. The maid directed him to the back garden and the "servants' entrance." Roger performed brilliantly, calling Miriam "ma'am" as he bowed slightly. He left us and headed back to the driveway.

"Mrs. Dougan" and I followed the maid into the foyer, stone-floored. Miriam's high heels tapped, echoed, tapped, echoed, inspiring the feeling we were breaking into an Egyptian tomb. The goddess statue should have prepared me for what lay beyond the door, but I had ignored her warning. Lorraine's house was a jarring jumble of Japanese modern and Mediterranean. To our left was the living room, the front window draped with heavy gold and olive-green curtains, drawn back with tasseled cords. A sectional grapefruit-colored couch ran the length of one wall, turned a corner, and ran halfway down the other.

The maid directed us into this room. "If you'll wait here, I'll announce you to Mrs. Hunt."

After she left, Miriam and I peered at each other.

"*What* have we gotten ourselves into?" Miriam demanded, eyes wandering to the towering fake cattails in a pale blue vase on the end table.

"It's too late to back out now," I said in a low whisper. "We're *here*."

We edged into the living room. In the center of the seating area a glass chrome-legged coffee table, littered with fashion magazines, sat on a faded Persian rug. Over an upright piano on the opposite wall was a large print, gold-framed, of an Italian villa overlooking vineyards on a hillside. On top of the piano were a ginger jar of silk eucalyptus, black-and-white oval-framed wedding photo, green banker's lamp, dish of paper-wrapped peppermints, and boxed set of the Romantic poets held upright by alabaster Buddha bookends. No wonder Jericho could not bear the thought of his father's painting in *this* house.

There was no sign of *The Cliffs at Etretat*. If Lorraine had bought into our story, wouldn't she have brought in the painting from the garage and cleaned it up for our inspection? I was turning to commiserate with an equally stunned Miriam when a shrill yapping emanated from the hall. With a click-click-clicking of hot pink painted nails, a gray poodle came careening across the stone foyer and, teeth bared, hurtled toward us. But the pooch was galloping too fast to make the turn into the living room. She skidded, sliding headlong into and under the Persian rug, halting her attack.

Lorraine, outfitted in a silky black high-necked Chinese dress, swept in, clapping her hands furiously. "Origami. Origami. Sit. Sit." The dog, dazed and humbled, crept on her belly to her mistress. Lorraine scooped her up and, tucking her under her arm, tapped two fingers on the poodle's nose. "Naughty. Naughty." She returned to the foyer and called down the hall. "Fifi. Fifi."

*Were we in Paris or Tokyo?*

I glanced from Lorraine to the fake bamboo tree in the corner and fought a rising sense of panic. Left of the piano I spotted an arched opening leading to a formal dining room. Maybe the painting was in there. I ambled closer.

Fifi appeared. Lorraine released Origami to her custody.

"Take her to her room," Lorraine said, "and then bring us some coffee."

*Her room?*

When Fifi left for the kitchen, I wondered if she would saddle Roger with Origami while she prepared coffee. We hadn't included a bad-tempered dog on our list of variables.

Lorraine lifted her red-framed glasses, suspended on a chain around her neck, and jiggled them into place on her pert nose. I tried not to gawk at her spectacular diamond ring—more carats than I could guess. Her hair, the color of French vanilla ice cream, was arranged in a flawless French twist. Her long nails were hot pink. To match the poodle's? Or the mythical bird embroidered diagonally across the front of her dress, its long yellow beak resting on her right shoulder, its body cascading down to fan out a rosy plumed tail over Lorraine's left hip.

Miriam recovered her composure before I did and stayed on script. She extended her hand to Lorraine. "Mrs. Hunt. I'm Miriam Dougan. It's a pleasure to meet you."

Lorraine took Miriam's fingertips between hers. "I'm always happy to meet another art lover," she said, her voice an octave lower than I had

## Chapter 18 ~ Alarms and Excursions

expected. "There aren't many of us in a town this size." She gestured toward the sofa. "Won't you sit down, please?"

Miriam navigated around the sharp corners of the glass coffee table and sat down. I craned my neck to get another glimpse into the dining room—no luck—and crossed the room to sit next to Miriam with the portfolio on my lap.

"As my assistant mentioned on the phone, Mrs. Hunt," Miriam said, "I own an art gallery and am planning an exhibit of artist soldiers. We'd love to feature your late father's work."

Lorraine lowered herself onto a rattan peacock fan chair to the right of the piano. She sat primly on the edge, right hand poised on the arm, with her black-ballet-slippered feet crossed elegantly at her ankles. The high round back of the chair might have made Lorraine appear regal if the setting had not been so bizarre. As it was, her shiny satin costume set against a backdrop of Early American Thrift Store with Asian overtones, complete with French maid and French poodle, produced an effect I found laughable. I couldn't wait to describe the scene to Agnes.

Lorraine's wary eyes darted from Miriam to me. "Tell me again how you met my stepmother."

Jericho had coached Miriam well. She didn't blink an eye. "I never met your stepmother. A friend of mine met Mrs. Greer at a veterans' reunion for their husbands."

Lorraine smirked. "And 'your friend' just happened to mention my father was an artist."

Miriam didn't flinch. "It came up in conversation. I told her I wanted to do an exhibit of soldier artists, and she remembered meeting your father at the reunion."

"Rose died over a year ago. And you're just now inquiring about my father's painting?"

"I've had a number of different shows in the last year, Mrs. Hunt. The inspiration for this one only recently occurred to me."

"You know my father is dead."

"I do," Miriam said. "And I was sorry to hear that."

"Does that give the painting more value?"

The glint in Lorraine's eye made me want to smack her.

To her credit, Miriam stayed the course, cool, clinical, and detached. "It would depend on the collector."

Lorraine examined her manicure. "So your friend gave you my father's number, and you called the house and got no answer. How did you end up here?"

"She also gave me the number of the shop. I called there next."

Lorraine looked askance at Miriam. "Oh, I see. And whom did you talk to?"

"I asked to speak to your brother."

"Stepbrother," she sniped.

Miriam ignored the jab. "He couldn't come to the phone. But he relayed the message that after your father's funeral, you asked for the painting and took it home."

"He said that, did he?"

"I don't want to take up much more of your time, Mrs. Hunt. If we could see Mr. Greer's work, we'll be on our way. We've brought all the necessary documents for you to approve."

This was my cue to produce our papers. Fifi returned with a tray and china cups and set them on the glass coffee table.

Lorraine stood. "I'll pour, Fifi. Thank you."

Fifi shot a quick glance in my direction—at least I thought she did—and withdrew.

Lorraine rose slowly; the rattan creaked. In the form-fitting dress which hugged her figure all the way to her calves, she had no option but to unpeel herself from the chair. I had to hand it to her—for a woman hugging 50, she was in great shape.

She poured coffee from a white ceramic pot and offered cream and sugar. I slipped my portfolio onto the couch. Inspired by the surroundings, I wondered idly if the coffee were poisoned. I snickered nervously at my "wicked queen" fantasy; Lorraine glared.

"Something wrong?" she asked.

I coughed. "No. I"—patting my paisley scarf—"frog in my throat. Pollen…"

Lorraine lifted a plate of cookies from the tray and offered them. "Pastry?"

Miriam shook her head. I perused the pile and took two from the top of the stack.

"Pepperidge Farm Chantilly," I said cutely. "My favorite."

Lorraine withdrew the plate. "They're from a local bakery."

"Oh," I said, chastened. "They look so similar."

## Chapter 18 ~ Alarms and Excursions

"They look delicious," Miriam said. "If you'll give my assistant the address, we'll stop by the bakery on our way out of town and buy a dozen to take with us."

Miriam was not about to be bested by this pretentious female. I, however, was way out of my depth and resolved to keep quiet. I popped the cookie whole into my mouth and set my cup on the table. Chewing, I rifled through my portfolio for a pen and legal pad and prepared to take notes or at least create that appearance.

Miriam stayed on track. Pinky raised, she stirred her coffee. "Did your father ever consider making art his profession, Mrs. Hunt?"

Lorraine, cup in hand, returned to her chair. "No. It was his hobby. He and my mother ran a bakery."

"My friend said it was a candy store," Miriam said, utterly calm. "Or did they expand?"

Sitting, Lorraine arched her perfectly drawn-on eyebrows. "Did I say 'bakery'? I suppose it was all the talk about the pastries. Yes, candy store. Still open, but hopelessly outdated."

She launched into the family history we already knew. But in her version, Rose was not a selfless woman who took care of a motherless girl. She had taken advantage of a lonely man's misfortune. Her father Ike wasn't a kind-hearted man who treated his employees like family. He was outdated and knew nothing about running a competitive business that could keep up with the times. As for her 'stepbrother John'—he had manipulated her father into selling him his half of the business and was now robbing her of her rightful share of the company *her* parents had built.

I felt my face go hot and was helpless to stop it. My cashmere sweater, the scarf around my neck, the coffee, the overcrowded room, this infuriating woman with her Lauren Bacall voice made me feel as if I were at the foot of Mount Vesuvius with molten lava encroaching. I thought I was masking my rising temper, but my pen tapping on the legal pad, my rapid breathing, half-snorting like a mad bull, crossing my legs, tugging on my skirt, all alerted Miriam. She eased her hand across the ugly yellow sofa and nudged my leg to calm me.

At least, that's what I thought she was doing—warning me to calm down.

But submerged in my murderous thoughts, I only half-heard Lorraine's closing question.

*You know that already, don't you, Mrs. Goddard?*

Had Lorraine called Miriam 'Mrs. Goddard'?

I looked up from my legal pad. "I'm sorry. I missed that. What did you say?"

Never have I seen anyone look as smug and self-satisfied as Lorraine in that moment.

She clicked her tongue, tut-tutting at me. "Mrs. Allgrove, *really*, the first rule of warfare is to know your enemy, and you and Mrs. Goddard have *severely* underestimated me."

I stumbled stupidly ahead. "I don't know what you're talking about. This is Mrs.—"

"Stop, Barbara," Miriam said. "She knows."

Lorraine rose and took a volume from between the Buddha bookends. She opened the book, taking out a stack of photos. Then she glided to the sofa and started through the pictures, narrating, as she dealt them one by one to Miriam.

"Nestor Carlyle, manager of the Magnolia Arms. His little wife, Agnes. Here's Roger Merriman." She smirked. "Part-time handyman." She peered over her red glasses. "I believe he's playing your chauffeur. I'll be checking the silverware after you're gone."

She droned mercilessly on and on. There were even photos of Bridey Ludlow and Ida. When she finished with her evidence, she leaned over and took the bogus documents from my lap. She examined them, humming, twisting her glossy red lips.

"Impressive," she said, tossing the papers on the table. "Might have worked, if Thorne hadn't developed his photos long before you hatched this pathetic little plan."

I considered grabbing the gold-fringed pillow at my elbow and hurling it at her. Miriam drew in a long breath and rose majestically.

"We won't take up any more of your time, Lorraine," she said in a perfectly marshalled voice. It crossed my mind—if she had been holding her cup at that precise moment, the coffee would have frozen solid.

Pretense out the window, I bolted up. The portfolio slid onto the Persian carpet. I was far from finished. "Okay. So we're trying to help Jericho, and we—"

Lorraine threw back her head and exploded with laughter. "Jericho? How stupid could he be using *that* as alias? And Fenton? Did he honestly think I wouldn't figure that out?"

## Chapter 18 ~ Alarms and Excursions

"He's *not* stupid," I said, near screeching. "He's brilliant. And he has a good heart. Something *you've never had*. And if your father's painting is *so* important to you, *where is it?*"

I was so loud, I startled us all. Lorraine took a step back. "It's in storage."

"Storage my hind foot," I said, spit flying. I licked my lips.

Miriam circled the coffee table to face our nemesis. "I won't pretend to know what it was like to lose your mother when you were a child, or how hard it was for you to accept your father's marriage…"

Spellbound by Miriam's unruffled demeanor, Lorraine faltered, her persona cracking. "That's ancient history."

"Exactly," Miriam said. "It *is* ancient history. The painting means nothing to you. What *you* need to do is stop acting like a spoiled child and sit down with your family and a mediator and settle this like adults."

"Adults?" Lorraine said, eyes blazing. She swished into the hall and called for Fifi. Then she folded her hands and levelled her chin. "If there's nothing else, you can take your papers and your errand boy straight back to that rattle-trap house you came from."

That did it. Insulting Jericho was one thing, but the Magnolia Arms?

"Rattle-trap?" I said, sweeping my arm around the room. "At least our house doesn't look like *Charlie Chan Goes to Paris*."

Lorraine called louder. "Fifi." Her voice cracked. "Come *now*. Show these people out."

Miriam kept inching forward. "I'm not finished."

"Oh, you're finished," Lorraine said. She turned on me. "And for your information, Japanese Modern is the trend now. And Charlie Chan was *Chinese*."

Miriam would not be ignored. "Your brother—"

"Stepbrother," Lorraine said.

"Your *brother*," Miriam insisted, "is a gifted artist. He's worked for months to make a copy of your father's work."

Fifi appeared in the foyer. Lorraine pointed to my portfolio on the floor. "Pick that up and hand it to the short one. I can't be bothered."

Fifi, looking sheepish, obeyed.

Miriam pressed ahead as if Lorraine were listening. "We brought Jericho's painting with us…quite honestly…as a back-up plan, which now we clearly need. We'd like to trade."

"You can't be serious," Lorraine sniped, her face glowing as red as her glasses. "You've come into my house, lied to me, *insulted* me"—she jerked her head in my direction—"tried to *swindle* me out of *my* artwork, and now you have the nerve to...*Fifi...show these people out.*"

To her credit, Miriam stayed on target. Her utter calm...that hypnotic tone. If I hadn't been trembling with rage, and near weeping because everything had gone so wrong, I could've watched her work all afternoon. But the battle was lost. Our plan had been doomed to fail before we got here. Lorraine was right. We had underestimated her. We were like *Abbot and Costello Meet Frankenstein*—that's how outmatched we were.

Lorraine marched to the foot of the stairs and laid her hand on the black wrought iron banister. She waited for her directive to be carried out.

I gaped at Miriam. "Is that it? We're just going to slink out of here like stray dogs?"

"There's nothing more to say." She motioned me to walk ahead of her.

Lorraine gloated as we made our way to the door. Fifi held out my portfolio.

"Where's Roger?" I asked.

"He's waiting for you at the car, ma'am," Fifi said.

"Don't call her *ma'am*," Lorraine said. "She's nothing but a thief."

I whirled to face her. Miriam pinched the back of my arm...hard. "Let's go."

Fifi opened the door. Without a backward glance, Miriam and I left the house, empty-handed except for the borrowed portfolio. The red door closed behind us. We stood, wrung out and defeated, on the porch.

"Well," Miriam said, "we tried."

"Yeah," I said. "I've met a lot of infuriating women in my life, but *never—*"

"Don't say another word," Miriam said. "She may be watching, and I have no intention of giving her the satisfaction of gloating while we creep away. Stand up straight."

I did as she said. We made our way back over the treacherous sidewalk. The minute I got in the car I was going to rip off this scarf, peel off this sweater, and pitch these new shoes onto the floor.

Roger—bless him—was standing at attention by the passenger door. I couldn't help smiling. He was going to play out his role to the end.

"Miss Miriam," he said, "would you like to ride in the front on the way home?"

"I would," she said, and walked around the front of the car.

## Chapter 18 ~ Alarms and Excursions

While he was opening the door for Miriam, I started tugging at the knot in my scarf. Roger settled Miriam in the passenger seat, closed her door, and circled around to my side.

"I'm sorry you got stuck with that dog," I said. "She didn't bite your ankle, did she?"

He opened my door. "No. The dog's fine when Mrs. Hunt's not around. She likes Sally."

I scooted into the backseat next to the painting. "Sally? Who's that?"

"The maid."

"You mean 'Fifi.'"

He shook his head. "Her name's Sally. Mrs. Hunt only calls her 'Fifi.' Sally puts up with it because she needs the job."

"Oh." I took off my scarf, damp with sweat, and laid it on the seat. "An hour ago I wouldn't have believed nonsense like that, but now it made perfect sense."

Roger closed my door, slid behind the steering wheel, and started the engine. He put the car in reverse and turned to look back.

"Can you help me back down to the street?" he asked. "It's hard to see."

I turned sideways to see out the rear window and coach Roger down the steep curved driveway. Twisting, I pulled my leg up onto the seat. My shin bumped the canvas. I glanced down and noticed black spots dotting the edge. Mildew?

We pulled onto the street and started home.

"So what did you do while we were talking to Lorraine?" I asked, slipping off my shoes.

"Oh, I helped out," Roger said. "When Sally brought the dog to the kitchen, I volunteered to take her out so Sally could serve the coffee."

"That was nice of you," Miriam said, slipping off her high heels. "That poor girl probably never gets a break."

"Mrs. Hunt isn't easy to work for," Roger said. "Anybody can see that."

Leaning forward, I slipped my sweater off my shoulders and let it drape down behind me. Then I reached back to hold the cuff and pull out my arm. The painting took up most of the floor space and made it hard to maneuver.

"Lorraine was so mad," I said. "I hope she won't take it out on Fifi the rest of the day."

"Sally," Roger said.

"Sally," I repeated. "What kind of woman won't call an employee by her own *name*?"

This new grievance brought me to the boiling point again. I jerked my sweater from behind me and yanked off the sleeve. My arm knocked against the corner of the canvas. *Why hadn't I taken off this sweater before I got in the car?*

"I guess we'll never know," Miriam said. "Maybe I should write to Fifi…Sally…and apologize for the trouble we caused."

Free of the sweater, I gave it a shake and held it up to straighten the sleeves and fold it neatly. It was, after all, cashmere.

"No need for that," Roger said. Reaching into his shirt pocket, he pulled out a piece of paper and held it up. "I'll find out when I call. She wanted to know we got home safely."

Miriam slapped his arm playfully. "Roger. Aren't you a clever boy? We couldn't have been there more than an hour. How did you win her over so fast?"

I brushed at the sweater with my fingertips and brought the shoulder seams together to match up the sleeves.

He shrugged. "To tell you the truth, I don't know. We just kind of hit it off."

I laid the sweater in my lap for the final fold and noticed a spot of white on the elbow. *From that dreadful couch,* I thought. I dabbed at the spot…filmy and sticky. I pinched it between my finger and thumb.

*Spider web. From Lorraine's living room?*

"I'm glad some good came of this day," Miriam said.

I pushed the painting forward, easing it upright. On the back, in the corner and along the top edge ran a spider web, a moth carcass and half a dozen smaller bugs, long dead, snagged in its weave. My mouth fell open.

"I can't believe it myself," Roger said. "We've got a date this weekend."

Trembling, I gripped the canvas with both hands and hoisted it up till the corner bumped the top of the car. I ran my finger over the black spots on the edge—it *was* mildew—and the bottom corner was tattered, stained with rust.

"Miss Barbara," Roger said. "Could you put that down? I can't see out the back."

I lowered the painting to the floor. Roger was gazing at me in the rearview mirror.

"*Roger,*" I said. "How in the *world*…?"

Miriam looked over her shoulder. "What's wrong?"

"Roger switched the paintings."

# Chapter 19

## New Friends and Old
### Dennisonville, North Carolina
### October 1979

Eager to put distance between us and the treacherous Lorraine, we left Bleakridge and headed for safety. Roger filled us in on the way, while we tried to ignore the 'elephant in the car'—the pesky notion that we might be pursued.

I finally brought it up. "Think Lorraine will send somebody after us…when she finds out we took the painting?"

Roger shook his head. "Sally said she never goes in the garage. Doesn't like to get her hands dirty. And besides that, she's afraid of spiders."

"There's a Howard Johnson's," Miriam said, pointing ahead. "Let's stop and eat. I think we'd feel better. I know I would."

"And I'd kind of like to clean up the painting before we give it to Jericho," Roger said.

We all agreed. There was nothing to be done about the mildew and rust, but at least we could brush off the cobwebs and dead bugs.

"If we could find a store," I said, "I could run in and get some shop rags or paper towels."

Roger pulled into the Howard Johnson's parking lot. "Don't have to do that. Sally gave me everything we need. It's in a bag in the trunk."

Sally. Another variable we had not figured on. A willing accomplice.

The meal revived us, and spirits lifted, we got back on the road for the final leg of our grand journey. Thirty miles from Dennisonville, we pulled into a rest stop and took out the painting. Roger carried it to a picnic table and held it upright, while Miriam and I tended to it with the same reverence cloistered nuns would give a sacred relic. Ignoring the strange looks we got from fellow travelers eating bologna sandwiches and potato chips, we chatted quietly as we worked, still marveling we had accomplished what we set out to do.

Late afternoon, autumn sun dimming, we crossed the city limits of Dennisonville. When Roger turned onto Belmont Drive, my stomach fluttered. I peered through the windshield at the Magnolia Arms, lights shining from the downstairs windows, and couldn't wait to get inside.

We got out of the car. I stood back to allow Roger the honor of carrying the painting. I was walking ahead to let him into the house when the front door sprang wide and Jericho bounded out. Roger eased up the porch steps and displayed the canvas. Miriam stepped next to me; Nestor and Agnes watched from the open door. No one spoke. Jericho reached out his hand and laid his finger on the sky, touching the cloud his father's hand had created. Then he rushed down the steps and swept up Miriam and me in a warm embrace.

"Thank you," he said. "You have no idea what this means to me." He released us and stood back, gesturing toward the door. "After you."

Roger led the way into the house and headed down the hall to the parlor.

"I'm going to change clothes," I said, starting up the stairs.

"Me, too," Miriam said, her high heels dangling from her hand.

"When you come down," Agnes said, "come to the parlor. I'll bring supper to you."

I donned my favorite pants and sweater, hung up my new clothes, wondering when I would wear them again, and sat on the bed. Then I flopped back and spread my arms wide, laughing out loud. We had done it.

Before I started downstairs, I wandered to the window and peered out. The white car was nowhere to be found. Hopefully, Thorne had fulfilled this part of his contract and we had seen the last of him, though Jericho's family problems were far from resolved.

By the time I came downstairs, everyone was in the parlor. The wingback chairs had been moved to either end of the sofa. Miriam, teacup in hand, sat in one; Roger, gobbling a sandwich, in the other. Nestor, holding Denver, was next to Agnes on the sofa. When she saw me, she edged closer to her husband and patted the empty place next to her. I scooted in, and she handed me a plate of food from the coffee table. And we sat, all lined up like visitors to the Louvre, eyes fixed on the painting propped against the piano.

## Chapter 19 ~ New Friends and Old

We gave an account of the day. Miriam, sparing no details, began by describing Lorraine's living room. Agnes observed, 'It's a good thing I wasn't there, because I *couldn't* have kept a straight face.' Nestor added, '…or your opinions to yourself.' Jericho, hearing his sister's treatment of us, shook his head, and reminded us, 'I tried to warn you.' I ended my part of the tale with discovering the spider web on my sleeve, and then Roger—the man of the hour—took center stage. Perched on the edge of his chair, he grew more animated with each word.

Agnes leaned over and whispered, "He's not the same person as when he got here."

"It started out pretty simple," Roger said. "I came to the back door. Sally let me in. I thought she looked at me kind of strange, but I thought I was just nervous. Then she floored me."

He had sat at the table; she offered coffee. Then Lorraine hollered for 'Fifi' to fetch the yapping dog. Sally excused herself and came back. With the dog tucked under her arm, she grabbed the leash looped over the back of the chair.

"She set down the dog," Roger continued, "put on the leash. Then, calm as could be, she said, 'Come with me. There's a side door on the garage. I've already unlocked it. The painting's in the back on the right. I'll hang onto the dog. Otherwise, he'll bark his head off. I'll wait on the back porch while you put the painting in your car.' I nearly spit out my coffee."

"And you believed her?" Nestor asked. "Just like that?"

Roger shrugged. "At first I thought it was some kind of trick. So I played dumb and asked what she meant. She got *real* put out and said, 'We don't have *time* for this.' Then she pointed toward the living room and said, 'that woman'—that's what she called her…*that woman*—had no intention of turning over Mr. Greer's painting, and it was still in the garage. That she already knew who we were."

"And you just got up and followed her out?" Agnes asked.

"I know. Sounds crazy, right?" Roger said. "It's not like me to trust people. But there was something about her…in her eyes. I knew she was telling me the truth."

Without a word, they stepped into the backyard. Sally stood guard at the door and pointed to the side door on the garage. Roger set out across the yard, opened the door, and maneuvering through yard tools and Christmas decorations, located the painting. Canvas in hand, he came out and glanced at Sally for the go-ahead. She motioned him to proceed. He slipped through the gate, and after a quick scan of the driveway and street, switched the paintings. He leaned against the rear car door to close it, checked again for onlookers, and eased through the gate.

Roger leaned back and folded his arms, a sly grin on his face. "You should've seen her face when I brought a painting *back* with me. Of course, she thought it was the same one."

Roger scooted back into the garage, slipped the canvas into place, and locked the door behind him before he rejoined Sally in the kitchen. The heist successfully pulled off, the pair of conspirators swapped stories while Origami snoozed under the table.

Sally had been working for Mrs. Hunt for three years, she explained, beginning part-time the summer after she graduated from high school. The oldest of seven children, it was up to Sally to put herself through college, and she was paying as she went.

'Good jobs are hard to come by in this town,' she said, 'and I can't afford to be picky. Why else would I put up with her calling me *Fifi*? I need the money.'

Mrs. Hunt was fickle and almost impossible to please, and the house, littered with random knick-knacks—'the décor of the month,' Sally described it—was not easy to manage. There was a constant flow of shopping bags and deliveries, all dictated by Mrs. Hunt's whims…her constant obsession to have what her neighbors had. Perfectly satisfied one moment, she could play bridge at a friend's house, notice something new—furniture, rug, curtains, floral arrangement—and Sally would be ordered to make room, take down, switch out, and haul away 'old things' to the thrift store in a never-ending cycle.

Jericho picked up his chair and crossed the room to join us. "But that still doesn't explain why Sally wanted to help you. It was a terrible risk for her."

"I asked her that," Roger said. "It was because of your dad."

"My dad?" Jericho said. "She knew him?"

Roger nodded. "She hadn't been working for your sister very long when one day your dad just showed up out of the blue."

"I remember when he did that. He just took off without telling anyone and drove to her house on a whim. He said he had to see her."

Roger continued. "Sally said she liked him the minute she laid eyes on him. Mrs. Hunt couldn't turn him away in front of Sally, so she felt obligated to invite him in for dinner."

## Chapter 19 ~ New Friends and Old

"He never told us that," Jericho said.

"It was the first time Sally had served a meal, and she was so nervous she knocked over a glass of tea. It spilled onto his lap. Mrs. Hunt was furious, but your dad just brushed off his pants, said they were old, and it didn't matter. Told Sally not to worry. She never forgot it."

Jericho smiled. "That sounds like him."

"Sally never saw him again, but she was still heartbroken when he died. Mrs. Hunt left for the funeral and stayed several days. When she came back, she had the painting with her. Said her brother wanted her to have it. Sally loved it and couldn't wait to hang it up."

Nestor scowled. "She met him *one* time and had more respect for him than his own daughter."

"She was really bothered when Mrs. Hunt never hung up the painting. It stayed on the floor of the dining room until her next party, and then she told Sally to move it out to the garage."

The audience erupted into a chorus of gasps and groans, lamenting this grievous sin.

"So it's been outside…in the *garage* all this time?" Agnes asked.

"Yes," Roger said. "Sally tried to leave it in a clean place, but there is so much junk in there that hadn't been touched in ages, it was almost impossible."

Sally began to overhear Mrs. Hunt on the phone discussing her father's business and other legal terms like probate, estate, and inheritance. From the sounds of it, Mrs. Hunt was either going to receive a large sum of money or become more involved in the family business. In that case, Sally feared Mrs. Hunt would move and she would be out of a job. She became more diligent about paying attention when her employer was on the phone, especially when a man named Thorne began to call. One day Mrs. Hunt told Sally Mr. Thorne was coming to the house.

"When Sally waited on them during the first interview," Roger said, "she figured out why he had been hired. John Greer had disappeared, and they couldn't settle the estate till he was found. She served coffee and then stayed in the hall to listen."

"Atta girl," Agnes said. "Exactly what I would've done."

Roger turned to Jericho. "That's when Sally knew you *hadn't* given your sister the painting, and she'd taken it without asking. Sally made up her mind right then, if there was any way she could help you get it back, she would. She was just waiting for the day you showed up."

"I might have, if I'd known I had an accomplice waiting," Jericho said, laughing.

"Poor old Mr. Hunt was long gone," Roger said, "so *Mrs.* Hunt had no one to talk to about her little scheme except Sally, and she told her everything. Sally played along, acting sympathetic. Mrs. Hunt even showed her all the photos Thorne took of our house and us."

"Did you hear that?" Agnes whispered to me. "He said 'our' house." We both grinned.

Sally kept up her subterfuge, listening to phone conversations when she could and hovering around when Thorne came with updates. Finally, he came with the news that he had found John Greer, who was not 'acting alone,' and had friends helping him.

"He told her about you, Miss Barbara," Roger said. "How you came out to his car and demanded to know why he was there and that you'd help if you had more information. Thorne told Mrs. Hunt if anyone called about the painting, it would probably be you."

A cold shiver ran up my spine.

"Lorraine was just waiting for you to show up," Agnes said, wide-eyed.

Thorne told Lorraine to expect a call and to play along. Because of the photos, Lorraine knew exactly who everyone was and what we looked like. Half an hour before we arrived, Lorraine took the photos from the table in the foyer and ordered Sally to come upstairs with her. She watched from a window and identified each of us as we stepped from the car. Then she sent Sally downstairs to place the photos on the piano, while she prepared for her entrance. Sally calmly did as she was told. The opportunity she had been waiting for had arrived.

"You know the rest," Roger said. "I couldn't have done it without her."

Jericho looked grave. "I hope she won't lose her job over this."

"I don't think there's any danger of that," Miriam said. "Even if Lorraine goes out to look at the painting, she's not sharp enough to tell the difference between the two, believe me. She wouldn't know good art if it bit her on the—" She put her hand to her mouth. "I shouldn't say."

"Even so," Jericho said, "It'd be just like Lorraine to stew over what happened today and send that poor girl out to find the painting so she could set fire to it."

Roger shook his head. "No. She's going to hold it over your head as long as possible. That's what Sally told me…and she *knows.*"

## Chapter 19 ~ New Friends and Old

The phone rang. Agnes hopped up. "I'll get it." She shook her finger at Roger. "Don't say anything else till I get back. I don't want to miss anything."

I tugged on her arm. "Let me get it. I know the whole story." I got up and started toward the hall. "But there's *way* more. Ask Roger where he's going Saturday."

I took the call in the kitchen. "Hello? Uh…Magnolia Arms."

"Babs?"

"Yes?"

I wasn't expecting to hear my name and didn't recognize the voice.

"This is Jussie."

A sudden storm of guilt billowed up and rained down on me. Absorbed with helping Jericho, I hadn't called home in two days. While I'd been playing James Bond, Justine had been home, fretting over her granddaughter's future.

"Justine. I'm sorry. I should've called," I said. "Are you okay? How's Topeka?"

"That's what I want to talk to you about."

I leaned against the counter, afraid the news was bad. "What happened?"

"What's 'happened' is I've had a wake-up call. I made up an excuse to come down here to Ruby's so I could talk to you in private. She says hi, by the way."

"Hello to her, too," I said. I was dying to know if Ruby and Hank were still "an item," but it wasn't the right time to ask. "I haven't seen Ivy Leigh yet. She's not here. And even after I talk to her, it's going to take time to tie up loose ends…about your mom's house."

"Oh, I'm not getting my hopes up about that. Once Ivy Leigh finds out we're not sisters, I don't expect she'll want anything more to do with me. She won't owe me a *thing*."

"You'll get *something* from Franny…just not the house."

"Babs…you and me both know I don't belong in that house. I never did, even when I lived there. I was always more at home in your house than mine. I still feel that way."

"My mother would've loved to hear you say that."

"She knew," Justine said. "I told her all the time."

"You're welcome to stay till you can get on your feet," I said. "It's not a problem."

"It's not that," Justine said impatiently. "Just let me *say* this." She paused, wheezing as she drew in a long breath. "I wanted to know…if you think Anne…would adopt Topeka."

My jaw dropped. I stretched the phone cord to its full length and snagged a chair so I could sit down. The room was spinning.

"Are...are you *sure* you want to do that?" I stammered.

"I haven't forgotten how I felt when I woke up in that hospital...so *scared*...for Toppy. I *can't* be her only hope. My health's not that great. Although...I will say your girl has me on a diet"—she laughed—"and we've been walking together every evening."

"That sounds like her," I said. "Is she making you drink more water?"

"I'm about to float slap away," she said. "And don't get me started on the lettuce I've eaten in the last few days." She laughed. "I gotta admit though, I haven't felt this good in years."

"It's the nurse thing," I said. "Anne does love to lecture about nutrition."

Justine grew silent and then spoke softly. "You know...I was just telling Ruby I came here to get help from my mother. I never dreamed I'd find it across the street."

"That's how it was when we were kids. Remember? Our moms were always sending us to borrow an egg or a cup of sugar. And our dads and all their tools..."

I stopped—getting downright weepy.

Her voice caught in her throat. "Yeah...I've been thinking about your mama a lot lately...being in her house...watching your Anne take care of my Toppy. She treats her like she was her own. That big heart of hers...reminds me so much of your mama."

Now we both fell silent, lost in the days when we were children and problems were solved by our mothers' bandaging a scraped knee or soothing a bruised heart.

Agnes, on her way to take Denver to his room, entered the kitchen and found me sniffing and wiping my nose. She stopped and whispered, "You okay?"

I gave a quick nod. She grabbed a napkin from the table, handed it to me, and kept going. "You still there, Babs?" Justine asked.

"Uh-huh. I...I just don't know what to say. But there is no doubt in my mind Anne would love to be Topeka's mother. She'll be honored that you trust her."

Justine breathed a sigh of relief. I could tell by her voice she was smiling. "Ruby said so, too, but I wanted to ask you first, what with you being her mama and all. It's only right."

"You go ahead and ask," I said. "She won't think twice. I promise."

## Chapter 19 ~ New Friends and Old

"All right. I'm going to walk right back over there and ask her. 'Course me and Dad won't go anywhere. I'll stay here in town to be close to Toppy. But I'll be her *grandma*. Not her mama. I'll have to find someplace to live. Can you help me with that when you get back?"

"Of course. Call me tomorrow and tell me how it goes. I wish I could be there to see the look on Anne's face."

"I will," Justine said. "And you call *me* after you've seen Ivy Leigh. And if she wants to talk to me even though I'm not her sister, tell her I'd like that. It's been way too long."

She hung up. I sank back, still holding the receiver, and remembered the day Justine, shabby and sweating, had come to my door. I'd tried to give her bus money to make her leave. I'd turned up my nose when her stale smell permeated my living room. I'd winced when she sat on my sofa. Her words about Anne...*reminds me so much of your mama*...repeated like a sweet refrain in my heart. My mother never thought twice about helping someone in need. The house *never* mattered as much as the person on the other side of the door.

What if I hadn't let Justine in? What if, sick as she was, and only moments from collapsing, she had walked away with Topeka in her arms?

The phone, off the hook too long, started beeping.

Agnes, on her way back from putting Denver to bed, took the receiver and hung up. Then she squatted down next to my chair and laid her hand on mine.

"Babs, what in the world is the matter?"

"Nothing," I said. "In fact, everything is perfect. No thanks to me."

We rejoined our friends, and the conversation resumed. Our focus turned from the tight-fisted Lorraine to the big-hearted Justine, who, for all her years of living, had but one treasure—a child, whom she was willing, for love's sake, to give up.

Miriam dabbed away tears with her napkin. "What a precious woman." She took her teacup from the coffee table and stood. "A wonderful way to end the day. I'll say good night."

Nestor rose. "Me, too," he said, reaching for Agnes' hand. "Roger and I have to be at the music school first thing in the morning. The reunion's over, and the last family's taking off."

"I forgot all about that," Agnes said. "My class is tomorrow. Who'll watch Denver?"

"I will," I said. "I want to stay here...for when Anne calls."

Roger stood up, stretched his arms over his head, and then crossed to the door. "It'll be good to get back to normal. See you in the morning. Good night."

"I'll go, too, Nestor, if that's okay," Miriam said. "Quite honestly, a day inside that beautiful house would be therapeutic. Cleanse my mind."

Jericho was taking a last look at *The Cliffs at Etretat*. "What time will you be leaving?" he asked, surprising us all.

"7:30," Nestor said.

"I'll be ready," Jericho said. "I owe you something for all the trouble I've been."

We parted in the hall, and Jericho, Miriam, and I started upstairs.

"What a day," Miriam said, walking ahead of me. "I haven't had this much excitement since I bailed my husband out of jail."

We stopped outside her door. "I hope I can sleep," I said. "I'm so wound up." Jericho walked past on his way to his room. I called to him. "Starting a new painting tomorrow?"

He turned. "Something else I have to do first." He entered his room and closed the door.

Jericho Fenton…mysterious to the end.

I lay down and turned out the light, resigned to a sleepless night, eyes on the ceiling, haunted by Lorraine. Instead, half-asleep, Justine appeared in my mind, leaving Ruby's house, almost skipping back to mine. She opened my front door and called.

*Anne? Could I talk to you a minute?*

The next thing I knew it was morning.

The six of us gathered at breakfast and chattered like school kids on the first day of Christmas vacation. Except for lingering concerns for Sally—"No news is good news," Roger observed—there was no dark cloud looming over the day. Miriam was looking after Denver, while Agnes gulped down another cup of coffee and checked her bookbag. Nestor was going over the "To Do" list with Jericho and Roger. I spooned strawberry preserves onto toast and thought of home, eager to hear Anne's reaction to Justine's request.

Truck keys in hand, Agnes paused on her way out. "If you don't mind, Babs, after my class, I'll go help out at the music school. Oh, and expect Bridey to show up today. She knows the reunion's over, and she'll want an update. So…let her in…or don't let her in. It's up to you."

"Since when does she *ask* before she comes in?" I stated.

Agnes exploded with laughter. "Good point."

## Chapter 19 ~ New Friends and Old

I took charge of the baby and watched from the kitchen window as Agnes drove one direction in the truck, and Miriam and the men went the other—all on their way to work. I had my own plans I confided to Denver.

"Come on. Let's put your swing in the office. Your mama doesn't know it, but I'm going to type on her manuscript today. She's never going to finish that book at the rate she's going."

He smiled. At least, I thought he did.

I bustled around, settled Denver in his swing, and cranked the handle to wind it up. As he swayed back and forth, gears clicking, handle turning, I sat at the desk and rolled paper into the typewriter carriage. Agnes had stopped at a chapter division: *Wedding Day*. I started typing, congratulating myself on my speed and accuracy. Though retired, I wasn't rusty. The pantry-turned-office transformed into Charlotte Wrayburn's mansion, filled with flowers, hors d'oeuvres, and wedding cake. I hummed "The Anniversary Waltz" as Monty played the accordion while the bride and groom—Jonas and Margaret Grinstead—danced at the reception.

The phone rang. I glanced at my watch—9:00 a.m. I knew it was Anne.

I hurried to the phone by the back door. "Hello?"

"Mom?" was all she managed to say.

"I know, sweetie. Justine told me last night."

She wept as words poured out. "All this time...trying to figure out *what* was wrong with me...and *what* to *do,* and a baby is left on our doorstep...just like in a movie."

"I know," I said. "Have you told Scott?"

"No. Haven't gotten hold of him yet. He's in meetings, and there's the time difference." She paused. "Do you know when you're coming home?"

"No. I'm sorry. I can't leave till I've seen Ivy Leigh...but she's due here any day."

"I understand. I just wish you were here. There's so much to do, and I want to get started."

A fresh wave of guilt crested over me. I took a stab at sounding upbeat. "Well, the first thing we have to do is find someplace for them to live. We'll start looking as soon as I get back."

"Them?"

"Justine and Hank. She said she wants to stay in town to be close to Topeka. Your brother knows all kinds of real estate people. We'll find someplace affordable."

"We may not need to figure Hank into those particular plans," she said.

"He's not leaving, is he?"

"Oh, no. He's not going *anywhere*. That's for sure."

Denver started fussing. "Can you hold on a second," I said, "while I check on the baby?"

"You're babysitting?" she asked.

"For the managers," I said. "Long story."

"It always is with you," she said.

I laid the phone on the counter and scooted back to the office. I wound up the swing and gave it a nudge to get it going, promising Denver I'd be right back.

As I breezed by the kitchen window on my way back to the phone, I noticed a white car in the driveway. *Not again. I thought we were done with Thorne.* The driver's door opened.

"I have to go, Anne," I said, whispering though there was no need. "Somebody just pulled up. Must be guests, and I'm the only one here."

"You're checking in guests, too? What kind of place is that? That guests do the work?"

"I'll explain later," I said. "Gotta go. Bye."

By the time I hung up the phone and returned to the window, the man was standing behind the raised trunk lid. He placed two suitcases on the driveway. Not till he closed the trunk and walked around the car did I get my first clear look.

Torbert Hampton. I recognized him from the wedding photos Agnes had showed me.

He opened the passenger door, and Ivy Leigh stepped from the car. She stood still, gazing at the Magnolia Arms, as if seeing the house for the first time. Torbert went back for the suitcases, and they started toward the kitchen door.

This was not the touching reunion I had imagined, where Ivy Leigh came to the *front* door and Agnes said, 'You'll never guess who's here,' and I swept down the stairs like a beauty queen, shouting, 'Surprise.'

There was no time to improvise. I backed up into the middle of the kitchen, smoothed my hair, and plastered a stupid grin on my face.

The door opened, and Ivy Leigh stepped in. "We're home," she said.

There she stood—the friend of my childhood, lost so long ago. Her face still wore the same placid expression, her eyes still shone with warmth and welcome. Here was a woman who had lived facing forward, not looking back with regret.

## Chapter 19 ~ New Friends and Old

"Hello," I said, waving feebly.

"Sorry," she said. "I thought you'd be Agnes." She walked toward me, hand extended. "I'm Ivy Leigh Ransom…" She giggled. "I mean *Hampton*. I just got married."

Torbert had followed her in. "Should I take these upstairs or—?"

"I know who you are," I said, throwing my arms around her.

A thousand reasons to weep caught up with me. I buried my head in her shoulder and half-laughed, half-cried, without considering she had *no idea* who I was or why I was clinging to her. But she politely yielded to my embrace.

"I'm sorry," she said, gingerly patting my shoulder. "I don't recognize you. Did you stay here once a long time ago?"

"No." I stood back and swiped my hand across my face. "But I've spent the night at your *other* house…many times."

Her expression changed from pleasant to puzzled to stunned in less than a second.

"Babs?"

"Uh-huh," was all I could manage.

She took me by the shoulders. "I can't believe it. What are you doing here?"

"Looking for you," I squeaked out.

Ivy Leigh grabbed my elbow and pulled me over to Torbert. "Sweetheart. You remember my telling you about Babs? My neighbor? This is *her*. *This* is Babs."

Torbert set down the luggage and took my hand in both of his. He was a bear of man, craggy-faced with an imposing square jaw, thin lips, prominent nose. But his eyes, green as the sea, sparkled with kindness and good humor.

"Torbert Hampton," he said. "My wife's told me a lot about you. The trouble you two would get into." His eyes were dancing.

"No need to bring that up," Ivy Leigh said, slapping his broad chest playfully. "But Babs, how in the world did you find me?"

Denver, tired of waiting, began to cry.

I gave Ivy Leigh a quick hug. "I'll tell you all about it, but I need to get the baby."

Reunion over, we transitioned seamlessly from the storybook reunion to everyday life. I brought Denver and handed him to Ivy Leigh, sending her to change him. Torbert asked where to put the luggage. I said 'upstairs,' explaining how I intended to let them have my room while they were here.

We were still debating good-naturedly when Ivy Leigh returned and assured me she would '*love* to stay downstairs for old time's sake.' After Torbert returned from taking their luggage to their room, he asked where everyone was. I explained, and he insisted on heading to the music school to help.

"Don't you need to rest?" Ivy Leigh asked, eyes fixed on the baby in her arms.

"Nah. I'll take a nap this afternoon." He kissed her on the cheek. "This way, you two can catch up. Bye, girls."

The first order of business was to hand a bottle to Ivy Leigh, so she could feed the baby. Agnes had told me Ivy Leigh had no children, so Denver was as close to a grandchild as she would come. So, while she took care of him, I offered coffee and cookies and bustled around the kitchen. It should have seemed strange—Ivy Leigh at the table, me—a guest in "her" house—taking cups and plates from the cabinet, but we were perfectly comfortable. She remarked that I 'knew where everything was' and asked how long I'd been here.

"Several days," I said, fussing with chores while I summoned my nerve. *How* was I supposed to bring up what I had come to say? I opened the silverware drawer. "You look great. You don't look like you've been sick a day in your life."

"Because of my husband," she said. "I would've been here sooner if it hadn't been for him. He *made* me take care of myself after the surgery."

I moved to the refrigerator and opened the door, feigning interest in the top shelf.

"Want milk in your coffee? Or we have half-and-half." A nervous chuckle slipped out. "Maybe we weren't drinking coffee by the time you left. We were only teenagers."

When she didn't answer, I peeked around the refrigerator door.

She was staring at me, eyes narrowed, lips straight as a pencil. She spoke calmly.

"There's only one reason you would've gone to all this trouble to find me." She paused. "My mother's dead. And you didn't want to tell me over the phone."

Her tone was a statement; her face a question.

Closing the refrigerator, I gave a quick nod.

"When?" she asked.

"Labor Day." I should have said: *When you were two.*

"Had she been sick?"

## Chapter 19 ~ New Friends and Old

"No." Thinking: *No. Clarissa was killed in a car wreck.*

I left the coffee unpoured and sat next to her. "It was a heart attack. She was gone before we could get her to the hospital."

"Was she at home?"

"In her kitchen," I said. "She was supposed to come for our cookout. You remember. We always had a cookout on Labor Day. We still do. She was five minutes late, so—"

Her face eased into a gentle smile. "Five?"

"Uh-huh," I said.

"So she hadn't changed. Always on time."

She fell into silence, dense, impenetrable, stranded in a thick fog, an arm's length...a thousand miles...a lifetime away. She set the empty bottle on the table and moved Denver to her shoulder. She pressed her cheek to his and closed her eyes.

The secret I had banished to the farthest corner of my mind rose to confront me, demanding center stage.

*Tell her. This is the chance you've been waiting for.*

"Did she say anything?" Ivy Leigh asked.

My mind was flitting from Clarissa to Franny, so I stared blankly, unsure what to say.

"Who?" I asked.

"My mother. Did she say anything about me? Tell me. No matter what she said."

"Yes." I reached for the empty bottle and made a dash for the sink.

"*Babs,*" Ivy Leigh said. "Come back and sit down. Tell me what she said."

I dropped the bottle in the sink and turned around, leaning against the counter. "She made me promise to find you and Justine...and take care of her house till you came home."

Ivy Leigh eased Denver to the crook of her arm and rocked him gently.

"*That's* what she said? 'Find Ivy Leigh and Justine'? *Both* of us? You're not making that up? She asked for *me*?"

"No. I mean...*yes*, that's what she said. No. I'm not making it up. 'Find my girls.'" I winced at the memory, still a painful, dull ache.

She rose. "Come on. Let's sit on the sofa. Bring a blanket for the baby."

"What about the coffee?"

"Leave it," she said from the hall.

The moment I'd been preparing for was here, and I was nowhere near ready.

I got a blanket from Denver's room. By the time I walked back, Ivy Leigh had settled the baby on an afghan on the sofa. Seated at one end, she had left a place for me at the other. I draped the blanket over the baby and eased onto the sofa, scooting back into the corner.

"What's that?" she asked, pointing at *The Cliffs at Etretat* still propped against the piano.

"Oh, that," I said, glad for the detour, "that's a long story if ever there—"

But the question was an idle one. She did not really want an answer.

"We were coming for Thanksgiving," she said, straightening the blanket. "Torbert said I'd never have peace till I made things right with my mother. I did try, Babs. I honestly did."

"Justine told me," I said, intending to comfort her, but with the opposite effect.

"You've *seen* her?" she asked, eyes flashing.

"She's at my house right now. Showed up the day after Franny's funeral."

Turning sideways, she put her arm on the back of the sofa. "She came *home*? Justine?"

"Yes." I swallowed hard. "She needed help…with her granddaughter."

"Which one?" Ivy Leigh asked. "The last time I talked to her, she had half a dozen."

"More now," I said. "This one's a baby. Justine has custody of her, but got overwhelmed, and decided to leave the baby with Franny."

"Where's the baby now?" she asked, alarmed. "Who *has* her?"

"My daughter. She's staying with them while I'm here. They're okay. All three of them."

"Three?" she asked.

"Yes. Justine…and Topeka…and…"

"Topeka?"

I nodded. "Yeah."

"And?"

"Hank," I said.

"Who?"

"Hank Merrier." I bit my lip. "Justine's father."

She leaned closer, fingering the locket she wore. "You mean… 'stepfather'? Do you mean to tell me Mother remarried?"

## Chapter 19 ~ New Friends and Old

"No," I said, gaining confidence. "That's not what I'm saying." I drew a lungful of air. "Hank was Franny's first husband. Your father...Cab...was her second."

She laughed...loud enough Denver jerked in his sleep. She pressed her fingers to her lips and lowered her voice. "Babs," she said, as if calming a mental patient, "I don't know *where* in the world you got an idea like that, but it's simply not—"

"I got it from Hank Merrier. At Franny's funeral. In Madison."

She sat back. "Madison? She's not buried with Daddy?"

"No." The road unblocked, I hurtled forward. "She wanted to be buried in Madison. Hank showed up. I was talking to him...and Ruby and the pastor said I shouldn't. I said we should have compassion for a homeless man, and Ruby said"—I paused to breathe—"Hank wasn't homeless. He was Franny's first husband."

The air rushed out of my lungs. The room. The house.

With one well-aimed blow, I had knocked her senseless. Her eyes darted around the room before settling on me.

At last she spoke. "You're sure what you're saying is true?"

"I have a whole box of pictures upstairs. Including a note from your mother." I scooted to the edge of the sofa. "I could get it and show you."

She held up her hand to stop me. "No. Just tell me."

"Where do you want me to start?" I asked.

"The beginning."

"Then we have to go back to Richmond," I said, remembering Hank, knees almost to his chin, in the front seat of the red VW on I-10, telling me the story.

She listened, doubtful, suspicious, but without interrupting.

While Denver slept between us, we journeyed north to Virginia. We attended Franny's debutante ball and then her wedding to Henry Fitzsimmons Merrier IV and then stood at the hospital nursery window to admire Justine Frances Merrier born two years later.

She nodded. "Right. December 1934. I was born in February the same year, but Mother never told me I was born in Richmond."

"You weren't born in Richmond. You were born in Madison, Florida."

She was struggling to calculate, fashion a tenuous whole from fragments of facts. "Are you saying Hank was *my* father? They were travelling when I was born?"

"No. They were in Richmond. They didn't move to Florida till later."

"I was born *before* Justine. In February," she repeated. "You know that."

Hopelessly stumped, she stared at me like a cornered animal.

"Yes," I said. "You were born February 10, 1934...to Cab Moore..."

She breathed out. "Thank you. I knew—"

I spoke over her, "And his wife, Clarissa...*your mother.*"

Before she could speak—terrible timing—the doorbell rang.

Ivy Leigh nodded toward the hall, dismissing me. "Would you get it?"

I charged down the hall, furious, thinking, *If that's Bridey Ludlow...so help me...*but even as I considered this, I knew it couldn't be Bridey. She never came to the front door and was certainly not polite enough to ring the bell.

I broke out in a cold sweat. *Get hold of yourself, Babs,* I said. This might be someone wanting a room. I fluffed my hair, hoping I looked presentable. Plastering on a quick smile, I opened the door to a familiar face.

"Hi," she said. "I got the day off, and I thought I'd bring this."

It was Sally, out of breath, with Jericho's painting tucked under her arm.

# Chapter 20

## Lost and Found
### Dennisonville, North Carolina
### October 1979

Decked out in denim skirt, perky red sweater, and loafers, Sally had left the role of 'Fifi' behind. This was no docile servant girl. The downcast eyes of yesterday were glowing with eagerness; the timid voice hoarse with suppressed excitement.

"Is Roger here?" Sally asked, breathless.

"No," I said. "He's working. Come in."

Stepping back, I opened the door. She handed the painting through. I held one side, and we brought it in, then leaned the canvas against the wall.

"That's a relief," Sally said and grabbed my arm. "When you were on your way back yesterday, did you feel like you were being followed?"

"Yes, but Sally, you shouldn't have risked your job to—"

"I kept telling myself I was being silly…I'm not *stealing* anything. I mean…once somebody puts something out for the garbageman to take, it's up for grabs. Right?"

Ivy Leigh approached us from behind. Old manager habits were hard to break, I supposed. She could not sit idly by while I welcomed a guest to "her" house.

She extended her hand to Sally. "I'm Ivy Leigh Hampton."

"Sally Meadows. I don't think Roger mentioned you."

"He wouldn't," Ivy Leigh said and spoke to me. "I put Denver in his crib. Where is this box you brought with my mother's…Franny's…photos and things?"

"Upstairs. In my room. On the dresser. Everything's there. But—"

"May I?" she asked, indicating the stairs.

I hesitated. I wanted to be *with* her, see her reaction when she saw the photo of Clarissa…read Franny's note. But I could not ask her to wait, and I could not leave Sally.

"Help yourself," I said. "I'm in Monty's old room. It's the one—"

She started up the stairs. "I know which one it is, Babs."

I shifted my attention to Sally. Hands clasped behind her back, she was strolling around, gazing wide-eyed into the dining room and then admiring the wall of photos that lined the stairs.

"So, this is the Magnolia Arms," she said. "It's so *different* from where I work. It's the windows. They're so tall. And *no drapes*. The light comes *in*. That's what windows are *for*."

Sally was like a wilted plant recently watered, on the verge of full bloom.

"Would you like to see the rest of the house?" I asked, when I really wanted to say, *What are you doing here, and do you have any idea how much trouble you're in?*

"No." She switched to all-business. "I have to talk to Mrs. Hunt's brother. He needs to know where she's gone."

"He's with Roger," I said, "and the others. We could call him."

"Do that first," she said. "He needs to start home right away."

"Let's use the phone in the kitchen," I said, leading her down the hall. "Would you like something to drink? You must be exhausted."

She paused at the parlor door. "What a beautiful room. I wouldn't mind being a *maid*"—the word twisting her upper lip—"if I could work in a house like this."

"After we call Jericho, we can sit in there, and you can tell me the whole story." I made a beeline to the phone and picked up the receiver. "What do you want me to tell him?"

Sally followed me into the kitchen. "Mrs. Hunt is on her way to see his wife."

"*What*? When did that happen?"

"When you left yesterday, she pitched a fit backwards. Said she was sick and tired of all this nonsense with John, and she was going to put an end to it once and for all. No more 'being Mrs. Nice Guy.'"

"When was she ever *that*?" I hung up, waiting for details. "Put an end to what?"

"The dispute…about the estate. She said she was going to her study to call her lawyer and for me to go upstairs and pack a suitcase for her…enough clothes for three days."

## Chapter 20 ~ Lost and Found

"Has she already left?" I snatched up the receiver again.

"Yeah. Otherwise, I wouldn't be here. I'd be working."

"What time did she leave?"

"This morning about 6:30." She stepped to the window and touched the white curtains. "So pretty. She took a cab to the train station. I waited till she left and then grabbed the painting from the curb and drove straight here."

Phone down. "The curb? Why was the painting—?"

Sally studied the African violets on the windowsill. "I was on my way upstairs to start packing, when she called me back down and sent me out to the garage to get the painting. Told me to put it on the street with the garbage. Some kind of revenge, I guess. Just pure meanness."

"And you *did* what she said?"

"Had to, didn't I? I knew she'd check. So I put it out and then did her packing."

"Why didn't you call us last night?" I asked, picking up the receiver again.

She took a glass from the dish drainer and turned on the faucet. "I live at home. When I told my parents what happened and that I was going to call Mr. Greer, my dad put his foot down. He said it was a family matter, and I shouldn't risk my job for something that was none of my business."

"Does your dad know you're here now?"

"No." She took a swig of water. "I said I had the day off…which I do…and I was doing a favor for a friend…which I *am*. I was awake half the night wondering if I could get back to the house before the garbagemen came. As soon as the sun was up, I drove to Mrs. Hunt's house, got the painting, and took off. I just hope the neighbors didn't see."

I dialed the music school. "There's coffee," I said. The phone started ringing. "Help yourself. As soon as I hang up, you need to call home and— Hello, Nestor? This is Babs. I need to speak to Jericho."

I explained the situation to Jericho. After I hung up, I turned my attention back to Sally, all the while wishing I were upstairs introducing Ivy Leigh to Clarissa. It was the longest twenty minutes of my life before Roger came through the door and made a beeline for Sally to see if she was 'all right.' Agnes followed, asked about Denver, and then where Ivy Leigh was, and charged upstairs. When I introduced Jericho to Sally, she was starstruck and said over and over how much she admired his dad. Miriam sidestepped the chaos, made a cup of tea, and settled at the table, eyeing the rest of us.

I sat next to her to ask about Torbert and Nestor and noticed she was drinking from a *Dennisonville, North Carolina* souvenir mug. I had seen them on a welcome table at the train station. Her china cup and saucer were unwashed by the sink.

"Sorry about your teacup," I said. "I meant to do the dishes, but then Ivy Leigh—"

She lifted the mug in a toast. "Tea is tea…" She nodded at Sally, who was repeating her story to Jericho and Roger. "Did you have a chance to talk to Ivy Leigh before Sally got here?"

"I had *just* enough time to tell her Clarissa was her mother before the doorbell rang. She's upstairs now, going through the box. I'm dying to get up there."

Miriam settled her gaze on Sally, talking to the men. "That 'polite maid' business is only a role for her. She's a feisty girl, isn't she?"

"You don't know how feisty. She brought Jericho's painting back with her. Lorraine made her put it out with the trash, but she went there this morning and got it."

"So now we have two," Miriam said, actually giggling. "After all that trouble…"

Sally was wrapping up her report. "It's not my place to tell you what to do, Mr. Greer," she said, "but you don't know your sister. Trust me. Your wife shouldn't face her on her own."

Jericho started toward the hall. "I'm going to go throw a few things in a suitcase. Can you take me to the station, Roger?"

"Sure. Want to come with us, Sally?" Roger asked.

She nodded eagerly.

"Call your dad first, Sally," I said, mother-like. She went to the phone.

Miriam drained her cup and plunked it down. "I'm going, too," she said.

Jericho stopped in the door. "That's nice, but I really don't need a send-off."

She stood and pushed her chair under the table. "No. I mean, I'm going with *you*." She spoke to me. "Could you help me pack, Barbara?"

I spluttered. "You're going? Why?"

In reply, Miriam addressed Jericho. "Do you have a good lawyer?"

"Friend of my father's. He did my dad's will. He's a typical small-town lawyer, good with the basics. I'm not sure how he'll do against Lorraine."

"You're going to need more than that," she said. "I'm not licensed to practice anymore, but I *know* the law. I can advise you." Her eyes twinkled. "And I won't charge you by the hour."

## Chapter 20 ~ Lost and Found

"I can't ask you to do that," Jericho said. "You've done so much for me already."

But her mind was made up. "You're not *asking* me to do anything. I'm volunteering. Come on, Barbara. We're wasting time."

If Ivy Leigh and Agnes, behind the closed door of my bedroom, heard the commotion when we came upstairs, they were too deep in conversation to be curious. I longed to tap on the door and see for myself how Ivy Leigh was. But I was too busy obeying Miriam's orders. As she ricocheted between her dresser and suitcase, opened on the bed, she muttered to herself and issued directions to me. *Not that dress. The suit. Navy blue heels. Slippers.* Was she really the same woman who had knelt on this carpet in the grip of a panic attack?

Roger came to the door. "We're ready. Can I carry your suitcase down, Miss Miriam?"

She snapped it closed. "Thank you, Roger." After he left, she kneeled down and pulled a brown leather attaché case from under the bed. "I'll need this," she said, standing. "To create a good impression."

"I don't think you'll need to impress Jericho's wife."

"Not her," Miriam said. "I'm going toe-to-toe with Lorraine."

I stood on the front porch and watched them drive away. Jericho was going home…with Miriam tagging along. Who saw that coming? Stepping back into the house, I gazed a long time at *The Cliffs at Etretat* still resting against the wall. Jericho had devoted months of his life to this work, cut himself off from everyone in the house—utterly isolated—as he labored over the scheme he was certain would fix everything. And now here sat the finished product, along with his father's painting down the hall, and he had rushed off without giving either a backward glance.

Alone in the foyer, I listened for any sound from upstairs. Nothing. Were Ivy Leigh and Agnes sorting through photos, assembling a timeline like the one Nancy and I had created on my kitchen table? Should I offer to help? Or let her piece together her unknown past with the friend she trusted? After all, Ivy Leigh and I were virtual strangers with decades of silence separating us. Why hadn't I tried to find her? Why hadn't she come home? The burden of unanswered questions, inexcusable behavior, overcame me. Approaching the staircase, I sank down on the second step.

The door to my room opened. Agnes started down the stairs. "What's going on?" she asked. "Where is everybody?"

I glanced over my shoulder. "Jericho's gone home, and Miriam went with him."

"*What*?" she said, sidling in next to me.

"Roger and Sally drove them to the station," I said, eyes on the floor.

"How cute is that? Has anyone checked on my son lately?"

"No... I should have." I peered at her. "I should've done a lot of things."

She understood I meant more than Denver and slipped her arm around my shoulders.

"That's true of all of us at one time or another." She stood. "Now get up there and help your friend. She's got a *lot* of questions, and you're the only one who has the answers."

Agnes stepped down to the first floor and held out her hand to help me up.

Standing, I gripped the banister and started upstairs. I knocked on my door; Ivy Leigh invited me in. She was sitting, facing the window, in one of the chairs she and Agnes had pulled to the side of the bed to create a makeshift desk.

Franny's life lay scattered on the white bedspread, haphazard, half-sorted, piled, tattered. Ivy Leigh's arm was draped over the arm rest, Franny's note on mauve paper, lavender scent long since evaporated, dangling from her hand...the note beginning "Dear Barbara," ending:

*Know that I've paid dearly for the choice I made—lived in constant fear they would find out. By now you'll know I died a coward leaving the secret with you alone. Do with it as you think best.*

She did not stir. I lingered in the open door.

"Is there more?" she asked, staring straight ahead.

"I have her will and other papers." I inched forward. "I haven't been through Franny's house yet. There hasn't been time." I babbled excuses. "Everything happened so fast. Justine showed up...and then left...without the baby...and then Nancy came, and I had to find Hank and the baby was sick and Justine was in the hospital, almost dead, and I had to find you and—"

She patted the chair next to her. "Come sit down, Babs."

She was perfectly composed. Exactly as I remembered her.

The years had only made her more of who she already was.

Trustworthy daughter. Level-headed sister. Wise friend.

I sat as she directed and studied her profile. She had the bearing of a classic Greek statue, serene, composed, resolute, one of those pristine white

## Chapter 20 ~ Lost and Found

marble goddesses still atop a pedestal, unperturbed by the rubble left by an earthquake or the centuries.

Leaning forward, I shuffled through the memories to locate the photo Nancy Crisp had left on my car a hundred years ago. I lifted the wedding invitation, playbill from Cherry Hill theater, Hank's postcard from Sweetwater, Texas...*I hope you can forgive me.*

The picture I most wanted to show Ivy Leigh was not here. Had I left it at home?

Growing frantic, I hopped up and scooted around the bed to search the floor.

"My favorite picture...you and your parents," I mumbled, kneeling down to peer under the bed, "I can't find it."

"Is this what you want?" Ivy Leigh asked.

Still on all fours, I peeked over the bed. The black-and-white photo of the Moore family was in her hand. She read the inscription on the back.

"Cab, Clarissa, & Ivy Leigh Moore. 1935," she said, like a newscaster reading off a cue card and then flipped the photo around. "Were you going to tell me I'm the spitting image of my mother? Or that you never saw my dad this happy? Because I can see that."

"Yes," I said, weakly, "that plus, you were awfully cute." Still on my knees, I propped my elbows on the bed. "When I saw that picture of Clarissa, I knew it was all true, before I ever learned the whole story."

"Come on," she said, re-arranging the chairs to face each other. "Tell me."

Rising, I circled the bed and took my place, face to face with Ivy Leigh.

Like Jericho, palette in hand, I was going to paint. Subject: a family of four cobbled together after a tragedy. Focal point: the stunning Francesca Elizabeth Hibbs Moore, who endured loss and the resulting small town gossip, and then seized the chance to start a new life where nobody knew her story...or ever would—neither her own daughter, nor the one she brought up as part of the deal struck to "save the children." Backdrop: Richmond? Where Franny waltzed at cotillions? Or Madison? Where the social highlight of the week for Clarissa was a picnic at Lake Frances.

I started there: "Clarissa (I could not bring myself to say, 'your mother') grew up in Madison...well, a few miles outside the city, actually."

When I described the Murphy family farm where Nancy Crisp still lived, Ivy Leigh interrupted. "I have an aunt?"

"Yes," I said, "and she can't wait to meet you."

"I've never had a family I didn't create myself," she said, like a child surprised with a new toy she had not thought of asking for.

Once the chasm between past and present was breached, the tale unfolded with surprising ease. By now, after hearing the story from Nancy and Hank, and then relating it to Justine, the Moores and Merriers were as familiar to me as my own family. In many ways, I knew more details about them than I did my own parents. Franny was no longer a near mythical character. I now realized her insistence on flawlessness, her preoccupation with propriety, were efforts to replicate the position she had once held—never regained—as Mrs. Henry Fitzsimmons Merrier IV, pinnacle of Richmond society.

I said as much to Ivy Leigh when I finished, and added, "She never stopped dreaming about her old life."

"That's better than what Clarissa did…throw away her child."

She drew the photo closer and examined it like a doctor reading an x-ray.

Again I waited, clueless what to say next. I had expected Ivy Leigh to resist, refuse to believe the truth, as Justine had…but she said nothing at all.

I watched the clock on the nightstand tick away 15 seconds. "Is…is there anything I can do? Do you want to…ask me anything?"

She laid the photo on top of the others. "I should have come home. After enough time passed, I should have ignored those hateful things Mother said and come home. Why didn't I?"

"You mean…what she said when Justine left?"

She nodded. "I got the *same* lecture every time I called…the few times she'd actually talk to me for more than a few minutes."

"You called her?"

"Oh, yes. Week after week." She reached for Cab and Franny's wedding photo lying by itself on the pillow. "Remember when I found this? Could make no sense of it. Why my proper mother got married dressed like *this* instead of a wedding gown? In somebody's living room?"

"I remember."

"Their faces." She laid her finger gently on the image. "Daddy's at least trying to smile, but look at Mother. I never understood why she looked so serious. I thought it was just her, trying to be dignified." She laughed bitterly. That's not it. She was in love, but not with *him*."

"I…I think she grew to love him, just…in a different way than she loved Hank."

## Chapter 20 ~ Lost and Found

She jerked her head up, eyes on fire. "Then why didn't she want to be buried with him?"

An accomplice to this crime, I was being interrogated and had no answers. So I changed the subject.

"I've always wondered if my mother knew. There were so many times I found her and Franny whispering. And when they'd see me, they—"

But it was not my voice Ivy Leigh heard. It was Franny's, whose memory had raided the room with such ferocity, it was impossible to hear above the fray.

"It was my fault," Ivy Leigh said. "That's what she said *every time* I called. It was my fault Justine ran away with 'that artist.' She mimicked Franny's tone. '*You* flirted with him, then you brought him into my house. You and those eyes of yours.'" Ivy Leigh shook her head. "I never understood why she *always* said that. 'Those eyes of yours.' But look here."

She snatched up her family photo again and displayed it. Clarissa's large, bright eyes—dazzling even in black and white—glistened with a hint of mischief and mystery. They were mesmerizing. Everything about Clarissa was captivating. And utterly unforgettable.

"Wonder what color they were," I said softy.

"I wonder if Hank took this photo," Ivy Leigh said, "and she was smiling at *him*."

I had studied the photo dozens of times and never entertained *that* thought. Stunned, I stared into the corner of the ceiling and watched them materialize. There they were: Franny holding Justine while Hank snapped the photo of their friends.

They were all laughing—all six of them, the Moores and the Merriers. Maybe Franny was hopping up and down, dancing with Justine to make Ivy Leigh smile. Then, maybe Cab took the camera while Hank and Franny posed with their daughter.

We sank into silence again, adrift in a sea of unknowns.

"I could ask Hank when I get home," I said. "We've gotten to be pretty good friends."

Even as the sentence slipped out, I winced at this absurdity. What did it matter? But she took no notice. Only placed the photo…face down…with the others.

"My poor father. Can you imagine what he went through all those years? His heart must have been as broken as my mother's…but you never would've known." She dabbed her fingertips at the corner of her eyes. "How's Justine? You said she was in the hospital? Is she all right now?"

"Yeah. On the mend. Doing even better now that my daughter is in charge of her."

As I reviewed my adventures with Justine, Ivy Leigh began to gather up her family history, lining up edges of pictures, refolding papers, asking questions, fitting pieces together.

"Poor Jussie," she said. "Sad as it is, Mother's death is going to leave her in the best shape she's ever been in, once the will is read." Returning her mother's life to the box, she closed the lid. "Who's the executor? Do you know?"

"Yeah. Me."

She buried her face in her hands. "I'm sorry for all the trouble you've had, when it should have been my responsibility."

"I'm sorry, too."

Standing, she picked up her chair to move it back to the table in the corner. "Well, you don't have to worry about this any longer, because I intend to—"

"No." I rose and carried my chair, placing it next to hers. "I'm not sorry about anything I've done for you or Justine." I nudged my chair under the table. "I'm sorry Franny never loved you the same way she loved Justine."

The truth we both knew as children, but never understood, needed to be acknowledged. Ivy Leigh walked to the window to gaze out. "For that, I crossed the street to your house. Your mom loved me exactly as I was." She smiled, unspilled tears pooling in her eyes. "You remember what she used to say, 'There's always room for one more.' That 'one more' was me."

On the second floor of the Magnolia Arms, two friends, who knew each other well and yet not at all, peered out, not speaking, as the postman, the neighbor walking his dog, the plumber taking tools from his truck, went about their daily chores. To these passersbys the day was ordinary. They were utterly unaware that above them, beyond the upstairs window, two women, driven into a storm, hearts pounding, feet shifting, were trying to stay afloat, like sailors clinging to the rails of a sinking ship.

From the moment the Moore family moved in, I had envied Ivy Leigh, dreamed what it would be like walking beside *her* mother into the Garden Club, instead of beside mine into the thrift store; dreamed of living in her house, lavish and unspoiled, instead of in mine where there was never enough of anything except people and racket. Never enough of anything

## Chapter 20 ~ Lost and Found

except love, which my rumpled and warm-hearted mother had bestowed freely on her own children *and* the Moore girls, while Franny was doting on her own daughter and doing her duty by Clarissa's daughter—hurting them both.

"My mom—," I almost said, 'never stopped missing you,' but thought better of it—"always wished I would be more like you," I said, "…more interested in recipes than—"

"What's Asa doing?" Ivy Leigh asked, still intent on the street below.

Glad for the distraction, I joined her at the window. Asa's cab was parked in front of Ida's house. With a large mallet he was hammering a huge white sign into the front yard.

*For Sale. As Is. Make Offer. Inquire at Magnolia Arms. 306 Belmont Drive. Contact Nestor or Agnes Carlyle.*

"That's sad," I said. "Think someone would buy it? Wrecked like that?"

"No idea," Ivy Leigh said. "Have you met Ida?"

"Oh, yes," I said. "We're best buddies since I saved Bernard's life."

"Well, I'll have to hear *that* story," she said, taking my hand. "Come on. Let's go downstairs. Agnes will be worried sick about me, and we need to put her out of her misery."

As simply as that we were drawn back to the present, safe in the Magnolia Arms.

Glancing at Franny's will on the dresser, I left it for later, and followed Ivy Leigh into the hall. We had covered enough ground for now.

We found Torbert and Agnes at the kitchen table. He stood when we entered and took Ivy Leigh in his arms. "You okay?" he asked.

"Better than I've been in a long time," she said.

Over her shoulder, he winked at me and mouthed, "Thank you."

Nestor was on the phone. "No problem," he said. "Go ahead and take her home. There's no need for her to pay for a train ticket after what she's done for us."

Torbert pulled out a chair for his wife and then for me.

"That's Roger," Agnes said, handing Denver to Ivy Leigh before she asked. "Nestor gave him the rest of the day off so he could drive Sally home. Talk about love at first sight."

We settled into ordinary conversation, inquiring first about the Hamptons' honeymoon trip—Paris, the Louvre, the Eiffel Tower. Then Ivy Leigh insisted on being filled in about her old neighbor, Ida, as well as Jericho, whom she had not met, and Miriam, whom she had. She was astonished I had made Miriam an ally, concluding, 'if anyone could have pulled that off, it would be you, Babs.' I repeated the account of our spy operation, assuring everyone I was not exaggerating the sinister atmosphere of Lorraine's house, and then mocked her mincing steps in her snug Asian garb.

Instead of fixing dinner ourselves, we piled into the Hamptons' car and drove to "Mollie's," the restaurant which had gotten its start in the dining room of the Magnolia Arms. Managed by the legendary Muriel Porter, who had known Agnes during her Brighton Park days, we not only enjoyed a sumptuous meal, but inside stories about Agnes as well. Muriel was also a longtime friend of Jonas Grinstead, having known him since he first arrived from Dennisonville, following his broken relationship with Margaret. I reflected—not for the first time—a lifetime spent with these people would be too short.

When we returned home, we found a note on the kitchen table from Roger.

*Sally home. Miriam called. Said they're meeting with Lorraine tomorrow. See you in the morning.*

We said good night. For the first time since I arrived, I went upstairs alone. I closed my door and walked to the dresser to take out my pajamas. There on top was the treasured photo—me, Ivy Leigh, and Justine on that windy day in Memorial Park. Lying next to it was Franny's will. Satisfying as the day had been, my task was not completed until I told Ivy Leigh that Franny's house belonged to her. Tucking the documents under my arm, I eased downstairs and slipped them under Ivy Leigh's door…her old room, the room Jericho had only recently vacated.

Next to the door was Jericho's painting, still propped unceremoniously against the wall.

Leaning back on the opposite wall, I peered at the canvas, faintly illuminated by the light from the upstairs hall. This was the work Jericho had guarded from prying eyes—like mine—so nobody would question his purpose. This was the canvas out of view when he glared down at me the night Ida's house burned. This was the reason he had left his wife behind to worry over him *and* the family business, while he carried out his reckless scheme to reclaim what his sister had stolen. This was his attempt to pay homage, keep his father's legacy alive.

## Chapter 20 ~ Lost and Found

And now the fruit of his labor sat, unadorned, on the floor for all to see. Exhausted, I closed my eyes, imagining what would happen if Ike Greer could walk through the door.

*What's this?* he would ask.

I would tell him the story.

*He went to all this trouble to get my painting back from Lorraine? Why?*

*It was precious to him. The work of your hands. Your legacy,* I would explain.

I knew—though I had never met Ike Greer—exactly what he would say. He would shake his head and chuckle. *That boy. Doesn't he know the best work I left behind was him?*

I left the will with Ivy Leigh, the painting with Ike Greer, and went upstairs.

# Chapter 21

## Till We Meet Again
### Dennisonville, North Carolina
### Jacksonville, Florida
### October 1979

When I woke up, Ivy Leigh was standing next to my bed, Franny's will in her hands.

"Good morning," she said. "You awake?"

One eye open, I rolled onto my back. "I am now."

"I thought you'd like to get an early start since it's your last day here. Agnes doesn't teach today, so we can—"

I blinked both eyes open. "Who said it's my last day?"

"I did," she said. "We'd go today, but I *can't* do that to Agnes."

"We?" Still groggy, I sat up. "You're leaving, too?"

She started toward the door. "There's a train that leaves at 9:30 in the morning. That'll be perfect. Think your daughter's up this early?"

I squinted at the alarm clock. "What time is it?"

"6:00."

"Yeah. She'll be up with the baby. Why?"

"Would you call her? Ask her to call your lawyer this morning"—she glanced at the label on the envelope—"Charles Hart? And make an appointment for me by the end of the week."

I swung my legs over the edge of the bed. "You're going home with *me*?"

"That's why you came, isn't it?" She held up the will. "To give me this…tell me Mother's house belongs to me."

I nodded. "Yeah…it was actually your grandmother's house. Clarissa's mother."

"Right. Mumsie wasn't my dad's aunt," she said, half-asking, half-stating. "What about Nancy? The sister. Did she get anything of her mother's? Because if she didn't—"

"She got the farm...in Madison."

"Hmm," she said, one foot out the door. "I'll have to see her while I'm there. How far away is Madison from Jacksonville? I don't remember."

"About an hour and a half."

"Think you could drive me over one day?"

I was getting more confused by the minute. "Sure. Could we talk about this after I've had some coffee? It's been a hard week."

"You've had a hard *month*," she said with a smile. "I shouldn't have sprung so much on you first thing in the morning. I forgot it takes you so long to wake up."

"Long to wake up? How long have I had? Ninety seconds?" I grabbed my bathrobe from the foot of the bed.

"Will I recognize the old neighborhood, you think?" she asked.

Standing, I put on my robe and tied the sash. "Yes. It's pretty much the same. You won't recognize my"—after her glowing tribute to my mother, I hesitated to tell her how much I had redecorated—"my house. It's been updated...a little."

She leaned against the door frame. "I can't wait to walk through your front door again. I thought about it last night. I'll tell you one thing," she said, eyebrows raised, "when I walk through Mother's front door, I'm *not* going to take my shoes off."

"What?"

"Don't you remember? *Shoes*"—she mimicked Franny's voice—"every time we walked in. Every time *anyone* walked in. Spring, summer, winter, fall. Rain or shine. Shoes *off*."

"I remember." I hadn't heard Franny say that in years. I guess there was less need...since few people came to visit.

"All that time..." She shook her head. "She was ordering me around my *own* house. It didn't even *belong* to her. That must have been so frustrating for her."

"I thought that, too...once I found out."

She shook off the memory. "Breakfast is ready. Let's get going."

"Let me get dressed first." I joined her at the door. "But we're going to talk about this 'leaving thing.' I told Agnes I'd help with her book. I've barely gotten started."

## Chapter 21 ~ Till We Meet Again

"Agnes understands," she said and started downstairs.

Rubbing my eyes, I ambled toward the bathroom and turned on the faucet. While I waited for the water to warm, I lectured myself in the mirror.

"Get hold of yourself, Babs. You knew you'd have to leave sooner or later. You came to find Ivy Leigh. You found her. And that's that."

I splashed warm water on my face. For that matter, I'd found Justine, too, *and* Hank. Franny wasn't the only one who had cemented together a family out of the rubble of bad choices. And now Topeka would connect the reunited Merrier family to mine.

When Justine came to my door, I never dreamed the baby she held was the one my daughter had prayed for. I pressed the towel to my face, picturing Anne, fussing over Topeka, Hank heading out the door with Caesar, Justine sneering at the bowl of raisin bran Anne had served instead of bacon and eggs.

There in my kitchen—my mother's kitchen—four people were finding comfort in each other. What had Ivy Leigh said? 'I never had a family I didn't create'? The home where I grew up was still doing exactly what a home was supposed to do—take in strangers and make friends of them—while across the street Franny's stately house stood pristine, good taste wall to wall, and empty…as it had been for decades. Home to two girls brought up with every advantage, the house sat silent, unstirred by the chaos visitors bring. *Why* had I longed to live there?

And when had I stopped wanting to?

Somewhere between the Madison cemetery, the Murphy farm, St. Vincent's ICU, and the bathroom on the second floor of the Magnolia Arms, I had stopped picturing *myself* in Franny's house and started imagining a "For Sale" sign in the front yard.

But Ivy Leigh had not reacted like I thought she would. Were we going to rush back so she could claim her inheritance? Did she and Torbert want to become "snowbirds," spending the winter in Jacksonville? They didn't seem like the type.

Would I now have to tell Justine our plan was out the window?

I got dressed and trudged downstairs to begin my last day. The hall was unearthly quiet, the kitchen sedate. Torbert, half-glasses perched on the end of his nose, was scratching away at the morning crossword puzzle. Ivy Leigh was cooing over Denver. The sun shone through the window onto the African violets. Agnes was scrubbing dishes, humming…what was the tune? "The Anniversary Waltz"? When I walked to the counter and picked up the coffee pot, I heard her sniffle. Turning, I saw a single tear course down her cheek. I put down my cup and stepped next to her.

She dropped the dishcloth into the sink and wrapped her arms around me, her wet, soapy hands soaking the back of my blouse.

"I knew you weren't going to stay forever," she said, voice breaking. "And I know you've only been here a little while, but you're one of my best friends."

"I feel the same way," I said.

"Come on, you two," Ivy Leigh said. "Stop that. You'll get me started."

Torbert, eyes glued to the newspaper, said with mock gruffness, "That's enough of that, ladies. I'm the only man here, and I can't handle *three* crying women."

"I'll come back to visit," I said, returning to my coffee cup. "And you could always—"

There was a knock; the back door opened. "Yoo-hoo. Babysitter's here." Gretchen Tate, a knitting bag over her arm, entered the kitchen.

Ivy Leigh hopped up and hugged her. "How are you and how's Moe?"

"Oh, he's fine. He and Roger had already started a checker game when I left."

The plan for the day unfolded. Roger was on loan to the Whispering Pines, manning the check-in desk *and* Moe, while Gretchen kept Denver. Agnes, Ivy Leigh, and I were to have the whole day together. Torbert had plans of his own.

Knowing how important the day was, Nestor had driven the car to school and left the truck for us. Ivy Leigh asked Torbert if he minded our being away all day. It was the first time they had been apart since their honeymoon.

"Don't you worry about me," he said. "I've got calls to make."

"You do, too, Babs," Ivy Leigh said. "The appointment with the lawyer?"

So I called Anne, who was delighted to hear I had found Ivy Leigh and was bringing her with me tomorrow.

"Wait till you see the baby," Anne said. "You won't believe how she's blossomed. Hold on a minute, Mom." She turned away from the receiver. "What? Yes. Okay…Mom, is Ivy Leigh there right now? Justine wants to speak to her."

"Yes. She's right here." I held out the receiver to Ivy Leigh. "Your sister wants to speak to you." She came to the phone and handed Denver to me.

262

## Chapter 21 ~ Till We Meet Again

"Hello? Hi, Jussie. It's good to hear your voice, too." One by one, the rest of us quietly left the room. The last words I heard Ivy Leigh say as I stepped into the hall were, "Of course we're still sisters. And we're going to start acting like we are."

I went to my room to start packing. At 9:00 we climbed into the truck, Agnes, behind the wheel, my short little self between my two tall friends. I asked where we were going.

"Raleigh," Ivy Leigh said. "I asked Justine what she needed. She said she didn't need anything and wouldn't tell me her size. Do you know?"

"When she first came, she was about a 22, but Anne's had her on a diet, so she may be smaller by now."

Ivy Leigh stared out the window. "Maybe a nice sweater. Or a new purse." She turned to me. "Does she have a nice purse?"

In an instant I was back at my house, opening the door to find Justine with Topeka in her arms and the smelly pink polka dot bookbag, ripped at one corner, over her shoulder.

"No. She doesn't have a purse. That's a good idea."

"And the baby. Topeka? I'll get a few things for her, too. She's my great niece, isn't she? I think that's right."

"You have to admire Justine," Agnes said, "trying to raise a baby at her age. That can't be easy. It's nice she has you to help, Babs."

"I'm not the only one," I said and shared the news about the adoption.

Agnes started crying again. "That's the sweetest story I ever heard. I'm going to *have* to come down there and meet them." She brightened. "Wait a minute. If you're going to be Topeka's grandmother, you two will be related…some way or other."

We shopped all morning, swapping stories about ourselves and our families as we sorted through pink dresses and sleepers, frilly socks and tiny patent leather shoes. Over lunch, bags on the seats between us or under the table, Agnes told Ivy Leigh she didn't know what she would've done if I hadn't shown up when I did. She credited me with winning Miriam over, undisguising Jericho, and helping Roger on the road to a new identity.

"Babs changed everything," Agnes told Ivy Leigh.

"So did you, when *you* came," Ivy Leigh said.

When we turned onto Belmont Drive late that afternoon, Agnes pointed at Ida's house. "What's going on there?"

The ruined section of Ida's house was disappearing, blackened timbers and debris piled high in her driveway.

"They've made a lot of progress in one day," Ivy Leigh said, leaning forward to peer through the windshield. "Drive down there."

We parked in front of Ida's house and got out. Torbert and Nestor, soiled and sweating, met us on the sidewalk. They looked exhausted, but were both grinning.

"What in the world are you doing?" Agnes asked.

"Demo," Torbert said.

"Demo?" I asked.

"Demolition," Ivy Leigh said. "So you were able to get a permit today?"

"No problem," Torbert said, wiping his face with a handkerchief.

"I know a guy at City Hall," Nestor said.

"When we remodeled our house," Agnes explained to me, "Nestor learned a few things."

"Does Ida know you're doing this?" I asked. "I mean…it's her house."

"Not for long," Torbert said. "She's coming back at the end of the week to sign a contract."

"Who would buy a burned-up house?" I asked.

"Me," Torbert said, tossing another board onto the pile. "I need something to occupy my time while my wife is in Jacksonville, and it will make the street look better."

"Ida needs the money," Ivy Leigh said to me. "I called her last night to tell her how sorry I was about her house, asked if there was anything I could do."

"That place her brother is living isn't cheap," Torbert said, closing the toolbox.

"And so, just like that, you decided to buy her house?" I asked.

"It's the simplest solution," Torbert said. "I've already talked to my boy Ham. He's going to help me, and I've hired Roger, too. I'm going to teach him as we go along. When we're finished, Nestor and Agnes can rent the house to a nice family and manage the property."

"In the meantime," Agnes asked, "who's got Denver?"

"Roger," Nestor said. "We've been taking shifts."

"I should check on him," Agnes said. "He may need help."

"Roger or the baby?" I asked.

"Both."

"I'll go with you," Nestor said. "I need to get the tarp from the garage."

Ivy Leigh stayed behind to talk to her husband. I walked with Nestor and Agnes back to the Magnolia Arms.

## Chapter 21 ~ Till We Meet Again

"Didn't you say Torbert was a retired janitor?" I asked when we were out of earshot.

"Uh-huh."

"How can he afford to buy a house…just like that?"

"He lives very simply," Agnes said. "Socks away his money. Only spends it on antique cars and people he loves. After Ivy Leigh told him Ida was worried about money, he said, 'I can fix that.' And that was that."

"A lot happened after I went upstairs," I said.

"It always does," she said, laughing.

That night we ate at home, huddled around the table, grim as a family waiting for news in a hospital waiting room. Ivy Leigh did her best to distract us with more questions about recent events, but none of us could cheer up.

Agnes stood. "I'm going to call and get a substitute for my class in the morning. I'm going with you to the train station."

Ivy Leigh tugged on her arm to make her sit. "No, you're not." Agnes plopped down. "I warned you about this when you took over as manager. If you run a house like this, you have to learn to let people go." She patted Agnes' arm. "Babs won't be back, but I will."

*Who says I won't be back?* I thought.

Anxious about the next day, I woke in the middle of the night. It felt strange being upstairs alone and in some kind of peculiar way, I actually missed Miriam. My thoughts shifted to Ivy Leigh. I glanced at the clock. Five minutes past midnight. I stared at the ceiling a while and then decided a glass of milk wouldn't hurt anything. I tiptoed downstairs and was almost to the kitchen when I heard her voice.

Hers was the only voice I heard, so I knew she was on the phone. I stopped beside the door and pressed my back against the wall and listened.

"We're leaving tomorrow…I'm not really up to a trip, but…uh-huh…I meet with the lawyer day after tomorrow…yes, the house is *mine*…I have the will right here in my hand…I know, right?…all these years I've *never* owned a house. Now I do. Who would've thought?"

I slipped back upstairs before she hung up. I didn't want to believe what I'd heard, but it must be true. Ivy Leigh had lived in this beautiful house for years, but it had never belonged to her. Maybe the satisfaction of owning Franny's home—where she had been shackled by a long list of "don'ts"—was irresistible.

We woke early to have breakfast with Agnes. In the cold light of day Ivy Leigh wasn't nearly so philosophical about leaving as the night before. Agnes hung on us both till Nestor gently took her arm and walked out with her. I watched through the kitchen window as he opened the truck door and then leaned in to kiss her goodbye while she sat behind the steering wheel. When I turned around, Torbert and Ivy Leigh, holding hands, were talking in low voices at the kitchen table. I made an excuse to leave so they could be alone.

*And* so I could be alone with the house. I stepped into the parlor, gazing around, imprinting the scene on my memory. Then I struggled down the hall, peeking into the dining room one last time, imagining us gathered at the table.

I had one foot on the stairs when I heard a knock at the front door. Since everyone was occupied, I answered it, and found Asa Ludlow, gripping the handle of a Stanley toolbox. Next to him, toting an army green backpack, was a short squarely built man, wearing black-framed glasses, thinning silvery hair, beard neatly trimmed. He wore a blue flannel shirt, pencil in pocket, khaki pants, at least one size too large, held up by a black belt, notches added, and scuffed hiking boots. In his arms, cradled like a sleeping child, was a battered violin case.

"Hello, Asa," I said.

Asa touched the bill of his newsboy cap. "This is Dr. Tuttle. Just got in town this morning. He met Mary Grace at the welcome table at the station, and she sent him over. You have a room, right?"

"Yes." I did a quick calculation. "One upstairs and one down here."

Dr. Tuttle spoke, low, as if someone might overhear. "I can move in right away?"

"Yes. Of course." I opened the door wide to allow him in.

He stepped closer. "Take this?" He held out his violin case. I took it without question. After he lugged in his backpack, he took the toolbox from Asa and dug in his pocket for a $10 bill. "Will that do?"

"Yes, sir," Asa said, then spoke to me. "Heard you're leaving this morning, Mrs. Allgrove. Will be you needing a ride to the station? I could wait."

"No, Ivy Leigh's husband is taking us. But thank you."

"Next time you're in town then," he said, "or maybe me and the missus will come to Florida to see you." I winced, picturing Bridey Ludlow banging on *my* front door, bulging suitcase in hand. At least she couldn't bring food with her.

I told Asa goodbye and closed the door. Dr. Tuttle was admiring *The Cliffs at Etretat.*

## Chapter 21 ~ Till We Meet Again

"Pretty," he said. "What's it doing on the floor?"

*How could I explain in a few words?*

"It was delivered yesterday," I said. "Belongs to a former tenant. He left in a hurry. Emergency at home."

"Hmm." He pointed to the violin case I was holding. "I'll take that now."

I returned it to him. "You're a violinist?"

He shook his head. "Geologist. Flannel shirt should have been a giveaway."

"Oh...I didn't know. I'll remember that."

"Inside joke," he said, straight-faced.

"But the violin?" I asked.

"My wife's," was all he said.

I eased behind the check-in desk. "If you'll sign here, I'll get the manager." I flipped the register around to face him. He printed his name. *Cosmo Tuttle.*

And to think I was *leaving* today and would have to wait to hear *his* story.

I found Nestor in the kitchen, where Torbert was reviewing the day's work. I told Nestor there was a new tenant and suggested he put him in the first floor room.

"You don't really want to move this guy in next to Miriam," I said. "Not a good idea."

Nestor met Cosmo, who took one look at the first floor room and said he would take it.

I climbed to the 3rd floor for one last glimpse out the tall arched window and made a farewell visit to my room. When I returned downstairs, I noticed the painting was gone from the hall. I asked Nestor about it when I said goodbye.

"Where's Jericho's painting? Did you put it with his father's?"

He shook his head. "No. Cosmo asked if he could put it in his room. So I said yes. After all, we do have *two*."

*Cliffs*, I thought. *Perfect painting for a geologist.*

Like it was here...waiting for him to arrive.

I told Roger goodbye and gave Denver a final hug. Torbert carried our luggage to the car, and I climbed in the backseat. When we reached the corner, I looked back at the Magnolia Arms, vowing to return. At the station, I promised Torbert I'd take care of Ivy Leigh and boarded the train to give them time alone. When Ivy Leigh joined me, neither of us spoke at first. I wanted to launch right into my questions: did she really need her mother's house and why was she in such a rush to claim it, when she never—?

"What do you think about my house?" Ivy Leigh asked.

Too far away in my own thoughts, I asked her to repeat the question.

"My house," she said. "What do you think about it?"

And just like that, she brought up the subject herself. I landed on it with both feet.

"I've always *loved* your house. You know that. So did your mother. That's why she trusted me to take care of it. I'll admit I once hoped to move into it myself, but that was before Justine came back." I paused, drawing in a deep breath to throw the final punch. "She has *nothing*. And poor Hank…lost his whole *family*. All he has is that dog."

"What in the world are you talking about, Babs?" she asked.

"Franny's house. *Your* house. I honestly thought you—"

"I wasn't talking about my *mother's* house. I meant the Magnolia Arms."

"Oh…" I managed a tiny smile. "I've never seen another house like it."

She turned sideways in her seat, forehead creased, and peered at me. "Do you honestly think I'm going back with you to get what's coming to me and kick Justine to the curb?"

"I heard you on the phone last night. You said you'd never owned a house and now you do. You said Franny ordered you around a house that didn't even belong to her…and…she did. I know that. And she *was* hard on you, and she *did* blame you for Justine leaving, and it *is* your house now. You have to feel vindicated."

"Vindicated? I don't feel any such thing. Do you honestly think I want some kind of revenge on the woman who fixed my meals and washed my clothes and made sure I had a clean bed to sleep in for my *whole* life?"

"Well…yeah…she hurt you badly enough you haven't been home in almost 30 years."

She let out a long sigh. "That was *her* decision. Not mine. I had to play the role she assigned me to play. I couldn't take a place in her life she wouldn't allow me to take."

"But it must feel good to know you're getting *something* from her after all these years. Especially the thing she loved best."

"Bless your heart, Babs. Have you been worried about that all this time?"

"Well, *yes*. If you could see Justine, you'd know she needs more than a sweater and a purse."

## Chapter 21 ~ *Till We Meet Again*

"I *know* that. Don't you think I've regretted it a million times that I brought that artist into my house? You and I were lucky. We escaped. Justine's the one he conned, and her life's been a mess ever since. I'm going home with you so I can sign over the house to *her*. I don't need it or want it."

"But on the phone you said…"

"I was talking to my friend Margaret. She lived with me at the Magnolia Arms for years. And how we're both married to these amazing men, and for the first time in our lives, we're not *renters*. We talk about it all the time."

I ducked my head. "I'm sorry. I feel like an idiot. I've just gotten so wrapped up with your family. I want to fix the mess they're in. The mess they *made*."

She patted my arm. "It's what you do. You did the same thing with Jericho's family."

I laughed. "I can't seem to mind my own business, can I?"

"You never could. But then…I don't either. It's what makes us loveable. Come on." She stood in the aisle. "Let's go the dining car. You obviously need more coffee."

We found the dining car and sat across from each other at a table.

"So," Ivy Leigh said, "you married Harry Allgrove. I knew you'd end up together."

I stirred cream into my coffee. "You're just saying that."

"No. He started talking about you when we were in 8$^{th}$ grade. I told him not to give up. I guess he didn't."

Before long we were gabbing like schoolgirls. I filled her in on the old neighborhood, my children's births, my parents' deaths, my life with Franny. She told about meeting Marshall Ransom in the VA hospital where she volunteered, marrying him, and moving to Dennisonville. She "introduced" me to her friend Margaret Hawthorne and shared the story about Jonas Grinstead—how he built the Magnolia Arms, lost Margaret, and then Agnes reunited them.

The trip home was half as long as the trip to Dennisonville.

We spotted our welcome committee before the train came to a stop. There was Anne, behind Topeka's stroller, holding a poster board: "Welcome Home, Mom." Next to her Justine, sporting new clothes and a perky hairstyle, had her own sign: "Welcome Home, Sis." Hank and Ruby, holding hands, stood next to them.

"A lot happened while I was gone," I said.

"Me, too." She squeezed my hand. "Thank you…for finding me."

## The Moores, the Merriers

We stepped off the train to a joyous jumble. The signs dropped while Anne wept on my shoulder—"I'm going to be a mom. Can you believe it?"—and Justine wept on Ivy Leigh's—"I can't believe you're here. You *still* want to be sisters?" Then we switched. Justine and I thanked each other. Anne told Ivy Leigh she felt like she was meeting a celebrity. And then Ruby nudged in to hug Ivy Leigh and say how much we had missed her, while Hank swept me up in his arms and asked how he could ever thank me enough.

Caesar was waiting to welcome us when we reached home. Ivy Leigh walked in, set down her suitcase, and stood still, surveying the house.

"It's good to be back," she said. "I keep thinking your mom's going to come from the kitchen, wearing that daisy apron. Mind if I look around?"

"Help yourself," I said.

Before she started upstairs, she gazed out my living room window at Franny's house. I couldn't read her expression and couldn't begin to imagine what she was thinking.

The ladies from the over-60s class had stock-piled enough food to last us three days. I had expected we would all have supper together, but after an hour Anne startled me by bringing Topeka to me to "say goodbye."

"You're not staying?" I asked.

"I moved home several days ago," Anne said. "Justine's idea. She wanted Topeka to get used to the idea of thinking of me as her mother and feeling like my house was her home."

"That's brilliant," I said. "I'd never have thought of it."

Apparently, I'd misjudged both Ivy Leigh *and* Justine.

Anne's was not the only surprise that night. Though she had hinted about Hank and Ruby becoming more than "friends," it was evident their romance had moved at lightning speed while I was away. They were inseparable. And while Anne had transformed Justine, Ruby had done the same for Hank. He, too, was wearing new clothes, had obviously been to the barber my dad used to go to, and literally had rosy cheeks. Ruby, perpetually proper, tried to appear as if Hank's arm on the back of her chair was nothing new. I tried not to stare, but I couldn't help it.

There was entirely too much ground to cover during one meal. We bounced from how Topeka had grown to Justine's weight loss to Ivy Leigh's honeymoon. After Ivy Leigh told how I had pulled off an art heist, all attention turned to me.

"Not tonight," I said. "I'm worn out."

## Chapter 21 ~ Till We Meet Again

"Me, too," Ruby said, standing. "I'm going to clean up these dishes and head home."

This, I discovered, was a pre-arranged plan.

Hank laid his hand on Ivy Leigh's. "If you don't mind, I'd like to take you for a drive, so I can tell you about your mother."

"You mean Clarissa?" she asked.

"Yes. You need to know there was more to her than…what happened between us. I don't want that to define her in your mind."

"I'd like that." She turned to Justine. "You want to come along?"

"No. Dad already told me…and about our mom, too. Back before everything happened. She was very different."

Ivy Leigh stood. "I'll get my purse." She stopped on her way to the living room. "Babs, be sure to call Agnes and let her know we're home."

# Chapter 22

# The Beginning
### Jacksonville, Florida
### October-November 1979

When I woke the next morning, I smelled coffee and found Caesar resting his head on the edge of my bed, his big black eyes beseeching me to get up.

"Aww," I said, stroking his head, "you missed me while I was gone."

I sat up and spotted his "baby," the floppy toy Hank had used to distract him at Franny's funeral, on the floor. Caesar sat at attention, waiting. I tossed the toy into the hall. He loped away and brought it back before I could put on my bathrobe.

I glanced at the clock—6:15. Early. But I was grateful I had slept at all after the news Agnes had shared when I called the Magnolia Arms the night before.

Downstairs I found Hank and Ivy Leigh in the kitchen. Justine, they told me, was on her way to babysit Topeka while Anne was at work. Ruby had driven her over.

"Were you two up late?" I asked, popping a slice of bread into the toaster.

"Not too late," Hank said.

Ivy Leigh asked if I called Agnes.

"I did," I said. "There's a *lot* going on."

"Eggs?" Hank asked, stationed at the stove.

"Just one. Scrambled."

"Tell me," Ivy Leigh said, pulling out a chair.

She had been crying. Eyes puffy, face pale, she was doing her best to sound nonchalant.

"She insisted on hearing about your reunion first," I said. "I gave her the rundown and told her you and Hank had gone out for a drive after supper. She was excited."

"So, she's okay?" Ivy Leigh asked. "She takes goodbyes so hard."

The toast popped up. I carried it to the table and reached for the butter. "I think there was so much going on yesterday she didn't have time to dwell on it."

"What happened?" she asked.

"When she came home from school, she saw a whole crew working on Ida's house. She was worried because she thought they had left Denver alone, but when she came in, Nestor was there. She said, 'If you're here, who's the other guy working on the house?' He said, 'Cosmo.'"

"Torbert put him to work that soon?" Ivy Leigh asked.

"No. Cosmo *offered*. After Nestor showed him around, he asked about the burned-up house down the street. Nestor told him, and Cosmo asked if he could help." I bit into my toast. "Torbert says Cosmo's every bit as good a carpenter as he is."

"I thought he was a geologist."

"He is…but his dad was a carpenter, and building is his *hobby*."

A gentle smile eased across her face. "That house. I've seen it happen time and again through the years. Somehow the right people always show up at the right time." She leaned back. "Have they heard from Miriam?"

Hank served my breakfast and sidled up next to Ivy Leigh.

"Not yet," I said. "But what about you two? Get a lot of talking done?"

Hank took Ivy Leigh's hand in both of his. "I'll tell you the truth. It took me a while to convince myself I was talking to the same little girl who used to play in my front yard."

"And how about you?" I asked Ivy Leigh. "What was it like getting to know Clarissa?"

I realized too late it was the *wrong* thing to say. She turned away and reached for a yellow legal pad in the center of the table.

"I think we need to take care of business first," she said.

"I'll let you get to it," Hank said. "I'm going to go see what Ruby's up to."

He zeroed in on me, giving a quick nod at Ivy Leigh as he stepped through the back door. I understood his meaning: *Take care of her.*

"Hank and Ruby," I said cheerily. "Who would've thought?"

Ivy Leigh said nothing. Head down, pen in hand, she began marking her list, doodling aimlessly, underlining as she talked, detached, like a secretary

## Chapter 22 ~ The Beginning

reading minutes of a meeting. She read, taut-voiced, willing herself to stay on task and move forward.

But the pain she was trying to outrun was stepping on her heels.

"Appointments with the lawyer will take priority," she said, clicking the top of the pen. "We'll plan around those. Will you go with Anne to her appointments…about the adoption?"

"We haven't talked about it yet."

She pointed to the next item, hand trembling. "I should visit Daddy's grave. And go to Madison to Mother's"—she closed her eyes—"I mean Franny's…and Clarissa's." She slammed down the pen. Her voice rose. "What in the *world* am I supposed to call *them*?"

Pushing back from the table, she stormed to the sink, planted both hands on the counter edge and leaned over, shoulders heaving as she tried to regain control. I hurried over and put my arm around her.

"I'm sorry," was all I could say. "It's going to take time—"

"It hit me last night," she said, "when Hank told me…about the wreck…when my mother died. I don't even *remember* her, but I felt like I lost her yesterday." She turned to face me. "I've lost *two* mothers, and I never knew *either one of them*."

Of all the heart-stopping moments I had endured since Franny died, this was the worst. My beautiful friend Ivy Leigh—I'd admired, envied, lost, found, brought home—needed answers from me. But what could I say that could possibly help?

"I've had more time to get used to the idea than you have." I took a glass from the cabinet and filled it from the faucet. "I truly believe Franny *thought* she was doing the right thing."

She took the water. "You mean cutting a deal with my father so she could put a roof over her daughter's head? Or lying to us for all these years?"

"I wouldn't put it that way exactly."

She gulped the water and set down the glass. "How *would* you put it?"

I leaned against the counter. "Times were hard. It wasn't like Franny could go out and get a job at Prudential. She didn't know how to *do* anything, except make a home."

She scoffed. "Some home. Beautiful dishes we never used. Vases we never put flowers in. More rules than a convent." She pointed out the window at her old home across the street. "She loved that house more than she loved me."

"I don't think that's true," I said, though I did.

"And all along it was mine. The house was *mine*. Do you *know* how that makes me feel?"

"How could I?" I said. "Come sit down." I guided her back to the table and sat next to her. "But don't you see? In some ways Franny made you who you are."

She bristled. "Don't say that. I'm *nothing* like her."

"That's my point. Sometimes a negative example is more powerful than a positive one."

"What do you mean?" she asked, sinking back into the chair.

"I've seen with my own eyes what you've done at the Magnolia Arms. That house is twice as beautiful as Franny's. It could've been a showplace, but because of you…who you *are*…anyone can walk through the door and feel at home, put their feet up. Grab any book off the shelf. Leave it on the coffee table when they're done. Play the chess game that's never over."

Feeling a twinge of homesickness, I stopped talking. No good for *me* to get weepy.

She raised her head slowly. "Surely you *know* where I learned that."

"Like I said—"

"From *your* mother. Don't you know how *jealous* I was of you? I would've traded places with you in a New York second. Why do you think I was over here all the time?"

"To see me?" I said.

"That, too." She brushed a crumb from the table and stood up. "I need to get hold of myself before I meet the lawyer. It's one thing to make a fool of myself in front of you. I can't do that in front of a stranger."

I got up and hugged her. "You didn't make a fool of yourself."

She stepped to the window to gaze across the street. "Hank told me as soon as we get back, I have to go into Mother's house. He said once he and Justine went in together and faced everything, they were better." She turned around. "I have to go home again."

I nodded at the pegboard by the door. "Key's right there, whenever you're ready."

"It *is* a beautiful house," she said, still gazing out the window. "I hope the right person will come along…give it new life and…be a good neighbor to you. That would be ideal."

Ivy Leigh said nothing as we left the neighborhood and drove down Riverside Avenue. I respected her silence, aware she was struggling to rein in her emotions before our appointment. The only time she breached the silence

## Chapter 22 ~ The Beginning

was when we crossed the St. Johns River. She leaned forward, peering at the Jacksonville skyline. 'Beautiful,' she said. 'I'd forgotten how much I love this view.' By the time we sat across from Charles Hart and legal jargon started flying, Ivy Leigh had transformed into a businesswoman. Despite my 'official status' as executor, I felt extraneous and kept quiet, nodding when appropriate.

"I feel better now that we've made a start," Ivy Leigh said when we got back in the car. "We'll have to find a realtor. Any suggestions?"

"I'll ask my son," I said, half-hearted. "He knows everything."

"You okay?" she asked.

"Yeah. I've known for a long time we'd sell Franny's house. I'm just...worried about letting it go. I want someone who'll appreciate it and take care of it. It's not just *any* house."

"You'll know when the right buyer comes along."

"I don't suppose you could stay till I find one?"

She laughed. "I'll stay long enough to put all the pieces in place and sign the papers I need to." She squeezed my arm. "And spend some time with you and Justine."

After lunch Ivy Leigh took the key to Franny's house and crossed the street. I watched from the window as she unlocked the door and went inside. I stepped to the table to put away the chicken salad we'd had for lunch. The phone rang.

It was Ivy Leigh. "I can't believe my eyes. Mother kept this."

"What?"

"The huge picture of me and Justine in our plaid skirts and those frilly blouses."

"There are pictures of you all over the house," I said. "Wait till you go upstairs."

"I've always pictured her methodically getting rid of any reminder of me, but they're still here. The house looks exactly the same as when I left 27 years ago."

"I *told* you...she said, 'find my girls'...*plural*...both of you."

She let go a long sigh. "I should've come home a long time ago. I wish I had."

"You're home now."

And so was I.

The next five days were packed with schedules, business appointments, visits from Franny's friends, staying up late to eat popcorn and tell stories with

Justine, packing up Franny's house, traveling to Madison to visiting the cemetery and put flowers on both mothers' graves and meet Nancy Crisp, who drove us to Cherry Lake, showed us where the Moores and Merriers used to live, and where the auditorium used to stand where one community theater performance altered so many lives. "Aunt Nancy" presented Ivy Leigh with a box of mementoes, including a baby sweater and her original birth certificate.

We called the Magnolia Arms every night. They were as busy as we were. The repairs on Ida's house, thanks to the skill of two master craftsmen, Torbert and Cosmo, and the assistance of Roger and Nestor, were almost complete.

"You can't tell the house was ever damaged," Torbert told her. "Everything's finished. We're just waiting on the buyers to choose appliances."

"Buyers?" Ivy Leigh said, and glanced at me, listening in at the kitchen table.

"Who?" I asked.

She held up her hand to quiet me as she listened. Her eyes grew wide with surprise. Then she held the receiver away from her face as she told me.

"Nice couple with two teenage daughters," she said, eyes twinkling. "Recently sold the family business. Want to start over someplace else. They're drawing up a contract."

"You can't mean—"

She grinned. "Uh-huh. Jericho and his family. But he's going by 'John Greer' now."

"They let Lorraine have the business. Jericho was okay with that?"

"Just a minute." She repeated my question to Torbert, then held out the phone. "He doesn't know anything about Lorraine. He's gone to get Agnes. Here. You talk to her. You know the story better than I do."

Agnes picked up the phone. "Hello?"

"Jericho is moving into Ida's house?" I asked. "You can't be serious."

She laughed. "It's true. After they wrangled with Lorraine a few days, Jericho's wife begged him to stop fighting. They're selling out to Sam Wilson."

"I can't believe it. What did Sam say?"

"He said to leave Lorraine to him. He had deep pockets, a bulldog for a lawyer, and on top of that, he'd fought Rommel and won."

"That's hilarious," I said.

"That's not the best part," she said. I could tell she was grinning.

"Go on."

## Chapter 22 ~ The Beginning

"It's Miriam. I *wish* you could see her. She's a different person. She said getting back into the 'legal realm,'—that's what she called it—"was the best she had felt in a long time. She's looking into becoming a paralegal."

"She's already got the degree. She told us that a while ago."

"Uh-huh. So, Jericho…uh, John's coming back, but Miriam's going home. She said she has to start living where she *is*, not where she used to be."

"Oh, Agnes, I'm sorry. That leaves you with a lot of empty rooms."

"Not really. There's a geology conference at UNC Chapel Hill next month. Cosmo invited his friends to stay here. Not long-term, but the house will be full for a week anyway."

So we all moved forward…valiantly at times…halting at others, dealing with the debris of the past, some we had created ourselves, some left behind by the flawed people we loved, each of us letting go, handing over something…or someone…to the care of another.

We were in and out of attorneys' offices: Justine, Anne, and Topeka in the care of family lawyers and adoption case workers; Ivy Leigh and I occupied with probate and inheritance. Tom recommended a realtor, who judged Franny's house 'breathtaking' and urged us to leave it as "staged" as possible, so a buyer could appreciate the potential. 'Leave the painting of the girls,' she advised. 'It's classic.' So we did…along with the antique furniture, Persian rugs, Tiffany lamps. When Ivy Leigh asked if there was anything I wanted… 'anything at all'…I asked for and received the Lenox nativity collection.

When Ivy Leigh announced the date she was leaving, Hank said, "There's one more thing you need to do before you go."

"What's that?" she asked.

"I want you and Justine to be my 'best girls' when I marry Ruby. Would you do that?"

With my family in attendance and Topeka serving as honorary flower girl—a wreath of daisies on her head—Hank and Ruby married in a small ceremony in my living room. I served as Ruby's matron of honor. After the reception, Ivy Leigh suggested we all parade to Memorial Park for wedding photos in front of the winged statue, *Life*, with our beautiful river, always different, always the same, in the background. The day was brilliant, one of those perfect crisp October days when the sky was clear and blue, and the clouds, white and billowing, looked painted.

The final photo, before Hank and Ruby left on their honeymoon, was of the three wedding attendants—me, Justine, and Ivy Leigh—trying to pose, but giggling as a stiff autumn breeze blew in from the St. Johns River.

A week later, our work concluded, Justine and I drove Ivy Leigh to the train station. We could not bear the thought of parting and hugged and cried, said goodbye, and then rushed back for another embrace. We vowed never to be out of touch again, our first reunion scheduled for Thanksgiving, the location yet to be determined. We stood on the platform till her train was out of sight and comforted ourselves with the knowledge she was going back to Torbert. I was jealous she was returning to the Magnolia Arms. We got in the car and started home.

Justine was quiet. *Just sad*, I thought, and did not disturb her. I was glad she didn't want to talk; I wanted to be alone with my thoughts anyway. We were almost home before she drew in a long breath and spoke.

"Anne asked me if she could change Toppy's name when she adopts her."

I did not say how relieved I was. As a longtime school secretary, I had already anticipated the trouble Topeka would have with questions and teasing when she started school.

"I'm…sure it was hard for Anne to ask you," I said. "What did you say?"

"I said it'd be hard for me to call her anything but Toppy. I'm worried now that I hurt Anne's feelings. Do you think I did? I wouldn't do that for anything in the world."

"She didn't say anything to me about it. She's so grateful to you…I'm sure she'll respect your wishes." I paused for a suitable amount of time. "Do you like 'Topeka' as a name?"

"Not really. My daughter was traveling at the time when Topeka was born early…*in* Topeka. She thought it would be funny, that she'd always have a story to tell. What could I say? The name was already on the birth certificate."

"True," I said. "What does Anne want to call her?"

"She wants her to go by her middle name. Hope. She said it fits her. Especially considering the circumstances. You know Toppy. Do *you* think it fits her?"

"I do." I turned onto our street. "Did Anne choose a new middle name?"

"Yes." She paused. "Francesca."

I turned to her so suddenly, my foot slipped off the accelerator. The car slowed to a stop. "She wants to name Topeka after *Franny*?"

She pointed at my house. "Don't you think we should get out of the middle of the street?"

Nosing into the driveway, I put the car in park. "Did Anne say *why* she wants to do that?"

## Chapter 22 ~ The Beginning

"She said my mom had always been a 'fixture' in your lives. That's the word she used. And she thought Mother was so sweet, she never understood why me and Ivy Leigh never came home and said she always felt sorry for Miss Franny."

"She never told me that."

"When I told her the whole story…about how Mother and Daddy got left and how they got married to bring up each other's children…she cried. Then, lo and behold, here she comes the next day to say she wants to honor my mom for adopting a little girl like she's doing now."

The tears I'd dried up after saying goodbye to Ivy Leigh were back.

"Hope Francesca," I said. "It's beautiful. And Franny would be so pleased."

Justine nodded. "Maybe I could call the baby 'Hopey.' Think Anne would mind?"

"She won't mind," I said. "I'm sure."

October turned to November. Hank and Ruby returned from their honeymoon, and Caesar moved down the street to his new home. Justine continued her diet and got a Florida driver's license so she could drive back and forth to Anne's house to be 'Hopey's nanny.' Anne's husband, Scott, came home from Beijing to finalize the adoption plans. Our realtor continued to show Franny's house. I'd watch from the kitchen window, grimacing at times, once trying to persuade myself it wouldn't be so bad having four teenage boys living across the street, if only they didn't all have their own trucks.

But that family didn't buy. Not enough space to park six vehicles. The couple with three school-age kids were not approved for their loan. Two elderly sisters decided the wood-block floors would be too risky. 'Might fall and break a hip,' they said.

But the pressure to sell the house was off. Hank had a home now, and Justine could live with me for the foreseeable future. We were, after all, going to be related…grandmothers of the same little girl. But Justine still needed financial security.

So we waited, hoping for the best.

Agnes and I exchanged letters once a week. The Greers had moved into Ida's house. Jericho's teenage daughters had, of course, taken an immediate liking to Denver, and soon became his official babysitters. Claire had been invited to join the Garden Club, and Bridey had presented her first peach cobbler. Agnes didn't know what Claire had done with it. Cosmo had moved upstairs into my old room. His wedding photo stood in place of the picture of me, Ivy Leigh, and Justine, which was now on my dresser. Agnes had made friends with all the visiting geologists and started a rock collection.

"For Denver," she explained. "If we start now, he'll have a great collection by the time he can appreciate it."

I knew perfectly well the collection was for her and that before long, she would be headed off to geology conferences with Cosmo.

When I would ask about Miriam, the reply was always the same. She was home, dealing with her husband's debts to his company, liquidating assets, and planning on a means to support herself in the future. I was so proud of her.

Two weeks before Thanksgiving, I had breakfast with Justine and then waved from the kitchen window as she 'left for work.' This was how she described her role as Hope's nanny, a self-imposed title giving her the dignity she had never enjoyed. Standing at the sink, hands submerged in suds, I gazed across the street at Franny's house. Sometimes the sight of it filled my heart to bursting, when I considered how her fractured family had been healed. Sometimes I grieved for her and the years she might have enjoyed with her adult daughters, if only…. Sometimes I simply missed her.

This was one of those mornings. I dried my hands and headed to Ruby's house to invite Caesar for a walk in the park. We strolled down Riverside Avenue, me and the dog that had once terrified me, now "Babs' best friend."

When we came home an hour later, I saw our beautiful blonde realtor, Patsy Spicer, standing on Franny's porch. When she spotted me, she waved vigorously, motioning me to join her. I dropped off Caesar and headed straight across the street.

She gripped my arm. "This is so exciting. I tried to call you several times this morning but got no answer. We have a *buyer*."

"When did this happen? When we talked yesterday, you said—"

"She's from out of state. Came in early this morning. Was at my office when I arrived. She asked if the property on Lomax Street was still available, and she was prepared to pay *cash*."

"That's amazing," I said. "But how in the world—?"

Franny's front door opened, and out stepped our buyer—Miriam Goddard.

I scared Patsy half to death when I screamed and grabbed Miriam.

"Miriam, I said, squeezing her. "No wonder Agnes wouldn't tell me anything. She's known all along what you were planning, hasn't she?" I let go

## Chapter 22 ~ The Beginning

and stood back. "But how can you afford it? With your husband's debts? How can you pay cash?"

"You're scaring the realtor, Babs," Miriam said.

"Sorry," I said to Patsy. "We know each other."

"So I see," Patsy said, only slightly alarmed.

"I'm using the inheritance my father left me. It's in my name only. I'm going to use it to start over. And Giles will need a place to live, when"—she glanced at Patsy—"you know…"

Patsy eased in. "How do you two know each other?"

I laughed. "I would say we were partners in crime, but I don't want to prejudice the sale."

"Would you like to show Mrs. Goddard around?" Patsy asked. "I'll start making some phone calls."

Miriam and I stepped into Franny's living room. She glided through the house exactly like Franny used to, stopping to admire the art, running her delicate hand over Franny's antiques. Then she stopped to admire the portrait of Ivy Leigh and Justine.

"Hmm," she said. "You can tell that's Ivy Leigh. The eyes."

I couldn't wait any longer to quiz her. "What about your husband? Does he know you're moving to Florida?"

"He knew we'd lose the house to pay off his debts. And, of course, he knew about my inheritance. He's the one who told me to invest in a house, rather than waste money renting. Funny thing is, he really is a keen financial advisor. Ironic."

"Well, I couldn't possibly be happier," I said, leading her upstairs. "Ivy Leigh said it would be nice if I could make a friend with the new owner of the house."

Hank, Ruby, and Justine were the first to meet our new neighbor. I said I knew her from the Magnolia Arms, but nothing else. When Hank asked Miriam if she was retired, she told him now that her children were grown, she was thinking of getting back into law.

"Not to practice, you understand," she said. "I wouldn't take the bar exam, but I recently had a chance to help a friend with some legal problems and I think I could do a lot of good as a paralegal. I'll have to get certified, of course."

"You should call Charles Hart," Ruby said. "He was Franny's lawyer."

"Have you thought about family law?" Justine asked. "Anne and I love our lawyer. Did Babs tell you Anne is adopting my granddaughter?"

"She did. I was there when Anne called to tell her," Miriam said.

Miriam became an overnight celebrity with Franny's other friends as well. Viola, Jean, Linda Faye, and Linda Jo thanked her again and again, her hand in theirs, applauding her for keeping Franny's house "the same," treating it with the respect it deserved.

When Miriam offered to host Thanksgiving dinner in her new home, Ruby politely resisted, informing her this was too ambitious a goal after just moving in, but Miriam gently insisted. Ruby gave in, but only if Miriam let her and Hank bring the turkey.

Justine got on the phone with Ivy Leigh, reminding her of her promise to spend Thanksgiving with us.

"Will you and Torbert come here?" Justine asked. "You can stay with me and Babs."

Ivy Leigh agreed.

Inspired, I called Agnes. "I know it's a little late in the game, and maybe your parents already invited you for Thanksgiving, but Miriam wants to host, and Ivy Leigh is coming, and—"

"We'd love to," she said. "I can't wait to meet everyone. I feel like I know them."

"They'll all be here," I said. "Tom will be with his wife's family, but Anne and her husband will be here. Hank, Ruby, and Justine. And you'll get to meet Topeka."

"Just one question."

"Yeah?"

"Can we bring Cosmo? Roger's having dinner with Sally, and that would leave Cosmo here by himself."

"Of course," I said. "There's always room for one more."

On Thanksgiving Day, we gathered at Miriam's dining room table, spread end to end with Franny's china and crystal. When Ivy Leigh, seated between Torbert and Justine, wept at the sight of it, they both slipped an arm around her. Miriam sat at the head of the table, Hank and Ruby on her left. Next to them were Agnes and Nestor, across from Anne and her husband, all hoping they could finish eating before their babies, asleep upstairs, woke up. I sat at the other end of the table, thinking about Franny and how happy she would be to see us all together.

Sitting next to me, Cosmo, sporting a new flannel shirt, tapped my elbow. "Barbara?"

I came back to the present. "Yes?"

## Chapter 22 ~ The Beginning

"Thank you for inviting me. This is my first Thanksgiving without my wife, and I was dreading it. But I feel okay…being here with all of you."

"I'm glad you're here, Cosmo. You know what they say. The more, the merrier."

The Dennisonville guests stayed through the holiday weekend.

On Friday Justine and I offered to take care of the babies, so their parents could start their Christmas shopping. Actually, Justine did most of the babysitting. I was busy typing Agnes' manuscript, which I had asked her to bring with her.

Torbert, Hank, and Cosmo offered to clean out Cab's workshop. Miriam said she had no use for the tools, and they were welcome to divide them up as they wished. They left the lawn equipment in place and surprised Miriam by creating a garden shed, which was of more use to her. Ruby and Ivy Leigh continued the process of packing up Franny's belongings. They shared their memories, talked about finding love again, and went on long drives around the city, reminiscing. Ivy Leigh made another trip to Madison to visit Nancy again, as well as both her mothers' graves.

On Sunday we said another tearful goodbye at the train station. The Hamptons were looking forward to seeing Jonas and Margaret. Cosmo and the Carlyles were headed back to Dennisonville. As usual, there was a lot to do. 'First thing' Monday morning Cosmo had a job interview. Nestor had recommended him to the academic dean of the community college in Bellport. Roger and Sally were driving him over. Sally was transferring there for her second semester. She had given Lorraine her two-week notice since she had found a better job at Claire-Rose Chocolates, the candy store the Greer family had opened.

When Agnes hugged me goodbye, she asked, "Are you sure you don't mind typing that manuscript? There's so *much* to be finished."

"My secretary fingers haven't lost their touch," I said. "I'm flying through the chapters. I'll head your way after Christmas. Then you and I can do a final read-through before we meet the publisher on January 4th."

"It'll be a dream come true," Agnes said.

"Sometimes they do," I said, kissing Denver's cheek.

Miriam met with Charles Hart and began the process of becoming a certified paralegal. She and I shared many a meal, many of cup of tea, and many a secret, but we never again posed as an art collector and executive assistant.

Justine continued to thrive. As I watched her transform, I often wished I had taken a picture of her during those first few days of recovery after her hospital stay. Sometimes I couldn't believe the difference in her, so I knew no one else would. Justine was already friends with Ruby from childhood, but she now called her "Mom." Ruby did not object. But I never anticipated Justine and Miriam growing close, which all started with Miriam's beginning her paralegal studies, brushing up on the law. When I was too busy typing Agnes' book, Miriam asked Justine to quiz her.

So Justine would go to "work" at Anne's, come home, have supper with me, and spend the evening with Miriam "tutoring" her. A few months ago, Miriam wouldn't have been caught dead with Justine. What would her Garden Club friends think now?

December dawned. Not only were we eager for Christmas, but for the New Year as well. The 1980 calendar was filling up. January: Agnes' book would be delivered to the publisher. February: Roger and Sally were getting married. March: Hope's adoption would be final. When Ivy Leigh wrote in her Christmas card that she and Torbert would like to visit "sometime" in the spring and bring Jonas and Margaret Grinstead with them, I immediately called Agnes to find out when spring break was. Maybe we could coordinate the dates, if they could find someone to manage the house a few days.

"I'll make that work," she said. "Ivy Leigh will make any adjustment to *her* schedule, if it means she can spend some time with Denver."

I laughed. "Okay, I'll let you take care of that. How is everyone?"

"Wonderful." She paused. "Have you gotten anything in the mail lately?"

"A lot of Christmas cards," I said. "Why do you ask?"

She hesitated. "No reason."

"Please don't tell me Bridey Ludlow makes fruitcake," I said. "She wouldn't send me one, would she?"

Agnes exploded with laughter. "Oh, no. They're way too heavy. She couldn't afford the postage. No. You'll like this. That's all I'll say. But keep your eye out for it."

The next day I found a notice in my mailbox. A package, needing my signature, was at the post office. I stood in line with the people mailing Christmas boxes, signed the required form, and the postal worker brought out a large flat parcel. There was no need to look at the return address. I knew at once who had sent it. And I knew what it was, having studied it many times on the easel in Jericho's makeshift studio on the third floor of the

## Chapter 22 ~ The Beginning

Magnolia Arms, as well as on the floor of the foyer after Sally brought it home.

I slid the canvas into my backseat and drove home, trying not to think how heartsick Cosmo must be. He had loved *The Cliffs at Etretat* from the moment he saw it. How had Jericho had the heart to ask for it back?

But I was thrilled he wanted me to have it. I pictured the painting in different places in my house. Over the piano? In place of my botanical prints? Dining room? I would ask Miriam for advice. She would know best.

At home I carried in my precious cargo and laid it face down on the dining room table. I snipped the twine and unfolded the brown wrapping paper. Jericho had taped an envelope to the back. Gingerly, I pried it loose and read his note.

*Dear Barbara: After I came home and our legal issues were resolved, Claire confessed she had hoped, after Ike died, that we could start a new life out from under Lorraine's shadow. As you know, I was unwilling to let go. Only Lorraine coming here to threaten Claire prompted me to make needed changes. I credit you with helping accomplish this. When we moved into our new home, Claire asked me not to display the painting that had kept me away from her for so long. I was willing to give it to only one person: you. Sincerely, John Greer*

Instead of flipping the canvas over, I stepped to the end of the table and bent down to examine the edges of the canvas. There I found them—rust spots and mildew from long weeks spent languishing in Lorraine's detached garage.

This was not Jericho's painting. It was Ike's.

I skittered to the kitchen to call Miriam.

She answered after one ring. "Hello?"

"Hi, this is Babs. Could you come over? I have something to show you."

"Sure. I could use a break from the books. Make me some tea?"

"Be glad to," I said. "Oh, and Miriam?"

"Yes?"

"Bring Mrs. Dougan with you."

Made in the USA
Columbia, SC
23 November 2019